# ACCLAIM FOR COLLI

### *Rosemary Cottage*

"Coble's fast-paced, atmospheric, and suspenseful second entry in her new romantic suspense series (after *Tidewater Inn*) is a sure bet . . . "

—*Library Journal*

"Coble's second Hope Beach book returns to the stunningly described Outer Banks locale. The suspenseful mystery, coupled with developing romance, creates a lively, page turning novel."

—*Romantic Times*, 4-star review

"Coble provides plenty of excitement for readers who enjoy her unique combination of cozy setting and action-packed mystery."

—*Publishers Weekly*

### *Tidewater Inn*

"Coble's atmospheric and suspenseful series launch should appeal to fans of Tracie Peterson and other authors of Christian romantic suspense."

—*Library Journal*

"Coble's mystery is intriguing and an ideal backdrop for the development of a romance. The plot moves briskly forward, providing an action-packed story along with wonderful development of the characters."

—*Romantic Times*

### *Safe in His Arms*

"A fiery redhead, a mystery man, and plot twists galore. What's not to love? Colleen has done it again . . . created a page-turner. Don't miss it!"

—Stephanie Grace Whitson, author of
The Quilt Chronicles series

"I so enjoyed the strong heroine and enigmatic hero in Colleen Coble's *Safe in His Arms*. What a fun story of learning to love, to trust, and to be safe in the arms of God, no matter the circumstances. You'll want to keep turning the pages on this one to discover what happens next!"

—Marlo Schalesky, author of the Christy
Award-winning *Beyond the Night*

"Colleen combines a rich, historical setting with real characters who reach out and grab ahold of you from page one. You won't want to put *Safe in His Arms* down until you turn the last page. Then you'll be sad the story ended so fast! I love Colleen's books and look forward to the next one!"

—Lynette Eason, award-winning, best-selling
author of The Women of Justice series

"Colleen Coble is an amazing storyteller who weaves stories I can't put down. In *Safe in His Arms* she combines a heroine I wanted to take to tea with a misunderstood hero and placed them in a historical setting I thoroughly enjoyed. Mix in romance and a touch of suspense and it is the perfect book."

—Cara Putman, award-winning author of *Stars in the Night* and *A Wedding Transpires on Mackinac Island*

# BUTTERFLY
# PALACE

# ALSO BY COLLEEN COBLE

Novellas included in *Smitten, Secretly Smitten,* and *Smitten Book Club*

### UNDER TEXAS STARS NOVELS
*Blue Moon Promise*
*Safe in His Arms*

### THE HOPE BEACH NOVELS
*Tidewater Inn*
*Rosemary Cottage*

### THE LONESTAR NOVELS
*Lonestar Sanctuary*
*Lonestar Secrets*
*Lonestar Homecoming*
*Lonestar Angel*

### THE MERCY FALLS SERIES
*The Lightkeeper's Daughter*
*The Lightkeeper's Bride*
*The Lightkeeper's Ball*

### THE ROCK HARBOR SERIES
*Without a Trace*
*Beyond a Doubt*
*Into the Deep*
*Cry in the Night*
*Silent Night* (e-book only)

### THE ALOHA REEF SERIES
*Distant Echoes*
*Black Sands*
*Dangerous Depths*
*Midnight Sea*
*Holy Night* (e-book only)

*Alaska Twilight*
*Fire Dancer*
*Abomination*
*Anathema*

# BUTTERFLY PALACE

COLLEEN COBLE

THOMAS NELSON
*Since 1798*

NASHVILLE DALLAS MEXICO CITY RIO DE JANEIRO

Published in Nashville, Tennessee, by Thomas Nelson. Thomas Nelson is a registered trademark of Thomas Nelson, Inc.

Thomas Nelson, Inc., titles may be purchased in bulk for educational, business, fundraising, or sales promotional use. For information, please e-mail SpecialMarkets@ThomasNelson.com.

Publisher's Note: This novel is a work of fiction. Names, characters, places, and incidents are either products of the author's imagination or used fictitiously. All characters are fictional, and any similarity to people living or dead is purely coincidental.

Unless otherwise noted, Scripture quotations are taken from the King James Version.

**Library of Congress Cataloging-in-Publication Data**

Coble, Colleen.
  Butterfly palace / Colleen Coble.
    pages cm.
  Summary: "Lily secures a job as maid in a grand manor in Austin, Texas. But even far from home, her past lurks around every corner. When Lily Donnelly arrives at the Cutlers' famed Butterfly Mansion in 1899, the massive house and unfamiliar duties threaten to overwhelm her. Victorian Austin is lavish, highly political, and intimidating, but with the help of the other servants, Lily resolves to prove herself to her new employers.Then, while serving at an elegant dinner party, Lily recognizes one distinguished guest as Andrew, the love of her life who abandoned her without a word back home. He seems to have assumed a new identity and refuses to acknowledge her, leaving her confused and reeling. Before Lily can absorb this unwelcome news, she's attacked. Could it be the sinister Servant Girl Killer who has been terrorizing Austin? Or is it someone after something more personal, someone from her past? Does she dare trust Andrew to help, or is he part of the danger threatening to draw Lily into its vortex?"—Provided by publisher.
  ISBN 978-1-59554-783-5 (pbk.)
  1. Housekeepers—Fiction. I. Title.
  PS3553.O2285B88 2014
  813'.54—dc23                                                           2013029518

*Printed in the United States of America*

14 15 16 17 18 RRD 6 5 4 3 2

*For my sister of the heart Diann Hunt,*
*who has grown more beautiful as she's lived out*
*the meaning of this novel—that struggle makes*
*us stronger and more fit for heaven.*
*Love you, Di! I'm in awe of your strength and*
*the way you shine Jesus every day.*

# PROLOGUE

*Larson, Texas, 1900*

Lily Donaldson tiptoed to the front door and winced when it opened with a creak. The last thing she wanted was to awaken her mother who was sleeping down the hall. Even though Lily was over twenty years old, her mother would take a switch to her if she knew she was sneaking out like this. The lights still shone from the livery attached to their house.

She peeked in the window as she passed. Her father sat at the desk with his partner as they pored over figures for the new expansion. There was a stack of money on the desk beside them. She stared for a moment at the stack of cash. It must have been a good day for the livery. It would be hours before their meeting came to an end. The talk of a new livery in the next town over had been going on for several weeks, and both men never seemed to tire of the topic.

The night air touched her heated skin, and she shivered as she hurried along the path to the barn. Crickets chirped as if to keep time to the ragtime tune tinkling from the tavern's piano down the street. The threat of discovery added another thump to her pulse.

The familiar scent of hay and horse greeted her when she stepped into the darkened building. "Andy?" She twisted the unfamiliar weight of the engagement ring on her finger. Her lips curved when Andy Hawkins stepped from the shadows. "I thought maybe you hadn't been able to slip away." She kept her voice barely above a whisper while she drank in his appearance.

He was a good head taller than most men, and his bulk made her feel tiny—and protected. His dark hair curled at the nape of his neck, and his eyes were the color of a buckeye nut.

His white teeth flashed below his perfect Roman nose. "I told Pa I wasn't feeling well. I'd much rather be with you." His warm hands came down on her shoulders, and he pulled her close for a kiss. "That meeting will go on for hours."

Heat ran through her at his words. She'd tried to resist the pull of their passion—they both had—but they'd been weak, so weak. The firm press of his fingers closed around her hand, and he pulled her to a comfortable stack of hay. She fell into his arms without a protest. His lips came down on hers, and she forgot everything but his touch.

He lifted his head and sniffed. "Do you smell smoke?"

Cries of alarm began to filter into her consciousness, muddied by the feel and scent of Andy. He helped her to her feet, and they both rushed to the door to view a scene that made her shudder.

Fire shot through the roof of the livery. "Pa!" Andy restrained her when she would have rushed forward.

More shouts came from town, and a line of men burst from the saloon and ran toward the burning building. The windows of the livery exploded, spewing broken glass onto the ground, then smoke poured from open frames.

Andy grabbed her hand, and they ran toward her front door. She stopped and stared at the fire. Which direction? Her mother was in the house. Their fathers were in the livery. Lily's chest was tight as flames consumed the livery.

Her fingers closed around the doorknob. "I'll get my mother. You get the men." The metal was already hot to the touch. How could the fire have grown so quickly?

She yanked open the door and plunged inside. Thick, roiling smoke choked Lily's nose and throat as soon as she reached the top of the stairs. She threw open the bedroom door and rushed to the bed. The smoke was thick in the bedroom too. Her mother slept, unaware of the danger.

Lily shook her. "Mama, wake up! You have to get out of here." Shouts and screams echoed from outside. What was happening to her father?

Her mother lifted her head and her eyes went wide, then cleared of confusion. She threw back the covers, then stumbled to the door with Lily. One hand around her mother's waist, Lily led her down the steps. Her chest burned both with the hot smoke and the need to escape.

"Almost there," she told her mother. She reached blindly for the door, and her fingers grasped the knob. She threw open the door.

The first brush of fresh air on her skin made her gasp and draw in the thick smoke. She coughed at the searing pain in her chest, then stumbled onto the porch with her mother. Lily led her mother a safe distance away before turning to see bright flames shooting into the night. A fire alarm clanged behind them, and the horses pulling the fire engine raced around the corner. As soon as it came to a stop, the firemen leaped into the yard and ran for the livery.

Her mother coughed and stared at the furiously burning structure. "Where's your father?"

But Lily didn't see her father's bald head. Dread congealed in her belly, and she shook her head. "I don't see them, but Andy went to get them out." She stared at the throng around the building. Was that Andy?

His soot-blackened face came into view by the light of the flames. He struggled with the two men holding him. "Let go of me! I have to find them."

"It's too dangerous," one of the men said. "The place is fully engulfed."

"Stay here, Mama." Lily hurried to Andy's side. "You didn't find them?" Her throat closed at the hopeless expression on his face.

She turned to stare at the inferno that had overrun both the livery and the attached house. The fire's heat scorched her face. The breeze blew stinging cinders against her skin. Andy renewed his efforts to free himself, but the firemen propelled him back to a safer distance.

The fire's roar was like a dragon from a fairy tale, monstrous and all-consuming. Flames licked out of the upper windows, straining toward the roof. More glass shattered, and the stink of burning bedding rolled over the lawn. With a groan, the building began to sag. The firemen shoved them back even more, and they all turned to watch it give a final shudder before the weakened timbers collapsed. Sparks and flames shot higher as the fire fed on the night air and began to consume the last of the building.

Lily sank to her knees, and Andy fell with her. They held one another as the fire took their fathers.

Andy stiffened, then pulled away. "It's my fault. I should have been there. I would have smelled it and gotten them out."

"It went too fast, Andy. There was nothing any of us could do." She tried to cup his face in her hands, but he flinched away, then jumped to his feet.

"Don't look at me. I can't even stand myself." He stalked off, and the dark swallowed him up.

# ONE

*Austin, Texas, 1904*

The train's whistle sounded as mournful as she felt as it pulled away from the station, leaving her on the siding with her valise at her feet. Lily brushed ineffectively at the soot on her serviceable gray skirt and squinted in the October sunshine. What if her new employer had sent no one to meet her? She didn't know how to get to her destination.

A dray pulled by two fine horses went past, and the driver stared too boldly for her taste, so she directed her gaze to her dusty black boots.

"Miss?"

She jerked her gaze back up to see a man dressed in a brown suit. A lock of reddish hair dipped below his stylish bowler. He appeared to be in his late thirties and was quite handsome.

He tipped his hat and nodded toward her luggage. "Is that all you have? You *are* Lily Donaldson?"

"Yes, yes, I am. You are from the Butterfly Palace?"

He picked up her valise and gave a vague nod her way. "This way."

People flowed around her as she followed his broad back to a fine automobile at the street. She hung back when he opened the door. "You didn't mention your name."

Amusement lit his pale blue eyes. "I'm not the killer attacking women here if that's what you're worried about."

She glanced around at the men loitering nearby. No one seemed to pay her any notice. "There's a killer?"

He shrugged. "A city is never as safe as it looks. Are you coming or not? I don't care either way. Mother asked me to fetch you when I objected to being forced to attend another of her boring balls, and I obliged. It's on your own head if you're late."

When he started for the driver's seat, she hoisted herself onto the plush seat. "I'm coming."

He grinned, and heat flared in her cheeks at his bold stare. His expensive suit proclaimed him to be much more than a driver sent to collect her. He'd mentioned his mother, so she assumed he was a Marshall.

The jerk of the automobile threw her against the leather seat and ended her speculation. It felt good to be away from the curious stares she'd endured on the train. Women didn't travel alone. She took off her bonnet and swiped some loose strands back into place, then replaced her hat.

She stared eagerly out the window at Austin. The state capital. It was much grander than she'd imagined. Electric trolley cars zipped by so fast they made her woozy. Houses larger than four or five homes back in Larson turned stately faces toward the wide street. Mercantile shops, printers, meat markets, and dress shops passed in a dizzying blur. Where did one start to find needed items? There were too many shops to choose from.

The scent of lilacs blew away the stench of the train's coal dust that lingered on her clothing. Her pulse beat hard and fast in her neck. Her new life was about to begin, and she had no idea what to expect. While she hoped to find a new life here, the recent death of her mother left her expecting only more heartache. Still, she had to support herself even if life seemed hard and dreary.

Didn't God care? She'd never expected him to let such terrible things happen. Ever since the fire, life had spiraled down in a disheartening whirlpool of pain.

The automobile stopped in front of a grand stone mansion illuminated by electric lights. The cobblestone drive was smooth under her shoes when the man assisted her out of the back. Lily stood, absorbing the huge edifice that would have been more at home on a French mountainside. Seeing it here on Texas soil felt wrong somehow, and something about the structure was off-putting in spite of its grandeur. Maybe it was the way the windows in the mansard roof seemed to leer down at her, or perhaps it was the dark brick that made it look stern and unwelcoming. A chill shuddered down her spine, but she picked up her valise. It would surely be more attractive in the daylight.

The man shut the automobile door behind her. "Welcome to Butterfly Palace, Lily."

His forwardness in addressing her by her Christian name made her straighten. "Why is it called that?" She craned her neck again and willed herself to admire the four-story mansion.

"My stepfather is a great collector of exotic butterflies. He employs a man to bring him the finest in the world. The sunroom is filled with them, and frescoes can be found everywhere." He pointed. "You'll want to go around back to the staff entrance, but I'm sure we'll be seeing more of one another. The name's Lambreth. I suppose I'll inherit this monstrosity someday." He winked at her.

The instructions and his wink took her aback. There was little distinction between servant and master in Larson, but then, no one in her hometown put on airs or flashed their wealth around. She took a step toward the side of the house, but Mr. Lambreth touched her arm and motioned her in the other direction.

"I'll have Rollo bring in your trunk. Mrs. O'Reilly will tell you where you're sleeping. See you around."

"Thank you." Gathering her courage, Lily followed a cobblestone path around the west side of the house.

Light spilled into a rose garden from large windows along the side of the house. Lily stopped and gaped. Women in shimmering silk dresses mingled with men in formal attire under a spectacular gas chandelier. The opulent scene was like something from *Godey's*. Houseboys and maids carrying trays offered food and drink to the guests, and piano music tinkled out the open windows.

She reined in her impulse to run back to the automobile and ask to be returned to the train. This life was far outside her experience, and she'd never fit in here. Would she be expected to wear a black dress and white apron and cap?

Tightening her grip on her small valise, she forced herself forward to the back door. The aroma of roast beef mingled with fish and cake as she knocked on the door.

The door opened, and a slim woman about Lily's age peered out. Her hazel eyes sparkled with life above flushed cheeks. "You must be Lily. I expected you an hour ago. We need you." She reached out and yanked the valise from Lily's hand. "We're shorthanded. Your dress will do for now, but take off your hat and put on an apron."

She left the door standing open and stepped back into a hall that opened into a large kitchen. Lily followed the young woman into the kitchen where the cooking odors grew stronger. The aromas of beef and fish vied with that of cinnamon and apples. Food covered a scarred wooden table, and several servants bustled around the room.

A tiny woman dressed in black orchestrated the chaos. The red hair under her cap was coiled in a bun tight enough to give her a headache. Her brown eyes assessed Lily, and she nodded. "So you're Lily?" Her brogue told of her Irish heritage. "I'm Glenda O'Reilly, the housekeeper. You may call me Mrs. O'Reilly."

"What would you have me do tonight?"

Mrs. O'Reilly pointed to a shelf and pegs. "Hang up your hat there. Emily, get her an apron."

The young woman who had opened the door nodded and reached into a cupboard. She handed a white apron to Lily. "You can take around the cider."

Lily pulled the pins from her hat and placed it on the shelf, then tied the apron around her waist. "You're Emily?"

The young woman nodded. "Sorry, love, I didn't introduce myself, did I? We'll be roommates, and there will be time to get acquainted later. *After* the party."

Lily's chest felt tight, and she wished she'd hidden out in the rose garden until the party was over. "When am I to meet Mrs. Marshall?"

"Tomorrow." Mrs. O'Reilly's brow lifted in challenge as if daring Lily to object.

"Yes, ma'am. I am just to offer the guests cider? I'll do my best."

"That's all I ask." The housekeeper pointed to a large tray filled with fine blue-and-white china cups. "Smile and let the guests take their own cup of mulled cider. Try not to spill it. When your tray is empty, come back here and get more."

Like Joan of Arc going to the stake, Lily squared her shoulders and picked up the tray.

Women in shimmering silks of every imaginable color danced by on the arms of men in sleek black suits. A mural over the fireplace depicted a butterfly in beautiful hues of blue and yellow. Drew Hawkes hung back in the corner and idly listened to the conversations around him, mostly about the recent murder of a servant girl. The unfortunate young woman had been discovered a few blocks from here, and the entire city was in a state. This was the third murder in two months.

Everett Marshall motioned to Drew, and he left the sanctuary of his corner to join him. Everett clapped a hand on Drew's shoulder. "This is the young man I was telling you about. Drew is quite gifted with investments, and you would do well to employ him. Drew, this is Stuart Vesters. He owns the stockyard on the west side of town."

Drew shook the man's hand, noticing the lack of enthusiasm in Stuart's grip. "Pleased to meet you, Mr. Vesters. I'm not currently taking on more clients though, sir. I'd be happy to put you on a waiting list." Dangling the carrot just out of reach tended to be much more effective than a hard sell.

Sure enough, the older man squared his shoulders and lifted a brow. "When could we discuss it, Mr. Hawkes? I might be persuaded to change investment companies. Everett here has been singing your praises for more than a month."

"I'm booked through the next three weeks, but I'd be happy to make an appointment after Thanksgiving." Drew had been trying to get close to Vesters for nearly six months. It wouldn't do to appear too eager. His supervisor wouldn't be happy if he ruined things now.

"That's much too far. I have some time on Thursday. We can meet in town."

Drew eyed the man's set jaw and read his determination. Good. "Let me see if I can rearrange my schedule." He whipped out a black leather calendar and pretended to peruse it. He pulled out a pencil and acted as though he were erasing something. "I can make that work. My other client may squawk, but I'll make it up to him with a new tip."

Vesters smiled with self-satisfaction, and Drew allowed himself a small smile as the man reached for a glass of cider. Drew looked at the young woman holding the tray. He blinked and looked again. All the blood drained from his head, and his knees went weak as he took in the blond hair and pointed chin.

Lily? It wasn't possible. She hadn't seen him yet as her attention was on Vesters. Drew's gaze drank in the face he'd seen only in his dreams for four years. Those delicate features and smooth skin hadn't changed in all this time. Her eyes were such a dark blue, and they grew even darker when she was angry. The glorious hair he'd loved to see released from its pins was hidden under an ugly maid's cap. The years had brought a new maturity to her beauty.

Drew turned on his heels and melted into the crowd. His pulse throbbed in his throat. He had to calm himself. If Vesters smelled something off now, it could ruin the whole thing. He spared a glance back at the group, but she wasn't looking his way. Maybe she hadn't seen him.

What was Lily doing here, so far from Larson? She wore an apron like she was a maid. Part of him longed to rush to her and announce himself. Did she hate him? He deserved it after the way he'd left without a word.

He was in the middle of the dancing couples, so he cut in on the man squiring Belle Castle. "I hope you don't mind, Miss Castle."

"Not at all, Mr. Hawkes." She flashed him a coy smile.

He'd known for weeks that the beautiful brunette held some fondness for him, and he hated to encourage it now, but Everett would be happy to see him dancing with his niece and would unlikely be upset at Drew's sudden departure. Everett would smooth things over with Vesters.

Drew was so distracted he didn't notice when the musicians struck up a reel. Belle picked up her pace but he didn't. Their feet became entangled. He tried to catch his balance, but everything was happening too fast. He released Belle so she wouldn't share his disgrace. In the moment he scrambled away, his arm collided with the soft body of someone behind him. The deep red Oriental rug rose to meet him, and they both went down in a tangle of limbs. The contents of the china cups darkened the red carpet to deep garnet.

The rest of the dancers stopped and stared. Someone snickered, and heat rose to his face. He quickly flipped the lady's dress over her lower limbs and sprang to his feet. "I'm terribly sorry. I—I—" His apology died when he stared into Lily's scarlet face.

Her eyes were wide and horrified. "Andy?"

He hadn't heard that nickname since his father died. "I'll explain later," he said low enough that only she could hear. After helping her to her feet, he knelt and put the cups back on the tray. Some of them were broken, and he prayed she wasn't blamed for the encounter.

She hadn't left when he stood with the tray in his hands. The rest of the guests began to move off, and the music tinkled out again.

Knowing his duty, he glanced at Belle. "I'm so sorry, Miss Castle. You are unharmed?"

"I'm fine, Mr. Hawkes." Belle smiled, and the amusement lit her eyes with a warm glow. "That was a much-needed bit of excitement for this too-dull party. I do believe I'll take my leave though and attend to my dress." She gestured to dark splotches on her gown. He opened his mouth to apologize again, but she held up her hand. "No harm done. I'll see you tomorrow for dinner."

He gave a slight bow. "I shall look forward to it."

Christopher Lambreth, Mrs. Marshall's son, gave a genial grin and held out his arm. "I'll escort you, cousin. I fear you've lost your usual fine sense of balance."

Belle laughed and took his arm. When her emerald skirt disappeared in the swirl of other gowns, Drew turned his attention back to Lily. She seemed rooted to the spot. His reappearance had to have rattled her.

He took her arm. "Let's get out of here. Make no sign that you know me."

She gave a slight nod. "Your past actions have already made it clear I don't know you at all."

His lips tightened, and he guided her through the crowd to the blessed cool of the hall outside the ballroom. "Lily, what are you doing here?"

She jerked her arm from his grip. "I think the better question would be, what are *you* doing here, Andy? And the first question begs the second. Where have you been for the past four years and two months?"

Part of him rejoiced that she knew so clearly how long he'd been gone, but that fact also revealed the depth of the pain he'd caused. "It will take too long to explain now. Can you meet me tomorrow afternoon at the park? Say nothing about my identity to anyone."

She shook her head. "I don't think I want to hear it. And besides, I don't know what my duties are yet. I just arrived tonight." Her eyes filled with tears. "Who are you really, Andy?" She turned toward the kitchen door.

"Wait, Lily, I want to talk to you." But the swish of her skirt was the only response he received.

# TWO

Somehow Lily managed to keep a pleasant smile on her face while she served the guests their after-dinner drinks and dessert. Andy, here? Had it been real? She fingered the sore spot on her arm where she'd fallen and knew it was.

Seeing him again had torn the scab off a wound she'd thought had healed long ago. The moment he looked into her eyes, she instantly remembered every moment spent skipping rocks in the Red River and every stolen kiss—and more—in the livery. Her emotions churned with the desire to resurrect the love she'd felt once. But it could not be. He couldn't be trusted.

She sidled behind a strange tree with a long scaly trunk topped by flat, spreading leaves and some kind of round, hard fruit that was planted in a wooden container. This party was unlike anything she'd ever imagined. The glorious silks the women wore made her fingers itch with the desire to touch them, especially the mauve ones. No homespun dresses here.

And the ballroom itself made her jaw drop. The great domed ceiling over the space made it appear even larger than it was. Gilded maids frolicked in the fresco with deer, and silk draped the massive windows. But what held her captive was the enormous stained glass window between the ballroom and the next room over. It was circular and at least ten feet across. The butterfly depicted in it seemed to glow from the intricately fused colored glass. Though it was beautiful, the beady eyes of the butterfly made her shudder.

She turned away and her gaze collided with Andy's intent one. She wanted to look away but couldn't until a distinguished gentleman stepped to the center of the room and tapped a spoon on his glass of amber liquid.

The man's smile beamed with pride. "I have something exciting to show you. I purchased the cocoon of what is reported to be a Red Glider."

A buzz of excitement started around the room, and Lily heard "Africa" murmured more than once. "Everett always knows how to make a splash at his parties," Mr. Lambreth whispered in her ear. She gasped at his nearness and sidled away. If her employer saw her talking intimately with him, she'd be discharged.

Mr. Marshall put his hand on the bark. "This is a coconut tree from Africa. I had it shipped here with the pupa still on it. The last few days, the outside has gotten translucent, which is the sign the butterfly is about to emerge. The butterfly began to try to break free nearly a week ago, a long time in the insect's life cycle."

"Why's it take so long?" a male voice asked. "I'd think the struggle would kill it."

Mr. Marshall nodded. "The butterfly needs the hardship to make it strong enough to fly. The struggle pumps fluid to its wings and gives it the strength to survive. If I were to help it by cutting away the chrysalis, it would die. So all we can do is stand back and observe its own efforts to free itself."

Lily stared as movement began in the small cocoon. The group crowded around to watch. Once it started, it all happened so fast. She held her breath as the insect, wet and ugly, crawled out and clung motionlessly to the leaf.

15

"It's letting its wings dry now," Mr. Marshall said. "That will take hours. That's the end of the show for now. Tomorrow this beauty will be up and flying around. I'll release it into my garden."

Even while he was smiling, the insect quivered and let loose of the leaf. It plummeted to the ground where it tried weakly to crawl before going motionless again.

Frowning, Mr. Marshall knelt and prodded it with the end of his spoon. "It's dead. I don't know what happened."

"Maybe the struggle was too much for it. I feel that way sometimes." A woman laughed and turned away.

Lily knew the feeling herself. She was so tired of the struggle to find a life for herself. Andy's desertion had changed everything for her. It had hurt her mother too, coming on the heels of Papa's death. Life seemed so hard. Would it ever get better?

One by one the others went back to talking and laughing. Lily watched her new employer touch the butterfly again with obvious distress. What caused him to care so much about those insects?

A pretty blond woman dressed in pink put her hand on his shoulder. "There's nothing you can do, Everett. Come along, darling." She saw Lily standing nearby and motioned to her. "Take this insect away and dispose of it."

Lily nearly pretended she didn't hear. She'd never liked butterflies, though she'd been fascinated by Mr. Marshall's obvious obsession. She nodded and moved closer. "Yes, ma'am."

"You're new. I'm Mrs. Marshall. You must be Lily Donaldson."

"Yes, ma'am."

The woman looked her over. "Who made your dress, Lily? It's cut very well."

"I did, ma'am. My mother was a dressmaker and taught me everything she knew."

"Do you know anything about hair as well?"

"Yes, ma'am. I like trying out the new hair fashions I see in *Godey's*."

"I hurt my arm in a fall from my horse and am struggling to do my hair. Perhaps you can help on a temporary basis. Come to my suite first thing in the morning."

"Certainly, ma'am."

"Please clean this up." Mrs. Marshall put her hand on her husband's shoulder again. "Your guests are waiting, my dear. Don't be distressed. You have plenty of butterflies in the garden."

"I don't know what happened," he muttered. "I'd like to keep it though and try to discern what went wrong. And it's still beautiful."

"Maybe it was just too weak to survive the emergence. It happens. I'll have the maid put it in your study." She motioned to Lily again. "Try not to damage it. Put it on a paper or something, and place it on Mr. Marshall's desk."

"And where is that, ma'am?" Lily trembled inside with the knowledge that she would have to touch it.

"Down the hall toward the kitchen. Fourth door on the left. It's not locked." She led her husband away.

Lily stared at the carcass. There was nothing beautiful about it in spite of what Mr. Marshall said. She tried to figure out what to put it on. She had no paper. A napkin? Maybe she could use a teaspoon to scoop it onto the napkin. A tray containing spoons was on the sideboard, so she grabbed one and found a soiled napkin. Holding her breath, she transferred the butterfly to the napkin without having to touch it. Carrying it gingerly, she took it away. It took several tries before she found the right room.

The study was dark, so she put the napkin on the floor and turned on the gaslights on the wall. She blinked when light flooded the room. Gaslights were quite wondrous. She put the butterfly on the desk, then lingered a moment to look around. More butterfly displays were on the walls and shelves.

No wonder this mansion was called the Butterfly Palace. It felt a little creepy to her though. She turned off the light and shut the door.

Belle kicked the soiled dress away from her, then pulled the bell to have one of the kitchen maids help her. Fuming, she sat on the embroidered stool in front of her dressing table. Her mirror reflected back the high color in her cheeks. Why hadn't Drew been more attentive? Instead, she'd been forced to attend that odious Vesters fellow. At least Christopher had been nearby to make her laugh with his dry humor.

Emily poked her head in. "Can I help you, Miss Belle?"

Belle pointed at the heap of green silk. "It's been ruined. You may discard it."

Emily smoothed the fabric with a gentle hand. "If you don't mind, miss, I'll see if Mrs. O'Reilly can get the stain out. The garment is too beautiful to destroy."

"Do whatever you like with it. I will never wear it again." Belle turned back to the mirror and yanked the pins from her hair. "My head aches. I'd like you to brush my hair."

"Of course, miss." Emily laid the dress over the back of the brocade chair by the door and moved to the dressing table. She picked up the horsehair brush and drew it through Belle's long dark hair.

Belle frowned as she remembered the way Drew had been so solicitous of the maid. "I've never seen that chit Mr. Hawkes fell on. Who is she?"

"The new kitchen maid, Lily Donaldson. Your cousin recommended her. She was a friend and neighbor."

"Oh yes, I remember now. You might warn her to stay away from the guests. She's just enough of a rube to think drawing attention to herself in that manner is allowed. She'll find herself unemployed if she isn't careful."

"I'll tell her, Miss Belle." Emily put down the brush. "Is that all?"

"Draw me a bath before you go."

"Of course."

Belle stopped her when she started toward the attached bathroom. "One more thing, Emily. I want you to keep your ears open around Mr. Hawkes. I mean to marry him, and I want to know everything you hear. Where he is going and what his plans are."

Emily's eyes were expressionless. "Of course, miss. Does your uncle know?" She bit her lip. "Forgive me, I spoke out of turn. It's none of my business."

Belle smiled, certain the girl would carry the tale back to the kitchen, just as she'd planned. She hadn't been oblivious to the way the servants fawned over Hawkes. "I shall tell my uncle when I'm ready. And the other man—the older gentleman with the whiskers who was talking to my uncle? Whatever you do, don't let me be alone with him. My uncle means to marry me off to him, and that won't do. It won't do at all."

"Of course, miss." Emily vanished into the bathroom, and the sound of the water began.

Belle tossed her hair away from her face. Her plans would fall into place. She would make sure of that.

*"Take the back stairway to the third floor and take a right. At the next hall take a left."*

Her chest tight, Lily crept through the dark halls and corridors.

The housekeeper's instructions had been vague, and this place was so large and intimidating. The hallways were poorly lit up here where only the servants resided. The plain plank floors were painted instead of stained, and the plaster walls were chipped in places. The painted molding was a dull green.

She paused at the first intersection, then turned right. Disembodied voices, too low to make out any words, added to her sense of disorientation. She hurried down the hall as if she knew exactly where she was going, even though she was terrified some monster would loom out of the shadows. She was even more frightened she'd open the wrong door and be sent packing. Lily reached the next junction and took a left. Her bedroom was supposed to be the last door on the right.

She opened the door and stepped inside, then shut it and leaned against it with her eyes closed. She'd made it. Opening her eyes, she stepped to the open window where she could see the lights of Austin glimmering on the water of the Colorado River. Wagons and horses still clattered past, and the laughter from a tavern down the street came to her ears.

Andy was here, *here*, in the least likely place she'd ever expected to see him. Why did this have to happen now when she was finally ready for a new life?

She glanced around the room. A metal bedstead held a double mattress that sagged a bit in the middle. A red, white, and blue quilt in a Texas star pattern covered it. The pillows were flat but covered by clean fabric. The wide wood floorboard was unpainted and bare. A crate acted as a night table and held a kerosene lamp. Several candles and matches lay beside it.

In other words, very much like home. Plain and comfortable. She would be happy here.

She opened the closet and found her valise. Her two dresses

were wrinkled from the trip, and she shook them out before hanging them on a nail in the tiny closet. She took off her skirt and blouse and hung them up, then pulled out her nightgown.

There was something scratchy on the shoulder, and she held it up to the lamplight. A piece of paper? She unpinned it and studied the single word: *Welcome.* Emily must have thought to do it. Or one of the other kitchen maids. She smiled in spite of the way her head ached, then found her brush. She pulled out the hairpins, then brushed out her long blond hair and braided it.

The door creaked open behind her, and Emily stepped into the room. "You're still up! I expected you to have found your rest by now." She shut the door. "Still no lock on this door, though I've asked five times. Ever since that wretched murderer started attacking women."

Lily glanced out at the dark and shuddered. She wouldn't sleep a wink. She stared at Emily. There had been no time to take the measure of her roommate when Lily first arrived. The other woman was tall, a good head taller than Lily. Her light brown hair was clean and glossy, and her clothing fit well. She took pride in her appearance. And Lily liked Emily's clear gaze and friendly smile. Perhaps they could be real friends. She needed a companion.

Emily frowned as she took in Lily's expression. "Aw, it's your first night, love. You'll get used to it. The Marshalls aren't so bad."

When Emily touched Lily's arm, she flinched and swallowed hard. Her eyes burned with the endeavor to hold back the tears. "So many people. Such lavish clothes and all. I hardly knew what to say to the guests."

"You're about to cry. I know you're feeling all alone, but we'll be friends."

At the woman's kind words, Lily lost the battle. Tears rolled down her cheeks, and she gulped. "Of course that's all it is.

Homesickness. I'm not used to the city. It's noisy here," she added when men guffawed again from the tavern. "And thank you for the note."

"What note?"

Lily picked it up off the bed. "Didn't you put this on my nightgown?"

Emily stared at it and shook her head. "Probably one of the kitchen maids." She patted Lily's shoulder. "Things will look brighter in the morning." She took off her hat and apron, then hung them on a hook by the door. "You're a small-town girl, just like I was. You'll get used to it. I heard you nearly got squashed at the ball."

Lily nodded as she sank onto the edge of the bed. The sheets and quilt smelled clean and fresh. "Mr. H-Hawkes fell on me."

Emily winked. "I wouldn't mind having him fall on me. All the girls want to bring him his breakfast when he's staying here."

"I-Is he staying here now?" The thought of running into Andy in the hall made her quail. She had to be careful to keep her distance from him at all times.

"He'll be here for the next month. He's in the west wing. I get to take his breakfast to him tomorrow."

"How long have you known him?"

Emily disrobed and pulled on a long cotton nightgown. "I wouldn't say any of us know him. He is a business partner of Mr. Marshall's, and he's much too upper crust for the likes of me. But he's a lovely man for sure. Always kind and polite."

"You said he's a business partner of Mr. Marshall's? What does he do?"

"He handles investments. Mr. Marshall says Drew has made him a wealthy man."

*Drew.* Lily tried to wrap her head around the different nickname. And Hawkes, not Hawkins. Why wasn't he using his real name? Because people might figure out he was a ranch hand from Larson, Texas? He'd always had an aptitude for mathematics, and it didn't surprise her he'd found his fortune that way.

"He's a little mysterious though," Emily said, plaiting her hair.

Lily's pulse sped up. "Mysterious?"

"He never mentions his family. I tried to find out where he's from, and he just said he's a Texan like everyone else." Emily frowned. "His accent is Texan, so maybe I'm making too much of it." Her expression cleared and she smiled at Lily. "What did he say when he helped you up?"

What had he said? Lily couldn't remember. She'd been lost in his dark brown eyes. Eyes she'd begged God to let her see again. Now here he was, and she was wishing she'd never dared ask for anything so presumptuous. It would be better not to know why he'd deserted her. Better to pretend his love had never failed.

Emily touched her arm. "You have a funny expression. Are you in pain?"

The pain was enough to suffocate her, but Lily shook her head. "I just have so many questions. What of Mr. Lambreth? I thought him a bit forward."

Emily lifted a brow. "He usually acts like we're fence posts. He's a nice enough chap. He's been here about six weeks, but he'll be going back to Spain at the end of the summer."

"How exciting. What does he do there?"

"He manages the estates there. A vineyard I believe."

Lily rubbed her head. "I'm just so discombobulated I hardly know where I am or if this is all a dream."

"You'll know at five that it's all too real." Emily crawled into the left side of the bed.

"We get up at five?"

Emily nodded. "You'll need to help in the kitchen, then prepare

Miss Belle's breakfast and take it up to her. She doesn't have a lady's maid. Her morning room will need to be freshly cleaned, and you can do that tomorrow. We take turns."

It all sounded quite overwhelming. "Mrs. Marshall asked me to attend to her in the morning. She hurt her arm and is struggling with her hair."

Emily's brows drew together. "Why would she ask you? She could have asked me or one of the other maids to help her."

Lily bit her lip at the censure in Emily's voice. "She looked at my dress and asked if I'd made it." She pulled back the threadbare sheets and slid into the bed. The slight sag in the middle made her roll against Emily.

"We should get some rest." Emily's voice was clipped. "It's nearly two. Put out the light."

"Of course." Lily put out the kerosene lamp. "Emily? I didn't mean to upset you." The darkness added to the silence for a long moment.

"It's all right, love. I'm not mad at you. Just a little jealous you've been singled out so quickly. Take advantage of tomorrow. I'd love to be a lady's maid, but I've never gotten the chance."

"It's only temporary until her arm heals."

"We'll see."

Lily gulped and tried to hug the edge of the bed. With all her heart, she wished she were back in Larson sewing dresses.

# THREE

Lily's eyes felt gritty from lack of sleep as she dressed in her black uniform and white apron before going off to find the kitchen. She'd lain awake listening to every creak outside in the hall and wishing there was a way to lock the bedroom door.

She made several wrong turns before she found the kitchen stairway in the back of the house. The large room teemed with activity as kitchen maids scurried around. Mrs. O'Reilly was dressed in a spotless white blouse and black skirt. Not a wisp of red hair had dared escape the pins. She was directing the efforts with a soft voice undergirded with steel.

Lily stepped closer. "Mrs. O'Reilly?"

The housekeeper looked up. "There you are. Emily has offered to take over your shift tending to Miss Belle so you can learn the ropes here in the kitchen." She pointed to the large wooden work-table. "That's for mixing the pancakes. The ingredients are in bins along the wood counter." She gestured to a butcher-block counter lined with tins of varying sizes.

Lily looked away. "I'm happy to do whatever you want. I'm to go see Mrs. Marshall this morning after breakfast. She wants me to help her with her hair."

Mrs. O'Reilly's face went blank. "So she told me. What did you do to finagle such a request?"

"Nothing, ma'am. She looked me over last night and asked who had made my dress. I made it myself. Then she asked if I was familiar with the current hairstyles. The next thing I knew, she was ordering me to help her this morning."

The housekeeper pursed her lips. "I won't have a maid who is scheming behind my back, Lily. Did you come here hoping to work your way out of the kitchen?"

Lily held the woman's gaze. "I am just grateful to have a job, Mrs. O'Reilly. I am unfamiliar with what a lady's maid even does. I only wish to be of service and earn my living. I came here expecting only to be a housemaid."

Mrs. O'Reilly's brown eyes softened. "Very well. I'll put aside my suspicions for the time being. There's nothing wrong with working your way up in the world, but I don't like connivers."

Lily glanced at Emily, then back to the housekeeper. "Neither do I, ma'am." She moved to the worktable to begin preparations for the pancakes.

As soon as Mrs. O'Reilly left the kitchen, Emily moved closer to Lily. Her hazel eyes were anxious and high color stained her cheeks. "I hope you're not upset, Lily. I know how Miss Belle likes things done, and I thought you'd have enough to learn today without more."

Was that the only reason for the change? Lily studied her roommate's expression but couldn't make up her mind. "I appreciate your concern. I'm sure it will be helpful to learn things one step at a time."

Emily ducked her head and moved back to her post at the stove when the housekeeper came back into the room.

It was going to take all of Lily's concentration to figure out her place here and who was friend or foe.

Lily's heart pounded as she entered Mrs. Marshall's room to wait for her as instructed. The bedchamber was enormous. Blue-and-white toile paper covered the expansive walls that rose to a domed ceiling at least twelve feet high. The fresco around the top gleamed with gilding. The Chippendale furniture was in impeccable condition. Her feet sank into thick carpeting the color of rich butter, and the sweet aroma of flowers permeated the room.

She touched the blue cover over the gigantic bed. Real silk. She whirled and put her hands behind her back as her employer entered from the balcony. Mrs. Marshall was dressed in a pale pink robe, and her hair was still on her shoulders.

She lifted a brow at Lily's appearance. "Ah, there you are. I'm finished with breakfast. You can take the tray away when you're done assisting me."

"Of course."

Mrs. Marshall walked to a door and pulled it open to reveal lustrous gowns of every imaginable color. "I'm going out with Belle for a ride with Mr. Vesters, but I'm not sure what I want to wear."

"May I?" When Mrs. Marshall nodded, Lily reached past her. "This is very fashionable. I've only seen it in magazines." She pulled out a pale gray walking skirt. "The shorter length will make it easier to get up and down from the carriage. And you have a lovely frilly blouse that will echo the frills on the hem." She pulled it out too.

"I haven't worn that yet. The skirt seemed scandalously short."

"It's only two inches higher than normal."

"Clearly you have studied fashion."

The tension began to ease from Lily's shoulders. "Yes, ma'am. My mother taught me well, and I've read every *Godey's* I could get my hands on." She caressed the fine fabric of the skirt. "This is very well made."

"It should be. It cost the earth. I'll trust your judgment and wear it."

"And these shoes." The skirt and blouse over her arm, Lily grabbed up a pair of white patent leather shoes.

"Indeed." Mrs. Marshall allowed Lily to dress her, then moved to the dressing table. "I'd like a chignon if you can manage it."

Lily gathered the woman's thick blond hair in her hands and began to style it. When she was done, she stepped away. "Does it pass muster?"

Mrs. Marshall put her hand to her hair. "It's lovely, quite lovely." She twisted on the stool and looked up at Lily. "Your talents are wasted in the kitchen, Lily. I think you would suit quite well as a lady's maid to Belle. I shall talk to her at once."

Lily's heart sank a bit. "I've heard she doesn't wish to have a maid." And Emily might not appreciate a fast promotion for Lily.

"That's true, but I'll prevail upon her. Leave it to me." She rose and slid her feet into the shoes. "Run along with the tray. We'll talk later."

"Yes, ma'am." Lily curtsied and went to the balcony to retrieve the tray.

The garden looked glorious in the morning sunlight. Blooms of every color imaginable burst forth from green leaves. The hedges were perfectly manicured. But her gaze fell on a familiar form. Andy stood with his hands in his pockets, an achingly familiar stance. It felt strange to see him dressed in such a stylish morning coat instead of work clothes.

She stepped away when he turned. Her heart couldn't bear to look in his eyes.

# FOUR

Drew mopped his brow and stared at the patio door. Butterflies swarmed the bushes in the garden that surrounded the stone patio. The sweet scent of some kind of flower filled the air. His eyes were gritty from lack of sleep. Every time he closed his eyes, he saw Lily's face. What was she doing here? Had she found him somehow? But no, he'd seen the shock in her beautiful blue eyes when she'd seen him.

He pulled out his pocket watch. Nearly eight. Maybe he could slip into the house and find her.

The door opened and Emily, one of the kitchen maids, stepped out of the large French doors onto the patio. She carried a tray. Her hazel eyes sparkled under her cap. "Good morning, Mr. Hawkes. I've brought your breakfast."

He waited until she set the tray on the table. "Thank you. I was wondering about the young woman I knocked down last night. Is she up? I'd like to make sure she suffered no ill effects."

Emily nodded. "Oh yes, she's been up for hours. Shall I fetch her?"

"Please do." He spread the white napkin on his lap, but his stomach clenched at the thought of swallowing anything. He'd been ready to blurt out everything last night, but in the bright light of day, he realized how disastrous that would be.

"I'll send her right out. She's fine though, sir." Emily stepped back through the French doors into the dining room.

Drew put down his fork and waited. What should he say to her? He couldn't tell Lily why he'd left her. Better to let her think he didn't care than to put her in more danger. Seeing her had knocked the props out from under him.

When Lily stepped into the sunshine, his heart nearly stopped in his chest. She was even more beautiful than he'd remembered from last night. The sun illuminated the planes and angles of her cheekbones and deep-set eyes. Her smooth skin looked soft and touchable. A hint of a blush ran up her neck. How was it possible she was still single—and that she was here and not in Larson?

"I like your hair down better," he blurted when the silence grew between them.

Her color deepened. "I'm a grown woman now, Andy. Not a callow girl to be taken in by your deceit."

Her words stung, but he couldn't let her see him flinch. He rose and thrust his hands into his pockets. "What are you doing here, Lily? Why aren't you home with your mother?"

"She's dead, and I have to earn my living."

A band of grief choked his voice. Her mother had been one of the sweetest women he'd ever met, and he loved her instead of the mother who had deserted him at the age of one.

Lily's eyes widened as she stared at him. The defiance on her face eased, and she touched his hand. "I know you cared about her." When he started to take her hand, she snatched it away. "At least you appeared to, though I now question how you could leave us without a word."

He would have to ask her not to betray his identity. "Please remember to call me Drew here."

She lifted a perfectly formed brow. "I hardly think so. I'm a servant here. If I were presumptuous enough to use your first name, I would be sacked. I shall call you Mr. Hawkins."

"Hawkes. I've shortened my name."

She clasped her hands together at the front of her oh-so-proper black skirt. "What's happened to you, Andy? The man I knew would not condone falsehood."

"The man you knew is dead." When she flinched, he softened his tone. "There are things you don't understand, Lily. I hope to explain myself someday, but it's impossible right now. May I have your word to keep my secret?"

Her gaze locked with his. "I can't promise that. What legitimate reason could you have for hiding your identity? I once trusted you with every fiber of my being, but you broke that trust. What right do you have to ask me to keep silent while you deceive my employer?"

*No right.* He gave a slow nod. "When is your next day off? I'd like to hear what's happening back home."

"I don't know. Mrs. O'Reilly has not told me my schedule yet."

He reached toward her but she stepped back. "Keep silent, Lily. There is a good explanation for my behavior."

"All of it?" Her words were barely above a whisper.

His gaze fell from her penetrating gaze, and he let his head drop.

"I see," she said when he didn't answer. "Very well. I will say nothing for now, but only because Mama loved you. As far as any relationship between you and me, you died to me long ago."

She turned and stepped back through the door. A faint scent of honeysuckle trailed her, a forgotten reminder of their love.

Lily fumed about Andy as she prepared coddled eggs and toast. The young mistress had sent word to the kitchen that she wished the new maid to attend her this morning. The kitchen was empty at the moment, though she heard Emily talking to Mrs. O'Reilly in the dining room.

The tea, brewed exactly three minutes per specification, was the perfect temperature when Lily loaded the items onto a solid silver tray and moved with haste up the back stairs to the main hallway on the second floor. Outside Belle's door, she balanced the tray in one hand and tapped softly.

"Come in." Belle's faint voice held impatience.

Lily stepped inside the room and spied the young woman outside on the veranda. Seated on a small iron chair at a round table, Belle barely glanced up from the book in her hand. The white cover she wore over her nightgown was the finest silk, and her dark brown hair lay loose on her shoulders.

The breeze, carrying with it the scent of grass and flowers, blew across the balcony railing. Lily eyed the flimsy look of the railing. She'd been afraid of high places ever since she got stuck in a tree trying to retrieve her kitten when she was five. It was a long way down to the stone patio from here.

She averted her gaze from the ground and set the tray on the small round table. "I brought your breakfast, miss."

"So I see. I'm not really hungry this morning." Belle put down her book and picked up a piece of toast. "You are the new maid?" Her tone held challenge.

Lily curtsied. "I'm the new kitchen maid, Miss Belle. Lily Donaldson. I arrived just last night from Larson."

Belle's gaze swept over her. "My cousin spoke quite highly of you."

Lily smiled and nodded. "Mr. Castle is a good man. He loves you very much."

Belle blinked fiercely. "I miss him. He is well?"

"Very well."

Belle looked down at the tray. "I suppose I must eat. I have to go on a carriage ride with Mr. Vesters." Her lip curled. "I can't abide the man, but my uncle insists."

Lily poured the tea into a nearly translucent cup. "He was at the party? I'm not sure which gentleman he was."

"He was the short fellow with the red face. And he's always perspiring." Belle wrinkled her nose.

Lily remembered him. He'd been talking to Andy and her employer. "He's looking for a wife?" She took the cover off the eggs, then spread the linen napkin on Belle's lap.

Belle put her book facedown on the table. "Unfortunately, my uncle seems determined I'm to be that bride."

Lily couldn't imagine being pressured to marry someone. Her mother had always allowed her to make her own decisions. She barely suppressed a shudder at the thought of sharing a bed with someone she didn't love. Heat raced to her cheeks at the memory of doing just that with Andy. And he'd betrayed her though she'd loved him with all her heart.

"I'd like some tea this afternoon. Please bring it up around three."

Lily hesitated. "I'll tell Mrs. O'Reilly. She'll make sure it's here."

"I want *you* to bring it."

Lily bit her lip. "I'll try, Miss Belle, but Mrs. O'Reilly directs my work." When Belle glowered, Lily gulped and retreated to the bedroom to pick up the discarded dresses and undergarments.

A shadow blocked the sunshine, and she turned to see Belle in the doorway. "Did you need something, Miss Belle?"

"I saw you speaking with Mr. Hawkes in the garden this morning. You seemed rather comfortable with him." Her eyes sparkled with accusation.

Heat seared Lily's cheeks. "He *did* knock me down. I think he wanted to assure himself I was unharmed." She draped the clothing over the back of the chair by the door.

"It appeared to be more than that to me."

Lily dropped her gaze. Had Belle seen her touch Andy's hand? It had been quite familiar. She'd promised not to betray him. A tiny white lie lingered on her tongue, but she couldn't bring herself to speak it. "Emily showed me the stain on your dress. I hope to be able to repair it later today. In the morning light, it's not as bad as we'd thought."

"Truly? I did like that dress." She waved a hand toward the wardrobe. "Now that you're here, you can button my dress. My aunt keeps telling me to hire a lady's maid, but I'm not at all fond of the idea. The creatures are usually scuttling around behind one's back telling tales. I don't suppose you know enough yet to carry stories to the kitchen."

"I wouldn't anyway, Miss Belle." Lily moved to the wardrobe. "What would you like to wear?" She tugged open the heavy door and surveyed the myriad options of colorful attire. A faint scent of cedar wafted from the interior.

Belle waved her hand. "I don't care. I hardly wish to impress Mr. Vesters."

"How about this silk?" Lily pulled out a deep garnet dress. "It would look lovely with your eyes and hair. The trailing skirt is very stylish."

"It's new." Belle allowed Lily to remove her nightgown, then drop the dress over her head and fasten it in the back. Then Belle sat on the small stool in front of the dressing table. "See what you can do with my hair. I want it up as tightly as possible. No curls, nothing to make me look too attractive."

Lily nodded and picked up the silver hairbrush. Belle's hair was thick and fine. Trying to be gentle, she managed to get it up in a tight bun at the back of Belle's head. "I think it's impossible to make you less attractive, Miss Belle."

Belle turned her head from one side to the other and stared at herself in the mirror. "No blush today, no powder. And maybe another dress instead. This one is too flashy. It screams, 'Look at me.'" She rose and went to the wardrobe again. "This one." She selected a dark brown one.

Lily helped her change, then nodded. "A good choice, but you are still very lovely." The darker color made Belle appear pale and fragile. A flower who needed tending. Any man worthy of the name would want to be the one to care for her.

Belle turned toward the still-open French doors. "I'm hungry now, Lily. Would you fix me some hot food? This is quite cold. And tea as well."

"Of course, Miss Belle." Lily retrieved the cold breakfast.

A tap sounded on the door, and Mrs. Marshall poked her head in. "Oh good, you're up." She stepped into the room and closed the door behind her. "Lily did your hair, I see. She's quite good, isn't she?"

Belle shrugged. "It's all right."

"I think it's time we hired you a lady's maid. In fact, I believe Lily will do quite well for you."

Belle's head came up and her eyes flashed. "I have no wish for a maid. I can call Lily when I need her."

Mrs. Marshall pressed her lips together. "I'm afraid your uncle insists. It's time you were married. Lily understands fashion, and she's quite a good seamstress. She will be an ally when you go to your married home too."

"She's much too pretty." Belle bit her lip as though she was sorry she'd let the words slip out.

Mrs. Marshall laughed. "She's no competition for you."

"I'll think about it."

"I'm not sure you have a choice. You'll have to discuss it with your uncle if you decide against my best advice." Mrs. Marshall opened the door.

Lily swallowed hard. Was this to be her life? Running after a spoiled young woman who didn't know her own mind from one moment to the next?

# FIVE

The stain on the green dress could no longer be seen. Lily hung it in the closet. Her gaze swept the room. She'd only been here a day, but she still gaped at the opulence. She allowed herself a chance to really take in the bedroom.

The curtains at the French doors were silk. The rich color on the wall was of the highest quality. The bedclothes were the softest satin. And the closet! Lily had never seen so many dresses and shoes.

Emily peeked her white-capped head in. "Mrs. O'Reilly sent me to train you." She stepped into the room. "I'll help you make the bed. The sheets were just changed yesterday."

Emily had taken the news of Lily's possible promotion with only a flicker of her lids, but Lily knew the other woman had wanted this position. "That would be lovely. Emily, I really don't want this job, you know. I'm hoping Belle says no."

Emily shrugged. "So you say."

"It's true. I—I need a friend here, and we are to share a room. It will be quite uncomfortable if you're angry with me."

"I'm not angry. Just perplexed over how you managed this so quickly."

"I did only what I was asked to do. Truly. Things just happened after that."

Emily lifted her head and studied Lily's face. "I think I'll be stuck in the kitchen forever." Her eyes brightened. "Could you teach me what you know? About hair and fashion, I mean?"

"Of course! I brought my *Godey's* books, and we can look at them at night."

Emily smiled and looked around the room. "Has Miss Belle given you instructions on how she likes things done yet? You'll need to know whether or not she takes you on as her maid."

Lily shook her head. "She went on a drive with Mr. Vesters."

"She likes her sheets washed every three days. The morning room floor is to be swept every morning with fresh linen laid before she gets up." She pointed. "Miss Belle calls the veranda her morning room though it's outside. Confusing, I know."

"I didn't get that done this morning. I wasn't sure what was to be done."

Emily shrugged. "You only had three hours of sleep."

"None, really. I never fell asleep last night. It was too loud and strange."

Emily's merry hazel eyes sparkled. "It's a lively city for sure. Anyway, she likes every gown cleaned after wearing. Just under the arms and any spots. She won't wear it any longer once she's worn it three times."

"Just three times?" Lily couldn't imagine such waste.

"We usually get her castoffs." Emily's smile widened. "Though where she expects us to wear something so grand, I have no idea. I've gotten three so far, and I've taken off trim and made them a little plainer so I can wear them to church."

"You're allowed to go to church?"

"We take turns. I get to go once a month. I'll let Mrs. O'Reilly know you'd like to go too." Emily moved to the bed and pulled off the sheets. "Miss Belle likes the bed made from scratch so the sheets are taut and without wrinkles."

Lily went to the far side of the bed and began to help Emily make it. Emily showed her how to make the corner tight. Lily had never seen it done so precisely. Suddenly, she wanted to get back on the train and ride it straight to Larson.

Emily stared at her. "You're looking a little blue. You'll get the hang of this soon enough, love. I've only been here a year, and I know everything about this house." She lowered her voice. "Including the gossip."

Lily smiled back. "Everyone seems quite proper. I'm surprised there is anything to talk about."

"You'd be surprised. Take Mrs. O'Reilly. Lovely woman. Fair and hardworking. But she likes a bit of wine on the evenings she goes out with her male friend."

"Does he work here too?"

Emily shook her head as she flipped the quilt onto the bed. "He manages the stable for the Karrs. Mrs. O'Reilly only gets to see him once a week, but she comes in blushing like a girl. I don't think he plans to marry her though. I've seen his kind. He pinched my backside once when she wasn't looking. Now I make sure I'm working in another room when he comes. She's too good for him."

"You didn't tell her?"

"Lord no, love. She's fair, but I'm not going to be the target of her jealousy. I just keep my head down and do my job."

Lily was beginning to like Emily quite a lot. Down to earth, kind, and unassuming. She didn't hide her feelings either. "Thank you for taking me under your wing, Emily. I'd be very lost without you."

"I try to do my part," she said cheerfully. "Let's see, what else? Oh yes, Mrs. Marshall. She took quite a shine to you."

"I don't quite know how it happened."

"She's a sweet lady. No airs, that one. She won't even have a maid do for her, and she cleans their bedroom herself. If she needs to be buttoned up, she has Mr. Marshall do the buttoning. But he's more likely to do the unbuttoning, if you know what I mean." Emily winked. "Those two hold hands like newlyweds. Well, they are newlyweds. They've only been married a year. She was the ambassador's widow."

"Only a year? I assumed they'd been married many years."

Emily shook her head. "The first Mrs. Marshall died in childbirth. It's been Mr. Marshall's greatest sorrow not to have children. He has me buy things regularly for the orphanage and run them by. They've doted on Belle ever since they took her in when her father, the dead Mrs. Marshall's brother, died. Which is probably why she's the way she is."

"Demanding?" Lily had seen enough of her new mistress to know serving her would be challenging.

"Poor chit deserves some attention though. Her mother doted on her brothers and barely noticed Belle's presence. Her dad did too, and he was overbearing to boot. At least so I hear. He lavished nice things on Belle, but she was no more noticed than the dog on the rug."

"And Mr. Marshall? It seems he could look right through you with his gray eyes."

"I'd marry the man myself if he were single." Emily smiled. "He's running for senator in the national election, and everyone loves him. He's got some great ideas, and he cares about the working class. Our wages are more than fair, and he often steps into the kitchen to see if we need anything."

"I didn't realize he was a politician. Belle seemed angry with him last night. She said he wants her to marry Mr. Vesters."

Emily rolled her eyes. "She adores her uncle. She was just angry with him last night. He wants her settled with some money. Her father was well-to-do, but he lost his money in a bad investment just before he died. Mr. Marshall would support her forever, but he wants her to be comfortable and in charge of her own home."

"How do you know all these things?" Lily was in awe of the information her roommate seemed to possess.

Emily tapped her ear. "I keep my ears open and my wits about me. You'd do well to do the same."

Belle was quite weary from dealing with Stuart by teatime. She took off her hat when she entered the drawing room. "I'm perishing for some iced tea and cookies."

The new girl, Lily, turned at her voice and smiled. "I just brought in a tray, Miss Belle."

She was unlike any other maid. Not that Belle had noticed the servants all that much. The woman seemed to have a strong sense of herself. Most of the housemaids looked at Belle with awe. This one looked calmly back as though she were equal. The circumstances of Lily's employment were unusual. Perhaps Belle should put her in her place and make sure she understood her role here.

"Where is the tea?"

Her maid didn't flinch at Belle's harsh tone. "On the chaise." She pointed to the lounge out on the private side terrace. "I brought fruit as well. Strawberries."

Belle's mouth watered at the word, but she wasn't about to let Lily know she'd pleased her. She handed her the hat. "Hang this up."

"Of course." Lily's smile never faltered. "Is there anything else I can do for you? I put your book out on the chaise as well in case you wanted to read before dinner."

"You seem to have thought of everything. I thought you'd never been in service before." Belle stepped to the French doors and opened them.

This side of the house was in shade in the later afternoon. The scent of roses and gardenias wafted up from the garden. A tray was on the table beside the chaise. She picked up her book and reclined on the comfortable seat. The iced tea was perfect with a sprig of mint in it.

Lily had followed her outside and stood watching with just a hint of concern. Finally. Belle wanted to find fault with what she'd done, but nothing was out of order.

"How is the tea?"

"Delicious. How did you know I liked mint in it?"

"Emily told me. I want to please you, Miss Belle."

"You mean so you'll get around me like you got around my aunt and uncle? How did you do it?"

Lily inhaled sharply. "I don't know what you mean. I did only what I was told. Your aunt liked the way I styled her hair and noticed I knew a bit about fashion. I assure you I didn't set out to become your maid."

"I might still say no. I'm going to discuss it with my uncle." Again, the girl was entirely too calm and self-assured. Belle took another sip of her excellent tea. "I didn't realize we were hiring a personal friend of my cousin's. That's never a good idea. If I'd realized that, I probably wouldn't have hired you."

"I'll make quite sure you don't regret it. Is there anything else I can get for you? A throw perhaps? The wind is picking up."

"It's actually quite warm. I want you to run out to the millinery though. A hat I ordered is ready for pickup." She gave Lily the name of the store. "Ask Mrs. O'Reilly how to get there."

"Yes, miss."

Her father had taught her it was important to always be the one with the upper hand. She dismissed Lily, and her uncle came in as the maid left. He was a fine-looking man, even if he was her uncle. The wings of gray at his temples only made him look distinguished. His morning coat fit impeccably, and his salt-and-pepper beard was neatly trimmed.

He pulled a chair closer to her chaise. "You're looking quite lovely today, Belle." His expression beamed approval. "Vesters was quite smitten."

"Was he? I didn't notice." She took another sip of her tea. "Listen, Uncle Everett, about the maid . . ."

His jaw hardened. "I'll brook no argument on it. A woman of your stature should have her own maid."

"Oh please, Uncle. In this day and age? It's 1904, not 1865. I could have a job, you know. Maybe I'll work as a secretary or a telephone operator."

"Things haven't changed much for a woman of wealth like you, Belle. And yes, yes, I know your father lost his money, but you'll be my heir. There will be no lack of property and wealth. I want you established with a good man who will know how to manage my many holdings."

She wanted to ask him why Vesters then, but she wasn't ready for that conversation yet.

# SIX

It had taken Lily forever to find the right store. Riding the street-car was a new experience, and she got off at the wrong stop twice. She'd barely gotten there before they closed. Hatbox in hand, she went to wait for the trolley, but she got turned around again and found herself wandering down an unfamiliar street. Darkness was falling fast, and a nearby moonlight tower flickered into operation. The dim light gave a bit of assurance to her steps.

The trolley came up ahead and she broke into a run. The hatbox thumped against her leg as she ran to attempt to catch it. Waving her hand, she tried to get it to slow, but it pulled away and lumbered down the street. She sighed and went to sit on the bench to wait for the next one.

A cat dashed across the street with a mouse squeaking in its mouth. The October night was pleasant, but the humidity intensi-fied the onion smell from an upstairs apartment. Mrs. O'Reilly was going to be upset with Lily's tardiness.

A scream came from somewhere behind her, and Lily leaped to her feet. Dim figures scuffled in the dark alley, and she realized a woman grappled with a man. Something shattered on the ground, and the sound broke her paralysis.

"You there, leave her alone!" She started for the alley without thinking.

The man broke away, and the woman crumpled to the ground as he ran off. Several unseen men shouted, and she heard running steps as someone chased after him. Lily ran down the alley to where the woman lay. She knelt by the woman's side and helped her sit up. The dim light of the moonlight tower was enough to see the victim was blond and in her twenties.

Lily dabbed ineffectually at the blood on the woman's forehead. "Are you all right? What's your name?"

"Jane. Jane White," the young woman muttered in a hoarse voice.

"What happened? Who was that man?"

"I don't know." Jane touched her forehead. "He cut me with a knife, but I shoved him and got out the back door of my house and ran away. I—I think he's the man wh-who's been attacking women."

Jane's clothes were rough homespun, and her speech held an accent Lily couldn't place. An immigrant? "Attacking women?"

"Three others so far. I'm the first to survive." Jane's voice trembled. "What if he comes back?"

Lily patted Jane's shoulder. "I'm sure the police will catch him."

Jane clasped herself. "They haven't yet. He's wily."

A police officer approached. A large man with red cheeks nodded to Lily. "You're her sister?"

Lily shook her head. "Just a passerby."

He frowned. "You two look alike. Best be on your guard, miss. Some monster has been attacking blond women."

Lily gasped. "Thank you for the warning." What kind of city had she found herself in?

"Ma'am, I need to take this young woman to the hospital."

"Of course." Lily stepped aside to allow the officer to help Jane

45

to her feet. He guided her toward a police wagon parked at the end of the alley.

Once he had Jane stowed, he turned back toward Lily. "What's your name, miss? We might need to talk to you about anything you saw."

Lily told him her name and where she resided, then ran to catch the trolley. The last thing she needed was a policeman coming to question her.

Mrs. O'Reilly's lips were flat as Lily flew in the door nearly an hour late. "I needed you to serve tonight, Lily. Dinner is over and they're eating dessert. I'm quite disappointed in you."

Lily took off her hat and put on her apron. The kitchen was warm and filled with the scent of freshly baked bread and goose. "I'm so sorry. I got lost on the trolley, and then I saw a young woman attacked. I helped her until the police arrived."

Interest erased the frown on the housekeeper's face. "Was she blond?"

"Why, yes."

Mrs. O'Reilly *tsked*. "There have been three women murdered in the past two months, all servant girls. The city is afraid the Servant Girl Killer is back. He terrorized the city back in '84 and '85. I've had a terrible time keeping servants since the first girl died. Was this one attacked with a knife?"

"Yes."

"Just like the last three. That poor girl." Mrs. O'Reilly straightened. "Get the glasses for the men's drinks and take them to the smoking room."

Lily hurried off to obey, praying all the while she wouldn't see

Andy or, rather, Drew. Now that she'd seen how different he was, it was easier to think of him as Drew. The Andy she'd known and loved was dead. She'd managed to avoid him for the past two days, though he was never far from her thoughts. Part of her wanted to hear his explanation, but the sane part knew she had to stay far away from the temptation he offered.

The dinner party had broken up by the time she carried the sherry into the room where the men waited. Drew tried to catch her eye, but she avoided him and slipped out of the room. She nearly ran into Mrs. O'Reilly.

"There's a policeman here to see you, Lily." Mrs. O'Reilly was frowning. "This is most unacceptable."

"A policeman? Did he say what he wanted?"

"He did not. I've put him in the butler's pantry to wait for you. I don't want Mrs. Marshall to think you've done something wrong. At least not yet."

Lily lifted her chin. "I've done nothing. It's probably about the attack I witnessed."

When Lily started in the wrong direction, Mrs. O'Reilly grabbed her arm. "This way."

The housekeeper marched her down a maze of hallways to the back of the house. The butler's pantry was a large space near the wine room. It held cabinets filled with china, cups, and crystal glasses. Fine silver filled felt-lined drawers that locked. The scent of cinnamon tea permeated the room.

The policeman turned when the women entered. He was about twenty-five, and he held his hat in his hands. "Ah, you must be Miss Donaldson."

"Yes, sir. You wanted to see me?"

He nodded. "I was told you were on the scene when Miss White was attacked. I have a few questions for you."

Mrs. O'Reilly visibly relaxed. She pressed Lily's arm. "I'll leave you to answer his questions. See me in the kitchen when you're done." Her voice was kind now.

Her attention on the policeman, Lily nodded. "I don't know how I can help you. It was so dark I couldn't make out much detail."

"Can you describe what you saw?"

She told him about running to catch the trolley. "I heard a scream and saw two figures struggling. When I shouted, he ran off. I rushed to help."

He looked up then, his brow lifted. "That's rather brave. Weren't you afraid he might harm you?"

"I didn't think. When I got there, Miss White was on the ground and bleeding from a wound on her forehead. She said he attacked her with a knife."

He scribbled on his pad of paper. "You didn't see the man at all? Any impression of his size?"

She hesitated. "It was too dark to see. He was taller than Miss White, but that's all I know." She shuddered. "Such a gruesome way to attack a defenseless woman."

"This monster has done the same and more to other women. Miss White is lucky to have survived."

Lily clasped her hands together. "So she did survive? I'm so glad. I wasn't sure what happened to her after she was taken to the hospital."

He nodded. "Can you think of anything else you noticed? Anything at all?" He thrust a drawing into her hands. "This is the last victim. She was killed two days ago."

Two days ago, the day Lily arrived on the train. She stared down into the face of the woman and shook her head. "I've never seen her."

The policeman sighed and put the drawing back in his pocket.

"This fellow has been targeting women who are of similar coloring and body type to you. I'd be careful if I were you, miss." He doffed his hat. "Thank you for your assistance." He headed for the door. "I'll see myself out."

She pushed away the uneasy feelings his words caused. No one knew her here. She was perfectly safe in this huge house.

The first five days had flown by. Lily's back ached as she climbed the rear stairway to the attic storage area. The box in her arms was heavy, but she would be rid of it soon. Dust motes danced in a shaft of sunlight streaming through the dormer windows. The "eyes" on this side of the house were just as disconcerting as when she'd first stood in the yard and looked up at them.

An assortment of furniture and old rugs crowded the space under the eaves. She found an empty space to drop the box of old books, then sneezed as a cloud of dust assaulted her nose. When she shoved the box closer to the wall and stood, her head banged against a board. A hollow sound echoed back at her. A crack appeared in the wall.

Her heart sank. If she'd broken the plaster, she'd be in so much trouble. She knelt beside the wall and ran her fingers over the smooth surface. There was definitely a crack. She nearly groaned until she realized it was much too uniform.

She shoved the box out of the way, then peered more closely at the wall. The crack ran all the way around three sides. It was a door, not a crack at all. A hidden door, at that. The mechanism for opening it was a lever just under a trim board that ran around the top of the wall where the roof turned upward.

Her pulse skipped in her throat. Did she dare open it? Before she could talk herself out of it, she gripped the lever and pulled. The wall groaned and swung inward instead of outward. A yawning black hole appeared. The stale scent of mouse droppings and dust rushed to greet her, and she backed away.

"Love, what are you doing?"

Her hand on her throat, she whirled to see Emily with a box in her arms. "You frightened me half to death. Look what I found. It seems to be a hidden room."

Emily crossed the attic floor and dropped her box onto the one Lily had brought up. "I've heard passageways wind their way all through this house. They were part of the original castle design, so Mr. Marshall had them reconstructed when he brought the stones over."

Lily peered into the fathomless void. "I wish we had a light so we could see."

"I can smell the mice, so you won't get me in there." Emily backed away. "I'm sure it's full of nastiness. Mrs. O'Reilly is on a rampage to get the rest of the books moved up here. You'd better shut that and come along."

Nearly a week had dragged by with no opportunity for Drew to catch Lily alone. Belle sought every chance to spend time with him, but Lily was as elusive as a bobcat. He caught her staring at him on occasion when she helped serve during dinner, but she quickly averted her gaze. Surely she would have a day off soon.

Thursday morning dawned with a clear blue sky that chased away the mid-autumn showers. The unusually cool temperatures were gone too, and he left his jacket behind in his room. His meeting with Vesters was at ten at the tea shop on Congress. Casual dress would be appropriate in the setting, and he wanted to make sure Vesters's guard was down. The economy of the entire country was riding on his meeting today.

Standing to the side of a mass of rosebushes, he waited for the car to be brought around. Movement out of the corner of his eye caught his attention, and he turned to see someone coming around the side of the house. Lily, dressed in a plain gray dress, strode through the garden toward the gate at the far side of the property. She hadn't seen him yet, and he allowed himself to take in her graceful form and the pink in her cheeks.

If only things were different. His blood surged when he remembered holding her, loving her. But his obsession with Lily had killed his father. It had been *his fault*. He didn't deserve her. And she didn't deserve a husband who could die any moment.

The best he could hope for now was to convince her to guard his secret.

The driver, Henry, pulled the 1903 Pullman Touring automobile to a stop in front of him. The young man was one Drew had seen around on occasion, and his gaze was focused over Drew's shoulder. He was watching Lily's approach, and Drew narrowed his gaze at the man. The driver looked away, a flush staining his cheeks.

Lily turned at the rattle of the engine. Her eyes widened when she saw him. He beckoned her, and she glanced toward the house, then approached him. Was that fear in her eyes?

He opened the back door of the open-riding sedan. "Heading to town? I have an appointment at the tea shop in town, and you can come along."

Her hands behind her back, she edged away. "I don't think Miss Belle would approve. She saw me speaking to you the other morning and questioned me."

His pulse kicked in his chest. "You said nothing, of course?"

She shook her head. "But you know how I dislike falsehood, Andy."

"Drew."

"Mr. Hawkes." She tipped up her chin.

Her spunk was one of the many things he'd always loved about her. Gripping her arm, he guided her toward the door. "Belle is out with her aunt, as I'm sure you know well."

"Someone may still tell her."

As she stepped into the automobile, it was all he could do to resist leaning in closer to sniff the faint scent of honeysuckle. He sprang up beside her, and the springs in the cushion groaned as he settled beside her. "Are you off work today?"

She shook her head. "Merely on an errand for Miss Belle. She wanted me to pick up some books for her."

The gas engine revved, and the automobile lurched forward. He plucked her hand from her lap. "Are you ever getting a day off?"

She pulled her hand away and edged toward the other side of the seat. "I don't know. Mrs. O'Reilly hasn't brought it up. She might be waiting until Miss Belle makes up her mind on whether I'm to be her lady's maid. Right now I'm doing a bit of everything."

The market wasn't far, and there would be no time to tell her all that needed to be said. "Then you must. You can't work every day."

She turned her head to look out at the passing scenery. "I'm grateful for the position. I can do nothing to jeopardize it."

With all his being, he wanted to tell her he'd take care of her. What did he have to offer though? The very danger he'd left to save her from. "You risk nothing by bringing up the terms of your employment."

"I'll ask Mrs. O'Reilly about it." She still wasn't looking at him. Edwards and Church Booksellers was just ahead. "Come to tea with me. For half an hour."

She turned to look at him, her blue eyes darkening to indigo. "You left me and never came back. Why? Though I doubt I can believe any excuse you tell me."

He winced. "I never lied to you, Lily."

"Your love was a lie."

"It wasn't!" He reached for her hand again and she flinched, so he clenched his hands together in his lap. "I have always loved you. I've never stopped."

Her lips parted in a faint gasp. Moisture made her eyes luminous. "You could not have loved me and put me through what you did. You've been gone for four years, Andy. *Four years!* Your professions of love are hollow. I could be in the grave like my mother, and you wouldn't even have known."

"I would have known. Grace wrote me every month. I got her letter about your mother the day after you arrived."

Her eyes grew wider. "She's known where you've been all this time? She's never mentioned a word."

"She's my cousin. I swore her to secrecy."

"But why?" The words were barely a whisper.

*Tell her.* He gritted his teeth to keep back the truth. Truth, though admirable, could get her killed. "Men were after me. Men I feared might harm you." *As they harmed our fathers.* It was as much as he could tell her.

The automobile stopped, and she thrust open the door on her side. "So you left me alone where anyone might have attacked me? That makes no sense, Andy. None at all. In fact, I think you're still lying to me." Gathering her skirt in one hand, she stepped down onto the sidewalk before he or the driver could assist her. "As far as I'm concerned, you are merely a guest at the Butterfly Palace. Anything that was once between us is gone. Belle can have you."

Her back ramrod straight, she disappeared through the door

to the booksellers. He leaped down from the auto and spoke to the driver. "I'll make my own way from here."

He glanced at his watch. His appointment was in fifteen minutes. There was no time to chase down Lily and make her listen. He turned back and climbed into the vehicle.

# SEVEN

Lily retrieved the volume of Dickens for her mistress, then tucked the leather book into her reticule. Her nerves still hummed from being in Drew's presence. Remembering his lies, she curled her fingers into the palms of her gloves. Did the man even know how to tell the truth?

The heat baked up from the bricks out on the sidewalk. She glanced down the street and saw the sign for the tea shop he'd mentioned. Who was he meeting? Though it was none of her business, she found herself moving in that direction. If he was up to no good, she owed it to her employers to find out. She had a bit of money in her purse, enough to purchase a cup of tea. It wasn't like he had the right to throw her out.

As she neared the café, she saw Drew sitting at an outside table with Mr. Vesters. Neither man had seen her yet, but she kept her head high as she quietly asked to be seated at the table next to theirs. A tall planter obscured her table from view. They were intent in conversation, but their voices carried as she settled into her chair with her back to them. The scent of cinnamon from the rolls on a tray filled the air.

A chair scraped on the pavement, and Vesters's voice rose. "So that's your game? I should leave right now."

"Look, I know what you're doing, and I want in on it." Drew's voice was hard and insistent. "You'll find me an asset to your operation. I have better contacts than you can imagine. I can double the money you're making now."

"How did you find out?" Mr. Vesters sounded a bit more relaxed but still wary.

"Does it matter? What matters is I can help you. I can expand your operation and your profits."

"Maybe."

Lily couldn't think, couldn't breathe. The words used made her uneasy. *Operation.* And *in on it.* Was Vesters doing something . . . criminal? And did that mean Drew was just as crooked? She didn't want to believe it, but the man behind her wasn't the man who'd held her hand in the moonlight and promised eternal devotion. He wasn't the man who'd lit her skin on fire with his touch.

She dared a glance over her shoulder, and her gaze collided with Drew's. His eyes widened, and the color drained from his face. He quickly recovered his composure and leaned forward to speak to the other man. So quietly Lily couldn't hear.

She blinked at the burning in her eyes as she drew off her gloves. The smile she slanted up toward the waitress was an effort. "Just tea, please. With sugar."

"Lily?"

She looked up at Drew's voice. He was alone. She'd been so lost in thought she hadn't seen Vesters leave. "I've concluded my duties and thought I'd have some tea." Her voice sounded high and strained. He said nothing as he stared at her. She'd never been able to mask her feelings. "What are you involved in, Drew? If you don't explain to my satisfaction, I will go to Mr. Marshall and tell him what I overheard."

Drew pulled out a chair beside her and sat. "What did you hear, Lily? We said nothing of consequence."

"It sounded as though you were forcing Mr. Vesters to allow you to join some nefarious scheme he's involved in."

He looked away, out toward the lorry clattering down the street, then back at her. "I can explain."

"So you keep saying. Yet no explanation has been forthcoming." Lily waited until the waitress set down her tea and left. "You can begin anytime."

"It's complicated, Lily. I don't want to be overheard." He rose and tossed some money onto the table, then held out his hand. "Come along to a more private place."

Eyeing his open palm, she considered his request. Tea could wait. She put her hand in his, and the touch of his skin against her palm tightened her chest. He still had the power to affect her like no other man. Gathering up her gloves, she went with him.

He led her down the street toward a small park. Children played on the other side of the grassy lawn, but no one was close enough to hear them as they settled on a bench under a tree. The branches screened them from any passersby. The sweet scent of flowers perfumed the air.

She arranged her skirts and listened to the birds chirp overhead. The scent of fresh-cut grass mingled with the roses rambling up a fence nearby. "Well?"

He sank beside her, close enough that his shoulder brushed hers. "I'm with the Secret Service."

"What? Why, when? You never told me." She studied his serious expression. His statement seemed ridiculous.

"You remember when I stalked off after the fire?"

She nodded, her throat tight. It was an image she still carried with her. "I never saw you again. Not until last week."

"I crawled into a barn to sleep. I didn't want to see you or anyone else. A man found me there. He told me our fathers had been killed because they'd discovered a counterfeiting ring."

The bench was hard under her thighs but not as hard as the lump in her throat. "The fire was deliberately set? I always wondered how it raged out of control so fast." She couldn't bear to think about the horrific night, so she concentrated on the birds chirping and the scent of freshly mown grass.

He nodded. "I agreed to become a Secret Service agent to bring the killer to justice. I had to do something about the guilt eating me alive."

Though she flinched from it, she thought back to that night. "There was a stack of money on the desk. Was it counterfeit?"

His eyes widened. "You never mentioned that."

"You disappeared. I couldn't tell you anything. Go on with the story."

"My superior told me there was a counterfeiting ring operating in the house next to yours. The Ballards."

She gasped. "That's ridiculous. Mr. Ballard was the nicest man. We were all crazy about him."

Drew's dark brown eyes were steady and resolute. "I believe that *nice* man killed our fathers."

Something squeezed in her chest, and she shook her head. "Where's the proof of that?"

"I saw stacks of money in his barn. That's where I was holed up when my boss offered me a job. I asked my boss to arrest them and he refused. The Secret Service wanted to get the entire gang. I was told to leave town, and they would send in another operative."

She struggled to reconcile what she knew with what he was saying. "Why didn't you tell me? I would have gone with you if you'd asked." Her heart had never recovered from his betrayal. She'd never been able to fully trust another man after he left without a word.

"I'm in a dangerous line of work. I couldn't keep you safe." His gaze dropped away. "And I didn't deserve you. Not after my actions killed our fathers." His lips flattened, and he looked off toward the children. "Ballard killed my father. I'll have revenge if it's the last thing I do."

Lammes Candies was filled with deliciously sweet smells when Belle opened the door and motioned her aunt inside. "Aunt Camille, you must taste their gem. It's icy and fruity, much better than ice cream." They passed a display of newspapers. The headlines held the lurid details of the last murder.

Men and women glanced their way from the long bar on the right. Candies of every type filled the glass display cases on the left. The women stepped to the wooden bar beside two policemen, and Belle ordered strawberry gems for both of them. Her aunt signed the tab to have the bill sent up to the house.

Belle took the frosty treats and carried them to the café tables out on the sidewalk. "I thought Uncle Everett would be here already." She pulled out her chair and settled onto it, then took a tiny taste of her gem.

Her aunt sat across the table from her. "You know how men are, darling. He likely got caught up in politics. Election Day will be here before we know it." Her eyes widened at the first taste of her gem. "It's delicious, Belle. I'll order some to be sent to the house for dessert tomorrow."

Belle's good humor evaporated. She'd had plans for Friday. "What's tomorrow?"

"Have you forgotten the fund-raising dinner already? We have fifty of Everett's best supporters descending on us. That reminds me—I ordered you a new dress. It's a daring shade of orange. We will stop and pick it up on the way home."

Belle had grown tired of all the new fripperies she was expected to wear. Ribbons, gloves, slippers. Dozens of dresses of every color packed her wardrobe. Many she hadn't yet worn. The thought of so many parties this year had seemed pleasant at first. Now she wished for something of more substance to do. She had no more purpose than the grass waving in the breeze.

"There's Uncle Everett." She waved at him. Many heads turned to watch him pass, including those of every woman in the area.

He lifted his hand in greeting and quickened his pace. The sidewalk was crowded, and he paused to allow two women to pass. The bushes lining the walk on the other side of the street by the park parted, and something glinted in the sun.

Belle squinted, then gasped. She leaped to her feet as the barrel took aim at her uncle. Time slowed as she instantly realized the shooter intended to kill her uncle.

She pointed. "Uncle Everett, get down! There's a gun!"

Uncle Everett looked up and paused. He smiled as if to assure her, but his smile faded as the gunman rose with the weapon in his hand.

There had been two policemen inside, and Belle shouted, "Help, police!" Unable to tear her gaze away, she took a step toward her uncle.

The bushes shook, and the gun became easier to see. A shot rang out, and Uncle Everett dropped to the ground. Aunt Camille leaped to her feet and screamed. The gun disappeared from the bushes, and a man rushed across the open park area. Other people screamed, and several men gave chase to the shooter.

Belle rushed toward her uncle, who began to stand and brush himself off. "Uncle, are you hurt?"

He embraced her. "No, no, my dear. Thanks to your warning, I escaped injury. Lucky for me you saw the scoundrel." He released her to hug his wife. "Don't fret, Camille, I'm fine. The police will soon catch the culprit."

"I knew this would happen." Camille pulled her hanky from her sleeve and dabbed her cheeks. "Ever since you announced you planned to support women's suffrage. You must stop, Everett. I don't want to be widowed."

Belle nodded. "It's not worth it, Uncle Everett. We don't want to lose you."

"You'd both have me forget my convictions? What kind of man would I be?"

Convictions. The word struck a chord in Belle's heart. Did she have any convictions of any sort? Her existence had been rather aimless and self-centered. But it was what was expected of women in her station of life. She didn't have to be some kind of crusader. Especially if it immersed her in danger or prevented her from achieving her goal of marriage.

She fell into step beside her aunt and uncle as they headed back to the candy store. "Do you know who these men might be, Uncle?"

He pulled out a chair for her aunt. "I've heard a few rumblings, but we have no proof. Was he familiar at all, Belle?"

She shook her head as he pulled out her chair. "I didn't get a good look at him. I saw only his back as he was running away. His hat obscured his face as he turned."

She looked across the street at the park. A couple caught her attention, and she frowned. Was that the new kitchen maid with a man? Narrowing her eyes, she studied the two in the shadow of the great live oak. Surely that wasn't Mr. Hawkes. She couldn't be positive with the sun in her eyes and the two of them half hidden by the leaves.

The police approached her, and she answered their questions. When they were through, she rose. "I think I'll take a walk in the park."

Her aunt caught at her hand. "Oh no, Belle. Not with that man still on the loose."

"I'll stay in the open area. I'll be back in fifteen minutes. Uncle Everett, you can have my gem. I haven't eaten any of it yet, and it's melting."

Shaking off her aunt's hand, she stepped into the street and dodged a lorry. All she needed was to get a little closer to see.

# EIGHT

Drew remained seated when Lily sprang to her feet and paced the grassy space under the tree. She had never been good at hiding her emotions. He probably shouldn't have told her the truth, but he couldn't let her betray him to her employer.

She spun around and stared at him. "The fire was set?"

He nodded. That night was so embedded in his memory he could almost smell smoke right now. He well remembered the look on Lily's face when she realized her father wasn't walking out of that inferno, as well as her mother's wails. A deep sense of responsibility still gnawed at him. The killer was still walking around. Justice had not been served.

Lily clutched his forearm. "But why? Why would anyone kill them? How were they involved in this?"

He stared at her hand on his arm. The familiar heat from her touch would only distract him. He stood up so her hand fell away. "A saddlebag of money was accidentally left in the livery. Your father was smart. He realized it was counterfeit and wrote a letter to the Secret Service. But before anything could be done, the money vanished and the fire occurred. That's when I was pulled into it."

Her blue eyes shimmered, and she blinked rapidly. "How close are you to putting the men responsible behind bars? It's been four years."

His gaze traveled over her perfect skin and luminous eyes. "Ballard has an uncanny ability to sniff us out. Every time I've gotten close, he's vanished. I tracked him here three months ago."

"Has he seen you? Are you in danger?"

He shook his head. "I've kept my distance. If he knew I was here, he'd vanish. The problem is I don't have enough hard evidence to convict him."

"Not even of murder?"

"Especially not of murder. What I've got is circumstantial. I need to catch him with the goods."

"Mr. Vesters is involved in the counterfeiting, so you're trying to get close to him?"

Her perception caught him off guard, but he wasn't going to lie to her. "That's right."

"Where is Ballard now?"

He could see her thoughts churning. "I don't want you anywhere near him, Lily. He's ruthless and has no conscience."

"If you don't tell me, I'll ask Mr. Vesters myself."

"You're going to tip my hand and put yourself at risk! Stay out of it," he said, sitting down on the bench again.

Her lips flattened, and she narrowed her eyes. "Then tell me where he is."

"Why? There's nothing you can do about this."

"If he killed my father, I have a right to help bring Ballard to justice."

Maybe she had a point. He felt the same. But she didn't know the type of man they were up against. Drew suspected Ballard had put more people in the grave than they knew. He didn't intend for Lily to be another victim. "I'll keep you informed, how's that? It's the best I can do, Lily."

She sank onto the bench beside him. "That's not good enough,

An—I mean, Mr. Hawkes. I want to help. I'm in a position to hear things. I could be of tremendous service to you."

He curled his hands into fists. The thought of her in harm's way was unacceptable. "No, Lily. Not going to happen."

"Then I'll do it on my own." She rose and took a step toward the sidewalk.

He couldn't let her do anything reckless. He caught at her hand before she could leave him, then tugged her back onto the bench. "People are noticing our argument. Smile. Try to relax like you're having a good time."

"No one is paying a bit of attention to us."

He nodded toward two men smoking cigars by the creek. A young woman sat on a boulder with a child in her arms. "Those two were watching with great interest."

Her eyes narrowed as she stared at them. "Who are they?"

"I don't know, but we can't afford to take any chances."

"You're just saying that to try to keep me from getting involved." She gave a small gasp. "That's the woman who was attacked the other day. Jane White." She stood and started toward the group.

Drew reached for her but missed. He leaped to his feet and hurried after her. They were too close to the group for him to stop her from speaking. He had noticed the men watching his discourse with Lily from the first moment. The young woman had a gruesome cut on her forehead, still purple and swollen.

Lily smiled when she reached the young woman. "Miss White, how lovely to see you up and about. Are you quite recovered from the attack?"

The woman gasped when she saw Lily, and she rose unsteadily. "M-Miss. How unexpected to see you." She glanced at her companions, then shifted the child to the other shoulder. "Yes, I'm fine now. Still a little stiff and sore, but very thankful to be alive. And please, call me Jane."

"Only if you call me Lily. I'm Lily Donaldson." She leaned close to look at the baby. "Who is this little one?"

"This is my little Hannah. She is six months old." A tender smile lit the woman's pale features with an unexpected beauty, and she brushed her lips across the baby's forehead.

"She's beautiful." Lily glanced at the grass. "What's this?" She picked up a glass globe containing a butterfly.

Miss White winced. "I received that a couple of days ago. The butterfly was alive, and I wanted to break the globe to set it free, but I was afraid I'd kill it. By the time my brother, Nathan, got home to help me, it wasn't moving. I probably shouldn't have brought it, but Hannah loves to see it. Even though the butterfly is dead, it's still beautiful."

Drew took it from Lily's hand. "Did you tell the police?"

Miss White shook her head. "I didn't think to mention it."

The taller man stared them down. He was about twenty-two with a trim brown beard and piercing green eyes. He was neatly dressed in brown pants and a white shirt. "Who are you, and why are you bothering my sister?"

Jane turned toward him. "This is the young lady who helped me after the attack, Nathan."

Nathan's gaze softened, and he took off his hat. His longish hair curled over his ears. He was probably attractive to the ladies with his soulful eyes and muscular form. "I thank you for that then, miss." He glanced at Drew. "This your fella?"

Lily colored and shook her head. "Just an acquaintance."

The pang at her words took Drew by surprise. He'd chosen his course long ago.

Nathan studied him. "I saw you talking to Vesters. Just a

friendly warning since you helped my sister. He's dangerous and you'd do well to stay away from him."

Drew lifted a brow. "Dangerous in what way?"

Nathan turned away. "I'm not saying anything else. Just be careful."

This might be the break Drew was looking for. He fixed his gaze on the other man, a fellow in his forties with a straggly blond beard and a rumpled white shirt. "And you are . . . ?"

The man shrugged. "Just a friend. This is none of my business." He folded his arms over his chest.

Lily turned to Jane. "We believe Vesters is associated with the man who killed our fathers. We need to know anything that might help us."

Jane put her hand on her brother's arm. "Please, Nathan. She was good to me."

Nathan turned back to face them. "I'm not surprised he would stoop to murder." His gaze went past Drew's shoulder. "We must go." He seized his sister's arm and propelled her into the trees. The other man followed them.

Drew turned to see Belle walking toward them with purposeful steps.

Belle had never seen the people with Drew and Lily before, but they slipped away into the lush green shrubs that lined the gurgling brook. They appeared to be of the unsavory sort, so she paid their departure no mind as she marched through the tall, damp grass toward the wayward maid. The chit would pay for the dampness on the hem of her new dress. Her slippers were soaked as well.

Drew's gaze caught hers, but his expression was inscrutable as he turned to greet her. He was so handsome in his gray suit that he nearly took her breath away. And it made her all the angrier that he was consorting with the *maid*.

He took off his hat and nodded. "Miss Castle, what a surprise to see you here."

"I'm sure it is." She stared at her maid. "Lily, I must say I'm quite disappointed to find you not attending to the duties I gave you this morning."

Lily didn't appear discomfited. She held up a book-shaped package wrapped in brown paper. "I completed my duties."

"Then you should have gone home!" Belle waited for her to explain her appearance with Drew, but the young woman kept her chin up and didn't appear to fear the tongue lashing she was about to get. "Who else were you with? I saw the other men."

"And woman," Lily said. "The young lady was the one I helped after she was attacked. I wished to make sure she was doing well."

"And I accompanied her," Drew put in.

Belle's gloved fingers curled into her palms. Why was he taking up for Lily? Was he one of those men who liked to trick maids into bed? But no, it was much more likely Lily had set her cap on him. "I see."

"Miss Jane is doing fine," Lily said. "She is still bruised but alive. Which is more than can be said for some of the villain's other victims."

Belle shuddered. Perhaps she would agree to having Lily for her maid after all. At least she would have direct contact in controlling her. "It's hardly a topic for polite company. Go back home at once, Lily. I'm sure Mrs. O'Reilly has other duties for you to tend to."

"Of course, Miss Belle." Lily's long lashes swept down, obscuring the expression in her eyes. "I'll see you there."

She didn't look at Drew, which was just as well, because Belle had had all she could take of the girl's impudence. How dare she even look at a cultured man like Drew? Once she got Lily alone, Belle intended to make it clear there would be no more of this type of behavior.

Once Lily hurried toward the street, Belle composed herself and smiled up at Drew. "I hope she wasn't too much of a nuisance. Thank you for taking care of her. I know it was your way of helping me and my uncle as well. We can't let any rumors fly about the integrity of one of our maids."

He offered his arm. "I'm sure you need to return home."

"My uncle is waiting for me at Lammes Candies." Drew smelled most divinely of bay rum as she took his arm. Her bad mood evaporated, and they strolled back toward the café. "Someone tried to shoot Uncle Everett."

He stopped. "He's all right?"

"Oh, of course. I saw the villain myself and warned my uncle just in time." She warmed at his expression of admiration. "The police are searching for the man, but I think he escaped. Did you see anyone running through the park? He came this way." She described what the fiend wore and what she could remember of his appearance.

She gasped, putting her hand to her throat. "One of those men you were speaking with. He had on a white shirt just like my uncle's attacker."

"There are many men with white shirts." He began to walk again.

"But that fellow was about the same height and build. Who was he? The police should interrogate him."

"I don't know his name. The other man was Miss White's brother. But it would be a kindness not to drag the fellow into something like that. I would have noticed if he'd run past us to where

Miss White was sitting. And he was not panting or showing any signs of exertion when we went to talk to his sister."

"That you noticed." She wasn't about to let him talk her out of such an important clue. "It can't hurt to tell the police. If he's innocent, no harm will come to him. And it might spare my uncle another attack."

"Any reason why he might be attacked?"

"He wishes to give women the vote. That's not a popular move."

"No, it's not."

He lifted a brow and smiled. "What is your view? Wouldn't you like to vote?"

Would she? She hadn't given it much thought. "Perhaps."

They reached the sidewalk and stood waiting for the lorries and drays to pass so they could cross. Her aunt and uncle were still sitting at the outside table. Her aunt gave a discreet wave and smiled. Belle knew her aunt would approve of Drew.

The street was clear, so she lifted her skirts free of the mud and dashed across to the café. Her fingers held tightly to Drew's arm, and if she had her way, she intended to make her claim on this man very clear to Lily.

# NINE

The two men, hands pocketed, strolled along the river walk in the fading light of day. Drew had requested the meeting, but now that he had Ian's attention, he was beginning to wonder if he'd overreacted.

The sunset threw brilliant colors onto the water, and the rich scent of river mud filled the air. They reached a vacant bench with no one around. Drew gestured to the seat, and the two settled onto it.

Ian's erect military bearing and muscular build were at odds with his age of about fifty. He'd been with the Secret Service since his late teens, first as a Pinkerton agent, then staying on when the real agency was formed. Even after all these years, Drew didn't know him well. The man kept his private life well hidden.

"What's this all about, Drew? You have new evidence on the counterfeiters?"

Drew shook his head. "Everett Marshall was nearly shot earlier today."

Ian absorbed the news, then frowned. "Political reasons?"

"I hear he plans to try to get through women's suffrage, and someone isn't happy. I thought you should know. There may be more attempts. It's possible it was an attempted political assassination."

"It might be our problem, but it could have been a random event that we wouldn't handle. Did they catch the shooter?"

"No, he escaped."

Ian took out his pipe and a pouch of tobacco. "That puts a different spin on it."

"And what if it's part of something bigger?" Drew had been unable to put his finger on why Everett's attempted murder had set all his alarms ringing. It was more than just a liking for the man. This felt bigger, more sinister than some random attack from a disgruntled citizen.

"How much do you know about Marshall?"

"Not much. He's been my introduction to Vesters. Rich as Job but he seems to be in politics because he cares about other people. He's in charge here of the big push to reelect President Roosevelt."

Ian lit his pipe, then took a puff. The scent of pipe tobacco mingled with that of the flowers across the walk. "I've met Marshall a few times. I recently heard he might be planning a run for the presidency after he wins his bid for a senate seat. I'm sure Teddy Roosevelt would support him. I assumed he might be involved with Vesters and the counterfeiting since they are friends, but we've found no evidence linking him to the others."

Drew shook his head. "He doesn't seem the type, and he's got plenty of money. No reason for him to do it."

"Did you ever figure out how he became associated with Vesters?"

"Vesters put a lot of money into his campaign."

"Why?"

"He felt he was more sympathetic to business. And I think he's had his eye on Marshall's niece."

Ian's gray eyes bored into Drew. "You seem more concerned than an initial look at this might warrant."

"It feels like it's the tip of something larger."

"Of what? I've learned to trust your instincts."

Drew chewed his lip. "The money Vesters used to donate to Marshall's campaign might well have been counterfeit."

"So you wonder if Marshall himself might be involved?"

"No, that's not it. Vesters may have some other ulterior motive for helping Marshall. And we know what a manipulator Ballard is."

"You did well to bring this to my attention. I'll poke around and see what I can find. I want you to stay out of it though. Your job is to get the counterfeiters. I'll handle anything else that comes up. That last ring you brought in has been helpful. The kingpin agreed to tell Vesters you've worked for him."

"That will help."

"Is that all?"

Drew hesitated. He owed his boss the truth. "My ex-fiancée is here."

Ian's eyes widened. "You've seen Lily?"

"I'm surprised you remember her name. It's been four years."

One gray brow rose. "I've seen the toll losing her has taken on you. Her mother died recently."

"You've kept tabs on her."

Ian shrugged. "Regret has a way of fueling obsession. If our budget hadn't been cut, I had meant to get some money to her anonymously. Then I heard she found a position and moved to Austin."

"Yet you didn't warn me."

"I would have. I had no idea you'd run into her so quickly. Where did you see her?"

"She works for Marshall. She's a housemaid."

"Well, that's an interesting twist. Has she seen you?"

Drew rubbed his head. "Not only has she seen me, but she's determined to help." He told Ian what Lily had overheard and how he'd been forced to reveal why he was in Austin.

Ian took another puff of his pipe. "Sloppy, Drew, very sloppy. This seriously compromises the investigation. She's likely to tell someone what she knows."

"Not Lily. And there's more." He told Ian about Jane White and how Lily had come to be acquainted with her. And about the warning her brother had issued.

Ian stroked his white goatee. "You need to find out what he knows. But I don't have to tell you that. You're good at your job."

"I'm going to see Nathan and try to convince him to trust me. His family seems to have fallen on rough times. Can I offer a reward?"

Ian shook his head. "Sorry, there's no money in the budget right now. If Lily wants to help, let her. They likely feel they can trust her a little since she helped Jane."

Drew clenched his jaw. "I don't want Lily in danger. I'll take care of it."

Ian gave a bark of a laugh. "Drew, you can't save the world. You walked away from Lily to save her once before. I've regretted encouraging that decision. I saw you as a bright young man with much to offer the agency, and I thought a wife would hinder your effectiveness. But I was wrong. A life lived without a family is a lonely one."

"You don't have a wife?" Drew wasn't sure if he was overstepping, but Ian had moved this discussion to something personal.

Ian looked down at his hands. "I did once. She was killed when someone shot at me. I thought to spare you that. But the happiest years of my life were the ones we spent together. I don't think she would have wanted to never have experienced that even if it meant a longer life. Some things are worth the risk."

"Not to me." He couldn't live with himself if he brought Lily harm. Losing his father had nearly killed him. "I did the right thing. I can't have her death on my conscience."

"You can't second-guess fate. All you can do is live your life one day at a time. You really should let go of that obsession with Ballard."

Drew clenched his jaw. "I'll get him behind bars yet."

"And if he slips away again, you'll just let her go a second time?"

"It's for the best."

For all his courageous words, Drew prayed he was strong enough to do the right thing.

The kitchen was a scene of pandemonium when Lily stepped inside. She'd tried to find a cab, but all she'd seen had been full and she had to wait for a trolley back to the Butterfly Palace. She was quite late. Kitchen maids scurried to and fro with bags of flour and sugar. Several stood at the stove stirring pots of something that steamed out delicious smells. Several apple pies stood cooling on the large wooden table, and another woman carved the turkey.

"Love, where have you been?" Emily tossed an apron at Lily. "Mrs. O'Reilly is on a rampage looking for you. The guests for the dinner party are arriving any minute, and the table still isn't set."

"I'll do that now." Lily took off her hat, then tied on the apron.

What would she do if she lost her job? She couldn't go back to Larson with her tail tucked between her legs. She had to do better, focus on doing her best for this job. Being around Drew distracted her.

Mrs. O'Reilly dusted the flour from her hands onto her already soiled apron. "Lily, there you are. You seem to be making a habit of tardiness."

Lily eyed the housekeeper, uncertain of the woman's deceptively mild tone. "Yes, ma'am. Sorry I'm late. I'm about to set the table."

"We'll talk later. There's no time now." Mrs. O'Reilly pointed to the kitchen door. "Go."

Lily went. The stack of china in her hands was heavy and cumbersome. Emily was in the large dining room smoothing the linen tablecloth on the massive table. Lily lowered her burden to the sideboard, then began to set the table.

She turned to see Mr. Lambreth leaning on the doorjamb as he watched her. "You needed something, sir?"

He shook his head, but his pale blue eyes looked her over. "I thought we might go for a walk after you get off work tonight."

She caught her breath. "I'm just the maid, Mr. Lambreth. I hardly think your father would approve."

"He's not my father, and I really don't care. Don't you ever feel smothered by social expectations? I've been watching you, and I like you. You've got spirit."

When he took a step closer, Lily backed up. "I'd better get back to work." His soft chuckle followed her into the hall. Could he seriously be attracted to her? He was very handsome, but if Miss Belle objected to her talking to Drew, she'd be doubly angry about Mr. Lambreth.

As soon as she stepped into the kitchen, Mrs. O'Reilly pointed at her. "Miss Belle wants you in her bedroom. At once."

Lily gulped and ran for the back stairs. Her pulse was galloping when she stepped to her mistress's door and turned the knob. "Miss Belle, you needed me?"

Still in her corset and underthings, Belle was seated in front of the dressing table. The curling iron and pins were laid out on top also. Her pout clearly showed in the mirror. "I've told my uncle I'm taking you for my lady's maid. You should have been here waiting on me! I'm going to be late, and it's your fault." She poked at her hair. "My hair is a mess. Do something with it."

"Yes, miss." Lily grabbed the brush from the dressing table and began to smooth out Belle's brown locks. The wind had caught and tangled it, so it took several minutes before it was ready to style. She gathered it into a loose chignon, then curled strands at the side of Belle's face. "You look beautiful. You could model as a Gibson girl."

Belle sniffed and tipped her head. "It's passable." She swiveled on the seat, then stood. "Help me dress. The new bronze silk is in the closet."

"Of course." Lily opened the wardrobe. She heard something thump in the closet and stepped back. "Did you hear that?"

"What?"

"I thought I heard something in the closet." The hair rose on the back of her head when she heard what sounded like fingers rapping on the wall. "That."

Belle stepped closer. "Are you trying to fool me? I need that dress, Lily."

"Yes, miss." Lily swallowed hard and pushed aside a couple of dresses to find the one for tonight. The bronze silk was as wrinkled as a new baby. "I—I need to press this, Miss Belle."

Belle was right behind her, and she grabbed Lily's arm roughly. "I've half a mind to send you packing! You *knew* this dinner was important, yet you were lollygagging with Mr. Hawkes when you should have been here preparing."

"I didn't know you were going to take me as your maid."

"If you'd been home when you should have, you would have been told." Belle's eyes spit fire. "Press it at once."

At least she wasn't fired. Yet. Lily removed the dress and hurried to the utility room where she eased the wrinkles out of the delicate fabric. Though she'd hurried, it was still nearly half an hour later when she returned to Belle's room.

Her mistress turned from her place by the window. "Nearly

everyone is here. I shall make a grand entrance, which isn't all bad."
A smile lifted the corner of her full lips. "Help me dress."

Lily hurried forward with the dress. "Yes, Miss Belle."

She hoisted the skirt over Belle's head and settled the bodice
over her slim shoulders. When Belle turned, Lily laced up the back
and cinched in the waist.

Belle spun around, and the dress swirled around her ankles. Her
long neck rose from creamy bare shoulders, and the dress accentu-
ated her figure. "How do I look?"

"Lovely, just lovely." Belle would attract the attention of every
man in the house. Even Drew. Lily pushed down her dismay and
managed to smile. "Your aunt will be fretting. I'm sure they're waiting the meal on you."

"Of course." Belle grabbed a wrap and draped it over one arm.
She started for the door, then turned. "Oh, and, Lily?"

"Yes, Miss Belle?"

"Let us be clear. The only reason I didn't discharge you on the
spot is that I like the way you do my hair. But if I find you dallying
with Mr. Hawkes again, no amount of hairdressing skill will save
you. Are we clear?"

Lily held her gaze. "I understand. Thank you for giving me
another chance. It won't happen again."

"I should hope not. You may accompany me downstairs, but keep
your distance from him tonight as well. Another maid can bring the
food to the table. If he even looks your way, I'll hold you responsible
for the consequences."

She inclined her head toward the door, and Lily sprang forward
to open it. Her throat ached from holding back the tears as she followed her mistress down the sweeping stairs to the first floor.

How was she to help bring her father's killer to justice if she
couldn't help Drew?

# TEN

Drew managed to get seated to the left of Vesters. The man was a veritable endless pit. The amount of food he consumed turned Drew's stomach. Vesters had ignored him for much of the meal, concentrating instead on his plate. It was going to take a few days for Vesters to come around to admitting Drew might be able to help him. No one liked his secrets being laid bare.

He'd seen Lily only once when she came to the doorway bearing pies that she transferred to another maid. When he'd tried to catch her attention, she turned her head and slipped away.

On his left Belle took a sip of her wine. "Uncle Everett, have you heard from the police?"

Across the table from her, her uncle put down his fork and frowned. "They did not find the villain."

"Did you tell them about the man I saw in the park?"

Drew tensed. He'd asked her not to say anything. Now the Whites would think he and Lily had turned them in. They would be unlikely to give them any other aid.

Everett shook his head. "Not yet. I will when they report back to me."

Maybe he could get to Everett and convince him to stay silent, but in the meantime, Everett might have other knowledge Drew needed. "You know everything about butterflies. Have you seen live butterflies encased in glass?"

Everett picked up his glass of port. "Oh yes. One of my companies makes them. The butterflies are common, of course. Why do you ask? I can arrange for you to have one if you like."

Drew couldn't imagine anything worse than trapping a living creature in glass. "I saw one today. The woman who was attacked the other day received one anonymously."

Belle shrugged. "Probably a suitor. The globes are quite popular, Aunt Camille says."

But Everett was frowning. "The police came to see me. The other three women who were killed had a globe among their possessions. I examined them, and they seem to have come from my business."

"A warning from the killer?"

"So the police suspect. The woman should report it to the police."

"And she should make sure she's not alone. The killer might come back," Belle said.

He eyed her. He would have pegged her as totally wrapped up in her own little world with no thought for those disadvantaged outside her small circle. She took a small bite of her pie, then dabbed her lips and smiled at him. The gleam in her eye made him uncomfortable. He was using her to get close to her uncle, and it made him feel like a cad. But then, wasn't he? It was clear he'd practically ruined Lily's life, and he had never intended to bring her harm. Quite the contrary, he'd wanted to protect her.

Instead, he'd destroyed any chance they had at a future. She should have had several children clinging to her skirts, instead she was slaving away in this big house. Lately he'd been questioning everything he'd done in the past few years. What had he accomplished with his life since he left Larson? Nothing really. He hadn't brought Ballard to justice, and the man's victims were still unavenged.

Lily entered the room and carried more dishes to the sideboard behind him. He tensed and wished he could speak to her.

He realized Belle had spoken to him. "I'm sorry?"

Her lips smiled but her eyes didn't. "I asked if you'd like to accompany me and my uncle on a ride along the river tomorrow afternoon. He's taking me for ice cream."

"I'd be delighted."

A light came on in her eyes. "We plan to leave about two."

"I'll be here." He watched Lily hurry from the room with her face pale. Had she overheard him making plans with Belle?

Chairs scraped as the guests rose. Everett beckoned the men to follow him to the smoking room while the ladies retired to the parlor. Drew took the opportunity to excuse himself for a moment. He had to find Lily to see what had happened when she'd gotten back. Something was wrong. He'd seen it in her tense shoulders and averted eyes.

Belle was speaking with another guest when he slipped out of the dining room and made his way down the hall to the kitchen. If he could just get Lily's attention without any of the other servants noticing . . .

But the kitchen buzzed with activity when he peeked in. He ducked back before anyone saw him lurking. The last thing he wanted was for it to be common knowledge that Lily and he were acquainted. It would elicit too many questions.

He took another glance into the room. This time he saw Lily scrubbing the big wooden table. She looked up just as his head poked into the room. Her eyes widened and she glanced around. He motioned to her, and she shook her head. Frowning, he motioned again. She sighed and took a step in his direction. He ducked his head back and went to stand in a small alcove in the pantry. Moments later footsteps sounded on the wood floors.

"Are you trying to get me fired?" she whispered.

"Fired?"

Her eyes sparked fire. "Miss Belle said I was not to speak to you again or she would let me go. We'll have to meet secretly."

His pulse leaped at the suggestion that she wanted to see him. "When and how?"

Confusion clouded her eyes. "I need to find out what Jane and her brother know. I'll visit them and manage to get a note to you."

She was talking about investigating, not anything personal. "Of course." He managed to hide his disappointment. Did she have no feelings left for him? Could he blame her after what he'd done?

"I have to go. If Belle catches me, I'm in trouble." She shot him another glance from her blue eyes. "Are you all right? You look a little pale."

"Just fine." He wasn't about to let her know she'd just stomped all over his heart.

The guests had departed, and the kitchen was clean. Lily stood in the housekeeper's small parlor with her hands behind her back. The scent of cinnamon from a bowl of potpourri filled the air. Her pulse hadn't stopped throbbing in her throat from the moment she'd been summoned here.

She glanced around the room. The brown horsehair sofa was threadbare. A battered lamp stand held a picture of Mrs. O'Reilly with a young man who had to be her brother from the resemblance. Two other chairs were crammed into the small space, and a basket of yarn and knitting needles sat beside the rocker. When did Mrs.

O'Reilly have time to knit? Lily had rarely seen her when she wasn't attending to household duties.

Mrs. O'Reilly stepped through the door. Her apron was spotless, but a few tendrils of red hair had escaped the tight bun. She gestured to the hardback chair. "Sit."

Lily obeyed. The hard wood bit into the back of her thighs, and she clung to the discomfort to sharpen her senses. "You wanted to see me?"

Mrs. O'Reilly sat in a rocker and clasped her hands in her lap. "I did. You're new here, Lily. You've never been in service before, so I think you need some things explained to you."

Lily sagged back in the chair. She wasn't getting fired. It was just a reprimand. "Yes, ma'am. I'll admit it's all quite new."

"Miss Belle can be a demanding employer. She has a good heart, but she's had everything handed to her. I've known her since she was a girl. You'll do fine if you keep your wits about you and mind her. One bit of sass and you're gone, though. I'd hate to see that happen."

"I don't plan to sass her, ma'am. I'm trying my best to please her. If she's complained about something, please tell me so I can do better."

"She hasn't complained, but when she wants something, she goes after it. And right now she wants Mr. Hawkes. If you get in her way, it won't be pleasant."

Heat scorched Lily's cheeks. *And what if there's a prior claim?* She bit back the retort. "I won't get in her way."

Mrs. O'Reilly lifted a brow. "I saw you go to town today with Mr. Hawkes. And then you left the kitchen tonight to speak with him. Miss Belle specifically told you to stay away from him, did she not?"

"She did. Mr. Hawkes insisted I ride with him to town instead of walking, and he had a question tonight about an incident in town."

"Hawkes is not your employer."

Lily clenched her hands together. "No, ma'am. He was insistent, and I didn't know how to refuse."

"Next time simply say you'll be fired if you fraternize with the guests." Her brown eyes sharpened. "And make no bones about it, Lily. If it happens again, you *will* be let go."

Lily wanted to tell the housekeeper that Drew had been hers. That he wasn't what he seemed. But she clamped her lips together and nodded. "I'll do that."

Mrs. O'Reilly studied her for a long moment. "Unfortunately, you're an attractive young woman. Mr. Lambreth seems to have noticed those attractions as well. Mrs. Marshall has plans for him. You'd do well to steer clear of him too." Her expression softened. "I like you, Lily. You're a hard worker, and you're trying your best with Miss Belle. That goes a long way with me. The poor child has been through so much, and I'd like to see her happy and settled. If she wants Mr. Hawkes, I intend to see she gets him."

Lily ignored the burst of pain in her chest. "Through so much? You mean her father's death?"

"Not just that. Her mother had little time for her, and when she died, Belle's father was gone a lot with his business. Her older brothers moved away as quickly as they could, and Belle was left alone too much. So now that she has her aunt and uncle catering to her every whim, she's spreading her wings a little. It's understandable."

Poor thing. Lily might not have had a lot of money, but she'd had her parents there to love and guide her for her growing-up years. "I'll try to help her all I can."

Mrs. O'Reilly's eyes narrowed. "With Mr. Hawkes as well?"

Lily managed a smile. "Her love life is not my business, but I will see she looks her best. The rest is up to her."

"And you'll discourage Mr. Hawkes's pursuit of you?"

Lily's cheeks warmed. "He hasn't been pursuing me! It's all quite innocent."

"An innocent friendship can quickly change to deliberate seduction."

Lily gasped and rose. "Really, Mrs. O'Reilly. Mr. Hawkes has no designs on my virtue." *He already took it.* At the housekeeper's quelling stare, Lily sank back onto the uncomfortable chair.

Mrs. O'Reilly plucked up a speck of lint as if outraged it had dared to appear on her sofa. "And you're naive if you think that. I've seen the way his gaze follows you around the dining room. If Miss Belle notices, you'll be out on the street. You must discourage him once and for all."

Lily swallowed. "Yes, ma'am."

"I know I sound harsh, but this is for your own good."

"And I'm grateful. I won't let you down."

"I hope not." Mrs. O'Reilly rose and moved to the door. "You're dismissed."

Lily escaped the close room and pulled the door shut behind her. She leaned on the wall and exhaled. How was she going to help Drew and keep her job? She needed the job, but she *had* to help avenge her father.

Drew was staying here. How could she stay out of his way? A small pulse of rebellion flared. And why should she? He'd been hers once. Belle had no right to lay claim on him just because she was wealthy. Drew wasn't a man who could be bought. At least Lily didn't think he'd changed that much. And what of his avowal that he still loved her? She hadn't dared to bring out his words and examine them.

She would not be hurt again.

# ELEVEN

The air was chilly when Lily awoke, but the birds were singing in spite of the rain pounding at the windows and drenching the yard. She felt a dull sense of unhappiness when she remembered her reprimands the day before. She'd only been here a week, and already her mistress was unhappy with her. Through no fault of her own. It seemed very unfair, but she should be used to unfair. It was unfair her father had been killed in the prime of his life. It was unfair her mother had been taken from her.

Her parents had been such good people. Why would God allow these things?

Emily turned from the stand that held the pitcher and bowl of water. "Good morning."

"Are you always so cheerful?"

"I try. What's to be gloomy about? I have life, a bed, food, and friends. That's all anyone needs to be happy."

Lily put her feet on the cool wooden floor and smiled. "I like your attitude, Emily. I usually look on the bright side, but it's a little hard this morning."

Emily's eyes held sympathy. "I heard a bit of the dressing down you got from Mrs. O'Reilly. It will be all right."

"Will it? I'm not so sure." Lily sat on the edge of the bed and undid her plait of hair, then tidied it into a knot atop her head. "Being with Mr. Hawkes was quite innocent."

Emily pressed her lips together as she tied on her apron. "I'm not a schoolgirl, Lily. You knew Mr. Hawkes before, didn't you? It's as plain as the nose on your face."

Drew hadn't wanted her to tell anyone, but keeping all these secrets quiet ate at her bones. She didn't have to tell Emily everything. "He's from Larson too."

Emily raised a brow. "Ah, I understand. Why not just tell Miss Belle the truth about that?"

"She's already let me know my friendship with her cousin has distressed her. She seems to think it might keep our relationship from being the proper mistress and maid one. Hearing I know the man she wants to marry is hardly going to endear me to her."

"But it might set her mind at ease about your relationship with Mr. Hawkes."

Lily slipped off her nightgown and pulled on her gray shirt-dress. "I'll just try to avoid him."

"Good luck. It's your turn to take him his breakfast."

Lily quailed in her boots. "Can't you take my place? If Miss Belle hears of it, I'm in trouble."

"She won't know anything about it. Mr. Hawkes likes his breakfast at five fifteen. There's a small sitting room in his wing of the house, and he goes there to eat on wet mornings. It's private enough no one will overhear you."

Feeling like she was about to face the gallows, Lily went down the hall. Something thumped behind a door, and she paused. Lily felt a presence too, as though someone listened to them. She tipped her head to one side and waited. Behind these doors was just storage. Maybe another servant had been sent to look for something.

"Hello?" She waited, but there was no answer.

She finally headed down the hall again to the back stairs to the kitchen. She took the tray that had already been prepared for Drew up the stairs to the second floor. She had never been in the guest wing, and she got turned around once before she found the sitting room. It was attractively decorated with a small navy rug and a fringed lamp on an end table by the settee. The dining table was in the corner.

Drew was seated at the table with a book open in front of him. When she neared, she realized it was his Bible. The same one she'd seen many times over the years. His grandmother had given it to him. It made her heart soften toward him to see the pages so thumbed and yellowed with use.

He looked up. His eyes were as warm and brown as a puppy's and just as eager. "Lily! I was just thinking about you." He rose and took the tray from her.

Why did he have to still be so handsome and solicitous? A black lock of hair fell boyishly over his high forehead. Her gaze drifted to his lips, and she found herself remembering the taste of him. It was not something she was ever likely to forget.

She backed away with her hands behind her back. "Well, you have your breakfast. If there's nothing else you need, I'll leave you to eat in peace."

"Don't go." His mouth twisted. "I want to listen to your voice and just look at you. I'm like a man lost in the desert who sees a pond ahead of him. I'm not quite sure if you're real or a mirage."

"I never went anywhere, Andy. You're the one who left."

"Tell me about Larson." He put a forkful of eggs in his mouth and looked up at her expectantly.

"You probably know all about it from your cousin. Let's not make small talk."

His smile flattened. "How did you end up here, of all places?"

She told him about the job offer she'd received through a friend who was Belle's cousin. It gave her the opportunity to drink in everything about him. There were tiny new lines at the edges of his eyes and a new maturity in his face. He'd been handsome in his teens. He took her breath away in his full adulthood. No wonder the rest of the servants mooned over him. No wonder Belle wanted him too. His broad shoulders filled out his white shirt. The planes and angles of his face spoke of strength, and even his neck was muscular. Where had he been all this time? Had there been other women? What woman could look at him and not want him for her own?

She realized she'd been staring and dropped her gaze to the carpet. "I should go."

He sprang to his feet and crossed the rug in three steps to block her escape. His hands came down on her arms. Her skin warmed from his touch, and the heat moved to her belly. She swallowed hard as the familiar desire enveloped her.

"Don't go," he said softly. "We're finally alone for a moment."

He bent his head, and without thinking, she tipped her face up and closed her eyes. She was nearly shaking from the desire to touch him, to feel his kiss. The sweet scent of his breath was so dear, so familiar.

A door slammed somewhere and brought her to her senses. She allowed herself to inhale one last taste of him before stepping away. "I must go."

He gave a grave nod, and his hands fell away. "I swore I'd treat you with more respect this time, and then I see you and all sense leaves me. I hope you can forgive me f-for losing my head when we were young. I want to be a better man than I was."

Heat flooded her cheeks. "There's nothing for me to forgive. I was as much at fault as you."

She turned and raced off. Hearing he regretted their love so deeply brought hot tears to her eyes. If only she could erase every memory.

Hyde Park was a streetcar suburb about a mile outside Austin's city limits. Belle sat in the back of the automobile with Vesters. Her uncle, driving cap crushed to his ears, drove the vehicle with a maniacal grin on his face. He rarely got the chance to drive, but he'd told Henry he could handle the driving himself. The automobile rumbled down streets lined by double rows of hackberry trees. Their destination, the pavilion, was just ahead.

"What a wonderful idea to watch the balloon ascension this afternoon," Belle said, forcing gaiety to her voice.

She'd hoped to spend the afternoon with Drew, but he'd been called away "on business," or so he said. Much to her dismay, her uncle had immediately invited Vesters to join them. He sat much too close to her on the leather seat, and there was no room for her to edge away.

The driver parked in a grassy lot next to the pavilion, and Vesters helped her down. She had to leave her gloved hand on his jacketed forearm, but as soon as they reached their seats on the third row, she removed it, ostensibly to smooth her skirt.

"I'll leave you two for a moment," her uncle said. "I see a man I need to speak with before we begin."

Her spirits sank as her uncle left her alone with Vesters. Out on the field men scurried around getting the balloon ready to launch. The balloon was brightly colored, but the basket where the balloonist would ride looked flimsy and unsafe.

"I've gone up in a balloon a time or two," Vesters said. "I surveyed storm damage to my castle last year. It was quite exhilarating."

She pulled her wrap around her arms. "I can't imagine."

"Would you like some punch?" Vesters nodded to the refreshment table set up along one side of the pavilion.

"That would be lovely." She looked around the seats as he left and hurried to the table. Several here she recognized.

A man and woman settled on Belle's other side. "Hello." The woman's friendly smile matched her comfortable blue dress that was rather worn.

"Good afternoon." Belle put warmth into her smile. Chatting with someone else might keep her from a distasteful conversation with Vesters. "Haven't we met?" She was sure she'd seen the woman's round face and rosy cheeks somewhere.

"I'm Molly Adams, and this is my husband, the Reverend Joshua Adams."

"Ah, you're at St. David's. I'm Belle Castle."

Her uncle interrupted. "I thought you'd save me a seat, Belle." He muscled his way into the row. "I'd thank you to move over a bit."

Belle barely managed to hide her shock. Her uncle was never rude or abrupt. She smiled apologetically at the minister and his wife as they shifted over one seat. Her uncle settled his girth onto the vacated seat without a word. He kept his gaze straight forward. In another minute, the displaced couple rose and moved over to another aisle.

"I don't want you fraternizing with them," he said as soon as they were out of earshot.

"It's a minister and his wife!"

"He's been working against my election."

She frowned. "That's hardly cause for such rudeness."

Her uncle pressed his lips together, and she knew she was getting no more information out of him. What could the minister possibly have said that upset Uncle Everett so much?

It had been Drew's good luck Nathan wasn't home when he stopped to talk to Miss White about the butterfly globe. She'd readily handed it over, and he went straightaway to the police station.

The officer he'd been ushered in to see turned the globe over in his hands. The man was in his fifties with a handlebar mustache that had more gray hairs than brown. "This is like the others. She received it two days before the attack?"

"So it would seem. The butterfly was alive when she got it. It had been left in a box at her door."

"I need to keep this." When Drew nodded, the officer put the globe down on his desk. "With one of the victims, it had been left on her bed beside her. The butterfly was still alive, but she wasn't. The other victim had found hers on the kitchen table."

"Was it found before the attack?"

The officer nodded. "About a week before. So the circumstances are slightly different. They might not be connected. All the women were single, and these globes are popular gifts."

Drew didn't buy it. "Surely not as anonymous gifts."

The officer shrugged. "I sent one to my girl without a card attached. She knew who sent it. We don't know if the other women knew who sent the gifts. Miss White doesn't know who sent this?"

"She has no idea. At first she thought it was a gift from her brother, but he denied knowing anything about it."

The officer leaned back in his chair. "I'll question her, but it's likely a coincidence." The man rose and opened his door with a finality that told Drew the conversation was at an end.

Drew stepped into the doorway. "Are you looking at Marshall? He makes those."

"We checked him out. Like I said, likely a coincidence."

Drew pressed his lips together and made his way out into the morning sunshine. The police had dismissed this all too quickly for his peace of mind. He liked Everett Marshall, but he still loved Lily. What if she was working for a killer?

# TWELVE

Lily's day off hadn't come too soon. Holding her hat in the breeze, she inhaled and looked at the ramshackle house behind a nicer two-story home. This shack was practically falling down. Peeling paint and missing shingles told the story of years of neglect. The smell of onions wafted out one of the ill-fitting windows. Somewhere inside, a baby wailed. Jane's little one? The owner should have kept it in better repair since it was part of his property. Perhaps he thought no one would notice it along the back side of the property past the orchard.

Lily rapped her gloved knuckles on the rotting wood of the door. "Hello?"

Did Jane live with her brother, or was it just her and the baby? And what about the child's father? The child wailed behind the door again, and the crying grew louder.

The door opened, and Jane's eyes widened. She shifted the infant to her other shoulder. "Miss Lily, what are you doing here?"

Lily lifted the basket in her hand. "I brought some things for you. I wasn't sure if you'd been able to work with your injury, and I was worried perhaps your baby needed a few items."

A shutter came down over Jane's expression. "I can care for my own."

"Of course you can. Friends help one another out. You'd do the same for me, I think. May I come in?"

Jane's eyes softened. "I'm forgetting my manners." She stood aside. "I'll get tea."

Lily followed her into a parlor. Though small, there was not a speck of lint or dirt anywhere. The sofa and chair were worn, but it was clear Jane took pride in her home.

Jane pointed at the sofa. "Please, make yourself comfortable. I'll prepare some tea."

"Could I hold your little one while you get it? I adore babies."

Jane hesitated, then passed Hannah to Lily. "She's sleepy and won't give up. She likes to be sung to."

Lily cradled the baby in one arm. "I can manage that. Here, you can put the food away. There's ham and a few other items. And some nappies for Hannah."

Jane's smile was shy. "Thank you, Miss Lily." She hurried toward the kitchen.

Lily settled the baby against her shoulder and began to sing "Amazing Grace" to her in a soft voice. The sweet smell of the infant grew stronger as the little one nuzzled against her. She kissed the baby's soft, downy head. For just a moment she let herself imagine holding her own baby—hers and Drew's. What a ridiculous dream. He'd made it perfectly clear how little he thought of her when he deserted her without a word.

Jane returned with a tray holding a chipped teapot and two cups. "I hope you don't mind your tea black. I'm out of sugar." She bit her lip and shot Lily an apologetic glance.

"That's exactly how I like it." Lily accepted the tea with her free hand. "Hannah's very sweet." She managed not to grimace at the bitter tea.

A tender smile lifted Jane's lips. "She's my world. I'd do anything for her." She glanced around the room. "I wish I could give her more than this."

"You work at the big house here? Are they good to you?"

Jane took a sip of her tea. "My mistress isn't the most understanding lady. When I had Hannah, she let me go but allows me to live here with my brother until I find another position. He works nights in the master's tavern. They don't want to lose him. I—I am having some problems finding another position. Most employers don't want to deal with an infant."

"How are you living?"

"My brother is helping me. I don't know what we would have done without Nathan." She let out a heavy sigh. "It's impossible to work right now anyway. Hannah needs to be fed and cared for. Nathan says he can watch her during the day while I work, but if he does that, he'll only get a few hours of sleep every day." She shook her head. "He says he doesn't need much sleep. We could use the money though."

"I'll ask around and see if the Marshalls need any help," Lily promised.

Jane's lips trembled. "Why are you being so good to me, Miss Lily? You hardly know me."

"I feel a connection to you, Jane. I hope you don't mind."

"I'm grateful for it. I could use a friend."

The back door slammed, and heavy footsteps came down the hall. Nathan stepped into the tiny parlor. His smile faded when he saw Lily. "What are you doing here? We don't want any trouble. You sent the police by."

She shook her head. "Miss Belle, my mistress, saw the fellow with you and thought he looked like the man who shot at her uncle. We all assured her it wasn't the same man, but she insisted her uncle report the incident. The police weren't worrisome, were they?"

Nathan shook his head. "I told them the truth about who we were and what we were doing there. They spoke with my friend, and he was exonerated. Your fellow came by this afternoon too. He took the butterfly globe to the police."

"Mr. Hawkes, you mean? I didn't know."

Nathan scowled. "We just want to be left alone."

Jane rose and extended her hand toward her brother. "Miss Lily brought some things by for the baby and me."

Nathan's fingers curled into his palms. "We don't need charity. I'm taking care of you, aren't I?"

Lily rose quickly. "Of course you are, Nathan. I like Jane though, and I could use a friend here. I'm new to town."

The tension in his shoulders eased. "You're not here to try to coax more information out of me about Vesters?" An edge of hostility still lined his words.

She shook her head and smiled. "That wasn't my reason for coming. If you'd like to tell me more, I will listen, but I care about Jane and little Hannah. Surely we can be friends?"

Nathan eyed her. "I don't think so."

She watched him stalk away. "I think I upset your brother."

Jane sank back onto the chair. "Most things upset him these days. Ever since he got involved with Mr. Vesters."

Lily shifted the baby to her other arm. "He's working for Mr. Vesters?"

Jane nodded. "Don't say anything though. I think Mr. Vesters is forcing Nathan to do things he doesn't want to do."

"What kinds of things?"

Jane bit her lip. "I wonder if your man friend could help Nathan. What if Nathan were to give him information? With Mr. Vesters in jail, maybe Nathan and I could start over somewhere else."

"Mr. Hawkes is not my man friend. But he might be able to help you. I can ask. Do you think Nathan would cooperate?"

Jane nodded. "I smell the fear on him every time he comes home. And he's afraid Mr. Vesters will do something to Hannah and me."

"Why would he bother with you and Hannah?"

Tears swam in Jane's eyes. "He's Hannah's father."

Lily left Jane's house and hurried down the sidewalk toward the trolley stop. She slowed outside Lammes Candies. A few dollars were safely tucked inside her bag. A bit of sweet might soothe the hurt that resided somewhere in the region of her heart.

She bought one chocolate, then took it to the café tables outside. A familiar figure waved to her, and she went to join Emily.

Emily smiled as Lily sat in one of the iron chairs. "What was your indulgence today?"

"Chocolate. I thought about ice cream."

Emily scooped up some. "It's very good." She eyed Lily. "You look rather glum. What's wrong? Is it Mr. Hawkes?"

Lily straightened. "What an odd thing to say." Her laugh sounded forced to her ears.

Emily lifted a brow. "I know there's something between you two. You already admitted you knew him before you came here. You can tell me the rest of it. I won't say anything."

Relief coursed through Lily. If she'd been back in Larson, she could have discussed everything with Lucy, but she'd felt so alone here. She exhaled and sat back in the chair. "We were engaged once."

Emily's jaw dropped. "To a swank like him?"

She wanted to tell Emily Drew's real last name wasn't even

Hawkes, but she clamped her teeth against the revelation. Though she trusted Emily, the other woman might inadvertently let something slip. She took a bite of her chocolate.

"My, my." Emily's eyes sparkled. "You just might put Miss Belle's nose out of joint. This is far more than just knowing him from your old hometown."

The pressure in Lily's chest intensified, and she swallowed hard. "I don't think he'll put up much resistance. She's quite beautiful."

Emily studied Lily's face. "You still care about him, don't you?"

A breeze cooled her heated cheeks. "It was long ago. We were so young."

"Yet you never married. You're a lovely girl, Lily. You never got over him, did you?"

"I was perfectly happy in Larson with my mother. I didn't need a man."

Emily inclined her head. "There they are now."

A carriage rattled past, and Lily spared a quick look to her left. Her gaze met Belle's, but only her uncle and Mr. Vesters accompanied her. "He didn't go with them after all. Listen, Emily, how well do you know Mr. Vesters?"

Emily blinked. "Not well. He's been coming around the house for about six months with his eye on marrying Miss Belle. She's not interested, but her uncle is pressing her. Vesters is filthy rich, and he is an avid butterfly collector just like Mr. Marshall. They belong to some kind of butterfly organization called Novo. It's Latin for 'change,' and it uses a butterfly as its logo."

Lily shuddered. "The butterfly conservatory is creepy. I don't like going in there. All those beautiful butterflies pinned into display cases . . . Why does Mr. Marshall do it?"

Her friend shrugged. "He thinks they're beautiful."

"They are when they're *alive*."

"Why are you asking about Mr. Vesters anyway? If you're hoping he'll attract Miss Belle away from Mr. Hawkes, you're quite wrong."

Lily shook her head. "I believe he may have had something to do with my father's death."

Emily's eyes widened. "Your father was in Austin?"

How much should Lily reveal? If she told Emily about the possible counterfeiting, there would be more questions. Questions that might lead to Drew's interest in the man. "Our fathers were killed in a fire. He heard a rumor it was set and one of Vesters's accomplices did the deed."

Emily's spoon clattered into her empty bowl. "I didn't want to speak ill of anyone, but I did see something the other day."

Lily's pulse stuttered, and she leaned forward. "About Mr. Vesters?"

Emily nodded. "He had a stack of money, and he threw it in the fire."

"He burned money?"

"Quite strange, isn't it? He stirred the fire until the bills were ashes."

Counterfeit money? She needed to let Drew know. "How much money did he burn?"

Emily held her fingers about two inches apart. "A stack like that."

"Did you see the money? Was there something odd about it?"

"I wasn't close enough to see any details. Just the bills." Emily lowered her voice. "Do you think it was fake money?"

"It seems likely. Who would burn real money?"

"What if it was stolen, and he was afraid he'd be caught with it?"

Lily paused at the thought, then shook her head. "Why not just hide it until it was safe to use? I bet there was something wrong with the money. This was in the parlor? Where were the Marshalls?"

"They hadn't arrived yet from a lunch engagement, and Mr. Vesters dropped by unannounced. I put him in the parlor and told him he could wait."

"He probably wants to marry Belle for the money. If he's desperate enough for that, he might be willing to step across the law to save his estate too. Did he see you watching?"

Emily shook her head. "I saw him in the hall mirror. It reflected his behavior clearly. I'm sure he has no idea he was seen."

Lily tried to hide her rising excitement. "Still, it seems odd he would burn it in our parlor. Why not take care of it at home rather than where his actions might be discovered?"

"It's strange, I admit."

Lily's attention was caught by a tall figure striding her way, determination stamped on his face. Drew motioned to her, then vanished behind a shrub. Though she told herself the heat in her cheeks was from the warm day, Lily couldn't explain away the throb of her pulse in her throat as she took her leave from Emily. It was several minutes before Emily finally let her go.

# THIRTEEN

The wind stiffened as dark clouds began to gather overhead. The days were getting short, and the clouds brought an even earlier dusk. Lily glanced behind the tree and along the side of the storefront but didn't see Drew. A boy on a bicycle saw her and waved, so she approached him. "Can I help you?"

He had a smudge of black on his upturned nose, and his hair didn't look like it had been combed in days. "Are you Miss Lily? The gentleman gave me a quarter to tell you to meet him in St. David's Episcopal Church." He pointed to the steeple. "In the garden."

Lily thanked him and hurried toward the church. The moonlight tower wasn't on this early, though it was dark enough that its illumination would have helped. The church was on the corner of Eighth and San Jacinto. No one was about when she made her way across the grounds to the garden. At least Drew had the sense to talk to her in a private setting. Someone would have been sure to notice their conversation at the candy store.

She paused near a bank of roses. "Drew?" The hair prickled on the back of her neck. The silence pressed in on her, and she peered into the gloom. She retreated a few feet. "Who's there?" Her voice trembled even though she knew there was nothing to fear here in the steeple's shadow.

She started to whirl at a footfall behind her, but a hard hand came down over her mouth and dragged her off the path and behind a line of shrubs.

He crushed her against his chest and kept her from turning her head. She caught a glimpse of something shiny and stilled. A knife blade. The cold metal touched her under the chin.

"So beautiful," the man crooned.

Lily's throat closed. This man intended to kill her. Had he been watching her? She quit struggling. Maybe he would loosen his grip. Her bag was still in her hand. Was there something she could use as a weapon? Her hand touched the hard clasp. It was sharp on one end.

She waited for her opportunity as the man dragged her farther into the shadows. His grip loosened on her right arm, and she brought the bag up with the point toward him. She hit his face with all her strength. She felt the protrusion sink into skin, and her fingers touched hair.

He swore viciously, and his hand left her arm. She wrenched herself out of his grip and ran toward the garden gate. A shriek burst from her chest, and she heard an answering shout past the arbor. Help was coming.

Footsteps went the other direction. She spared a glance over her shoulder and saw a bulky form hurtling over the trimmed hedge like a track and field runner. Her strength left her, and she sank to her knees on the grass. Could Drew have lured her here on purpose? She rejected the notion, but it kept insinuating itself into her thoughts.

What did she really know about the man he'd become? Her presence in Austin may have made him fearful she would ruin whatever plans he was pursuing. She wasn't sure she believed he was with the Secret Service. Could he have fed her all those lies to make her trust him?

A policeman arrived and helped her to her feet. "Are you all right, miss?"

She burst into tears and nodded. "A man—he had a knife." She gestured toward the garden. Another policeman arrived, and he ran into the garden where the hedge had been disturbed.

The policeman guided her to a bench at the front of the church property. "Can you describe him?"

"I didn't see him very well. Taller than me and muscular. Maybe five ten. He could have been anyone though. It was too dark to see clearly, and he attacked me from behind."

"You're very lucky. I'll escort you home. Where do you live?"

"I'm a lady's maid for Mr. Everett Marshall's niece."

He straightened and looked at her with respect in his eyes. "Ah, the Butterfly Palace. I know it. Mr. Marshall is well liked in the city."

Lily managed a watery smile. "Thank you for your assistance. I feel quite shaken."

Several people approached from across the street, and Emily hurried toward her. The sight of her friend nearly made Lily cry again.

Emily's cheeks were pink when she reached them. "Lily, are you all right? What happened?"

"I was attacked." Lily shook her head quickly when she saw Emily's expression. "N-Not that kind of attack. He held a knife to my throat. If I hadn't hit him with my bag, he would have killed me." She held up her flimsy purse and laughed. "It doesn't look like much of a weapon, but I used the clasp."

The policeman looked it over. "Would he carry a wound from this, miss?"

"I believe so. I felt it sink into his skin." For the first time she was hopeful they might find her attacker. "I think it hit his scalp."

"I'll let the men know to be looking for someone injured that way." He stared at Lily. "And what were you doing in the church garden?"

The acceptable answer would be to say she was praying. She didn't dare tell him she was meeting Drew.

Emily glanced at her and shrugged. "What does anyone do at a church, Officer? That's a silly question."

He reddened. "Can you escort your friend home? I'd like to help search."

"Of course." Emily held up her purse. "We are both armed and dangerous."

Drew was only inside the store a moment, but he was beginning to think he must have missed Lily when he stepped inside for a drink of water. Or else she'd ignored his request to speak to her. He sat on a stone wall in the alley and watched for her familiar form. When she hadn't come fifteen minutes later, he rose and stretched. Might as well head back to the Butterfly Palace.

There seemed to be a commotion near the church as he walked that direction. The rain began to fall, fat drops that soaked his coat and shoes and left a tang in the air. He pulled up his collar and hurried faster. As he drew abreast of the church, he squinted at the two women exiting the grounds. His pulse kicked when he recognized Lily. What was she doing here? And why were policemen roaming around looking grim?

He ran after them and caught at Lily's arm. "What's happened?"

She shook off his hand. "Why didn't you meet me?"

"What? You never showed up."

Rain sluiced over her soaked hair and face. "I got your message to come to the church, but you left me to be attacked by some maniac! Did you purposely lure me there, Drew?"

He held up his hand. "Wait, I never told you to meet me at the church. I was waiting where I motioned you to. Why would you think I wanted to meet at the church?"

Her eyes widened and she took a step back. "A boy said you'd asked him to give me a message. I had no reason to disbelieve him."

"You were attacked here?" There was a red mark on her neck, and she flinched when he reached out to touch it.

"I'm fine."

Emily smiled and held up her bag. "He'll know better than to try to hurt this one again. She had a lethal purse."

Lily's cheeks reddened. "I got lucky, Emily."

Emily still smiled inanely as she swung her purse around. Drew bit his lip to keep from laughing with her, even though the thought of Lily facing an attacker with only her bag was enough to make him quake in his boots.

He took her arm. "Let's get you home."

She pulled away again. "I'd rather you didn't escort me."

Emily nodded. "If Belle sees her, she's out on the streets. I'll get her home."

The rain tapered off to a drizzle. He willed her to look at him. "You believe me, don't you? You know I'd never do anything to hurt you."

Her lush lashes swept to her cheeks, then back up again. Her eyes blazed out of her white face as she studied him. "I don't know what to believe anymore, Drew. It was all very . . . convenient."

His chest tightened, and he curled his fingers into his palms. If she wanted to think so poorly of him, he couldn't blame her. What had he done to deserve her trust?

She wiped the water from her face with the back of her sleeve. "I must go. I'm quite chilled."

"Of course." He knew his formal tone hurt her when she bit her lip and turned away.

As soon as she was out of sight, he went to speak to the police still milling around the church grounds. "I'm a friend of the young woman who was attacked. Did you find the culprit?"

The policeman was young, around twenty-five, with a pimply complexion. He shook his head, but his gray eyes studied Drew. "We recovered his knife where he dropped it as he jumped over the hedge. It was a nasty one, sharp as the dickens. She's a lucky girl."

Drew suppressed a shudder. He didn't like to think of Lily terrorized and hurt. "Could I see it? I might be able to identify it."

"You some kind of metalsmith?" The policeman motioned for Drew to follow.

The knife lay on the steps to the church. It glinted in the sunlight beginning to shine through the clouds. The thing was easily eight inches long. He'd seen something like it before, but he couldn't quite remember where.

The policeman picked it up. "It's an uncommon piece. Real whalebone handle."

Whalebone. Ballard carved whalebone, and that's where Drew had seen a knife like this. But Ballard didn't know Lily was here. Did he?

It was Emily's turn to take up Drew's breakfast, but when she heard Lily needed to talk to him the next morning, Emily quickly traded days with her. Lily didn't want to do this, but Jane needed help. Seeing Drew grew more painful every time she heard his voice.

He was at the table with his Bible again. She set his tray on the table in front of him. "I need to speak with you a moment, if you don't mind."

His gaze went to her neck. "You still have a mark. Does it hurt?"

She touched her neck. "Not really. There's much more to worry about than this."

He put down his fork. "Like what?"

"I took Jane a few items for the baby. She wants our help to extricate Nathan from his association with Vesters. According to Jane, Vesters is forcing him to do something he doesn't want to do. Nathan is afraid of him."

"What's he afraid of? Did Jane say?"

She shook her head. "She also told me something else very disconcerting. Vesters is the father of her baby."

He rose and took her by the shoulders. "I don't want you involved in this. The tentacles are spreading everywhere. Let me handle it."

She lifted her chin. "Jane is my friend. I'm not going to desert her."

His gaze searched hers. "It's wonderful how you want to help her. In the old days, we were both pretty selfish. I love the way you help other people." His hands fell away, and he turned back to the table. "What does she want me to do?" He sounded resigned.

"She's going to try to talk Nathan into working with you. He'll feed you information, and you can gather the evidence to put Vesters behind bars."

He picked up the fork. "I must say that seems rather odd she would want Hannah's father in jail."

"I thought of that but didn't want to ask too many questions."

She watched him eat for a moment and allowed herself to imagine them eating breakfast together at a cozy nook in their

own home. Such a silly schoolgirl dream, yet she'd never success-
fully quashed it.

"Did the police come by last night to ask for more information?" he asked.

"No, but I was glad. I didn't want to talk about it." She fingered
the soreness at her throat. She'd been very lucky the man hadn't cut
her more deeply.

"If you can talk about it this morning, I'd like to hear more.
What did he look like?"

"I didn't see him well. It was much too dark. He grabbed me
from behind."

"Did he say anything?"

Her face heated. "Just two words. 'So beautiful.'"

Drew's gaze heated. "He was right. I don't think you realize
how beautiful you are." He stood and stepped toward her. His
hand touched her hair. "Your hair is as soft as down. I've never seen
another woman with eyes as dark blue as yours." He thumbed the
skin on her cheek. "Your skin is so soft."

Her pulse raced in her neck, and she knew she should step away
but couldn't. Not while he was touching her. Not while his chestnut
eyes were staring into her soul with what looked like love.

He ran his thumb over her lower lip as if testing its softness. As
if measuring how it would feel to kiss her. Her eyelids drifted shut
of their own accord, and she lifted her face toward him. His breath
touched her face, and she smelled the mint from his tooth tonic. Her
heart felt as if it would burst from her chest as she waited for the
touch of his mouth on hers. It had been so long.

She heard him swallow and felt cold. She opened her eyes to
find he'd stepped away.

"I find it so hard to resist you, but I must," he whispered.

"Lily?"

Emily's voice shocked her out of her stupor at Drew's words. She backed away so fast she nearly fell.

"Miss Belle just rang for you. You know how she is."

"Of course, I'll go right now." Lily turned and flew down the hall toward Belle's room.

It was only when she was standing outside the door that she remembered she hadn't gone to the kitchen for Belle's breakfast.

# FOURTEEN

Belle's aquamarine dress shimmered in the sunlight as she entered the state capitol, a temporary structure until the new building was completed. She clung to her uncle's arm and smiled at the gaping man who opened the door for them. His admiration raised her spirits immensely after being ditched by Drew the day before. She was still smarting over how quickly he had made his excuses.

"You can wait in my office while I attend to a bit of business," her uncle said. "Since it's Saturday there won't be hardly anyone here."

She nodded and stepped through the door into his office. He had promised to take her shopping after his brief meeting. She settled in his chair behind his gleaming walnut desk and picked up a book, but it was a boring law manual so she tossed it back onto the desk. Maybe she should have stayed home until he was done. No telling how long this might take.

Voices muttered on the other side of the wall. She paid no mind until someone cried out. Alarmed, she leaped up and pressed her ear against the wall.

A female voice sobbed, "You're hurting me."

"I'll do more than inflict a bruise if you don't do what I'm telling you." The male voice was harsh and grating. "He should have been dead by now. We can't wait any longer. Take this gun. He'll be exiting his meeting in a few minutes. You can hide around the corner by the side door. You'll have a clear shot."

Belle curled her fingers into her palm. Could they be talking about Uncle Everett? Her pulse throbbed in her throat. Why would anyone want to hurt him? He was a good man, the best. Not many men would have been so kind to an orphaned niece. She sometimes complained when he insisted on his way, but deep inside, she always knew it was because he wanted the best for her.

She tiptoed to the door and opened it, wincing when it creaked a bit. No sound came from the next office over. The side door was ahead, just past the room that contained the man and woman. There might be a door from that room to the hall, so they may not come out this main one. Where was Uncle Everett? She should have watched to see where he headed.

Trying to act unconcerned, she walked briskly toward the row of offices on the far side of the building. She heard no voices. Surely there were some security men around. Or other state representatives. The place couldn't be as empty as it felt. She had to get help.

She scurried down the hall to the first door and rapped softly. When she heard no answer, she went to the next and the next. With each room she tried, she grew more agitated. Where was her uncle?

The doorman. She hurried back to the front door, pausing long enough to peer down the side hall. Still empty. At least no woman with a gun was lurking about. She reached the front door and pushed it open, then motioned to the doorman.

"Miss?"

"Do you know where my uncle was meeting? I need to speak with him. It's most urgent."

"I believe he was in the room just past the side hall. On the left."

"I tried there."

"Did you go inside? Maybe he didn't hear you."

"No. I'll try that." Should she enlist his help? But no, she didn't know whom she could trust in here. This man, nice looking though he was, could be in cahoots with the people in that room. "Thank you."

She backed away and let the door shut her off from his curious expression. As she went to the office he'd suggested, she glanced again down the hall. This time a shadow moved at the back of the hall, near the door. Her throat tightened and she rushed on past.

This time when she rapped on the door, she used more force. "Uncle Everett?" She twisted the doorknob, and it turned easily.

Three men on the far side of the large room turned to look at her. Her uncle frowned and rose. "Belle? I told you I'd be along as soon as I could."

"Might I have a word with you? It's important." Her gaze swept the other two men. They looked vaguely familiar, both state representatives. Her uncle had served two terms as a state senator. This election would boost him to the national senate level.

His brow furrowed, but he stepped to meet her by the door. "What is it, Belle? This meeting is important."

"Uncle Everett, there's a woman with a gun in the side hallway outside. I fear you might be her target. A man was insisting she hide there to shoot someone he said should have already been dead. Doesn't that sound like another attempt on your life?"

His eyes widened, and his hand came down on her shoulder. "You were right to tell me."

She leaned closer to whisper, "Trust no one. We have no idea if one of these men is involved too. Tell them there's a family emergency and you must go. Is there another way out instead of the front or side door?"

He nodded. "Out the other side of this room. I'll go that way. Thank you, my dear." Facing the men, he cleared his throat. "I'm

afraid I've been summoned home for an emergency." He held up his hand when the men murmured in dismay. "I'm sure it's fine. Let's meet again on Monday at three. Does that suit?"

The men muttered and nodded as they began to gather their papers on the table.

Belle smiled and apologized for interrupting, then led her uncle across the room. "We'll just go this way." She unlocked the door and twisted the doorknob. The fresh scent of the pines lining the building spurred her on.

"Let's get out of here." Her uncle closed the door behind him. "We'll stop to tell the police on our way home."

Belle glanced over her shoulder as they hurried to the automobile. Only when they were halfway down the street did she ease back against the cushion.

Belle sat at the piano in the music room. "Adjust my skirt before everyone gets here, Lily."

Lily tugged here and there on the pink skirt until it draped perfectly around the bench and onto the floor. "I think that looks lovely, Miss Belle." The pink dress shimmered in the electric light. "You'll be the star of the opera house tonight."

Belle smoothed the fabric over her stomach and turned to view herself in the large mirror on one wall. "You did a marvelous job, Lily."

Lily's cheeks heated at the praise. It wasn't always easy to please her employer. She tucked a few strands of flowers into Belle's hair.

"I'm quite exhausted after explaining what I heard to the police."

Lily froze, then resumed the hair arrangement. "Police? What happened?"

"I suspect I overheard a plot to murder my uncle. I managed to warn him, and we left the back way."

Lily gasped. "How brave of you."

Belle tipped her head to one side and examined her reflection again. "I was in no danger, but I was certainly fearful for Uncle Everett."

"Do you have any idea why someone would want to harm your uncle? He seems such a kind man."

Belle shrugged. "I assume it's political. I've suggested he hire a bodyguard for now."

"Will he?"

"I hope so." Belle's gaze met Lily's in the mirror. "Mrs. O'Reilly told me you had a mishap at the church yesterday yourself. What happened?"

Lily tried not to be hurt that Belle didn't so much as ask if she was all right. "A man attacked me in the churchyard." She launched into an explanation of the incident.

Belle shuddered delicately. "He had a knife? How terrifying! Did he cut you deep?"

Lily shook her head. "It left a mark though." She tipped her chin up to display the thin line of the cut.

"The city is getting to be a frightening place. I've half a mind to accept Stuart Vesters and escape to New York."

"Is securing a husband your primary goal in life?"

Belle lifted her chin. "Of course. I want to be like Mrs. Astor. I would even like to travel to New York and meet her in person someday."

"I'm afraid I don't know who that is."

Belle's glance held pity. "She's just the most famous woman in all of New York society. Her husband is one of the richest men in the world. Women who marry power can do so much. I want to see the world, experience everything. The right man can give me that."

"And is Mr. Hawkes that right man? He doesn't seem to have enough power or money for that." Lily held her breath to see how Belle would respond.

Belle stared at her. "Why do you care?"

Lily adjusted a glittering diamond pin in Belle's hair. "I don't care at all. It's just he has no power that I can tell."

"He's a handsome devil though." Belle's fingers rippled across the keys. "But you're right. I've been realizing he's not husband material. But I don't think Stuart Vesters is either. I am going to look around for a man with Hawkes's good looks and Vesters's wealth."

"What about love?"

A smile lifted Belle's lips. "I'll be happy to love the man who can give me everything I want out of life."

"You don't believe in a love that transcends things like money and power? What if you fell in love with a servant?"

Belle's laugh tinkled out. "You're too funny, Lily. How utterly ridiculous. I would never allow myself to get close to someone in that position. Even our relationship knows its boundaries, though I tell you just about everything. But we're not *friends*. You're my maid, and that's all you'll ever be."

Belle's dismissive words stung more than they should have. "Of course, Miss Belle." Lily pressed her lips together. "Do you want your wrap?"

Belle nodded. "What about you, Lily? Do you believe in all that happily ever after?" She chuckled as if the thought was nonsense.

Did she? Lily wasn't sure anymore. "I did once. Life gets in the way sometimes though. And then it's hard to know what another person really feels or thinks." She adjusted the wrap around Belle's bare shoulders.

"Men will say anything to get what they want. Our job is not to let them have it until we get the rings on our fingers."

The other woman's brazen statement took Lily's breath. Was that all love was—a dance around the bedroom? Maybe Andy's desertion was her own fault. She hadn't resisted his appeal, and though God had forgiven her, she hadn't forgiven herself. "I think there are good men out there. My father was a wonderful man who treated Mama and me like queens."

"They are few and far between. I just want a man who is rich enough to allow me to travel and who isn't overly domineering. I will vet that well." She pinched her cheeks.

"Who is escorting you to the opera tonight?"

"Stuart. But he has a rich young friend who is meeting us there, and I plan to check him out." Her silvery laugh tinkled out. "Don't look so disapproving, Lily. You're in the city now. We do things differently here. When you and I are traveling in Paris, you'll thank me for keeping my head about me."

The doorbell rang, and Lily hurried to escape before Mr. Vesters arrived for appetizers before the event.

Maybe Belle was right. Love hadn't worked out well for Lily herself. Maybe it would be worth absorbing Belle's very different ideas. After all, she was in the city now. Things weren't as black and white as they seemed in Larson.

Her thoughts drifted to Mr. Lambreth's blue eyes, but she shoved that inappropriate thought away. If Drew was forbidden, Mr. Lambreth was doubly so.

# FIFTEEN

The opera rippled with movement—women in silk gowns of every color and men dressed nattily in suits mingled in the aisles before they found their balcony seats for the performance. Drew tugged on his tie and glanced around for Vesters. He'd hoped to discover the man's partner tonight.

Drew jammed his hands into the pockets of his jacket and clenched his teeth. He had to figure out where Ballard was. The man had to be behind the attack on Lily. The ominous words the attacker had said reverberated in Drew's head. *"So beautiful."* As if he'd been watching her and knew her.

Camille Marshall waved at him from across the room. She made her way through the throng to grasp his forearm. "I didn't expect to see you, Drew. If you're looking for Belle, she's with Mr. Vesters." She smiled slyly and inclined her head. "In our seats."

He shifted and looked away, unsure how to deal with the family expectations. Maybe he would have considered an arranged match before Lily disrupted his world again. He'd tried hard to forget her, but now here she was again and smack-dab back in the middle of a dangerous situation.

He smiled at Mrs. Marshall. "I'll just go say hello then." Vesters was the real reason for the meeting. Taking his leave, he made his way to the Marshall seats.

Belle looked beautiful tonight, as she always did, but his gaze went to Vesters. The vest buttons were strained across the man's chest, and he mopped his face with a hanky. Pity stirred in Drew. Belle would have the upper hand in that relationship, and Vesters would be dancing to her whims.

Drew stepped into the row and bowed. "Your aunt directed me here to say hello."

Belle glanced at Vesters, then smiled prettily as she took his hand. "Sit with us, Mr. Hawkes. There's plenty of room."

Vesters nodded and pointed to the chair on his other side. "Sit here and we can talk a bit."

Belle bit her lip, then recovered her smile. "Of course."

The opera was about to start, so Drew moved to his seat. He allowed his gaze to wander the balconies. He would know Ballard's shape and the set of his ears anywhere. What would he do if Ballard had moved on from Austin?

His gaze swept the room again. Then he saw a man lean forward to whisper in a woman's ear. The slant of the chin, the hooked nose. Ballard. He was here. He fisted his hands and wished he could leap over the balcony and bring the man down. There was no proof though. But at least he knew Ballard was still here working on whatever plan he had in mind.

The man turned his head and their gazes collided. Ballard's eyes widened, and he looked away quickly. Drew exhaled. His enemy knew he was here, so he needed to be on his guard.

Was Ian right? This obsession could get him killed. But he was close, so close. And what if he brought Ballard to justice? Pursuing the man had given Drew his purpose in life. With Ballard behind bars, what then? More tracking of counterfeiters and murderers?

Now that he'd seen Lily again, he realized how lonely he'd been. His life had been a series of empty hotel rooms and lousy food.

He could offer her nothing though.

Lily's breath came fast as she descended the cellar steps on Friday night. The butterfly room keys hung from her fingers. She'd tried to talk Emily into making this trip for her, but none of the maids liked to come down here. The thought of what she might see here made her pause outside the door.

All the staff talked about this room, but she hadn't seen it yet. She would have liked to have kept it that way, but Mr. Marshall was waiting on her. She inhaled and forced herself to insert the key. It twisted in the lock, and she opened the door, then turned on the lights. The glass cases sprang into sight. Her gaze went from one case to the other. All those beautiful creatures pinned into glass coffins made her shudder. Mr. Marshall had instructed her to go to the small room at the back. He had requested she bring the Queen Alexandra's Birdwing specimen up to show the guests.

"You doing all right?" Mrs. O'Reilly's voice spoke from behind her.

Lily sagged with relief as she turned. "I'm so glad you're here. It's quite creepy."

"I felt bad I'd sent you down here on your own for the first time." The housekeeper glanced around the space. "You'll get used to it. Mr. Marshall is so proud of these insects. And you must admit they're beautifully colored."

"I hadn't dared to look at them." Lily shuddered but walked to join Mrs. O'Reilly at a glass case. She much preferred the insects fluttering around. The card on the display read *Bhutanitis lidderdalei*. She couldn't even pronounce it.

"See how they have tiger-like spots? It's to frighten predators. They live in Bhutan. That's in South Asia." Mrs. O'Reilly moved to the next display. "And this one is the *Ornithoptera chimaera*."

"They're so green. They almost look like orchids."

Mrs. O'Reilly smiled. "See, they aren't so terrifying. Over here is what Mr. Marshall sent you after." She walked purposefully to the door at the back of the cavernous room and opened it.

When Mrs. O'Reilly flipped on the light, Lily took a step back. "They're gigantic!"

The bluish-green butterfly was stretched out to display the full size of its wings. A black vein contrasted the color. Its wingspread was close to ten inches. Seeing the creature flying about would be rather daunting and scary. What if it became caught in a woman's hair?

"Why does he collect these?"

Mrs. O'Reilly's smile lingered lovingly on the huge specimen. "He says all beautiful things should be displayed. You must admit the butterflies are quite spectacular."

"They're dead."

The housekeeper's smile faded. "Well, yes. But their beauty remains." She picked up the display case and thrust it into Lily's arms. "Take this to the parlor and be quick about it. He's likely growing impatient already."

Carrying the butterfly carefully, Lily rushed up the stairs and down the hall to the parlor. She was breathless when she stepped into the large room filled with people. Women sat in a group chatting and the men stood by the fireplace as they most likely discussed politics and the economy. The hum of voices stopped when she entered with the case.

Mr. Marshall held out his hand. "Ah, there you are. I'm eager to show off my prize specimen."

Lily was only too glad to hand it over. Her gaze briefly collided with Drew's before she quickly looked away. Belle narrowed her eyes meaningfully and jerked her head toward the door. Lily started that direction.

"Stay put, Lily," Mr. Marshall said. "I don't want this out of the vault for long."

Lily retreated to a space by the wall. Her gaze darted to Belle, and when she realized her mistress had moved to see the butterfly, she glanced at Drew. He was staring at the case, and Lily allowed herself to drink in the strong planes and lines of his face. A lock of black hair had fallen over his forehead, and his cheeks were flushed by the warmth of the room. She curled her fingers into her palms. If only she had the right to brush that soft hair off his face, to trace the roughened line of his jaw.

He glanced her way and transfixed her in place. The emotion blazing in his eyes was clear for anyone who looked that way. She wanted to flee, to forget the pain there. Could his tale possibly be true? She couldn't imagine anything that would have made her desert him, so it seemed unlikely.

She finally managed to look away. No one seemed to have noticed the intense interlude between them. Belle was laughing with her head thrown back, revealing the fine line of her throat and chin. At least she hadn't seen. Lily exhaled and edged farther out of the throng.

She felt like a calf cut from its mama. Alone, bewildered, afraid. If she could mount the next train for Larson, she would. Back home she knew what was expected of her. Every day was like the next without the dizzying highs and lows of life here.

The group had finally quit admiring the giant butterfly, and Lily took it without looking at the poor dead thing. The sooner it was tucked away, the happier she would be. She hurried back to the basement stairs, but it was scarier this time. Darker somehow with the shadows leaping and moving like gargoyles. She raced to the vault at the back of the room and thrust the case back in among the other valuable specimens.

When she slammed the door and locked it, she heard a sliding, slithering sound like a foot. *Or a snake.*

*But that's ridiculous.* Her breathing felt tight and labored as she started back across the room. Something swooped toward her, and she ducked instinctively with her heart pounding. Squinting in the dim light, she made out what appeared to be a cloud of colors. Black, brown, orange, violet. Her throat was too tight to scream as she backpedaled.

She closed her eyes and raised her hands instinctively as wings came again. The soft touch of wings on her face and hands broke her paralysis, and she shrieked as she ran for the door. Again and again screams tore from her throat as delicate wings whispered over her skin.

A hand grabbed her arm, and Drew's voice was in her ear. "Lily, it's okay."

The panic ebbed as she burrowed into his chest. His hand smoothed her hair. "There's something here. Bats maybe." She shuddered and closed her eyes, reveling in the comforting press of his arms and the scent of his bay-rum cologne.

"Not bats, just butterflies. Look, it's just butterflies."

She peeked open an eye and glanced around. Dozens of butterflies rested on everything. "What are they doing down here?"

With his arm still around her, he guided her toward the door. "Maybe Mr. Marshall will know."

# SIXTEEN

Butterflies covered every bush, every shrub. The brightly colored insects coated the table and chairs on the patio as well. Lily didn't want to step outside the French doors onto the brick in case she stepped on one. After last night, butterflies made her tremble.

"See, nothing to worry about." Mr. Marshall's smile was kind. "This type of migration happens occasionally. The American Snout butterfly is common here, and after heavy rains, their numbers surge. We will probably have close to twenty million passing through here."

Mrs. Marshall's head bobbed, and she put her gloved hand on Lily's arm. "Mr. Hawkes will be joining Belle for breakfast in the dining room. Put him in there to wait."

"She's running a few minutes late, Mrs. Marshall," Lily said. "And she doesn't like me to speak with Mr. Hawkes."

"That girl is being ridiculous. Serve him some tea or coffee until she comes down. Mr. Marshall and I have an appointment in town. Make sure he needs for nothing."

"Yes, ma'am." Inside, she quailed at the thought of being alone with Drew. If Belle came in and found them talking intimately, her job here would be gone.

The Marshalls were barely out the door when Drew stepped

onto the terrace. He smiled at her. "I've been working on my catlike skills. You didn't even hear me coming."

She had to smile, but she shot a glance into the house to make sure Belle wasn't coming. "This way, Mr. Hawkes."

His lips tightened, and she knew he didn't like her addressing him so formally, but she had to get used to calling him that so she didn't slip in front of Belle. He said nothing though as he followed her into the empty dining room. Food steamed on the sideboard.

She moved toward it. "Coffee?" She lifted the silver coffeepot.

"Please." He went to the head of the long table, clad in fine white linen. "May I sit here?"

"Wherever you like." She poured coffee into a fine china cup. "Milk or sugar?"

"Black." He studied her over the rim of the cup. "Where's Belle?"

"Running a bit late. I can go check on her." She put down the pot and started to turn, but he caught her by the wrist.

"I'd rather you stay and talk to me."

Her skin was hot where he touched her. "You'll get me fired."

"We'll hear her if she comes this way. Another one of my catlike skills." He kept hold of her wrist.

"Another servant may report it."

"Have you recovered from the butterfly attack last night?" His expression made it clear he didn't intend to let her leave, though he released her wrist.

She rubbed where he'd touched and stepped back two steps so if anyone peeked into the dining room it wouldn't appear as if they were deep in conversation. "Yes, I'm fine. There are more butterflies everywhere outside too."

He nodded. "My wheels crunched over some in the road. I wanted to rush out and shoo them away."

She gestured to the French doors. "They're all over the patio."

125

He took a sip of coffee and leaned back in his chair. "I want to hear more about the attack the other night. You distracted me."

"*I* distracted you? I don't think so."

His grin widened, then an intense expression came over his face. "I meant to ask if you recognized the voice."

She shook her head. "Not at all. Who do you suspect?"

He released a heavy exhale. "I got to wondering if it could have been Ballard."

She thought about the figure running away. "I suppose it's possible."

"I saw him at the opera."

"Did he see you?"

"Yes, and I followed him too. He's staying at the Driskill Hotel."

His gaze seemed to devour her. Did he still think she was beautiful? She'd felt lovely in his eyes once upon a time, but since he left, she didn't walk with her head as high as she used to. His desertion had taken her confidence.

She heard a rustle in the hall and hurried to the sideboard. Lifting a tray of sweets, she turned toward Drew with a distant smile. "A sweet roll, Mr. Hawkes? I'm sure Miss Belle will be down shortly."

Belle swept into the room with a sweep of silk skirts. "I'm right here. I hope you haven't been waiting long."

Drew rose and pulled out a chair for Belle. "I've only had time to have my coffee poured."

"I hope I was worth waiting for." She batted her eyes at him.

"Absolutely." He scooted her chair in and sat back down.

Lily blinked her burning eyes and offered the tray of trifles to Belle. "Eggs and ham should be ready now. I'll fetch the rest of your breakfast."

"Don't bother. This is plenty, don't you think, Mr. Hawkes?"

Drew lifted a brow. "I'm not sure this will sustain me all day. I wouldn't turn down some ham and eggs."

Belle's lips tightened. "Fetch the other food, Lily. And don't dawdle. We have a lot to do this morning. While we're gone, I want you to have my new dress ready for tonight."

"Yes, miss." Lily escaped from the room. Why was he complimenting her and then catering to Belle in practically the same breath?

The police station bustled with activity on Monday morning when Lily detoured from one of her errands. She asked to speak to the officer in charge of the case and was shown back to a cramped room with only a desk and two chairs. It smelled of stale smoke and liniment. The man at the window turned, and she recognized him as the policeman in the churchyard.

"Miss Donaldson, what a surprise. I'm Officer Pickle." He limped a bit as he rushed to the chair and swept the papers from it. "Have a seat."

She thanked him and settled onto the hard oak seat. "I wondered if you've tracked down the perpetrator yet?"

He looked her over before he shrugged. "Not yet. I was going to find you today since I had a few more questions."

"Questions?" She didn't much care for the skepticism in his eyes.

"A passerby told us you greeted the man with a hug. Is there something else you wish to say? Or maybe you want to retract your accusation?"

Lily gasped and stood. "Absolutely not! What you heard is an absolute falsehood." She yanked the kerchief from around her neck. "And what about this? It's clearly a mark left by a knife."

"So you had no assignation in the churchyard?"

She hesitated. Perhaps she should have told him the entire story. But what if he told Belle? "A boy told me Mr. Hawkes wanted to see me. He's a frequent visitor at the Butterfly Palace, so of course I hurried to obey the summons."

"Mr. Hawkes? He arrived a bit later." The officer's expression grew crafty. "Was this a usual assignation?"

"If you mean did we meet for a romantic interlude, you couldn't be more wrong. It was an innocent meeting."

"If that's true, why didn't you tell me about this meeting?"

She clutched her handbag tightly in both hands. "Because I feared you would have exactly this reaction. You need to focus on finding the man who attacked me. I can assure you it was no one I knew, and it certainly wasn't Mr. Hawkes. He's a gentleman."

"You had to see something. You've given us no description. Surely you can see how suspicious that is."

"But he attacked me from behind! And it was getting dark."

"So you say."

Rage pooled in her chest. "There's someone out there attacking women. I saw another attack, and you're doing nothing to stop this man."

"What attack?"

"Miss Jane White. I cared for her until she was taken to the hospital."

He nodded. "An entirely different matter. The man attacks women in their own homes. You were in the churchyard."

She wheeled and stalked to the door, but her lids quivered with the desire to cry. How could they suspect she was lying about this? She bore the marks on her throat.

Her head high, she rushed out into the sunshine, then down the street and around the corner to the church. The churchyard was empty, but then, it was Monday. Lily stood on the walk and debated whether to go in. The vicar might not even be around, but no, a shadow passed in front of the window. Someone was there. She opened the gate and walked to the front door.

"Can I help you?"

Lily turned to see a woman of about fifty in a plain gray dress in the flower garden. The woman wore muddy gloves and held a pair of pruning shears. The floppy hat she wore obscured all but her smile. "I was attacked here last week, and I wanted to see if anyone happened to witness it."

The woman's smile vanished. She took off her gloves and approached with her hands outstretched. "I'm so sorry. You're Miss Lily Donaldson, then."

Lily knew the encounter had been in the paper. "That's right."

"You weren't hurt?"

Lily shook her head. "I'm fine, actually. But I have to admit I'm looking over my shoulder every time I go out now. I'd feel better if the police had found the attacker."

"I'm the reverend's wife, Molly Adams." The woman took Lily's arm and guided her to a bench. "I'm sorry to say I wasn't here. My husband was though, and he spoke with the police. Did you talk to the detective about what they've found?"

Lily nodded. "I just came from there." The woman's kindness made her want to cry, and she gulped. "The police seem to think I had some kind of assignation and my lover attacked me."

"I'm sorry to say the police insinuated such to me as well. I can see you're not that kind of woman though. Your pure soul shines out through your eyes." Molly's gaze went to Lily's neck. "The attacker did that?"

"Yes, with a knife. What did your husband see?"

Molly laid her gardening gloves on the bench. "He thought the two of you were embracing at first. Then he heard you scream. He'd already locked the door. The key often gives him trouble, so by the time he was able to get into the yard, you'd left."

"And he told the police he thought we were a couple?"

"Yes. I'm afraid so. I'll tell him what you've told me." Molly put her hand on Lily's arm. "I'm sorry if he's brought you trouble. I'll make sure he rectifies it."

"I don't know if it will make a difference. The police don't seem to be treating this attack seriously. Did your husband get a look at the man?"

Molly shook her head. "His eyesight isn't very good, and he'd just lost his glasses for the third time that day. He wasn't much help to the police." She rose and turned back toward the porch. "I found something that might belong to you." She opened the door and reached inside.

Lily's gaze went to the object in her hand. A butterfly in a globe winked in the sunlight. She swallowed hard. "Where did you get that?"

"It was in the yard. I can't imagine where it came from. Is it yours?"

Lily didn't want to touch the thing, but she forced herself to rise from the bench and reach for it. "I—I think my attacker intended to leave it by my dead body."

"Oh dear," Mrs. Adams whispered.

The globe was oddly warm in Lily's fingers. "I'll take it to the police. Thank you for your time. I must be going. My mistress will be expecting me back. If your husband remembers anything, you can find me at the Butterfly Palace."

A strange expression crossed the woman's face. "You work for Mrs. Marshall?"

"I'm her niece's maid. Is there something wrong?"

Molly shook her head and backed away. "No, no, nothing's wrong. Have a good day." She turned on her heel and practically ran for the door of the church.

# SEVENTEEN

Drew glanced at his pocket watch. At this time on a Monday afternoon, most of the household would be out except for the servants. They would be beating rugs and cleaning everything in preparation for the week ahead, which meant he might be able to have a private conversation with Lily. He fingered the note he received an hour ago.

He went around the side of the house to the backyard. Smoke belched from the open windows of the back room. The odor of lye made his eyes water. He caught a glimpse of her head through the window of the laundry room. She was alone. He tapped on the window and she turned.

Her smile was quickly shuttered, but she stepped to the door and opened it. "You came." Her tone was cautious, and she glanced toward the interior door. "Keep your voice down. I don't want Mrs. O'Reilly or Emily to see us."

"Of course." He brushed past her and closed the door.

The strong odor of soap and bluing hung in the steamy air. Perspiration instantly broke out on his forehead. The open windows failed to vent much of the heat generated by the boiling water on the stove and in the large tubs of clothing. A basket by a large wringer contained clean, wet clothes.

She stepped toward the basket. "I need to hang up these things. The line is around the side where no one can see us."

"I'll take it." He lifted the basket of clothing and carried it through the door.

She followed him outside, and he dropped the basket under the clothesline, located away from the garden in the side yard, then turned to face her. "Your note said it was urgent. What's wrong?"

She blew a strand of hair out of her eyes. Her cheeks were pink from the heat and exertion. "The police think I made up the attack."

He hated seeing her working so hard. She should have her own servants and be dressed in the finest silks he could buy. What she said finally penetrated when she stared at him as if waiting for his reaction. "What?"

"I went to the police station this morning. Officer Pickle thinks you and I were having an assignation and concocted the story to cover our affair."

His mind wandered there for a moment before he reined it in. He wanted Lily forever, not just for a fling. Never again would he dishonor her that way. His gaze went to the mark still visible on her neck. "He thinks I attacked you with a knife?" He wanted to touch it but curled his fingers into his palms instead.

"He implied it." She wet her lips. "There's more. I went to the church, and the minister's wife found this." She thrust her hand into her apron and held it out.

The butterfly in the globe beat its wings ineffectually against the glass that imprisoned it. He took it from her fingers. "The butterfly is still alive."

"Can we get it out?"

"I can break the glass. Not sure if the stress will kill it though."

"It's better than leaving it trapped in there."

The thing gave him a bad feeling. "So it wasn't Ballard who

attacked you. I don't like this, Lily. You've caught the attention of a killer."

"I'll be careful. We should tell the police about this."

"I don't think they'll listen."

"I'll stop by and tell them myself."

He knelt in the garden and grabbed a rock. The first blow was too timid and glanced off the glass globe. The butterfly fluttered to the bottom of the globe and was motionless. He hit the glass with more force and small cracks spidered out. He tapped it again, and the pieces of glass separated.

The butterfly was motionless, and he touched it with a gentle finger. The wings drooped and Lily whimpered.

He shook his head. "I think it's dead. Maybe we didn't free it in time." Picking it up, he carried it to the flowers and laid it at the base of a rosebush.

Her eyes were filled with tears when he turned back around and began to pick up the glass. "We need to talk to Jane and Nathan. I need to wrap this up before my cover is blown. When could you go with me?"

She inhaled, her eyes on the glass, then she looked at the laundry. "If you can secure a cab, I could slip away for about two hours as soon as these are hung up." She knelt to lift a heavy skirt to the clothesline. "You said you saw Ballard. Are you close to arresting him?"

"Not by a long shot."

"You said he's at the Driskill?"

"Yes, that big hotel on Brazos." He realized she'd gone still. "You're not thinking of going to see him, are you?"

She shook out a blouse and pinned it to the line before answering. "I might."

He took her arm and turned her to face him. "Lily, you can't do that. He's dangerous."

"So you keep saying, but I've never felt any sense of threat from him. What if he might tell me something, something that would bring justice to our fathers? I'm not frightened. It would be in a public place. He's not going to harm me."

He wanted to shake some sense into her, but instead he pulled her close. His heart thudded in his chest at the sweet smell of her hair and the way she relaxed against him. "I can't run the risk of losing you." He pressed his lips against her head.

She pulled away slightly. "You threw me away long ago. There's nothing left."

He searched her eyes for some sign she still cared about him, but her expression was shuttered and aloof. She shifted as if to move away, but he tightened his grip on her upper arms. He bent his head but she didn't flinch. Brushing his lips against hers was like coming home. The sweet scent of her breath, the softness of her lips, the feel of her in his arms reminded him of all he had lost.

She didn't kiss him back, at least not at first. He deepened the kiss and pulled her closer until her lips moved and she responded. Her right hand moved to his chest, and her breath came faster. She melted against him, and he touched her hair, pulling her even tighter against him. Passion and tenderness choked him, and he wished he'd never let her go. He wished he'd married her and could take her back to his apartment forever.

He'd been such an idiot to let her go.

She pushed his chest with her hand, and feeling cold and bereft, he let her go. "I'm not sorry. Not one bit. You still care about me, Lily. You can't deny it."

Her lips were pink and swollen from their kiss, and her eyes were luminous. She took a step back, and her hand went to her disheveled hair. "You left me, Drew. I can't ignore that. You offer me a kiss in secret while you go about your merry way."

She was right. What could he offer her? A life spent traveling from one place to the next in pursuit of the next enemy of the government? It was all he knew. If he wasn't employed by the Secret Service, how could he support a wife and family? She deserved more than what he could offer.

He'd been reaching toward her again, but he dropped his hand and stepped back. Nothing had changed, not really. She was being practical and had seen the obstacles still in their way. All he could do was hurt her more.

Nathan didn't glare at them like last time. Lily took the tea Jane gave her with a smile of thanks. Jane gave Drew his tea, then retreated to her chair. She folded her hands in her lap and said nothing, but her gaze darted to her brother.

Nathan cleared his throat. "Jane has asked me to help you. Let me start by saying I'm helping myself and my sister, which is all I'm really interested in."

"We understand." Lily shot a glance at Drew. "We appreciate any assistance you can give us. I'll let Drew ask you the questions he most needs answers to."

Drew set his tea on the battered table in front of them. "How long have you worked for Vesters?"

"About two years."

"How did you come into his employ?"

Nathan let out a heavy sigh. "I was working part-time for Karr's Fine Spirits. I work full-time as an engineer at his construction firm, but I needed some extra money. Vesters came in one day and had dinner. He paid with a twenty-dollar bill and told me to keep the change."

Lily blinked. "That's quite a large tip."

"Exactly. He did the same thing for several nights, and you can understand if I came to regard him in a kindly light."

"Of course." Drew nodded. "Go on."

"After a couple of weeks, I noticed the bill he gave me was a little wet. I thought nothing about it until the ink came off on my hands. Then I realized it was counterfeit. I told him about it, expecting him to be indignant someone had passed him a forged bill. Instead, he laughed and told me he could use a smart chap like me."

"He lured you in with the thought of easy money?"

Nathan shook his head at Drew's question. "He told me Mr. Karr had suggested he bring me in on it. He and Karr belong to that Novo group, and Mr. Karr is great friends with him so I had no idea he was lying. Once I'd gotten involved, I found out Mr. Karr knew nothing about it. But by then, I'd dropped several parcels for him and several other men had seen me. He'd have no trouble pinning the forgeries on me."

Jane leaned forward. "And then there was me. Vesters told Nathan if he didn't do like he said, he'd make sure I disappeared. Nathan would never see me again."

"What an evil, evil man," Lily burst out.

"He's all that and more." Jane's voice was choked. "Nathan is in so tightly now, he'll go to prison if it's all uncovered. Vesters had made sure of that."

Drew glanced at Lily, and she could see he wanted to tell them both the truth. They both knew he couldn't. Maintaining his cover was too important.

"If I can get the evidence against Vesters, I have a friend who might be able to help," Drew said. "I'll make sure you are cleared for testifying once he's arrested."

"What evidence do you need?"

"It's easy enough to arrest him when he's at his printing facility, but unless we want to worry about reprisals from the people he's working with, we need them all. I want his partner too. Do you know who that is?"

Nathan shook his head. "I've never seen him."

Drew leaned forward. "I need to catch them all red-handed."

Nathan glanced at Jane. "I'll see what I can find out. I want you to promise me if anything happens to me, you'll take care of Jane and Hannah."

"I promise," Lily said quickly. "I heard today our assistant cook is quitting. If she goes through with it, I'll send word right away for you to come for an interview."

Jane brightened, then slumped. "When they find out I have a baby, they won't hire me."

"Mrs. Marshall is a fair woman. Let's wait and see what happens."

# EIGHTEEN

Belle strode in a very unladylike way to the butterfly conservatory where she knew her aunt would be. The Monday afternoon ride had been unending, and she'd barely held her smile in place. Though the man had seemed promising when she met him at dinner, he had a wandering hand she'd had to keep in check.

Her aunt was on a white chaise. Christopher was on a chair beside her. He had his mother's poodle on his lap.

Aunt Camille looked up from the book she was reading. She looked quite lovely in a pale green gown. "Whatever is the matter, Belle? You're behaving like a hoyden."

Belle dropped onto a chair near Aunt Camille. "Remind me never to go out with him alone again. He fancied himself quite the Casanova."

Christopher scowled and put down the dog. "He didn't harm you?"

His mother slapped his arm with her fan. "Christopher, stay out of this. And brush your hair out of your face. I quite dislike that new hairstyle."

Rage flashed over Christopher's face but quickly vanished. Belle shot Christopher a sympathetic glance, then removed her hat and threw it onto the floor. "Of course not. I wouldn't allow it."

He grinned and sat back in his chair. "Of course you wouldn't."

Her aunt closed the book. "Lily, get us some tea," she told the maid who was dusting glass display cases. "Belle, dear, you should accept Mr. Vesters and be done with it."

Belle sighed. "I'd hoped for someone more dashing."

"He has money and political aspirations. That's dashing enough."

Lily moved to a tray on the table and retrieved a white envelope. "Before I go for the tea, I should give you this from Mr. Vesters."

Belle took the thick envelope and read the contents. "He would like to take me to the theater on Friday." She smiled but her heart felt no real joy. Her plan to marry well would come together, but why, oh why couldn't Vesters look like Mr. Hawkes?

Aunt Camille stared at Lily. "You went out today. I saw you leaving the police station. What were you doing there?"

Lily colored and glanced at Aunt Camille. "I don't know if Miss Belle told you, but I was attacked in the yard of St. David's Episcopal Church on Friday."

Her aunt bolted more upright. "You don't mean . . . ?"

Lily's cheeks grew redder. "No, no, but he had a knife." She unbuttoned her collar to reveal a red slash against her white skin. "I escaped before any real harm was done. The police have not caught him."

Christopher leaped to his feet. "The cad!"

Aunt Camille winced at the lurid mark. "It seems my son is right for once. I'm so sorry, Lily. And, Belle, why didn't you tell me?"

"I'm sorry but I forgot, Aunt Camille." Belle eyed Christopher, who was pacing the floor. Why would he care about a servant?

Lily turned away. "I was unharmed so I thought not to worry you."

"You really should have told us," Aunt Camille said. "I'll have my husband talk to the police himself."

Lily shook her head. "I'd rather you didn't, Mrs. Marshall. I don't want any special attention. I stopped by the church to see if the minister or his wife had seen anything. Mrs. Adams seemed rather peculiar. Have you ever attended that church?"

Her aunt picked up her book. "No, we attend the Presbyterian church. What do you mean about her being peculiar?" Her voice seemed a little high and strained.

"When she discovered I worked here, she rushed off as if she was frightened."

Belle laughed. "I've heard people say my uncle worships butterflies. They're quite ignorant. The ornate frescoes seem rather heathenish to some people. I wouldn't worry about it."

"Yes, miss."

"What exactly did the minister's wife say?" Aunt Camille asked.

"She asked if I worked for you, ma'am."

"How strange. I'm sure I don't know her." She rose and went to the door. "I'll have one of the other maids fetch the tea." Her aunt hurried out of the room. "Come with me, Christopher."

He sighed and followed his mother. He paused near Lily as though he wanted to speak, but then scurried out the door.

Belle stared after them. "Aunt Camille has only been married to Uncle Everett for a year. She was an ambassador's widow. My uncle thought her connections would enhance his political ambitions."

"An arranged marriage?"

"Of course. My uncle has his sights on getting to Washington eventually. Aunt Camille knows the political arena quite well. Her husband left her penniless, so she needed a wealthy husband. It's been quite advantageous to both of them."

"They seem quite fond of one another."

"Oh, they are! It's a love match now, but it didn't start out that way. I'm sure I can do the same. I will be able to love my husband

140

eventually, whoever he is. As long as he brings the right expectations to the marriage."

When Lily pressed her lips together, Belle laughed. "You're so charming, Lily." Belle slipped her feet out of her shoes. "What you don't seem to understand is that I have few options. Once I'm married, I can go where I want and do what I like. Right now my uncle controls my every movement. I'm ready to manage my own house."

"You could travel, go to the university if you pleased. You don't have to marry, Miss Belle. You said you wanted power, but isn't it better to have power over your own destiny rather than have to fall in with your husband's wishes? Especially if it's a loveless marriage? Your husband may not cater to your every whim like you think."

Belle touched the glass housing a very colorful butterfly. "That's very progressive thinking. Would you go to college if you could?"

Lily ran her dust cloth over another case. "My father owned the town livery, and we were quite comfortable. I dreamed of going off to college, but when he died, my mother had to find a way to support us, so she started a dressmaking business. I quit school to help her."

Belle hadn't thought about how her maid grew up. She glanced at Lily's hands, roughened from needlework and scrubbing. "This is as far as you've ever traveled? What if you could go to London, Paris, Madrid? Would you marry someone for that?" Lily smiled, and Belle was struck with how attractive her maid was. Was Mr. Hawkes interested in her as a woman? Maybe even Christopher? "What if you could marry someone like Mr. Hawkes and travel the world?"

Lily turned red, then white. "Mr. Hawkes is in Austin. He's not traveling the world."

"He's quite the cosmopolitan traveler though. He spent nearly a year in Paris before he came here."

Lily blinked and moved to the next case. "How exciting for him. But I thought you'd decided against Mr. Hawkes."

"I haven't decided anything. All I know is I intend to forge my own destiny. I won't be ordered about the way my mother was."

Lily held her gaze. "Then you should think twice about accepting Mr. Vesters."

"Why would you say that?"

"He seems the forceful type, Miss Belle. I think once the bloom wore off the marriage, he would insist on his own way. I think he might even strike you."

Belle laughed at the thought of anyone daring to lift a hand to her. "You let me worry about how to control Stuart Vesters."

The Driskill Hotel was on Sixth Street and Brazos. Its massive stone edifice was almost enough to make Lily turn tail and run as soon as she stepped off the trolley. She shrank back and turned her head as Mrs. Marshall sailed out the door. Once the woman was in her car and out of sight, Lily moved toward the hotel again.

A doorman held open the glass door. She clenched her hand around her bag and moved onto the marble floor of the entry. Brass gleamed everywhere on ornate wood. Her shoes echoed with the ceilings that seemed to go on forever. It was so grand it took her breath away.

Quaking inside, she went to the front desk. "Is Mr. Ballard in?"

The clerk, a mousy man with a thin mustache, looked her over with a brow lifted. "He just went to the salon." He pointed down the hall. "He's eating lunch."

She nodded and walked across the cavernous lobby to the salon before she lost her nerve. Her heart thudded in her chest, and her throat was so tight she struggled to swallow. She couldn't have asked for better circumstances. He would think she just happened to see him here rather than know she'd sought him out.

She paused in the doorway and surveyed the room, paneled with rich wood and furnished with plush leather seating. Waiters discreetly brought drinks to the patrons. She saw him at the far table by the window. He was alone with a newspaper. A half-empty glass was in front of him.

She took a deep breath and stepped into the room. The distance to his table seemed enormous, and with each step, her pulse increased. A few people looked at her curiously, and she knew her modest dress was out of place in this setting. She finally reached his table and stood quietly a moment until he lifted his gaze from the newspaper.

She smiled with as much enthusiasm as she could muster. "I couldn't believe my eyes when I saw you sitting here. Mr. Ballard, how lovely to run into you."

He went white, then scrambled to his feet. "Miss Donaldson, what are you doing here in Austin? I never dreamed you'd ever leave Larson." He jerked a chair out from the table. "Please, have a seat. Have you had lunch?" He snapped his fingers for a waiter. "Bring my guest a sandwich. Is roast beef all right? That's what I'm having."

"That would be lovely. And some tea, please." She settled into the leather chair and pulled off her gloves. "It's wonderful to see someone from home. How long have you been in Austin?"

He sat back down and folded his newspaper. "About six months. I have a knife business that's doing quite well, and, well, one thing led to another and I just purchased some property here. We are going to move in tomorrow. My mother is with me, of course. She is in her room with a headache. She'll be sorry to have missed you."

He'd always had a way of making her feel she was the most

important person in the room. His intent gaze never left her face, and he leaned forward slightly as though he didn't want to miss a syllable. His beard was mostly gray now, and his gray hair just brushed the collar of his white shirt. She thought he was about fifty-five, but his erect carriage gave the impression of someone younger.

She'd liked him from the moment he moved in next door. He and his wife had often been at her house too. She'd died in a fall from a horse when Lily was sixteen. He talked politics with her father and joked with her mother. How could he be as evil as Drew proclaimed? How could he possibly have killed her father? Yet Drew had been so adamant about it.

His smile faded, and he reached out to take her hand. "I heard about your mother. She was a wonderful lady."

She returned the pressure of his fingers. "Thank you. I miss her."

He sat back and took a sip of his drink. "How have you come to be here, Miss Lily?"

"I'm employed by the Marshalls. I tend to their niece, Belle Castle."

He lifted a brow. "I know Everett Marshall. Good man. I supported his bid for the state senate, and I plan to vote for him in the upcoming election. He'll make a fine U.S. senator. I hate to see you in service though."

"I don't mind it. I like being independent."

"You always did." He drummed his fingers on the tabletop. "My mother could use a lady's maid. I'd rather see you among friends than with strangers."

His grin reminded her again of their long history. How could she get to the truth? She wet her lips. "Thank you, but I'm quite happy where I am, though I would be glad to help you find someone. I can ask some of the staff. And I'm glad to have run into you. I've been thinking about my father's death. You were his good friend. I've heard the fire might have been set. Can you think of any enemies who might have wanted to harm him?"

His eyes clouded. "That's a rather far-fetched accusation. Your father had no enemies I'm aware of. Perhaps someone else was the target and your father and Mr. Hawkins were unfortunate victims as well."

She decided to gamble it all. She nodded and leaned forward. "There were rumors of a counterfeiting operation going on in Larson."

He blinked but betrayed no emotion. "Counterfeiting? I heard no such rumors. That's really quite outlandish."

She wanted to believe him. "I thought so too."

"I am intrigued by such accusations, however. I'm going to look into it. When could we meet again to discuss my findings? I'm quite unwilling to lose touch with you now that I know you're here in the city."

"I'm off on Wednesday afternoon."

"Let's meet here for lunch in a week. I'll see what I can find out about the fire. Perhaps I can dig up whatever evidence they have."

What if he went to the police and heard Drew was here too? This might not have been a good idea.

# NINETEEN

The basement of the old building smelled moldy, and Drew sneezed as he made his way into the bowels of the counterfeiting operation. The sharp tang of ink was a familiar smell, and he could hear the clatter of the presses. He ducked under the floor joists and stepped into a large space. The low ceiling made it feel smaller than it was, and it was packed with presses. Several men were working the presses, and they briefly nodded before getting back to work. He wasn't sure what kind of game Ballard was playing. Ian didn't seem to know either.

Vesters swept his arm out to encompass the room. "This is my little operation."

"It doesn't look so little." Drew wagered there was more than a quarter of a million dollars in counterfeit money stacked around the space. "First off, you need more space. We could easily double the number of presses."

Vesters opened his mouth, but Drew held up his hand. "I know you haven't had distribution outlets for more cash, but let me remind you I have the resources."

Vesters smiled. "Excellent. I have a building in mind. It's an abandoned barn, two levels and out in the middle of nowhere."

Drew calculated how long it would take to get his associates in here. He needed a stack of money for proof too. Stepping to a nearby table, he picked up a couple of bills. "Can I start with this?" He shook his head, answering his own question. "This is too wet."

"This way." Vesters beckoned him toward a doorway on the far side of the basement. Through the door was an office with a desk and a large wooden filing cabinet. One of the men yelled for Vesters. "I'll be right back." He shut the door behind him.

Drew put his ear against the door, but it was too thick to be able to hear more than muffled voices. He turned back to stare around the small room.

Stacks of money were bound together and lined the walls. More money lay on the desk. Drew pocketed a couple of bills quickly. His glance fell on a stack of papers. Vesters was still talking to one of the workers so Drew pulled the top paper toward him. It was a document about distribution of the counterfeit money. He memorized it and moved it back into place. When he did, another paper dislodged and floated to the floor. When he picked it up, the first sentence of the second paragraph leaped out at him.

*Marshall will be shot as he leaves the party. Have an alibi ready.*

"What are you doing?" Vesters snarled from the doorway with a gun in his hand. He stepped to the desk and snatched the note from Drew's hand.

Drew shrugged. "I happened to see it, that's all. But you don't have to worry about me giving anything away. I want to see him brought down myself."

Vesters frowned. "I don't believe you."

Drew leaned forward. "Believe this. It's his fault my father is dead, and I mean to have revenge. We'll see who kills him first."

Vesters stared at him as if trying to see what made him tick.

"You are staying at Marshall's, and now you're telling me you want him dead? Forgive me if I find that difficult to believe." The gun in his hand never wavered.

"From the outside you seemed to be his friend as well. No one will suspect either of us when he turns up assassinated."

Keeping the gun level, Vesters shook his head. "I either trust you or kill you, Hawkes. I haven't quite decided which one yet."

Drew picked up a stack of bills. "I'll take this money and prove myself. When you have fifty thousand dollars in your account, maybe then you'll trust me."

"A friend of mine has vouched for you." He stared at Drew for a long moment, then put the gun atop the desk. "Okay." He picked up a satchel and began to stuff it with stacks of money. "You've got one month."

"And then what?"

"Then we execute our plan for election night."

Election night. It made perfect sense. "And then the governor will appoint someone to take his place. You?"

Vesters shrugged. "Everyone will be focused on finding out who killed him, and my appointment will skate under the radar."

"Isn't that a little risky? Lots of people around. I want him dead, but I don't want to hang for it."

"We have a foolproof plan."

"*We?* Who else is in on this? You're smart and I know you would have thought this out, but I'm not so sure about your partner, whoever he is."

"All in good time." Vesters zipped shut the satchel and shoved it across the desk to Drew.

Lily was used to a large group at the dinner table, but when she carried in the soup, the flickering candlelight showed only the Marshalls, Belle, Mr. Lambreth, and Mr. Vesters. Belle sat next to her beau, and he leaned on one arm as he talked with her. Their close conversation made Lily uncomfortable.

Biting her lip, she set down her burden and went back to the kitchen. Cook was pulling individual pies from the oven. The delicious aroma of cinnamon and apples made Lily's mouth water. She hadn't eaten since breakfast. The day had been much too busy.

Lily wiped her hands on her apron. "What next?"

Mrs. O'Reilly took a pie from Cook and set it on the sideboard to cool. "I really must hire a new kitchen maid. We're so short-handed, but no one seems to want to work in the kitchen. The city is terrified of that killer. I would even settle for someone to help only with dinner."

"I'd take someone like that too," Cook said. "I can't continue to do this by myself."

"We've all pitched in to help."

"Of course, Mrs. O'Reilly." The cook bent over the oven to retrieve another pie.

Lily looked toward the door. "I sent a note to the young woman I mentioned, Jane White. She should be here anytime."

"Is she a hard worker?" Cook dusted her hands on her apron. "I won't have any slacker around my kitchen. And can she cook too?"

"It would be good if she could start at once," Mrs. O'Reilly said. "We could use the help with tomorrow's dinner party."

"I believe she would be a hard worker." Lily turned toward a timid knock at the back door. "That is likely Jane now." She smiled reassuringly at Jane through the glass in the door before she opened it. "I was just talking about you. Come in."

Dressed in a demure gray dress with her hair scraped back, Jane stepped into the kitchen. Her gaze darted to Mrs. O'Reilly, then veered back to Lily as if to take strength from her.

Lily took her arm and pulled her toward the housekeeper. "Mrs. O'Reilly, this is Jane White."

She looked Jane over. "What experience have you had?"

Jane clenched her hands in front of her. "I was the assistant cook for the Karrs."

"I know of them. It pleases me you can actually cook. So I can assume you know how to make delicacies such as duck and puddings?"

Jane brightened. "Yes, ma'am. Cook was ill quite often with the rheumatism, and I cooked about eighty percent of the time."

"Quite good. Can you provide references?"

Jane's smile vanished. "I—I don't think so."

"You were let go? Why?"

Jane hung her head. "I had a baby."

Mrs. O'Reilly gasped and dropped onto a chair. "I see."

Lily curled her fingers into her palms. "Please give her a chance, Mrs. O'Reilly."

"I'm a good worker, ma'am. Let me prove it to you." Jane's voice was hoarse. "I can start tonight."

"How old is your child, and who will care for it?"

"She's six months. I've found a young girl in the neighborhood who has agreed to care for her while I'm at work. My brother will help some too."

"Is she weaned? She's very young to be left alone."

Lily took hope at the housekeeper's caring words. "If she did some of the cooking, you could attend to running the household. Finding a good cook's assistant has been very difficult."

"I know that better than you, Lily." Mrs. O'Reilly continued to stare at Jane. "Well, answer the question."

Jane swallowed. "No, ma'am, she isn't weaned yet. But I've started feeding her a wee bit of mashed potatoes and porridge."

Mrs. O'Reilly sighed. "I don't hold with a mother leaving her children." She pressed her lips together. "But I desperately need help. How far away do you live?"

"About half an hour on foot."

"Too far." The housekeeper sighed again. "There is one possible solution, but I will have to speak to Mrs. Marshall about it. There is a small house on the back side of the property. It's not in very good shape, but if Mrs. Marshall is agreeable, you could stay there. It would be close enough for you to feed your baby when necessary."

Jane's eyes widened. "I will work hard for you. You won't regret it."

"It's not done yet. I will have to tell all to Mrs. Marshall. She may decide she won't employ you, Jane. You must be prepared for that as well."

"Yes, ma'am. When might I hear an answer?"

"She'll be in here in a few minutes to let me know when to serve dessert. I shall talk to her then. You may wait in the butler's pantry in case she wishes to speak with you personally. Lily, show her where that is."

"This way." Lily led Jane to the small room and shut the door behind them. "There's something we didn't discuss, Jane, and I'm not sure what to do about it. Mr. Vesters is often here. In fact, he's dining with the Marshalls tonight."

Jane went white. "He's here?" She backed away until she was against the wall. "I can't see him!"

"There's no real reason for you to run into him. He wouldn't enter the kitchen. But you should know Miss Belle is entertaining him as a suitor. It's possible she might marry him."

"Oh, she mustn't, Miss Lily! He's an evil, evil man." Jane clutched Lily's arm. "You must warn her."

"I'm her maid, Jane. I can't tell her who to marry." The panic on Jane's face unsettled Lily. Maybe she should at least try to warn Belle. "What could I say if I warned her? Do you have any specific accusations against him?"

Jane's hand dropped away, and she ducked her head. "Nothing anyone would believe."

"I would believe you."

Jane's chin came up and she blinked. "You're a good woman, Miss Lily. I know people think I was his mistress, but it wasn't like that. Not exactly." She bit her lip. "He came to see my brother, but Nathan was gone. H-He stayed the night. Mrs. Karr told him he could." Tears shimmered on her lashes. "I was afraid Nathan would lose his job, so I–I went along with it. And with every other night he came by, even though I wanted to run there was nowhere to go."

Poor girl. Lily couldn't imagine being in a situation like that.

"He should at least be paying for Hannah's support. Have you tried to get him to provide for her?"

"No, miss, I wouldn't dare."

Lily squared her shoulders. "Well, I would. And I'll take the first opportunity to approach him. If he's fearful of the truth getting to Belle, perhaps he will assume his responsibility at least."

# TWENTY

Belle's face hurt from the fake smile she'd pasted on all evening. She drew her shawl tighter against the late October chill. Listening to Stuart boast of his accomplishments should have helped her decide to accept him if he proposed, but instead, she found herself wishing she could be anywhere but beside him.

She sipped the last of her apple cider as Lily removed the remains of the small apple pie. "It was delicious." Glancing at Lily, Belle frowned. Was that pity in her eyes? She knew her maid thought her political aspirations were unworthy, but she'd fire the girl before she let her look at her that way.

She swept her lashes down to cover her irritation. "Shall we retire to the salon, Mr. Vesters?"

"I've told you to call me Stuart." He pushed back his chair, then pulled out her chair and took her hand to escort her from the dining room.

His hand was slightly sweaty, and she disliked his touch on her skin. Smiling, she managed to hide her distaste. "Would you prefer to smoke with my uncle?"

"I'd much rather talk to this lovely lady." He squeezed her hand and smiled.

Her aunt smiled her direction and added a conspiratorial wink. Belle frowned, hoping the expression meant nothing important. But when her aunt and uncle made excuses not to join them, her pulse began to throb against her temples.

The gaslights cast a warm glow over the parlor. She pulled her hand away and hurried to the chair. He'd started for the sofa and stood with a bewildered expression when she didn't join him.

He pointed to the cushion. "I'd like you to sit here beside me."

His dictatorial tone put her back up, but she smiled to cover her anger. "We're alone, so I thought it best to maintain appearances."

He glowered, then cleared his throat. "Soon it won't matter, my dear."

His intent was clear, and her cheeks burned. "I heard there was a robbery at the bank today. Is there any news about it?" Surely he would be derailed by such important news.

"I heard it as well, but I believe they caught the robbers. I saw two men in handcuffs being marched into the police station."

The tension eased from her shoulders that her ploy seemed to have worked, but then he cleared his throat and stood. Her chest tightened when he stopped by her and dropped to one knee. "Why, Stuart, have you hurt yourself?"

He pressed his lips together. "Of course not, Belle, what a notion. You're being very skittish when I'm trying to say something to you."

There was no help for it. She would have to listen to his proposal. "Of course, Stuart."

He took her hand. "You're a lovely young woman, and I've come to care for you a great deal. I've already spoken to your uncle, and he's given me permission to ask for your hand in marriage. I think we would suit very well, and you would make a lovely senator's wife. Would you do me the honor of becoming my wife?"

*A senator's wife.* Washington would be hers. Even so, she badly wanted to refuse him, but there was no one else offering for her, especially no one of this caliber.

"Belle?"

She'd left her answer a fraction too long. "Of course, Stuart. Forgive me for being so tongue-tied. I'm overwhelmed with how dear you are." She cupped her hands around his fleshy face and looked into his eyes. "I would be honored to become your wife."

His florid face grew redder, and he leaned forward to press a kiss against her lips. She recoiled just a little. Would she always feel such distaste? She hoped not. It would be a hard marriage if she wanted to turn away every time he approached her. She forced herself to hold still and accept the caress until he pulled away.

He was breathing harder, and his smile made her feel soiled. She wanted only to get away so he couldn't kiss her again. She jumped to her feet. "We must tell my aunt and uncle the happy news!"

He heaved himself to his feet as well. "Of course."

His jovial tone was at odds with the disappointment in his eyes, and she knew he'd hoped for more kisses, something she planned to avoid at all costs. "They're probably still in the dining room. I'll call for some champagne, and we'll bring them back here to toast our engagement."

"Wait one moment. I nearly forgot." He thrust his hand into his pocket and pulled out a velvet box. "Allow me." He opened it and lifted it into the light for her perusal.

The most exquisite ring she'd ever seen glittered in the light. She gasped and touched it. "It's so lovely, Stuart."

He beamed. "It's three carats, Belle. Only the best for my wife."

That sounded good to her. The finest of everything might make up for what she'd have to endure in the bedroom. *Might.* "Would you put it on me, please?" She held out her left hand.

He lifted the ring from its box and slid it onto her finger. It went over her knuckle easily. "Does it fit properly?"

She tugged on it with her right hand, and it stayed seated nicely. "I think so." Her hand felt heavy and unfamiliar with the ring on it. Her friends would gasp when they saw it. Their admiration would go far toward making her at peace with her choice.

Mrs. Marshall's eyes were kind as she looked Jane over. "We think a lot of Lily, Miss White. Ordinarily I wouldn't consider employing someone of questionable character, but on her recommendation, I'm going to hire you. Please don't make me sorry."

The approving glance the mistress of the house sent her way made Lily square her shoulders.

Jane clenched her hands in front of her. "I won't, Mrs. Marshall."

Mrs. Marshall glanced at Mrs. O'Reilly. "Please arrange for the old carriage house to be cleaned and repaired. Get it done as cheaply as possible."

"I can clean it myself," Jane said.

"I'll help her on my day off," Lily added. "Thank you so much, Mrs. Marshall. I don't think you'll be sorry."

"I certainly hope not." Belle called for her aunt from the dining room, and Mrs. Marshall turned toward the door. "I'd like you to start as soon as the place is habitable." She paused and looked back. "And I assume there will not be a repeat of your, um, indiscretion?"

Color ran up Jane's neck and into her cheeks. "No, ma'am."

Lily exhaled when Mrs. Marshall left and Mrs. O'Reilly followed her out. Jane's eyes were shining. "Nathan will be so relieved. I don't mind admitting things have been very hard lately. It costs money to raise Hannah."

"After I've cleaned the kitchen, let's go take a look at the carriage house and see what needs to be done."

"I'll help. Hannah won't need to be fed for two hours."

Emily and the other housemaid had already done most of the dishes when they stepped into the kitchen. "We'll finish," Emily said. "The lantern is by the back door. I'll join you soon."

Warmed by her friend's kindness, Lily nodded and went to the back door where she lit the lantern, then turned down the wick until the soft glow beamed into the night. "This way."

Holding the lantern aloft, she followed the stone path around the side of the house and past a gate into an area where she'd never been. She'd caught glimpses of the structure over her weeks here, but she'd assumed it belonged to a neighbor since no one ever went this way.

She stopped in front of the stoop and stared. The front door hung ajar, and animal droppings littered the steps. "This is disgusting." Craning her neck, she looked up at the low-slung roof. Slate shingles appeared to be missing, and Lily wasn't sure she wanted to go in while it was dark.

"It will be fine, Miss Lily." Jane mounted the single step and pushed on the door. It creaked open the rest of the way.

Lily held the lamp higher until the light pushed back the edges of the darkness. She followed Jane across the threshold. Debris crunched under her shoes, and shadows danced on the stained walls. The room was about twelve by twelve. A dry sink was against one wall. There was a doorway to another room on the left, so she stepped forward to inspect it. The other room was smaller, about nine feet square.

"This is a bedroom, I think. It's all in rather bad shape. I'm not sure Mrs. Marshall knows what condition it's in." Then Lily took another look. The bedding was new and fairly clean. "It seems like someone might have been living here."

Jane was smiling. "Probably someone with nowhere else to go. He'll see it's occupied." She glanced around. "A little elbow grease, and it will be as good as where I'm living now."

"You've got a very good attitude about it. I don't think I would want to live here, but maybe it will look better in the daylight. I'll slip out and take a gander tomorrow. There's really nothing we can do tonight. It's too dark."

"At least I have a position." Jane's smile was brilliant. "I can't thank you enough, Miss Lily."

"Just call me Lily." Smiling, she turned to go when she heard a slithering, sliding sound. "What was that?"

"I didn't hear anything."

The door creaked open from somewhere, and a breeze touched Lily's flushed cheeks. "Who's there? Emily, is that you?"

The darkness felt thick and menacing. Lily raised the lantern higher, but it only pushed back the shadows about five feet. "Emily?"

A soft laugh came to her left. It was a male voice. Gooseflesh prickled along her back, and she took a step back. Jane's hand squeezed her arm hard as she exhaled.

"We have to get out of here," Jane whispered. "Run."

Lily felt frozen in place. The hostility in the man's laugh made her chest squeeze. What if it was the man who'd already attacked Jane once? Who attacked her? They shouldn't have come out here in the dark without a protector.

"Go, Lily." Jane gave her a little shove.

Lily leaped for the dim glow of moonlight coming through the door. As she raced forward, a scuffle sounded behind her. Whirling, she held up the light and saw Jane pinned to the floor by a man. He faced away from Lily, and she couldn't see anything but the breadth of his back.

She screamed at the top of her lungs. "Help! Somebody help

us!" She looked around for a weapon. There was a broken chair and she put down the lantern, then grabbed it. She slammed it down on his back.

He cursed and rose toward her, but it was still too dark to see his face.

"Lily?" Drew's voice came from outside the carriage house.

"Drew, in here! Help us!"

The man growled, then turned and lunged away. Moments later a back door slammed.

Drew burst into the building and snatched up the lantern. "Lily, are you all right?"

She staggered toward him, and he caught her with his left arm. Leaning into his strength restored her courage. "I'm fine. He got away."

She snatched the lantern from him and held it high. Jane sat up and pushed her hair out of her face. "Jane, did he harm you?"

"Not this time." Jane took the hand Drew extended and got to her feet.

Lily swallowed and lowered the light. "You mean it was the same man who attacked you before?"

"I think so. I never saw his face either time, but I smelled his breath." She shuddered. "It was minty just like the man who attacked me."

Drew took the lantern from Lily's unresisting hand. "Let's get out of here and summon the police."

# TWENTY-ONE

Though the night was warm and moist, Lily couldn't stop shivering. The policeman who had looked at her with such disdain on Monday had taken down the particulars, but she saw his skepticism. And he'd eyed Drew as well. The police had escorted Jane home, and the kitchen was nearly empty now.

Mr. Marshall put his big hand on her shoulder. "You go on to bed, Lily. You're still pale."

"I need to see to Miss Belle."

"Miss Belle can see to herself tonight. You go on up."

"Yes, sir." She glanced at Drew. They hadn't had a moment alone to talk, but there would be no opportunity tonight.

"If Mr. Hawkes needs anything, one of the other maids will see to him."

"Yes, sir. Good night."

She slipped through the doorway of the back stairway and went up the steps to the second-floor landing where she paused. Belle would be expecting her, and the thought of going to her dark, cramped attic bedroom was unappealing. She needed company, someone to distract her from what had happened. Her mind made up, she hurried down the dark hall.

Belle's door was half open. She was sitting in front of the dressing table with her hair down on her shoulders. She hadn't taken off her evening dress yet.

Lily tapped on the door. "Miss Belle? Sorry I'm late."

Belle turned. "Lily, are you all right? I heard there was a dreadful attack tonight. I was frightened for you."

Lily shut the door behind her. "Jane and I escaped unharmed." She began to unbutton her mistress's dress. "You look a bit flushed."

Belle extended her left hand. "Look." An enormous ring sparkled on her hand.

Lily bit her lip. Any warning she might offer was too late. "You accepted Mr. Vesters?"

Belle gave a hollow laugh. "Don't sound so disapproving. It's not your place to approve of my choice."

"Of course not, Miss Belle. I—I just think you could do better."

"Like who? Mr. Hawkes?" Belle wrinkled her nose. "He came rushing to your defense again tonight. I won't have it, Lily. I've warned you about setting your cap for him more than once."

"I haven't, truly." Picking up the brush, she avoided Belle's gaze and began to run the bristles through her mistress's silky dark hair.

"You must admit it was most peculiar he turned up tonight when you screamed. Was he following you?"

"I'm sure he just happened to be in the yard taking some fresh air."

"Or maybe you and he had an assignation."

She couldn't let Belle go on with that line of thinking. Not if she wanted to keep her job. "It's not true. Not at all. I was helping Jane, the new cook's assistant, see what needed to be done to make the carriage house habitable. You can ask your aunt."

Belle held her gaze in the mirror. "I hope you're telling me the truth."

Lily refused to look away. "I am, Miss Belle." Belle rose, and Lily helped her out of her dress and into her nightgown. "When is the wedding?"

"We haven't set a date. I hope it's a long way off." Belle wrinkled her nose and sighed. "I don't much care for his kisses."

Lily's cheeks burned at such talk, but she heard a forlorn note in Belle's voice. "It's not too late to refuse him."

"And why would I do that? He's rich and politically minded. He'll be a senator someday. Exactly what I was looking for."

"You've tried to avoid him for weeks. You can cover up your feelings with others, but I know better, Miss Belle."

Belle flopped back onto the stool. "All right, fine, it's true he would not have been my first choice. As soon as I'd said yes, I wished I hadn't. But no one else of his caliber is offering, Lily. I must get my future settled. I want my own home, and I want to move in political circles. Stuart can give me those things."

"At a steep cost." Lily began to braid Belle's hair. "You'll be married to him the rest of your life. Please make sure it's what you want to do. Just because he's your uncle's supporter doesn't mean he's a good man."

Belle grabbed her by the wrist and stared at her. "Whatever does that mean? Do you know something about Stuart?"

Lily tied a ribbon at the end of Belle's braid. Did she dare tell her the truth? If she did, Jane would likely be fired before she ever started. And it wasn't her story to tell anyway. It was Jane's place to speak if she so desired. "I know nothing from personal experience about Mr. Vesters."

Belle released her and frowned. "You may not know anything for certain, but you've heard gossip. What is it?"

Lily turned away and pulled the covers back on the bed. "How long have you known Mr. Vesters?"

"Long enough. Several months, actually. Uncle Everett thinks the world of him."

"What if he never achieves his political goals?"

Belle climbed into bed. "What's gotten into you, Lily? You've become quite bold in your opinions."

"I care about you, Miss Belle. I don't want to see you make a mistake."

Belle yanked the sheet up to her shoulders. "I think I know which direction my life should go much better than you. Turn out the light on your way out."

Lily extinguished the light and stepped out into the hall. Even if Belle knew the truth, would she care? All she saw was her goal of power.

She pulled the door shut behind her, then went up the back stairs to her room. As she reached the last hall, she passed by the doorway to the attic. A thought struck her. What if the sounds she'd heard were from someone in the hidden passageway she'd found? And what if the passage went all the way to the shack out back?

She rejected the idea as preposterous, but her pulse thumped in her chest. The idea would haunt her until she checked it out. But not in the dark. She hurried to her room and nearly tripped over a box in the doorway.

It was wrapped in bright paper and tied with a bow. Drew? Smiling, she untied the bow and lifted the lid. A pair of butterfly earrings lay nestled in tissue. A chill shuddered down her spine. Drew knew she hated butterflies. He would never do this.

She looked at the card inside. *"So beautiful."*

A strangled cry burst from her throat and she dropped the box, then ran into her bedroom and shut the door behind her.

This spot along the river walk was deserted, and after the attack two days ago, the solitude had Lily peering into every shadow. According to Drew's note, she was supposed to meet him at one, and it was already one fifteen. She wandered into the flower bed and sniffed a yellow rose. She'd wait fifteen more minutes before giving up.

Almost as soon as the thought formed, she heard boot heels clicking along the brick walk. Walking fast, Drew came into view. His steps paused a moment when he saw her, then he smiled and hurried toward her.

His concerned gaze swept over her. "No ill effects from the attack?"

She hesitated, then shook her head. "I received an odd gift though." She told him about the earrings made from butterfly wings and the card. "I—I think he knows where I live. I checked with the butler, and he said it was delivered by a boy he'd never seen."

His eyes were grave. "I don't like it, Lily. You must be careful."

"I will. You said you needed to talk to me. I only have a few minutes until I need to hurry back. Belle will be looking for me by two."

He took her hands in his and pulled her to a nearby bench. "I didn't want to involve you, but I have no choice. I have uncovered a plot to kill Mr. Marshall."

She gasped and gripped his hands, taking strength from his touch. "Who plans to kill him? Ballard?"

The muscles in his neck contorted. "Stuart Vesters."

Pulling her hands away, she leaped to her feet. "That can't be true. He's marrying Belle."

Drew caught her left hand. "I know, but I assure you it's true. The plan is to kill Marshall the night of the election. He's expected to win by a landslide. Vesters will then be appointed senator."

"I'm sure Belle doesn't know he's such an evil man." She sank back to the bench beside him. "What do you need from me?"

"I think we have to tell Belle and enlist her help. Though I've told him I want Marshall dead too, Vesters doesn't trust me, not fully. I suspect he may change his plans now that I know."

"What can Belle do?"

"She can snoop through his things and listen for snippets of conversation."

Lily shook her head. "She's impetuous, Drew. I don't believe she can keep the knowledge to herself. You don't know her as well as I. She's never one to hold her tongue."

"If her uncle's life hangs in the balance, she will. She's flighty, yes, but she loves her uncle a great deal. There's no one else we can go to. If we don't risk this, Marshall is as good as dead."

"Can't you just warn him?"

"He won't believe me. He'll think I am trying to discredit Vesters because he beat me out for Belle's hand."

Lily chewed on her lower lip. "Very well, I'll talk to her. But I need to pick the time and place carefully so there is adequate time to explain it to her. And now that I think about it, she's been able to convince Vesters she cares about him when in reality she is repulsed. So perhaps she could hide her feelings."

The sun cast dappled patterns on the walk and river. Birds chirped, and it would have been an idyllic day if not for the menace Lily felt everywhere since she'd arrived in Austin. "I'm so tired of fighting. Why can't we have a little peace? Is that too much to ask?"

His fingers tightened on hers. "I think life is always about striving against evil. It's what I do."

She sighed and didn't answer. He wasn't going to like what she had to tell him. She exhaled and looked away from the tenderness in his eyes. "There's something you should know."

"About Vesters?"

"No." She dragged her gaze from the sparkling water and stared up at him. "I went to see Ballard."

He shot to his feet. "Lily, you didn't! I told you to stay away from him." His voice vibrated.

"I went to the hotel hoping I might run into him, and I did. As far as he knows, we merely ran into one another. He offered me a job working for his wife."

"You didn't accept?"

She laced her fingers together. "No, of course not. I told him I was happy with my position. But, Drew, I don't believe he had anything to do with Papa's death. He was our friend and neighbor for years. I think you are mistaken about him."

"Lily, I forbid you to get involved in this."

She rose to face him. "You forbid? You lost any right to tell me what to do long ago. I'm not going to stand by and let you send a good man off to jail. He didn't attack me at the church. We have the globe to prove it was the killer. You have no proof you've been able to offer me about his guilt. It's all supposition."

"It's much more than that." His voice matched the spark in his eyes. "I have evidence linking him to the fire."

"What evidence? You've given me nothing solid. I'm not willing to condemn a man I've known nearly all my life."

"So you discount what I say in favor of a man who killed your father—and mine! I thought I knew you, Lily, but the girl I loved would have moved anything in her path to bring her father's killer to justice."

She managed not to wince at his contempt. "And I will! But I don't believe it's Ballard, Drew." How could she get him to listen? Together they might be able to discover who had killed their fathers, but not if he remained focused on the wrong man.

He took a deep breath and stepped back. "What do you have to go on, Lily? Tell me that. Do you have anything more than mere sentiment? You *feel* he isn't the villain I say he is, but you're unwilling to listen to evidence."

"What evidence? You keep saying you have evidence, but you've given me nothing."

His jaw hardened. "I wanted to spare you, but you leave me no choice. Ballard's wallet was clutched in your father's hand."

Her confidence faltered. "How do you know it was his wallet?"

"There were several charred pieces of identification left inside."

She swallowed. "Someone could have planted it there to implicate Ballard."

Pity crept into his eyes. "He has completely persuaded you, hasn't he?"

"Have you ever asked him how his wallet came to be there?"

"Of course not. I didn't want him to know we were trailing him."

"Very well." She would ask him herself.

# TWENTY-TWO

The brilliant reds and golds of the sunset had faded by the time Belle shut her bedroom door and turned her back to let Lily unbutton her dress. Her face hurt from smiling, and all she wanted to do was crawl into her clean sheets and forget how bleak her future appeared.

She rubbed her gritty eyes. "It's so wearing to have to listen to that man prattle on about himself. He never shuts up. I can only be admiring for so long."

Lily's hands paused, then resumed the march down Belle's buttons. "He's to be your husband, Miss Belle."

"I know that," Belle snapped. "You overstep yourself, Lily. Draw my bath."

"Yes, miss."

Belle followed her to the bathroom and watched as Lily turned on the tap. "You are much too outspoken for a lady's maid." A vague sense of curiosity stirred about her maid's past. Lily seemed to have a good sense of her own worth, something Belle admired.

Lily's cheeks were flushed when she straightened from her position over the tub and turned to face her. "I want you to be happy. I fear Mr. Vesters is not the man you think he is."

Belle frowned at the certainty on Lily's face. "What do you

mean? And don't try to wiggle out of telling me. It's clear you know something."

Lily's hand went to her stomach, and the color washed from her face. "I have to know you trust me. That you will not discount what I'm about to tell you."

"You sound very serious."

Lily nodded. "I know you love your uncle."

"Of course I do. He's been very good to me." Belle shucked her dress and kicked it away from her ankles, then stepped into the steaming tub. She sank into the bubbles up to her chin. "What does Uncle Everett have to do with this? He's delighted with my choice for a husband."

Lily handed her a long-handled bath brush. "He wouldn't be so pleased if he knew what Mr. Vesters is planning."

Belle rolled her eyes. "You're sounding more and more melodramatic. If this is about your position, you'll come with me, of course. You don't need to fear losing your job." Lily actually shuddered at her words, and Belle frowned. "Get on with it. What do you have against Stuart?"

Lily clasped her hands in front of her. "He plans to murder your uncle." She bit her lip and held Belle's gaze. "I know it's a serious accusation, but you know I wouldn't make such a charge frivolously."

Belle sat up. "Lily, that's ludicrous. Where did you get such a notion?"

Lily pulled up a stool and sat beside the tub. "Mr. Hawkes is not who you think he is."

"So now everyone is plotting against my uncle?" Belle's initial alarm faded, and she began to suds her arms. Perhaps her maid wasn't quite right in the head. She was seeing conspiracies around every corner.

Lily looked down at her hands. "You were right when you

noticed there was something between us. I've known him all my life. I was engaged to him once."

Belle squeezed the soap so hard it escaped from her fingers. "That's impossible. He's a gentleman."

"He is the son of the Larson blacksmith. His father was a part owner of my father's livery. He is with the Secret Service and is here investigating a counterfeiting ring."

Belle started to object, then saw the certainty on Lily's face. Hawkes had been very elusive and mysterious. He'd been very reticent about his past. Could Lily be right? "Go on."

"Mr. Vesters is part of that ring, and Drew finally managed to infiltrate it. While he was at the office the other day, he discovered the plot to kill your uncle." The words poured out of Lily in a rush. "We must do something to protect your uncle."

Belle knew truth when she heard it. She rose and reached for the towel. "I'll tell my uncle at once."

Lily gripped her wet arm. "You mustn't! If Vesters gets wind his plan has been exposed, he'll go underground with it, and we won't know what's happening. We need to put him behind bars and break up the plot." She reached for Belle's robe and draped it around her.

*Plot.* And *murder.* It was so dire and serious. Belle wrapped the robe around her. "What is the motive for this?"

"Vesters wants to be senator. He knows he can't win, but he's close friends with the governor and believes he would be appointed to take your uncle's place. So they plan to kill him the night of the election, once his win is announced."

"Senator?" For an instant, Belle had a vision of herself in the White House, hobnobbing with President Roosevelt. She pushed the thought away. Though everything in her longed to fulfill that dream, it wouldn't be worth her uncle's death. "What can I do?"

"Stay close to Vesters. Ask to tour his house and see if you can find any clues to exactly what he intends."

"You don't know the exact plan?"

Lily shook her head. "Just when it's planned. Your uncle would never believe Vesters would harm him. He dotes on the man."

"He does indeed. It will take strong proof to convince Uncle Everett. I'm not fully convinced myself. I think I should speak to Mr. Hawkes myself." Her pulse fluttered at the thought of being involved in something so thrilling and a little dangerous.

Perhaps Hawkes would be so impressed with her daring he would develop tender feelings for her. And if this did all turn out to be true, where did that leave her? Without a fiancé and right back to trying to find a wealthy husband. She was tired of seeing the pity in her friends' eyes. She was nearly twenty-three. Before too long the rumor would be going around that she was unmarriageable.

Lily glanced at Belle out of the corner of her eye as they stood under a tree in the yard of the old shack out back. Her employer seemed uncommonly composed—and lovely. Drew was bound to be impressed with her willingness to help them.

Belle glanced at the dilapidated building. "This seems an odd place to meet Mr. Hawkes."

"No one comes back here, and we don't want to be overheard."

"I've certainly never been here. Why has my uncle allowed it to fall into this state?"

"It's not been used in years, and it can't be seen from the street. It's being repaired for one of the new housemaids to use." Lily shut her mouth quickly before she could be tempted to tell Belle all about the new housemaid—and her child.

"Someone will live here?" Belle shuddered. "It looks rat infested."

"It might be, but it's better than where she's living now." Lily wanted to shake her. Did Belle live in some dream world where she never noticed those with fewer advantages?

"Is there no room in the attic? Surely that would be better than this."

"She has a child as well. Her brother helps her care for the child, and they all need a place to stay."

Belle dusted a nonexistent speck from her skirt. "Mr. Hawkes is late. If he doesn't come soon, I'm going back to the house. This place makes me feel quite unsettled."

"There he is now." Lily lifted her hand in greeting. No one would ever know how her pulse leaped at the sight of Drew's lazy smile and broad shoulders.

He took Belle's hand. "Sorry I'm late. Thank you for coming, Miss Castle. And for not dismissing us out of hand."

Belle withdrew her hand. "Please tell me what this is all about."

"I thought Lily explained it to you."

"I'd like to hear it from you. You must admit the entire concept seems rather far-fetched."

Drew nodded. "I can understand your skepticism, but it's all true, I assure you."

"You really work with the Secret Service?"

"I do."

Belle lifted a brow. "Can you prove it?"

"I could have my superior contact you."

Lily touched her arm. "I think you have enough discernment to know the truth when you hear it, Miss Belle."

Belle jerked her arm away and scowled at her. "Let Mr. Hawkes speak for himself, Lily. This story is like something out of a dime-store novel. Is it any wonder I have trouble believing it?

You're both asking me to trust you when doing so will disrupt my entire life."

Lily hadn't stopped to think about how this news would derail Belle's life. No more engagement parties, no more newspaper articles in the society pages, no exciting days of trying on lovely white dresses and planning an elaborate wedding. And when this hit the news, Belle would be subject to titters and gossip. She would be made to feel she'd been very foolish—something that would grate on Belle.

"You're being very brave," Drew said, echoing Lily's thoughts. "I don't blame you for questioning us. A man by the name of Ian will be contacting you discreetly. I beg you to be just as circumspect. You could do him great harm by telling anyone about him."

"Of course. I have some questions for you."

"I'm here to answer them." He glanced over his shoulder. "Did you hear something?"

Lily listened but heard only the distant sound of the wringer washer. "The housemaids are doing the laundry."

Drew's shoulders relaxed. "We can't be too careful. Mr. Marshall's life depends on us."

Belle paced the rough stone path. "You keep saying that! But I find it very difficult to believe Stuart would harm Uncle Everett."

"You must admit you don't know Vesters well," Drew said.

"But my uncle does. They've been friends a long time."

"About six months," Drew corrected. "I've been watching Vesters awhile now, and he deliberately arranged to be introduced to your uncle at a fund-raising event. He's had this planned out awhile now."

"Why couldn't he just run for senator himself? He's a well-known businessman."

Lily had wondered that herself. While she disliked Vesters, he could be charming when he exerted himself. Then it hit her. "He has something in his past to hide, doesn't he? And he feared the press would discover his secret if he announced his candidacy."

Drew's glance was warm and approving. "Exactly." He inclined his head as though he caught her silent plea to hold his tongue about what that secret might be.

If a reporter talked to Jane and the news got out about Vesters's relationship with her, he would be ruined. She needed to talk to Drew alone.

"So you want me to spy on my own fiancé." Belle sighed and turned to gaze at the butterflies sitting on the bushes. "I don't like it."

Drew pocketed his hands. "None of us do, but if we can uncover the full extent of the plot, we can arrest all the key players. Your uncle will be safe."

Belle sighed. "Very well. I'll see what I can find out, though I hardly expect Stuart to bare his plot to me."

"You are smart and resourceful," Lily said. "See if he slips away to talk to anyone. Follow him when you can and try to overhear. Time is of the essence. The election is in three weeks."

"When will we next meet to discuss this?"

"You can pass along anything you hear to Lily, and she'll tell me. It's probably best if we don't run the risk of being seen together too often. It might tip off Vesters."

Belle pressed her lips together. "Very well, but it makes me feel like an outsider. I'd rather we worked together on this."

Lily knew what she was up to—Belle's attraction to Drew had always been obvious. She waited for Drew to see through it too, but he inclined his head and agreed to meet together in two days. If her engagement came to a disastrous end, Belle would surely seek his attentions again.

Lily curled her fingers into her palms. It was nothing to her if Belle set her cap for him.

# TWENTY-THREE

Lily walked away from the shack with Belle, but she glanced behind her and tried to signal to Drew to wait. He nodded and stepped into the shadows of the shack's interior. Now she had to figure out how to get away from Belle.

When they reached the house, Mrs. Marshall hailed Belle from the garden. Lily waited until the two disappeared behind the box hedge before rushing back into the old building in the back.

She squinted in the dark interior. "You waited."

"Of course."

She took a step closer. "I know what Vesters is trying to hide." Her eyes were beginning to adjust, and she was close enough to see his eyes widen.

"What have you found out?"

"I mentioned Vesters is the father of Jane's baby."

He nodded. "That's hardly enough to stop his election."

"There's more. He gave her no choice, forced her basically. And it was with Mrs. Karr's arrangement. I'm sure Mr. Karr would have known as well. The scandal would affect both of them."

He winced. "You're sure of this?"

"Jane told me herself. Talking about this made me wonder if he could be behind the attacks on Jane. With her out of the way, no one would ever know what he did."

His lips flattened. "It's possible. The man is scum."

She nearly shuddered at his grim tone. "I fear for Jane."

"I am uneasy she'll be living here. It's remote and screened by shrubs."

"She's already been attacked here once—and while I was here as well. The man was very brazen. I don't know how we're going to keep her safe."

"Her brother will be living with her. I'll have a word with him and tell him of our concerns."

"But he works at night. She'll be here alone." She squared her shoulders. "I'm going to move in with her."

He took her by the arms. "You can't do that, Lily! I won't have you in such danger."

She stared into his face and willed him to understand. "There is no one else to help. Can you get me a gun, Drew?" The tenderness in his face nearly made her melt against his chest, but she held strong. "You taught me how to shoot when I was fifteen."

"That was nine years ago. Have you shot one since then?"

"I'm sure it's not something easily forgotten." She relished the feel of his hands on her arms. When she was with him, she was strong. "Will you get me one?"

"I have one in my pocket." He continued to stare into her face as if memorizing her features. "But I don't like it. What you're doing is very dangerous. If Vesters is determined to get rid of Jane, he won't let you stand in his way."

"But I'm going to. We are going to best him, Drew. We have to. He's an evil man."

His right hand left her arm and traveled up to cup her cheek. "You're so beautiful. I can't get enough of you, Lily. I don't know how I lived without you all these years. You're like the air I breathe—fragrant and necessary. And yet I wouldn't want you in the danger that is always around me."

He bent his head and his lips brushed hers, tentatively at first, as if he thought she might push him away. She closed her eyes and inhaled the scent of him: bay-rum cologne, soap, and man. A heady blend of intoxicating fragrances. Wrapping her arms around his neck, she kissed him back. In those few moments, she forgot the danger surrounding them, his desertion, and her position. His lips were firm yet tender, passionate but controlled.

*Yet he hurt you.*

She ignored the insistent voice, but it was enough to make her stiffen just enough for him to pull back.

He dropped his hands to his sides. "You make me forget everything, Lily, even my duty to my country. I can't put you in danger, but I could almost walk away from all of it."

She took a step back. "Almost." If they had any kind of future, she would always have to accept the fact his duty would come first. With his kiss still warm on her lips and the imprint of his fingers still lingering on her arms, she wanted to convince herself it was enough.

Another almost.

He put his hand in his pocket and pulled out a revolver. "I have extra bullets in my room. I'll slip you some, though I hope you never have cause to use them. One look at this and any intruder should run."

She stared at it, then plucked it from his palm. "It doesn't look very fearsome."

"It's a Remington derringer." He showed her how to cock it. "At the first sound, get it ready to shoot."

She liked the feel of it in her hand. "Where can we go to practice shooting it? It's different from the rifle I used."

"On your day off we could go out of town and let you hit some tin cans on a fence."

He was close enough for his scent to still waft over her. What would he think if she leaned closer and sniffed? She stifled a smile.

He looked down at her and grinned. "You look rather cheerful. Is it the thought of shooting someone?"

She laughed then, sure it was going to be all right and quite certain she could handle this little gun and any intruder. "I have to admit I feel empowered."

He sobered then. "A gun can make you too cocky if you're not careful. One slap at your wrist and the gun could be on the floor. You're better off never getting into a position where you have to use it."

"Then let's get Vesters behind bars." She looked back at the shack. "I found a hidden passageway in the attic. Do you think it could run out here?"

"That's a long way. I doubt anyone would tunnel that far. Have you explored it?"

She shook her head. "Want to go with me?"

He took her arm. "Wouldn't have it any other way."

Drew held the kerosene lantern aloft. It pushed back the shadows by about two feet. "You sure you want to do this tonight?"

Lily's face was pale but she nodded. "Everyone is asleep. I don't want anyone to know we're looking around. What if whoever attacked Jane is using this passageway? They could be creeping around the mansion and no one would know. Miss Belle might even be attacked. Or Emily." She swiped the air inside the entry to the passageway with the broom in her hand. "I'm ready."

He bent to look into the cavity behind the wall. "This may not go much of anywhere, but there's only one way to find out."

Holding the lantern out, he stepped into the tight space. Lily walked close behind him. In another two feet, he was able to walk upright. The space was over six feet high and about three feet wide. The odor of mouse and dust was unappealing. Cobwebs hung from the ceiling, so he handed the lantern to Lily and took the broom. The passageway wandered left, then they reached some steps down.

Lily shone the light out over the narrow stairs. "It's dark down there." Her voice was hushed.

"I'm not sure how safe these steps are either." He tested the first one with his left foot. It held strong. "Let me have the light."

They exchanged items again, and he began to descend. He could only see a few feet at a time, so he eased his weight onto each tread before going on. When he reached the bottom where the path yawned to the right in the dark, he turned and called up for Lily to come down.

He heard her scuffling down the stairs much too fast for his peace of mind. "Be careful."

Her eyes were wide in her white face when she joined him. "I'm totally turned around."

"I think we're on the second floor on the west side."

"Near Belle's room?"

"Yes." He lifted the light and looked around. "What's this?" Another door was on this side of the wall.

"I bet that opens into Belle's closet. I heard something the other day when I was fetching her dress." Lily ran her fingers over the wall. "Put the light here a minute."

He did as she asked, and she touched the wall. "I think this is a peephole." She moved a small piece of metal out of the way to reveal a hole. "Look."

He watched as she put her eye to the hole. "See anything?"

"No, it's too dark. You'd only be able to see something when the closet door is open."

"Maybe that's how an intruder could tell it was safe to get into the closet. I don't like this, Lily."

She hugged herself and stepped away. "It's scary to think someone is creeping around back here. Let's find the stairs down and see if it goes across the yard."

He took her hand, and they plodded along the passage. It seemed to go on forever, and they went down two more flights of stairs. They found multiple doors and offshoots to the secret halls. Then the path veered to the right.

He placed his hand on another door. "I think the back of the kitchen is here." He pointed. "So that means this passage goes across the backyard."

Her fingers tightened around his. "It might go all the way out to the old servant quarters."

"Let's find out." He led her over the rough, uneven floor. It seemed like hours before they reached a final door and the end of the passage, but he knew it was only minutes. "This must be it."

She reached past him and twisted the release. The door swung open, revealing the bed with its new sheets. "So that means whoever has been living here has a way to get into the house."

She stepped into the bedroom, and he followed. "I think this means whoever has been using the passage isn't a member of the household, which is some comfort."

She turned back to face him. "If Jane is going to stay here, we need to figure out how to make her safe."

"And you." She looked so beautiful standing there. He couldn't resist reaching out and wrapping an escaped curl around his finger.

She caught her breath, and he looked into those eyes he loved so much. He wasn't consciously aware of moving until she was in his arms, and his mouth was on hers. She tasted of cinnamon and something sweet. He crushed her against him, and she burrowed deeper as if she couldn't get close enough either.

The bed was right there, and he took a step toward it, then caught himself. He tore his lips away from hers, though everything in him resisted the restraint he knew he had to have. "I'm sorry," he whispered against her cheek. "We'd better get back."

She nodded, and the disappointment between them was as thick as smoke.

Mrs. O'Reilly wiped her hands on her apron, then draped the towel on the front of the cookstove. The scent of the morning's bacon hung in the air. "I must say, I don't see the need for you to move in with Jane. And what will Miss Belle say if she needs you and I have to send someone clear to the back of the property to fetch you?"

Though Mrs. O'Reilly had already capitulated the night before, Lily felt the need to reassure her again as she headed toward the back door with her suitcase of meager belongings. "She never awakens in the night. I'll wait to go to the cabin until she's asleep."

"It's a nasty place, Lily. I don't feel right about you staying out there. Not with the attacks and all."

"You'd feel worse if something happened to Jane when she was all alone."

Mrs. O'Reilly sighed. "Very well. You seem determined. Do you need any help?"

Lily shook her head. "This is all I have."

"Get on with you, then. And be careful."

Smiling at the housekeeper's concern, Lily hurried through the darkness. Once she stepped past the shrubs, she could see the dim glow of a candle in the window. Jane must be there already. She touched her lips. There would be no kisses from Drew tonight.

The door stood open when she reached the shack, and Jane's dim figure flitted about in the shadows. She whirled when Lily's heels clattered on the rough wooden floors. "There you are, Miss Lily."

"Just Lily." She set her suitcase on the floor. "Where's little Hannah?"

"Sleeping in the bedroom." Jane put her hands on her hips. "I don't feel right about taking the bedroom and making you sleep out here in the main room."

"I have a cot we found in the attic." Lily's gaze sought and found it in the corner. "There are three of you with your brother here part of the time. This works fine."

Jane swallowed and put her hand to her throat. "I still can't believe you'd do this for me. I've never met anyone as kind as you. Most people cross the street to avoid seeing someone in need. Why are you doing this?"

"I could have been in your situation, Jane. One unfortunate circumstance can change our lives for the worst, and all it takes is an act of kindness to turn it around the other way."

"I'll never forget this. Never." Jane blinked rapidly, then grabbed the handle of Lily's suitcase and hefted it onto the sofa.

Lily studied the soft curve of her cheek. They were so much alike. "I have to confess, Jane." When her friend looked up and turned, she hurried on. "I told Drew who Hannah's father is. And what he did to you."

Jane's eyes went wide. "Oh no." The words were barely audible.

"I had to. I fear Mr. Vesters is behind the attacks on you."

Jane took a step back. "That's not possible."

"There are things you don't know. He has political aspirations.

If what he and Mrs. Karr did to you got out, he'd be ruined. The only way to prevent the possibility is to eliminate you."

Jane went white. "That's quite horrible. I don't think I believe he is quite that despicable."

Drew would be upset if she told, but Lily didn't care. Jane needed to know how evil Vesters was. "He plans to murder Mr. Marshall and be appointed senator in his place. What he did to you is only the tip of his evil nature."

Jane said nothing for several long moments, then she blinked and shook her head as if bemused. "How do you know this?"

"Drew has uncovered it all." While she trusted Jane with the truth of Drew's true profession, Lily had promised to keep it silent. It was bad enough they'd had to tell Belle.

Jane's lips trembled. "My poor little girl. Such a father."

"He should be supporting her, but I fear if we pursue that, his efforts to eliminate you will get stepped up."

"I don't want anything from him."

"I don't blame you." What would he say if she ever confronted him? The thought of his dark eyes made her gulp and push away the notion, though she'd once thought to confront him.

"Are you all right? You look pale."

Lily forced a smile. "There should be room in the little dresser I had sent over." She glanced around and saw it behind the folded-up cot. She arranged the furniture the way she wanted it with the dresser against the secret door. Just in case.

Jane pulled open the drawer and began to load the clothing into it. "Wait, what is this?" She turned with something in her hand.

Lily stepped closer to examine the item. The light revealed earrings made from butterfly wings. "Those horrible things!" She shuddered and pushed them away. "Someone sent them to me, but I threw them away."

The back of her neck prickled at the thought that someone could do something so malevolent. Whoever it was likely knew about her fear of butterflies. Emily? There had been some rivalry between them, but Lily had thought it was past. Was she wrong, or did she have another enemy in the house?

She forced herself to pick up the earrings and drop them into the pocket of her apron. Right beside the gun. Her fingers touched the cold steel barrel. Its hard strength gave her courage.

Whoever wanted to harm them would have to face this gun first.

# TWENTY-FOUR

Since Stuart was going to be family, dinner was in the smaller dining room. The chandelier sparkled above the table set for seven. Belle stared at the spare plate, unsure who that seventh guest might be. When the doorbell rang, she thrilled at a familiar deep voice. Her uncle had invited Mr. Hawkes. It would be hard to keep her attention on Stuart.

She straightened her garnet silk dress and smiled as both men stepped into the room. "Good evening, gentlemen."

Stuart flushed and pawed at her hand, then kissed her cheek. "You look lovely tonight, Belle."

She arched a brow his way. "Just tonight?"

He went redder. "Always, Belle, always."

She gently pulled her hand away. "Would you care for a glass of wine? Uncle Everett will be down any moment. Aunt Camille has been gone somewhere all day, so I don't know if she will be able to join us or not."

"I'm right here." Her uncle, with Aunt Camille on his arm, stepped into the dining room with Christopher trailing behind. "Glad to see you're taking care of our guests, Belle."

"Of course." Her smile felt stiff at his unspoken rebuke. It was as if he wasn't sure he could trust her in his absence.

Christopher shot her a glance, then stepped forward to take her arm. "Is that a new dress, Belle? The color is most becoming."

The rough fabric of his jacket under her fingers helped settle her. "Yes, Lily made it."

"She's quite talented. Such a good choice of a maid for you."

The men in Belle's life noticed Lily way too much. It was on the tip of her tongue to tell Christopher how unsuitable Lily could be at times, but she restrained herself. Mr. Hawkes glanced at her, and she caught the warning in his eyes. He jerked his head a bit toward Stuart, so Belle strolled over to grasp her fiancé's forearm as he stood talking with her uncle.

"How's the campaign going?" she asked.

Her uncle raised a brow. "You usually show no interest, young lady. Are you picking up Stuart's obsession?"

She laughed. "It's a wise move for a wife to take an interest in what pleases her husband."

Stuart patted her hand on his arm. "And I approve." He glanced at her. "Your uncle is sure to be elected. His opponent has hardly any support. I wouldn't be surprised if Everett garners twice the votes."

His tone held such jubilance she sneaked a peek at his face. Was that avarice in his eyes, or was she reading things into it? Could he possibly be as evil as she'd been told? "Have you ever met the governor, Stuart? I wondered if he was as honorable as he seems."

"He's been a friend of mine for many years. We served on several committees together."

Confirmation of his friendship with his own lips. "You're looking quite sour, Uncle Everett. You don't care for the governor?"

"Our policies differ," her uncle said, his voice clipped. "I expect we will butt heads quite frequently once I'm elected."

She nudged Stuart. "I'm surprised you support Uncle Everett since he's a Republican."

"I'm more an Independent. Your uncle has many good ideas I'd like to see instituted."

She knew if she asked him what those policies were, he'd rattle off a list. The man was collected and prepared. "Have you ever met the governor personally, Uncle Everett?"

"Once."

"And . . . ?" She pushed on even though it was clear her uncle wished she'd change the subject.

"The man is corrupt," her uncle barked. "If he had his way, Texas would be provincial."

Stuart stiffened. "You're being harsh, Everett. The governor sees the wisdom of taking careful thought of any radical change."

"I've seen no evidence of his wisdom," Uncle Everett said sourly. "Let's move to a more pleasant topic of conversation, shall we?"

Stuart's eyes went dark, and he nearly gritted his teeth. Her uncle didn't see because Stuart turned away to pour a drink. Stuart's expression was almost—murderous.

Belle pressed her hand to her stomach. "I'm feeling a bit indisposed tonight. May I be excused to go lie down? I'll try to come back for dessert if I'm feeling better."

Her aunt took her arm. "Of course, Belle! I'll send Lily to you at once with some tea and toast. Should I call the doctor?"

"No, I'll be fine. Thank you." Belle practically ran from the room. She nearly collided with Lily in the hall.

"You're white as a ghost," Lily said. "What's wrong?"

"It's Stuart." Belle gulped and closed her eyes. "It's all true. I could just tell tonight as they discussed politics. There was such rage in his eyes when Uncle Everett criticized the governor. I didn't believe you, not totally. But it's true." She swallowed hard. "We have to stop him."

"We will. Calm yourself, then go back to the dining room. Ask him to allow you to see the house so you can make a list of changes you'd like. It's a perfectly normal request for a soon-to-be wife."

Belle felt faint at the thought. "I could never marry him. Not now. Not even if he were to become president." She clutched Lily's arm. "What if we can't find out the details? I don't think Uncle Everett would believe me if I tried to tell him."

"Your aunt might."

"But he would still go to celebrate with his supporters. And he'll be shot." This panicked feeling must be hysteria. Belle tried to stuff it down, but it kept bubbling into her throat. The very thought of what faced them seemed too overwhelming.

Lily took her by the shoulders. "Courage, Miss Belle. We'll manage. You'll see. Drew has many resources."

"Belle?"

They both turned at Aunt Camille's voice. "Lily was just helping me to bed." Belle winced at the way she stammered. Her aunt was sure to be suspicious. What maid practically shook her mistress?

"Help her to bed, Lily. And thank you for taking care of her."

Belle let out her breath when her aunt returned to the dining room. "What if I go over when he's not there? Then I could look around in peace."

"How could you do that?" Lily sounded hopeful.

"I could pretend I didn't remember he would be gone and stop by. Then I could tell his servant I wanted to look around. He wouldn't refuse me."

"It might work." Lily's blue eyes were lit with admiration. "Tomorrow?"

Belle nodded, though her throat tightened. "Tomorrow afternoon."

The small cabin still smelled of carbolic and vinegar from the vigorous scrubbing Jane and Lily had given it. The night sounds came through the cracks around the windows in a comforting cacophony of katydids, crickets, and cicadas that nearly drowned out the sound of tree frogs.

Lily could hear the even tone of Jane's breathing through the doorway into the bedroom. Every muscle ached, and she rolled over on the narrow cot to try to get comfortable. Being out here in such a remote location still lifted the hair on the back of her neck. Who might be lurking out there in the night? No streetlights, not even the moon, lifted the inky blackness.

The springs squeaked when she sat up and swung her feet to the floor. Maybe warm milk would help her sleep. She padded to the cookstove, an old one she'd worked on for three hours before it was clean enough for her standards, then opened the old icebox to retrieve the milk. The ice was nearly gone, and she would have to ask Mrs. O'Reilly for more.

She set the battered pan of milk on top of the stove, but a pinging noise behind her made her whirl. The sound came again, then she heard a male voice call her name. Her knees went weak when she recognized Drew's deep tone.

She rushed to the door and threw it open. "What are you doing here? It has to be after eleven."

"I've been watching Vesters. His lights went out about an hour ago so I came to check on you. All is quiet?"

She hugged herself, suddenly aware of her feet peeking out from the hem of her simple cotton nightgown. Backing into the cabin, she snatched the blanket from the bed and draped it around her. Her face was hot when she stepped back outside.

He grinned. "I can still see your toes."

She tucked them away and lifted her chin. "It's hardly proper you're here. But I have to admit I'm glad to see you. It feels very deserted and unsafe back here. I'm sure I'll get used to it though."

He sobered and touched her arm. "You have your gun?"

"I do. It's beside the bed. I fear sleep isn't coming easily though. I'm so afraid there will be a sound I'll miss."

He tried the door. "The lock is solid?"

She nodded. "Nathan strengthened the door, and the lock is new. The back door is a bit rickety though."

"Show me."

She led him through the shack to the narrow back door. It opened even without unlocking it. "I must not have gotten it latched properly."

"I'll fix it tomorrow. Tonight I'll sleep on the floor right here."

"I can't let you do that!"

He touched her arm, then his hand moved to her cheek. "I won't leave you out here alone."

"Like last time?" The words were out before she could stop them. She wanted to back away, but that would mean leaving his comforting touch.

His thumb moved back and forth across her skin. "I wish I could go back and change what I did, Lily. Can't you forgive me?"

Her mouth was dry, and she couldn't think with his warm hand on her face. "I forgive you."

He was leaning closer, his intention clear. She closed her eyes, unable to avert her head. His breath whispered across her skin, light as goose down and so fragrant she would inhale him deep inside if she could. When his lips finally brushed across hers, something in her chest loosened as if she'd come home after a long trip. She clutched his shirt with both fists and pulled him closer in a most unladylike way.

He deepened the kiss and crushed her against his chest. She let her guard down, all the way down, and burrowed deep into the passion pouring from him in waves. The love welling in her heart overflowed into a kiss that held more passion than she'd ever dreamed. His hand went to the back of her head and pressed her tighter still. Then he let her go and stepped back, his breathing labored.

She stood staring at him in a tiny bit of light from the candle. She couldn't deny how she felt anymore. She still loved him. What he did and said mattered to her and always would. Her farce of not caring fell off like a cocoon, and she felt alive, truly alive, for the first time in years. She'd follow Drew anywhere, suffer any kind of uncomfortable situation, just to be with him, to be able to go into his arms at the close of the day.

She felt quite wanton as she reached out and touched his roughened jaw. "Drew?" Had her passion put him off?

He caught her hand and held it away from his face. "Give me a moment to collect myself, Lily. I—I don't want to compromise you in any way. Not ever again."

Her touch had caused this. She wanted to kiss him again, to taste the power she had over him. It was exhilarating to know she could affect him so strongly. But she pulled her hand away and stepped back, away from the fire.

He shuddered, then took a deep breath. "I didn't hurt you?"

She shook her head as shyness swept over her. She still loved him. The realization made her eyes burn. Loving him could lead to more hurt. She backed away. "I'd better go in."

# TWENTY-FIVE

The Vesters house was a pompous building looming over the passersby. The mansard-style roof hooded the attic windows in a frown. Drew scowled at it as he went up the brick walkway. He rang the doorbell with more assurance than he felt. Any moment he expected Vesters to figure out he was being investigated.

The butler ushered him to the parlor where Drew found Vesters perusing the newspaper. The man ignored Drew for a full minute before folding the paper and laying it on the table. Drew felt like a supplicant with his hat in his hands waiting to be invited to be seated.

He didn't have to let Vesters intimidate him though, so he dropped into a seat by the door without waiting for an invitation. "You wanted to see me?"

Vesters frowned before masking his irritation. "Have you got your contacts in order? The first of the bigger orders of twenty-dollar bills is ready to roll off the presses."

"Everything is prepared." Drew leaned forward. "But I'm more interested in your plans for Marshall."

The suspicion on Vesters's face deepened. "It might be best if you forget what you saw. You seem too fond of Marshall."

"We both hide our intentions very well. I'm your best ally. I want him out of the way too." He smiled. "Have you checked your bank account today? That fifty thousand should be there. That should prove something to you."

Vesters leaned back. "We'll see. I'll make a call."

He stepped into the hall, and Drew heard him ring through on the telephone to the bank. He glanced around the parlor while he waited. Belle planned to come by this afternoon, and he needed to make sure Vesters was gone. Maybe a trip to the bank would be in order.

Footsteps sounded on the oak floors, then Vesters stepped back into the room. "They haven't seen it yet."

"It should be there by this afternoon. In fact, let me take you to lunch, and we'll stop by the bank to check on the deposit. I'm certain it will be there."

Vesters lifted a brow, then moved to the table and poured himself a Scotch. "Are you trying to avoid the subject? I'd like more details of your vendetta with Marshall." He tossed back the drink with a grimace.

Drew had rehearsed this in his head, but it would take his best acting to pull off the lie. "I believe he lured my father into that building and set fire to it while blocking any escape. I want him to suffer the way my father suffered."

"I never would have guessed Marshall could be so cold-blooded. You're sure?"

"I'm positive." Ballard's features flashed through Drew's mind. Ballard's time would come, once this problem was put to rest.

"This changes things."

"So what can I do? I want to be part of this."

"As I said, I'll talk to my partner. I can't promise anything though. We'll see."

"Can you tell me a bit more about what is being planned? I'd like to look for any problems and be prepared."

"You're putting the cart before the horse, my friend." Vesters dropped back onto the sofa with his drink in his hand. "Let's concentrate on the money, shall we?"

Looking at the man's disinterested face, Drew knew he didn't have a chance of prying out more information. Maybe Belle would have more luck. "Congratulations on your engagement, by the way. Belle is a lovely woman."

"Thank you. I agree."

"And it's a smart move on your part. No one would suspect you had anything to do with the assassination when you're engaged to Marshall's niece. You'll seem the logical choice as well."

Vesters grinned. "I'm glad you approve, but we're not going to talk about this anymore." He pulled out his pocket watch. "I believe it's about lunchtime. I'll take you up on your offer, and we'll check on that money after we eat." He put his empty glass on the table.

Drew had to give the man credit. He was cagey and knew how to handle himself. Drew rose and reached for his hat. "And we can stop by the factory and arrange for me to take shipment of that new money coming off the presses."

He had most of the evidence he needed to arrest Vesters for counterfeiting, but he couldn't do a thing until Marshall was safe. And he still had no proof to arrest Ballard for a thing. Could he be wrong about the man? He was a counterfeiter, but maybe he'd had nothing to do with the fire. And it didn't appear he was the man who had attacked Lily.

And what was he going to do about Lily? She'd admitted she still loved him, but now that he was away from the temptation of her kisses, he saw all the obstacles clearly again. She could be killed like Ian's wife. And what about children? His entire family would be in harm's way. How could he live with himself if he put them in danger? He rubbed his chest. And he could drop dead at any moment himself.

Though walking away from his job was an option, it was something his soul cringed from. He'd found his calling. Justice ran in his blood. How did he reconcile the two loves of his life?

Belle's pulse pounded in her ears as she stepped from the cab onto the walk in front of Stuart's house. It was such an ugly place. If they'd married, she'd have convinced him to sell it and buy something more stylish. At least now she wouldn't have to move into this monstrosity.

Her head high, she sailed to the front door and rang the bell. When his man opened it, she gave him her most superior smile. "Let Stuart know his fiancée has arrived."

The man blinked. "He's out, Miss Belle. I don't expect him back for another couple of hours."

"It's no problem. I wanted to take a look at changes I plan to make before I move in. I can do that without him here."

The servant shifted uneasily. "I've not been given permission for that."

"Oh, for heaven's sake!" Belle pushed past him and drew off her gloves. She pulled paper and a pencil from her bag. "This will be my home. I have every right to inspect it. Go on about your duties. I can do this by myself."

Was her color too high? She turned her back on the servant and marched down the hall toward what she assumed was the kitchen. Three women leaped to their feet when she stepped into the room. A large wooden table held the makings of dinner. Flour spilled onto the floor, and there was a smudge of white on the older woman's face. The scent of apple pie emanated from the wood cookstove.

"Can we help you, miss?" The older woman, presumably the cook, rubbed her soiled hands on her apron.

"I'm Belle Castle. I've come to inspect the house." She glanced around the kitchen. "The stove is rather old, isn't it? I'd like to get a new one with a proper oven. I'm particularly fond of pies."

The cook bristled. "Wait until you taste my apple pie. You'll have no reason to turn up your nose. But I wouldn't say no to a new stove."

"Any other needs here in the kitchen?" Belle jotted down *stove* on her list. There was unlikely to be any clues here, but she wanted to establish her presence and motive. The male servant hovered in the doorway behind her, and she hoped he'd leave her alone in a few minutes.

"No, miss. We're quite happy here, aren't we?" The cook nudged the woman beside her who nodded vigorously.

"Excellent." Belle moved past her. "What's this way?"

"Just the laundry room, miss."

Belle peeked into the back room. "We must get one of the new wringer washers. They do a much better job than a washboard."

She could see by their smiles that she'd made allies in the house. "Sorry for disturbing you. I'll let you get back to dinner preparations."

Mouths gaping, the women watched her go. She had to push past the male servant, still in the doorway. "You needn't follow me around. What's your name?"

"Jasper, miss." His voice was colorless.

Could he be involved with Stuart? The man seemed a bit smarmy with eyes set too close together and a suspicious manner. "Jasper, go on about your business. I'll be here awhile."

"I don't think I should, miss."

"I'm giving you a direct order. Mr. Vesters would not like it if you disrespected me."

He took a step back. "No, miss. Call me if you need anything."

"You can bring me tea in about half an hour."

"As you wish." He bowed, then disappeared back into the kitchen.

Belle exhaled, then moved with determination to Stuart's office. Heavy curtains blocked the sunlight from the room, so she shut the door behind her, then moved to the windows and pushed the curtains out of the way. Light filled the room so she could see. The large desk was clear of papers. Shelves filled with books covered one wall. She glanced at them. They were mostly law books.

She stepped to the desk and opened the first drawer on the left. More books were heaped inside. She lifted them out and examined them carefully but found nothing of interest. A clock on the desk chimed one o'clock. After going through the other drawers, she was forced to admit defeat. Maybe there would be something in his bedroom.

She opened the door and walked upstairs as though she had every right. After several false starts, she found the master bedroom. It was a large room at the back of the house. There was no private bath so she jotted that on her paper so it would be clear to Stuart of her purpose. Shutting the door behind her, she first made note of the colors and fabrics she would change, then she slid her hand under the mattress. Nothing. She went to the other side and did the same. Not a scrap of evidence. Had she risked the trip for nothing?

The only place she hadn't looked was the chest of drawers. She opened the top drawer and shuddered at the male undergarments. She closed her eyes and forced herself to riffle through them without looking. Her fingers closed around a piece of paper tucked into the far back right corner. She pulled it out and unfolded it. When she scanned it, she realized it was from someone who called himself "L" and seemed to be a friend.

*Meet me next Thursday at the river walk. Ten p.m. I'll bring the gun. Ballard will be there too.*

Ballard? Who was that and what role did he play in this? She thought she heard something and thrust the paper back into the drawer. She'd barely gotten it shut and had turned toward the door when it opened and Stuart stood staring at her with a troubled scowl on his face.

"What are you doing, Belle?"

She flashed him a brilliant smile and hurried to brush a kiss across his whiskered face. "I've been having a lovely time deciding on the changes to our bedroom. And some other changes as well. A wife's duty, you know."

His scowl eased and he flushed. "Excellent, my dear, but you should have waited until I could escort you."

She showed him her notes. "What do you think of sky blue in this room? It's so relaxing. I suspect we'll be spending a great deal of time here, and it's my favorite color."

His eyes went a little glazed. "Whatever you like, Belle. Come kiss me again."

She danced away as he reached for her. "We're in your bedroom and quite unchaperoned, Stuart. Let's go down for some tea. I'll see about *one* more kiss."

# TWENTY-SIX

Mr. Marshall's office was huge with a high, coffered ceiling. Lily put her fingers to her lips as she pulled Belle inside and shut the door.

"Why did you want to come in here?" Belle glanced around her uncle's office.

"Drew wanted to make sure he wasn't missing anything your uncle was working on that might impact the murder plot." She watched Belle pacing back and forth across the thick carpet. "You're quite tense, Miss Belle."

"You would have been tense too! I was nearly discovered in Stuart's bedroom with the letter in my hand."

"You found a letter?" She needed to get word to Drew. Her pulse still fluttered at his ardor last night—and her own.

"It was in his unmentionables drawer." Belle wrinkled her nose. "He's meeting this person and someone named Ballard too."

Lily gasped. "Ballard? Are you sure?"

Belle sat on the stool and stared at her. "The name is familiar to you?"

Lily nodded. "He's a neighbor from Larson. I—I'd heard he moved here to Austin."

"Does Mr. Hawkes know him as well?"

Lily nodded. "He believes the man is responsible for the deaths of our fathers."

"Both of them?"

"They were killed in a fire." She bit her lip. "I must admit I'm not convinced. Drew is passionate about bringing him to justice, and I would be as well if I were sure he was guilty."

"He seems to be involved in this messy business in some manner. We must tell Drew."

Lily glanced away at Belle's use of Drew's name. And the proprietary way she'd said it.

Belle arched a brow. "What are you thinking, Lily? You want Drew for yourself, don't you? Surely you don't think he would settle for you."

Belle's words stabbed at Lily's core. "I love him. I've loved him for most of my life."

"Surely you want what's best for him. With an infusion of money from an advantageous marriage, he could go anywhere, do anything." Belle's laugh tinkled out. "Passion fades, and then what do you have? Not much without money. He would resent you eventually. He'd know you kept him from his true destiny."

"Why do you care?" Lily burst out. "You want him for yourself, don't you?"

Belle shrugged and rose to face her. "I could bring him many advantages."

"You don't love him. You just like his looks and manner. You don't really know him."

"If you'd step out of the way, I could know him better."

Belle's tone was inflexible, and the determination in her eyes told Lily there would be a battle. But she wasn't going to back away, not now that she knew how she felt about Drew. Not now that he'd kissed her with his soul unbarred.

"I'm not going to step out of the way."

"I could discharge you."

"But you won't. We must save your uncle, and that will take all of us working together. Besides, if you put me out on the street, Drew would marry me at once."

But would he? It might derail his investigation. Lily was suddenly unsure of how the future she envisioned would play out. She lifted her chin and stared at Belle as if showing determination would quell her misgivings.

How could Drew prefer her to this beauty before her? Belle was so lovely with her dark hair and flashing brown eyes, complemented by her lovely gowns. She had money and power to offer as well, while Lily had nothing but herself. What man with his full faculties would choose her over Belle? If Belle were a butterfly, Lily would be a moth.

"You're very impertinent, Lily."

"I'm sorry, Miss Belle, but you don't understand how much Drew means to me. I won't give him up. Not for you or anyone else."

Belle's chin tipped up. "Maybe I'll take him from you, then."

"Is that a declaration of war?" Lily smiled to try to defuse the tension. The last thing she wanted was to battle with her mistress.

Belle's laugh was a derisive tinkling sound. "Oh, Lily, you are so funny. I'm only teasing you. You can have your precious Drew. I have many other men to choose from. And Drew has no interest in politics. I'm quite determined to be the wife of a senator or governor. Maybe I'll even be the First Lady someday."

"Y-You were joking?"

Belle nodded. "I wanted to see if I could rattle your devotion. It appears I can't." She stared at Lily. "I don't even know what your kind of love is like. I've never seen it. My father was rather domineering and crushed my mother's spirit because she loved him so much. I will never kowtow to a man like that. Love makes you vulnerable."

"It also makes you strong, Miss Belle. Together you can do much."

Belle moved to the desk and flipped through the papers there. "You'd have to find the right man, and how do you know when it's the right one? I am never allowed to get to know the real man inside. Not with the chaperone sitting right there."

For the first time, Lily began to understand what Belle's life had been like. What it still was. While money hadn't been something Mama could provide much of, Lily had seen love displayed in front of her. She hadn't been boxed into a life she didn't want. She'd been allowed to have enough freedom to go fishing with Drew and to learn to love the real man inside.

She touched Belle's hand. "I'll pray for you, Miss Belle. That God shows you the man who will love you for who you are."

Tears sprang to Belle's eyes. "How blasphemous to think God cares about such mundane things, Lily. But thank you."

Lily opened a drawer. "God always cares."

Jane was rocking the baby by the light of a candle when Lily stepped into the shack. The sight of mother and baby always brought a lump to Lily's throat. "Is she sleeping?"

Jane shook her head. "Wide-awake and waiting for Aunt Lily."

Lily gently lifted the little one to her chest and brushed her lips over Hannah's soft hair. "How's my good girl tonight?"

Hannah cooed and waved a chubby fist in the air. Lily kissed her fingers, and the baby grasped a loose strand of hair.

"She knows you," Jane said.

Settling little Hannah into the crook of her arm, Lily joined Jane on the broken-down sofa. "How are you settling into your job?"

"Just fine. The Marshalls seemed to like the spiced oysters I made tonight."

The thought of such fancy food filled Lily with admiration. "Mrs. O'Reilly thanked me today for recommending you."

Nathan's bulk filled the doorway from the bedroom. "And I'd add my thanks to hers, Miss Lily. I've never seen my sister so happy. And she's safe here from Vesters."

"I'm glad it's all working out." Lily glanced at the door. "Mr. Hawkes repaired the door?"

Nathan moved closer in the dim candlelight. "He said to tell you he'd stop back by about ten." He seized his hat. "I'm off to work. Keep a lookout. And keep the gun close."

"We will."

"What time is it?" Jane asked.

"Nine thirty," he told her.

"Miss Belle nodded off early."

The baby began to squawk and root for milk so Lily passed her over to her mother. "She was tired. Do you have a minute before you go, Nathan?"

"About five is all. Is something wrong?"

"Do you know a man named Ballard?" Why was she asking him? He hardly ran in the same circles as Ballard. "Never mind."

"I do know him, actually. Good man. He pops into the pub on occasion."

"Have you ever seen him meeting with Mr. Vesters?"

Nathan shook his head. "He can't abide the man. They got into a fistfight several months ago. Vesters tried to take liberties with one of the waitresses, and Ballard ejected him from the bar."

That didn't sound like someone in cahoots with Vesters. "Thanks, Nathan."

There was a knock on the door, and Nathan opened it. He grinned at Drew. "I'm on my way out so you can take over protecting the women."

"Have a good night."

Before Drew could shut the door, Lily jumped up and took his hand. "I need to talk to you outside for a moment."

"I like the sound of that." Drew winked at Jane who laughed, then ducked her head.

"I'll be putting the baby to bed, so don't go outside on my account." She scurried from the room and shut the bedroom door behind her.

Lily's face burned, but she wouldn't be averse to another kiss like last night. She shook her head to clear her bemused thoughts. "Belle found something today." She told him about the note and the mention of Ballard. "I know you think this implicates him more, but I don't think Mr. Ballard is the evil man you think he is, Drew."

His smile vanished. "Why would I lie about something like that?"

"I didn't mean you were lying. Just that he might not be guilty of all you think he is."

"Why are you so resistant to hearing the truth about him?"

Lily heard the inflexibility in his voice and knew she'd get nowhere. "Let's talk about something else. The truth will come out sooner or later."

Drew's lips flattened. "Fine. Anything else from Belle?"

"She was nearly caught." She told him about Vesters's reaction to finding Belle in the bedroom.

"Does she think he was suspicious?"

Lily shook her head. "She thinks her story was believable."

"I don't understand why he'd be meeting Ballard," Drew muttered.

"I know. Nathan told me the two despise each other."

Drew frowned as he listened to what Nathan had told her. "I'll try to find out what it's all about. Vesters might tell me."

"Did you get any closer to finding out what he's planning? You talked to him this morning, right?"

"Not much. He's got a partner who is opposed to bringing me in on the plan. He demanded to know why I wanted Marshall dead. When I told him he'd killed my father, he promised to discuss it with the partner."

"Marshall killed . . . I don't understand."

"I had to have a personal excuse for a vendetta against him, so I chose one I had passion for."

"Ballard."

He nodded. "Exactly."

She willed him to take her in his arms and ease the tension between them. Did he regret the words and kisses they'd shared? But no, studying his dear face, she knew he loved her. Knew it with every fiber of her being. Every couple had disagreements.

Then why hadn't he talked of marriage? There was still something holding him aloof. And she feared he had secrets he hadn't told her.

Drew took a seat at the stern of the steamboat on Lake McDonald. Ian would find him before the vessel left. Not many sat back here since the goal was to view the scenery as the boat circled the lake. The air horn overhead blew loud enough to pierce his eardrums, and the stink from the steam engine made him slightly nauseated.

The boat rocked in the water as passengers boarded. He heard a footfall and saw Ian making his way toward the back of the boat. His supervisor was dressed in a navy blue blazer with a straw boater shading his face. His gray beard was as neatly trimmed as always.

Ian settled on the bench beside him. "I came at once. Your note seemed quite urgent. Something new on Vesters?"

"You might say that." Drew told him about the note he found about the murder plot to kill Marshall. "He is planning on being appointed in Marshall's place. I'm having trouble tying him to Ballard, though it makes sense they would be partners. He professes to dislike Ballard." Drew told him of the attack and how Lily had gone to see Ballard.

Ian listened intently. "We knew when we came here this was a hotbed for counterfeiters. Let's get Vesters first. Maybe we can prevent Marshall's murder."

Drew shook his head. "But Ballard knows I'm here. He'll be gone in a heartbeat. I think they're connected somehow." What if Ballard bolted again? Drew wanted to put an end to his obsession, not be forced to follow his enemy to a new location.

The paddle wheels began to turn, and the boat pulled away from the dock. The spray of water from the wet paddles drifted to Drew's face on the wind.

Ian wiped the moisture from his cheeks. "You said he just bought a house, correct? I suspect he plans to stay here. I think he feels invincible. We can take this one step at a time."

"At least he's in one place. I can stake out his house and follow where he goes. He'll lead me to his hidey-hole."

Ian frowned. "I think you're too obsessed with this, Drew. I'm going to put another agent on this. You concentrate on Vesters."

"This is my case! Someone else won't supplant me. I'm too close to let him go now. I'm convinced the two are connected. Let me handle it."

Ian stared at him, then nodded. "I see there's no deterring you. Are you fearful for Lily's safety?"

"Yes, I'm very worried about her. And I just want this *over*. Once Ballard is behind bars, maybe I can go on to some kind of normal life."

Ian pulled out his pipe and lit it. The smoke swirled about his head as he puffed, but the wind carried away the odor. "You want to marry Lily."

"If I'm convinced it's safe."

"Life is never safe, Drew. You can't second-guess what will happen tomorrow. You plan to stay with the service?"

"Yes, if you'll have me."

"It would grieve me to lose you. But what will Lily say about that?"

"I haven't asked her. I think she would feel it was worth the danger."

But would she? She'd been on the periphery so far and hadn't seen the things he'd seen in the past four years. Did he put her through that, or did he walk away from the job he loved? It would be a hard decision.

# TWENTY-SEVEN

On her next day off, Lily clutched the address Mr. Ballard had given her and stared at the house from the sidewalk. Decorative iron fencing rimmed the property, and the lovely Victorian presided over the green lawn like a queen.

Drew would be angry with her, but she had to help figure this out.

She opened the iron gate and started for the house when a female voice hailed her. She turned to see Mrs. Ballard cutting roses. She wore a casual blue gown with a straw hat and had gardening gloves on her hands.

Mrs. Ballard smiled as she approached with a rose in her hand. "Lily, how lovely to see you. My son mentioned he'd run into you at the hotel. Have you changed your mind and decided to come work for us?"

The tone put Lily's back up. Mrs. Ballard had always taken every opportunity to let the rest of Larson townspeople know she came from money. Her parents lived in Boston, and she still had the New England accent. At times—like today—she played it up even more. She'd never seemed to like Lily either. Her warmth seemed forced, and there had been times when Lily caught her glaring.

Lily smiled past her discomfort. "I'm happy where I am, Mrs.

Ballard. I stopped by to say hello and see if there was anything I could do for you. I'm beginning to know my way around Austin quite well, and today is my day off." She glanced around. "Is your son home?"

Mrs. Ballard's smile vanished. "He's not here at the moment." She lifted her chin.

"I wanted to thank him for his kindness. Please pass it along."

The front door opened, and Mr. Ballard stepped out. Mrs. Ballard went pink. Lily tried to act as though the woman hadn't just told her a bald-faced lie and stepped toward him with her hand outstretched.

He was smiling as he encased her hand in both of his. "Lily, how wonderful to see you. Come in, and I'll have the maid bring some tea and cookies. Norris stopped by too, but you just missed him."

"I'm sorry I missed him." Aware of Mrs. Ballard's gaze drilling into her back, Lily smiled and followed him into the house. The coolness of the interior was a welcome relief from the heat outside. She took off her hat and placed it on the walnut table in the entry, then joined him in the parlor where he was giving orders to the maid for tea. Some kind of baked pumpkin smell wafted from the back of the house.

"I'll be just a moment," Mrs. Ballard said from the doorway. "I want to clean up." Her voice was cold.

Lily settled on the armchair. "I like your new house very much."

He went to the window and pushed open the drapes so sunlight streamed into the room. "I do too. My mother is slightly less enthusiastic. She wanted a larger one on a higher-profile street." He went to the sofa and sat at one end.

Lily smiled and didn't respond to his comment. Her gaze roamed the parlor. "She's done a lovely job decorating."

"Thank you." Mrs. Ballard stood in the doorway. She'd shed her gloves and hat. Glancing at her son, she settled on the sofa beside him.

The tension in the room was palpable. Lily folded her hands in her lap and tried to think how she might defuse the hostility emanating from the woman in waves. What had Lily ever done to deserve it?

Mr. Ballard sent a swift glance at his mother, then laced his fingers and inhaled. "I wondered if Norris and I might escort you to the opera one night. You could use a fun night, I'm sure."

Lily blinked at the sudden request. Was he trying to arrange something between her and his son? "I—I seldom have time off."

"If not the opera, then perhaps dinner one night. Surely you have a day off now and then?"

Her pulse fluttered, and she felt pinned to the chair by his attention. This wasn't what she'd expected. "I will have to see when my next day off is. We've been shorthanded at the house, and I'm not sure when I'll be free at night. I will let you know." She exhaled when a maid brought in tea and cookies. She selected a lemon square to compose herself. At least he hadn't asked her to go tonight when she was clearly off work.

Mrs. Ballard's displeasure pruned her lips even more, but she said nothing. Mr. Ballard looked displeased as he poured the tea.

Lily rushed to fill the void with chitchat about the news and weather. It was only when she finally escaped the house that she realized he hadn't brought up the fire.

The Friday night guests had retired to the parlor after dinner, and Lily stacked the dishes in the dining room, then carried them to the kitchen. Drew and Vesters had come to dinner, and she'd been tense as she helped serve them. She'd managed to whisper the news to Drew that she'd found nothing at the Ballard house.

Mrs. O'Reilly took the dishes from her. "Mr. Marshall wants his butterflies again. He received a new one this morning he wants to show off. Get case number three."

Lily backed away with her hands behind her back. "I'd be glad to wash the dishes if you want to go get them."

Mrs. O'Reilly put her hand on Lily's shoulder. "You need to get over your fear. It will be fine."

"I'll go with you," Jane offered. She had a smudge of flour on one cheek and a long trail of white on her black skirt.

"I would appreciate it. I hate going down there alone." She inhaled and took the key Mrs. O'Reilly held out, then went toward the door.

Her legs were weak and shaky as she twisted the key in the door to the butterfly room. The lantern only pushed back the darkness a few feet. She turned on the lights and finally exhaled when the illumination pushed away the shadows. The dank odor of the basement added to her unease.

Jane gasped at her first sight of the butterflies. She hovered over a display case. "How lovely!"

Lily shuddered. "I think they're creepy. Poor dead things. I don't know why he collects them. They were once flying free and beautiful in a forest somewhere, and he hired someone to kill them."

"I suppose you're right." Jane wandered closer to the first case and stared. "There is one in here from Africa. He probably spent a lot of money on these butterflies."

"I'm sure he did." Lily went toward the third case. The new butterfly was beautiful, about six inches across with wings a lovely shade of blue. It was almost iridescent. She picked up the case and carried it toward the door. "Would you lock up behind us?"

"What's that?" Jane's voice held panic.

Lily turned to see a woman's foot sticking out from under a display case. A sick feeling started at the back of her throat. She put down the butterfly and approached. Kneeling, she touched the woman's ankle. It was cold.

She snatched her hand away and scrabbled back, then stood. "We must fetch Mr. Marshall at once."

"I-Is she *dead*?"

Lily swallowed hard. "Yes." She rubbed her hand against her skirt, trying to erase the feel of the woman's clammy skin.

"Who is she?" Jane whispered.

"I can't see her very well, and I don't want to disturb anything for the police." Lily grabbed the case of butterflies and rushed toward the door. "Would you guard the door while I fetch Mr. Marshall?" Jane was still staring at the body when Lily turned back halfway up the stairs. "Jane?" She retreated a few steps to see why her friend was frozen in place.

Jane turned toward her with an agonized expression. "I think it's Mrs. Karr."

"Are you sure?"

Jane's lips trembled. "Not certain since I can't see her face, but I think so." She came toward Lily.

The two went up to the kitchen. Lily left Jane to tell Mrs. O'Reilly and Emily what they'd found while Lily rushed to the parlor. She stood awkwardly in the doorway. Drew saw her first and lifted a brow. He knew her so well he was sure to see her distress. Mr. Marshall finally glanced up from where he stood by the fireplace speaking to Drew.

She clasped the case of butterflies to her chest. "May I speak to you for a moment, sir?"

He excused himself. "Ah, you have my butterflies." He took the case from her and started to turn away.

"Sir, we have a situation."

He swung back around to face her, a frown of displeasure wrinkling his brow. "I have guests. Can't it wait?"

"No, sir. The police need to be called. Th-There's a woman in the butterfly room. She appears to be dead."

His head came up higher. "One of our servants?"

"I don't think so, Mr. Marshall. I don't know how she got there."

Drew joined them. "What's wrong, Everett?"

"Belle's maid informs me there's a deceased person in the basement." Mr. Marshall frowned. "You believe there was foul play? You mentioned calling the police."

"She doesn't appear to belong to the household. I didn't disturb the body, but she's lying half under one of the butterfly displays."

"How on earth did she get in? It's always locked. Was it secure when you went down? Maybe when the new specimen was delivered, the door wasn't locked."

"I didn't check, sir. I just put the key in the lock and turned it."

Drew touched her arm. "Are you all right, Lily? You look a little pale."

Mr. Marshall shot him a startled look, then stared at her. "Yes, you do. I'll take it from here. Get some tea. I'm sure it's been a shock."

"Thank you, sir." She badly wanted to burrow into the sanctuary of Drew's arms, but she turned and rushed down the hall toward the kitchen.

Drew called her name from the parlor, and moments later he caught her by the arm. "I don't like this, Lily. Surely you know more than you told Marshall."

She shook her head. "I came up at once to inform him." She told him about Jane's possible identification of the woman. "What was she doing here?"

"It sounds quite ominous. Could you tell how she died?"

She shook her head again.

Mr. Marshall joined them. "The police will be here shortly." His gaze lingered on Drew's hand on Lily's arm.

She started to step away, but Drew tightened his grip and stared at Mr. Marshall. The doorbell rang, and two policemen rushed into the hall.

"This way," Mr. Marshall said.

# TWENTY-EIGHT

Drew stood back and watched as the police finished examining the body. Lily stood with her arm around Jane as she identified the woman as Sarah Karr, Jane's employer until she'd been dismissed.

"What's the cause of death?" Drew hadn't been able to see with so many people crowding around. This place gave him the willies too. All those beautiful dead butterflies.

The younger policeman was the same man who'd been investigating the attack on Lily in the churchyard, and he stared at her with a contemplative expression before turning his attention to Drew. "Her throat was slashed. With this." He held out a bloody knife similar to the one Lily's attacker had dropped.

Drew's gut tightened and he glanced at Lily, who wore a stricken expression when she saw the knife. "Did you have any luck tracing the last one?"

"We did not."

Everett moved closer. "Last one? What are you talking about?"

"Lily was attacked in the churchyard, and the man dropped a knife like this one."

Everett glanced at Lily. "Why was I not informed of this?"

She still stood with her arm around Jane who was weeping. "I was unhurt, Mr. Marshall. I didn't want to bother you with it."

The policeman turned his attention to the mansion's owner. "Mr. Marshall, did you know the deceased woman?"

"I did. What is your name, young man?"

"Officer Pickle." The man lifted his pimpled chin as though daring them to laugh. "Do you have any idea how she happened to be down here?"

Everett shook his head. "Only my butterfly collection is kept here, and I keep the key unless I send a maid down to fetch a specimen. Which is how this unfortunate woman came to be discovered. The only other person with a key is the housekeeper."

"Perhaps her husband will be able to shed light on how she came to be here." Pickle directed his attention to Lily. "Was this the first time you'd been down here today?"

"It was."

"You're about this woman's height, and your hair color is the same."

"Blond hair is hardly unusual," Drew said.

The officer glared. "I must ask you to be quiet while I conduct my investigation."

Drew held up his hands. "Proceed."

"Could the killer have mistaken Mrs. Karr for you? The victim was wearing a black dress. Though it was of a finer material than yours, in the dark it might have been easy to mistake her for you."

Jane was blond too. Lily bit her lip. "I hardly think so. The bigger question is, why was she here?"

Everett clenched his hands into fists. "I'll tell you why! She came to steal my new specimen. Karr has envied my collection for years. He was furious when I was asked to show my collection at the museum instead of his."

"He collects butterflies too?" Pickle asked. "Is his collection as extensive?"

Everett's nostrils flared. "Not even close. He probably has a tenth of what I have. Though I will admit he owns a few rare specimens."

Pickle glanced around. "What here could he want badly enough to steal? Couldn't he just buy what he wanted?"

Everett's smile could only be called joyous. "I just received the most beautiful iridescent butterfly today. I've never seen anything like it. It's a very special Blue Morpho from South America with unusual powers. There isn't another one like it in the world. It's upstairs in the parlor. I'll show it to you. Lily, would you fetch it?"

She nodded, hugged Jane, then started up the stairs.

"I'll go with her. I don't think it's safe for her to wander alone." Drew followed Lily and caught up with her in the kitchen.

Her eyes widened when she saw him. "What are you doing? You're going to get me discharged."

He took her elbow and escorted her toward the parlor. "This place isn't safe for you, Lily. I'll not stand by and let anything happen to you."

She stopped in the hall and looked up at him, her blue eyes as soft as thistledown. "I'm fine, Drew. Really. I have the gun you got me."

"You don't have it on you at the moment, do you?"

"Well, no, it's in the carriage house. But I don't need it when I'm working."

"I'm sure Mrs. Karr thought the same."

She winced. "We don't know yet what that's all about. She may have been stealing Mr. Marshall's butterfly."

"Maybe. I would like to believe that, but I'm not convinced." He cupped his hand around her cheek. "I couldn't live if anything happened to you, Lily."

A pretty blush climbed her cheeks, but she held his gaze, looking deeply into his eyes as if trying to read his inner thoughts and feelings. He turned away. What did he have to offer her? "Let's go find that butterfly and get it to Everett before he comes up here himself." He led her by the hand into the parlor. "Where did he put it?"

"On the piano, I think." She moved toward the polished surface of the grand piano in the back corner. "It's not here. Maybe I'm wrong or someone moved it."

Drew helped her search, but minutes later they had to admit the truth. "The butterfly case is missing."

Lily knew Jane hadn't slept much last night because she'd lain awake most of the night herself and had heard her moving around restlessly in the bedroom. They both bolted down the last of their porridge. Hannah played on the floor at their feet.

Lily took her last sip of tea. "We'd better get to work." Her yawn matched Jane's. "Are you doing okay?"

Jane nodded. "Poor Mrs. Karr. I hope the police get to the bottom of this." She looked toward the door. "I don't know where Nathan is. I shall be late if he doesn't arrive soon."

"I'll let Mrs. O'Reilly know. He should be along any moment."

Lily opened the door and nearly barreled into the policeman with his arm raised to knock. "Officer Pickle."

His narrow-set eyes looked her over. He smelled of tobacco. "I would like to speak to Miss White."

Jane stepped forward with Hannah in her arms. "I'm right here."

"You're to come along to the station for questioning. Now."

"What's this all about?" Jane's eyes held a hint of fear.

"We have some questions."

Lily's gut tightened at his somber expression. "I'd like to come with her."

"Very well. We'll likely have some questions for you too. Come along."

Jane's eyes widened. "B-But what about my baby?"

For the first time the officer looked uncertain. "Surely someone here can watch her."

"There's no one I can ask," Jane said.

"Then you'll need to bring her, I suppose." Officer Pickle didn't meet her gaze.

"I need to let the big house know where we're going." Lily walked ahead of them along the rough path.

Belle came around the corner of the house. She was wearing a riding dress and boots and carried a riding crop. She glanced from Lily to Jane and the policeman. "What's going on?"

"The officer is taking Jane in for questioning." Lily sent her mistress a pleading look. There probably was nothing Belle could do, but Lily wanted to spare Jane if she could.

Belle blocked the path. "I think that's hardly necessary. Feel free to use the parlor, Officer."

Officer Pickle looked uncomfortable. "I'm sorry, Miss Castle, but I must take her in."

Belle frowned. "You're arresting her?"

The officer shuffled. "It depends on her answers."

Lily's mouth went dry. The police obviously thought Jane was guilty. "W-We aren't sure what to do about Hannah."

Belle glanced at the baby, then stared hard at Jane. "I'll take her." She held out her arms. "I'm sure I can coax Mrs. O'Reilly and Emily to help."

Jane burst into tears. "You're a good woman, Miss Belle." She passed her daughter over into Belle's arms.

Belle held the child awkwardly. "We'll take good care of her, Jane." She gave the officer a stern look. "Don't keep her too long."

He looked away without answering. Jane wept as the policeman led them to the buggy. The ride to the police station was silent, broken only by Jane's occasional cough.

Pickle led them inside to a small room filled with the stench of tobacco. "Please be seated." He sat at the desk and took out a pencil and paper. "I've spoken to several servants in the Karr household, and it appears Mrs. Karr went there to steal the butterfly, just as Mr. Marshall suspected. How long did you work for the Karrs, Miss White?"

Jane folded her hands in her lap. "Three years."

"You worked in the kitchen?"

"Yes, sir."

"You knew the deceased, Mrs. Karr, well?"

Jane nodded. "As well as a servant can know her employer."

"So you admired her?"

Jane bit her lip. "I wouldn't exactly say that, sir."

Pickle lifted a brow and put his pencil down. "You were enemies?"

"Sh-She did me wrong once."

Lily glanced at her sharply but said nothing. From the look of satisfaction on Pickle's face, it was clear he knew of the animosity.

"I heard you despised Mrs. Karr and hated her enough to kill her."

"I would never harm another person," Jane said, her voice barely audible. "She wasn't a good person though."

"Where were you last night in the hour before Mrs. Karr's body was discovered?"

"Working in the kitchen."

"Alone?"

Jane twisted her hands in her lap. "It was Cook's night off."

"Answer the question," he barked.

"Yes, sir. Alone."

"Did you speak with Mrs. Karr? To get to the butterfly room, she would have had to come into the kitchen."

Lily leaned forward. "She didn't see her, Officer Pickle! None of us know how she got down there. And her body was cold. I touched her ankle."

Pickle quelled her with a cold look. "Please be quiet, or you'll have to leave."

She sank against the hard chair back. *Lord, keep Jane calm. Let this man see she had nothing to do with this.*

Pickle turned his attention back to Jane. "Did you speak to her? Remember, if we find you've lied to the police, any trouble you're in just got worse."

"I—I . . ." Jane gulped. "Yes, sir. I spoke to her." Her shoulders slumped and she shuddered.

Lily couldn't hold back a gasp. She stared at her friend. What was going on? Then she remembered Jane had pointed out the body first. She didn't want to believe Jane could have had anything to do with this. She was a kind, gentle soul.

"What was the conversation about?"

"She told me if I didn't let her go to the butterfly room, she would tell my employer a lie about me."

"What lie?" Pickle's voice was hard.

Tears hung on Jane's lashes. "That I'd been a prostitute and that's why I had a baby."

"Was it true?"

Jane shook her head violently. "She knew it wasn't true because it was her fault I became pregnant. She and her husband sent a-a man to my room. I'm a good girl, Officer Pickle. I had never even held hands with a man." She swallowed hard. "She and her husband ruined my life."

Pickle's expression was stony. "So you killed her. I understand. She deserved it, didn't she?"

Jane hung her head. "I didn't kill her."

"So what happened then?" His icy gray eyes bored into her.

"Mrs. O'Reilly gave me her keys to get some wine. I still had them when Mrs. Karr came to the door. I—I let her go to the butterfly room."

Lily gasped and stared at Jane. "Oh, Jane."

Jane twisted her handkerchief in her hand. "It was wrong—I know that! But I couldn't let her destroy the new life I was trying to make. She said she just wanted to take a look at it and make sure the new butterfly was really all Mr. Marshall claimed it to be. She went down there smiling like she'd won." Jane's voice held distaste.

"And then what happened?" Pickle demanded.

"Nothing. I did my work and kept wondering where she was, but I didn't have time to look for her. Not when I was doing the cooking by myself. Then Lily came and said she had to go get that butterfly for Mr. Marshall. I suddenly realized just how long she had to have been down there, so I went along."

Even Lily could see Jane's argument was weak. So she wasn't surprised when Pickle stood and said, "Miss White, you're under arrest for the murder of Mrs. Karr."

# TWENTY-NINE

Lily couldn't remember when she'd been so angry as she paced the kitchen with Hannah in her arms. Nathan had gone down to the police station to see what he could do, but the baby would be crying soon for milk.

"The police actually locked her up?" Emily flipped the mound of dough over and began to roll it out.

"She was crying when they dragged her off to the cell. It was horrible." Lily brushed her lips across the baby's soft hair. "What am I going to do about Hannah?"

"Our neighbor has a goat," Mrs. O'Reilly said. "I'll ask for some milk. Emily, you run to the general store and buy a couple of bottles. It will have to do."

Emily dusted the flour from her hands onto her apron. "What about preparations for lunch?"

"We have ham and cheese in the larder. I can whip up sandwiches when I get back."

"Won't we get in trouble?" In spite of her protest, Emily's eyes were gleaming as she took off her apron.

"I'll explain to the missus. No woman could stand back and let a baby go hungry."

Hannah swiped a tiny hand at a wisp of Lily's hair. Lily kissed

223

the small fingers. What would happen to the little mite if Jane went to prison? Not that she could possibly be guilty, but the police didn't seem to care about the truth. They thought they had their murderer all sewed up and wouldn't be looking around for the real culprit.

The women had barely gotten out the back door when Belle stepped into the kitchen. "Where is Jane?"

"It's been a trying morning." Lily told her what had happened at the police station.

Belle's face softened as she listened. "You can't take care of the baby, Lily. Surely you see that. Jane worked part-time in the kitchen so she could pop back and forth to the little house when she needed to. That won't work long-term." Hannah stared up at Belle, then smiled a toothy grin. Belle smiled back. "She's the sweetest thing." She held out her arms and took Hannah.

Hannah grabbed her necklace and yanked.

"Careful, she might break it."

Belle extracted her necklace from the baby's chubby fingers. "How will you feed her?"

At least Belle wasn't ordering her to give the baby to the orphanage, which was what she'd expected in spite of Belle's earlier agreeability. "Emily went to get a bottle, and Mrs. O'Reilly stepped next door to ask for goat milk."

"Does the child have any other clothing?" Belle wrinkled her nose.

"She smelled quite sour earlier so I bathed her, but the gown has been mended a dozen times. I think she needs to be bathed again. She has one other gown. It's clean. I can run get it and give her another bath."

"I'll start her bath. You go get the gown. We'll go shopping for more clothing this afternoon." Belle carried the baby to the sink.

"Let me help you." Lily grabbed the hot water from the stove and poured it into the sink, then pumped cold water until it was a comfortable temperature. "I'll go get the clean gown."

She raced to the empty shack and grabbed the gown and a clean diaper. By the time she got back, Belle had Hannah in the water. The baby was cooing and splashing. Maybe the other house had running water, but Lily had only seen Jane sponge the baby clean.

Belle's face shone. "She's very pretty, isn't she?"

Lily smiled. "She looks like her mama. Her big blue eyes are very appealing."

Her smile faded when she remembered how Jane came to have the baby. What a terrible thing, to be betrayed by someone you knew well.

"I need a towel," Belle said.

Lily grabbed a clean dish towel. "This will do. She's small."

Belle lifted the wriggling, dripping baby from the water, and Hannah wailed with protest. Lily dried her off while Belle held her still, then together they managed to get her into a clean diaper and gown.

"What is all the caterwauling?" Mrs. Marshall stood in the doorway to the kitchen with her hands on her hips. She wore an elaborate pink gown with a matching hat. She had her gloves on too, so either she'd just come in or she was preparing to go out.

"Aunt Camille, the most terrible thing has happened!" Belle told her aunt about the morning and Jane's predicament.

"I should have known better than to hire a woman like that. I trusted her." Mrs. Marshall stared at Lily. "And you. You recommended her."

"I stand by that recommendation. This is a terrible mistake, Mrs. Marshall. You'll see."

The older woman pursed her lips. "To think we harbored

someone who would help steal Everett's prized possession. She will no longer be in our employ, even if she didn't murder that poor woman."

"Yes, ma'am."

"Isn't the baby darling though?" Belle hugged Hannah to her chest. "I want to help take care of her until Jane is released. And if she never gets out, I'll keep her."

"You'll do no such thing! You're taking on a huge responsibility, and your future husband may have something to say about it."

"We'll see." Belle's chin tipped up. "I'm sure Stuart will have no objections."

The open draperies did little to block the afternoon sun slanting into the drawing room. The space felt stifling, and Drew tugged on his tie.

Dressed in a gray morning coat, Everett stepped into the room with an abstracted air. He shook Drew's hand. "It's a nasty business, Drew. You heard one of our housemaids was arrested?"

Drew's next breath hitched in his chest. "No, I hadn't heard. What's happened?"

"Our cook's assistant, Jane White, let that woman in to steal the butterfly I'd just received. She and Mrs. Karr were at odds in the past, and the White girl has been accused of the murder."

Drew exhaled. At least it wasn't Lily in trouble, but he liked Jane and knew Lily would be distressed. He couldn't imagine quiet Jane killing anyone. "I'm sorry to hear it. Has your butterfly been found?"

Everett shook his head. "I told Karr if I got it back safe and sound, I wouldn't press charges, but he looked me in the eye and denied he had it." He moved to the table and poured himself a drink. "Scotch?"

"No, thank you." Everett glanced at the window, then frowned. Drew turned to look too and saw Lily and Belle getting out of the carriage. Belle was carrying something, and a closer look revealed she held Jane's baby. Lily had several bundles in her arms.

"What the devil is she doing?" Everett muttered. The entry door opened, and he called his niece's name.

When the women entered the room, Drew moved to help Lily with the bundles. The items were soft, likely clothing. He tucked them under his arm.

"This is Hannah, Uncle Everett." Belle's smile was coaxing. "Isn't she adorable?"

"Where did you get this child?"

"Her mama is Jane White, who is in jail. Someone had to take charge of her, so I decided to do it." Belle kissed the little one's cheek.

His brow raised, Drew glanced at Lily, who shrugged. While it was good news for Hannah that Belle had taken such interest in her, he had to wonder how long it would be before her interest waned. She didn't seem the motherly type, but maybe he was wrong.

"I bought her some things, and I'm putting her in my old nursery. My old baby bed is being scrubbed and assembled."

Everett tossed back another Scotch. "I'm surprised at you, Belle. The child's mother is a common thief."

"Where's your charity, Uncle? The poor waif must be fed and clothed. I'm not turning her over to the orphanage." She smiled and turned the baby to face him. "And while I was in town, I stopped by the newspaper office. They're sending out a photographer to take a picture of you with the baby. Your generosity will be front-page news the week before the election."

Everett stared at her, then smiled. "You will be the consummate wife of a politician. I'm astonished at how well you think things through."

Belle smiled and went to sit on the sofa with the child. "Stuart doesn't know what he's getting yet, does he?"

"Does he know you've taken on this child?" Drew asked. They had to get more details from Vesters. The election was approaching much too quickly, and they still didn't know how he planned to murder Everett.

"Not yet. He's coming by this afternoon, and I'll tell him them." Belle reached forward and selected a cookie from the silver tray on the table.

The baby squawked, and Lily hurried to take her. "She is hungry. I'll feed her in the kitchen."

"Bring her back to me when you're done."

"I'll go with you." Drew was eager to find out what had brought about the transformation in Belle.

Belle smoothed her hair, then pinned on a smile and stepped into the parlor. She should go on the stage. It was quite clear she had acting ability. "Hello, Stuart, I've been counting the minutes until you arrived." She offered her cheek to him and managed not to grimace when his whiskers ground into her skin.

She skittered away as quickly as possible. "I've ordered tea. A reporter from the newspaper is coming soon to take a picture of me."

His eyes went wide in his round face. "Whatever for?" He smiled. "It seems I came at the right time. Is it for an engagement announcement?"

"Partially. I don't think you've met our kitchen maid Jane." She told him about the events that had transpired since dinner the night before.

Stuart absorbed the news silently at first. He turned his back and went to pour himself a drink at the sideboard.

"Tea is coming, as I said."

"I think I need something stronger than tea." He turned with the glass in his hand. "Let us get something straight right now, Belle. I expect my wife to consult me before she makes any major decisions."

"Helping care for a baby is hardly major." She attempted a laugh, but it came off hollow. Even though she knew she wouldn't marry him, his hostility took her aback. "And the picture will be good for Uncle Everett's election."

He waved his hand. "That hardly matters when I'm discussing what I expect from a wife."

She had to bite her tongue to keep from spitting out a tart reply. The maid came in with tea and cookies. "Put the tray on the table." She took a couple of deep breaths to regain her composure and think about how to answer.

Emily's gaze darted from her to Stuart and back again as if she felt the tension in the air. "Anything else, miss?"

"Bring the baby to me when she awakens."

"Of course." Emily scurried away.

Belle sent a coaxing smile Stuart's direction. "Once you see the baby, you'll understand why I did this."

"I have no desire to see the squalling brat." He gulped down his drink in one big swallow.

"I find your attitude most peculiar. It gives me pause about our engagement. I want to have children, of course. I thought you would like children and would make a loving father."

His stern expression softened. "Our own children will be quite different, of course."

"Will they? And how will I know that? The poor little mite has been left all alone, and yet you would deny her love and support for the few days Jane will be in jail. I thought better of you, Stuart."

"The child is not the point. Doing this without asking me is the base of my objection."

She lifted her chin and narrowed her eyes. "I am a modern woman with a mind of my own. I find no need to ask permission for every decision. And furthermore, I refuse to do it. If that's going to be a source of conflict, then you can take your ring back right now." She wrenched it from her finger and held it out.

He backed away and held his hands up. "No, no, Belle. I love your independence. But can't you see how any couple needs to discuss decisions of great import? I wouldn't make a major decision myself without talking to you. I would not have taken on the care and support of a child without making sure you had no objections."

She let the silence hover between them a moment before she nodded. "I see your point. Perhaps I should have let you know what I was thinking, but there was no time. The child was hungry, wet, and in need. It was the Christian thing to do."

"Of course, of course. I was speaking without thinking. I see now I was wrong."

She let him take her hand and lead her to the sofa. "I accept your apology."

He swallowed hard. "Let's put it behind us, my dear. It was a very minor spat."

Lily stepped into the parlor with little Hannah in her arms. "She's awake, Miss Belle. I swear, she was looking around as though she missed you. I changed her and brought her down."

Indeed, the little mite appeared to brighten when she spied Belle. She reached pudgy fingers toward her, and Belle stood to catch her as she lunged. The baby smelled deliciously of talcum and soap. "I assume she'll be hungry soon?"

"I fed her when she awakened."

Belle had been looking forward to cuddling the little one while she took her bottle. "Next time I'd like to feed her myself."

"Of course." Lily's gaze locked on Stuart.

Belle glanced at her fiancé and found him staring at the baby. His expression was most peculiar—part repulsion and part fascination. "Are you all right, Stuart?"

He blinked before his gaze moved to her. "Of course. Sh-She looks like her mother."

Belle's pulse jumped in her throat. "You know Jane?"

"I've seen her, of course. The blond woman. In fact, she and Lily look quite a bit alike."

Belle turned to stare at Lily. "You're right. I'd never really noticed." She glanced back at Stuart and frowned. He was staring at Lily with an almost murderous expression.

It was all most peculiar.

# THIRTY

Lily had waited in the wings while Belle posed with Hannah for the picture with her uncle. Stuart had stared at her nearly the entire time. He'd then sat with Belle for the engagement photograph. His glower cast a pall over the day until the door finally shut behind him.

Belle had changed into her gray silk for dinner and sat in a chair in the conservatory. She looked lovely with her hair up except for one long curl hanging over one shoulder. Lily hated being in here. Too many butterflies stared at her from their frames on the walls. Some were even suspended from the ceiling.

Lily straightened the cushions. "Will Mr. Vesters be back for dinner?"

"Unfortunately, yes." Belle gave a heavy sigh. "It's an important dinner for my uncle's campaign. The election's in a week. Uncle Everett is trying to rally all last-minute support to seal his certain victory."

"Things seemed a bit tense when I came in with Hannah. Did you discover anything?"

"Only that he seemed to have an inflated view of his importance in my decision making." Belle picked a thread from her skirt. "The very idea that I should have to ask his permission for something like that."

"I noticed he stared at Hannah quite a lot." Lily made sure to keep her voice neutral.

"I saw that. I think maybe he hasn't been around babies very much."

"Perhaps."

Belle stared at her. "Do you know something? Your tone is very strange."

"I'm just tired." Lily wished she could tell Belle the truth, but it wasn't her story to share. The truth would come out sooner or later. "Did your uncle hear anything when he went to the police station?"

"He's very angry. Jane can't come back here, of course."

Lily's eyes burned. "Can you not prevail upon your uncle for mercy? Jane was put in a very bad position. She didn't know Mrs. Karr wanted to steal it. She was threatened. All she was doing was trying to save her job by what seemed a harmless peek at the butterflies."

"I can try, but surely you can see the position Uncle Everett is in. How can he trust her? He has very valuable things in this house. And the butterfly *is* missing."

"Jane didn't steal it. I know she didn't."

Belle's gaze softened. "You're a good friend, Lily." She rose from the damask seat and wandered to study an orchid petal. She picked a bloom and handed it to Lily. "Put this in my hair, please."

Lily secured the fragrant white flower. "You look beautiful. Who are you trying to impress tonight?"

"Stuart, of course. If I bewitch him, maybe he will let something slip."

"You did well to find the note about next Thursday. Just five days away. Perhaps Drew will uncover everything."

"I'm not hopeful. The conspirators seem to be very good. Their plan isn't easily discovered. I'll have to tell Uncle Everett."

Lily knew Drew wouldn't want her to encourage Belle to do that, but she nodded. "I agree. Drew thinks it will do no good to try to dissuade your uncle, but we can't let him walk into a trap with no warning."

"What if I came right out with the question to Stuart? I could tell him I'd heard a rumor there was a plot to kill Uncle Everett. I won't say he was under suspicion. He might leave here and go straight to see his associates. It might tell us something."

Lily frowned and tried to examine the idea from all angles. On the surface, it appeared to have value. "Drew won't like it."

Belle turned and smiled. "Drew doesn't have to know."

"We'll need someone to follow Mr. Vesters."

"We can do it."

"Your uncle wouldn't want you out that late. I'll do it. I can dress like a man and follow from a distance."

"Only if I go too. There is safety in numbers. We'll take the buggy. It's quieter than the automobile. He'll never notice us behind him."

Emily stepped into the doorway. "Our dinner guests are arriving. Mr. Vesters has asked for you, Miss Belle."

Belle groaned. "Coming." She put her fingers to her lips. "Stay close, Lily. And be ready."

The sun was beginning to set as Lily packed the last of her things in a crate to take to the big house, then handed it to Drew, who stacked it by the door. She couldn't stay here with Jane in custody, so she would be moving back to the third floor with Emily, at least until Jane was released. Nathan was living here, and it wouldn't be proper for just the two of them to be here alone.

She tipped her head and listened. "Are those footsteps?" She went to the door and flung it open. Nathan stood on the doorstep, his green eyes desolate. He swept a cap off of his brown hair.

She stepped aside to allow him to enter. "Any news? I'd hoped to see Jane with you."

He shook his head. "The police seem sure she killed Mrs. Karr. I know my sister, and it's impossible." He flung himself onto the broken-down sofa, then put his head in his hands. "I don't know what to do. There's only me and Jane left. I can't let her go to prison."

Drew took her hand and squeezed it. "What evidence do they have, Nathan? Did they tell you?"

"The servants have told the police lies. I don't know how to counteract them."

*Lies?* Was there more Lily hadn't heard? "What did the servants say?"

Nathan's head was still down so the words came out as a mumble. "Mrs. Karr told the servants Jane had stolen before."

"Jane is no thief!"

"That doesn't even make sense," Drew said. "Mrs. Karr came to the house for a reason. I suspect she came to steal the butterfly. So she's the thief, not Jane."

Nathan raised his head. "I told the police the same thing. Officer Pickle agreed with me, but he said Mr. Karr said Jane had given stolen goods to sell to a middleman. It's his word against hers, and who do you think they'll believe?"

Lily clutched Drew's hand to keep her outrage in control. "It's so unfair!"

"And it's not true. My sister was a good girl. It's not her fault she's in this situation—it's all the Karrs' fault." Nathan's voice vibrated with rage. "Because of them, Jane is rotting in that jail without Hannah."

"Did you get to see her?" Drew asked.

Nathan sat up. "No, but I'm sure she's never stopped crying for Hannah. Where is my niece?"

"At the big house. Miss Belle has taken a shine to her." Lily told him how Belle had bathed the baby and bought her clothing. "She plans to care for her until Jane is set free."

Nathan rubbed his forehead. "I don't feel right taking her charity. Hannah should be here with me."

"And how will you take care of her without Jane? You have to work and so do I. Jane was the only one with the flexibility to come and go a bit."

Nathan dropped his head into his hands again. "I have to fix this, but I don't know how. Jane will go mad in jail. She is afraid of tight places. Besides, she's never been apart from Hannah, not even for one night. Has the baby cried for her?"

"Luckily, she's familiar with me. She refused the bottle for a little while, but once she was hungry enough, she took it. She seems content." When Nathan hunched into himself even more, Lily rushed to reassure him. "Of course she'll be missing Jane more tomorrow, but she's a resilient little one. She's used to being cared for by several of us. By the time she's too fractious, Jane will be home. I'm sure of it." She put more certainty into her voice than she felt because she wasn't at all sure the police would investigate to find the real killer.

"I hope so." Nathan jumped to his feet. "I'm going back to the police station. I have to make them listen."

Drew let go of Lily's hand and blocked Nathan's path. "Let me go with you tomorrow. In your state, you're more likely to do more harm than good."

"Why do you care? You don't even know Jane all that well."

"Jane is important to Lily, and Lily is important to me. And even a casual acquaintance can tell what kind of person Jane is. Let me help."

Nathan stared at him, then nodded. "Maybe you can get them to let me see her."

"You'll have to go to work soon," Lily said. "I'd like to come too. Then if you have to leave, I can report to you how she's doing."

"Thank you for being so good to her. You've been a good friend."

Lily blinked back the moisture in her eyes. "I wish I could do more. Do you have any idea what happened to the butterfly? If we could find who took it, we might get the police to listen."

Nathan hesitated. "There's a man who sells valuable insects to collectors. He might know if the Karrs were looking for this specific butterfly."

"Do you know how we could contact him?" Drew asked.

Nathan looked down at the floor. "I'll do it in the morning." He headed for the bedroom door.

Drew moved closer, and Lily wanted to sink against his warmth and comfort. "How could this happen, Drew? I know she's innocent."

He draped his arms around her and pulled her close. "I love how you care about injustice in the world. Life seems unfair, but you never stop trying."

"For all the good I manage to do." She stayed in the circle of his arms until he touched her chin and tipped her mouth up to meet his. While his kiss didn't make the injustice go away, it gave her strength to deal with it. "I want to come with you tomorrow."

"I'd rather you didn't."

"I have to see her and make sure she's all right."

He hugged her. "I love your heart. But if it's too bad, I want you to wait in the automobile."

She bit her lip and nodded. Nothing would keep her from seeing Jane.

Belle smiled at Stuart over the rim of her glass. "I'll be so glad when this election is over. It's actually a little scary."

He tugged on the neck of his shirt. His face was scarlet above his tie. "Scary, my dear? Hardly. It's quite exhilarating. And don't be fearful. Your uncle is sure to win."

"It's not the winning I fear." She eyed him, unsure if she should continue. What if this was the wrong way to approach it? But they had to flush him out. Her uncle's life was at stake.

"Then what?" He motioned to Lily for more wine, and she hurried to refill his cup.

Good. Perhaps he would be too inebriated to think through her questions. She leaned closer to whisper in his ear. He smelled sweaty, but she managed not to recoil. "I've heard a rumor, Stuart. It's quite terrifying. Have you heard anything about a plot to assassinate my uncle after he's elected?"

He gasped and began to cough. She slapped him on the back. "Are you all right?" The rest of the guests were staring, and she smiled. "He swallowed his wine the wrong way."

He wheezed, then his breathing eased into a more normal pattern. "I'm fine, fine." But his eyes were cold and wary as he stared at Belle. "Where did you hear such nonsense? Did you hear who might be involved in this so-called plot?"

She shook her head. "I have no idea. I overheard a snippet of conversation."

"Between whom?" He took a cautious sip of water.

Reckless bravery. That's what was required here. "Between Mr. Hawkes and another man. I don't know who he was."

Stuart went white, then red. He cast a venomous glare across the table at Hawkes. Had she gone too far? If he was too angry with Hawkes, might he try to harm him? But she'd thought if he suspected Hawkes wasn't on his side, he might let something slip.

He rose and tossed his napkin to the chair. "I'm afraid I'm not feeling well, Belle. I am going to take my leave now, and we'll talk more tomorrow. Put this ridiculous nonsense out of your mind though. Your uncle is perfectly safe." He made his excuses to her uncle, then headed for the door.

She bent to whisper in her aunt's ear. "I'm not feeling well myself, Aunt Camille. I'm going to go on to bed. Please make my excuses with your guests later."

"I'll send Lily to tend you."

"Thank you." Belle hurried from the dining room and turned to see Lily on her heels.

"Quick! I have a buggy waiting out the side door." Lily rushed down the hall and wrenched open the door that opened onto the side street. Moonlight peeked from behind the clouds scudding across the dark sky. "There he goes." She pointed as a carriage emblazoned with an eagle rattled by.

Lily helped her into a buggy hitched to a black horse. "We have to catch him." She hoisted her skirt and clambered onto the seat of the open buggy.

Belle climbed onto the seat. "You should have had Henry here. We'll never catch him."

"Watch me." Lily seized the reins and urged the horse into a canter.

The buggy sped down the street in the direction where they'd last seen Stuart. Belle was impressed at how Lily handled the horse. "Were you close enough to see Stuart's reaction?"

Lily shook her head. "I saw his face go red though, and then he left. He was upset you'd heard the rumor?" She slapped the reins on the horse's rump.

"It was more than that. I told him I overheard Mr. Hawkes telling someone else about the plot."

Lily gasped and glanced at her before turning her attention back to the horse. "Miss Belle, you didn't! He might harm Drew. Oh, this is terrible."

"I think it might flush him out. We'll warn Mr. Hawkes to be on his guard. I'm sure he would be quite willing to be bait."

"You should have discussed it with him first." Lily urged the horse around a corner. "There, is that Vesters ahead?"

Belle squinted. "I think so. That looks like his coat of arms on the back. But he's not going in the direction of the house. See, he's turning off."

"I suspect he's going to see his associate. Maybe to discuss getting rid of Drew." Lily's voice was tight. "We must find out what they are doing and warn Drew."

"Drew will be fine. We must save my uncle."

# THIRTY-ONE

Belle's mysterious disappearance hadn't escaped Drew. When Vesters rushed off, Drew had stepped into the hallway and had seen the two women hurry out the side door. He caught Emily in the hall and asked her to make his excuses to Mrs. Marshall, then he followed Lily and Belle into the fragrant night air.

The buggy was already far in the distance by the time he stood along the side of the road. How could he follow them? He spied a bicycle leaning against a bush, probably left by one of the servants, so he grabbed it and pedaled after the buggy as fast as he could. The muscles in his thighs burned as he kept the wheels spinning faster and faster. He would not be able to catch them, but he hoped to at least keep them in sight.

What were they thinking to rush off into the night after Vesters? What had he said to trigger such reckless behavior? Drew worried the questions around in his head but didn't come up with a suitable answer. The buggy veered to the left ahead of him, and he frowned. They weren't going to Vesters's house as he'd expected. The buggy turned again, down an unfamiliar side road. It seemed to be slowing, then the vehicle pulled to the right and stopped. There must be a house there.

His thighs were on fire from the exertion, but he forced himself to go faster until the buggy was close enough for him to see the two women clamber down. He pulled off the road and dismounted behind the buggy. The women stood talking softly when he stepped around the end of the buggy.

"What are you two doing? Trying to get killed?" It was too dark to see their expressions well, but he saw Lily turn toward him.

"Drew, what are you doing here?"

"I just asked you the same thing. It's not safe out here by your-selves." He reached them and took her by the arm. "What's going on?" The fragrance of honeysuckle in her hair made him want to hold her and make sure she was all right. "You scared me out of a year of life."

"Belle tried to flush out Mr. Vesters tonight at dinner. I think it worked."

"Flush him out." He listened to Lily's explanation of the dinner conversation. "That was pretty brilliant, Belle. Now he's going to come after me, and I'll be able to figure out who he's working with."

"That was the plan." Belle's voice held a lilt. "You're not frightened?"

"I can handle myself. Where is he?"

Lily pointed down the street. "He parked his buggy, then walked on down the street. Mr. Ballard lives on this street, Drew. We couldn't tell which house Vesters went into though. The moon went behind the clouds when he got out of his buggy. I know it's not the first or second house, but we couldn't see beyond that. Lights are on in all the houses, so we can peer in the windows until we find him."

He released her arm. "You go back home. I'm going to find out."

"If you think we came all this way to miss the excitement, you are wrong, Mr. Hawkes." Belle started down the street with deter-mined steps. "Come along, Lily."

He sighed, recognizing when he was whipped. "Stay close to me, Lily. I don't want anything to happen to you."

Her fingers crept into his. "I'm more fearful for you. What if he ambushes you?"

"This is what I do. I'll be fine." He quickened his steps and fell in beside Belle.

The lights in the second house went out as they approached the sidewalk. He strode along the iron fence to the third house in the row. All the houses here were well kept and rather grand. Not as fancy as the Butterfly Palace, but beautiful all the same. The third house was a Georgian with manicured shrubs and a large rose garden. Lights shone from what appeared to be a parlor.

"Stay here." He opened the gate and slipped into the yard, then approached the window. A man and woman sat sipping tea on the sofa. No sign of Vesters. He retreated to where the women waited. "He's not there."

"Th-The next house belongs to Mr. Ballard." Lily's voice was tight. "Let me check it."

He shot her a glance. "I'd rather you didn't."

She quickened her steps to the gate. Without answering him, she opened the gate and sidled through the yard. He pressed his lips together and followed her. She hurried to the large window where light spilled into the yard.

Vesters, the movements of his arms punctuating whatever he was saying, stood talking to a man with his back to Drew. Then he turned. "That's Ballard's son, Norris." This had to convince her Ballard was as black as the night sky. Vesters was in the Ballard house.

"Someone's coming!" Belle's hushed voice came out of the darkness. "Hide."

He glanced around to see her dive into the bushes. He dragged Lily into the shadows, and they crouched behind a yew shaped like a sheep. The front door opened, and a woman stepped into view.

"It's Mrs. Ballard," Lily said in his ear.

"Is someone out here?" the woman called.

Norris joined her in the doorway. "What's going on, Grandmother?"

"I thought I heard a voice."

"No one's there. It was probably a passerby." He pulled her back inside and the door shut.

Lily exhaled. "Could Norris be involved in this?"

Drew pressed his lips together. "I'm going to find out."

Belle found her uncle perusing the paper over his eggs and toast. "Good morning, Uncle Everett. Is that a new morning coat? You look very dashing. I like the gray stripe."

"It is." He folded the paper and laid it aside. "What happened to you last night? Half the dinner party disappeared. Surely it wasn't the food."

"Stuart and I had a—a little spat."

He frowned. "It's all resolved now?"

She seated herself beside him and rang for her breakfast. "Oh yes. He's taking me for a ride in the park this afternoon. You know how these things can blow up out of nothing."

His expression cleared. "Very good. I want you settled, my dear. Have you set a date yet?"

"Not yet. I'm thinking next fall though." For the first time, her lies bothered her. Her uncle loved her, and it was painful to deceive him. She wanted to tell him about the assassination plot, but Lily had convinced her to hold her tongue for one more day to try to discover the co-conspirators.

Lily brought in a tray of coddled eggs, toast, and jam. She poured the tea and set the food in front of Belle, then backed off and stood at a discreet distance.

Uncle Everett picked up his knife and spread jam on his toast. "That's a bit far off, don't you think?"

"Not at all. It will take time to have the wedding dress made as well as all the clothing for the honeymoon. We're going to Europe."

His smile was soft and reminiscent. "Camille and I went to the south of Spain for our honeymoon. It was quite lovely."

"I think we'll make a visit there as well." She studied his face. "There's something I'd like you to do for me in lieu of a wedding gift, Uncle."

His expression went wary. "This sounds serious."

"I don't want little Hannah to grow up without her mama. Would you visit the police station and see if you can get Jane released?"

He slammed his fist down on the table. "Absolutely not, Belle. Have you forgotten my butterfly is still missing? I believe she is in this nasty mess clear up to her neck. That child is better off without a mother like that."

She put her hand over his. "Please, Uncle Everett. I don't believe Jane had anything to do with the theft of your butterfly. She thought the woman only wanted to look at it. I believe her story."

He glared at Lily, who was standing by the wall. "Come here, Lily. Come on, I won't bite."

Her head high, Lily approached the table. "Would you like more toast, sir?"

"I want to know why you would recommend someone like that into our employ. You knew she'd had a baby out of wedlock, correct?"

Lily nodded. "There were unusual circumstances though, sir. Jane was not at fault." Spots of color stained her cheeks, and she looked at the carpet. "She was—forced into the situation."

His mouth dangled open several seconds before he shut it with a snap. "I find myself quite disbelieving of such a story. It makes a convenient excuse."

Lily bit her lip but held his gaze. "It's no excuse, sir. Jane is an honorable woman. All she wants is to be left in peace to work and raise her daughter. She asks for nothing beyond that."

Belle put her hand on her uncle's arm. "Please, Uncle Everett. See what you can do to get her out. Hannah has been quite fretful, and I know she misses her mother."

"What are you going to do with that child? I suspect Miss White will either hang or go to prison for the rest of her life."

"Not if you can intervene. Otherwise, I'll raise her myself."

He scowled. "That's not a good idea. What do you know of raising children, especially the child of a murderer?"

"The baby had nothing to do with that woman's death!" Belle took a sip of her tea. "You're being very obstinate. You could help, but you refuse to because of a silly butterfly."

"That butterfly is worth a great deal of money." He rose and threw his napkin to the table. "I'm not going to discuss it anymore. And you need to make alternate arrangements for the child. She isn't going to stay here for long."

"The phone has already been ringing with people congratulating you on your largesse," Belle said. "Caring for Hannah will win you votes. Interceding for her mother would win you even more votes as it will show your strong support of women."

"I doubt that. Men will say I'm too soft to send a woman to the gallows. I have no choice in this, Belle. You don't understand politics."

She rose and faced him. "I understand it perfectly well. You are hardhearted and cruel." She burst into tears and rushed from the room.

Lily followed Belle to her bedroom, where she found her staring out the window with Hannah in her arms. "I want to go see Jane. If your uncle won't help, maybe the police would listen to you. Drew is bringing the car around at nine."

"We can try, but I'm not hopeful." Belle kissed the top of the baby's head. "Let's go now before I lose my courage. We'll take Hannah. Maybe that will sway the police."

They rode in silence with Drew and Nathan to the jail. After nearly half an hour of arguing, Lily and Nathan were finally let in to see Jane, but they refused to let them take the baby, so Belle stayed behind with Hannah. When they stepped into the cell block, Lily saw her sitting on a cot with her head down, the picture of despondency.

She rushed toward her. "Jane!"

Jane looked up and joy lit her features. She leaped to her feet and rushed to the bars. "You came to get me out? Where's Hannah?" She was dressed in a shapeless gray gown the police had given her, and her hair hung out of its bun onto her shoulders. Though disheveled, she looked beautiful and vulnerable. Lily ached to make it right, to get her out of there. The injustice of it all nearly did her in.

"Stand back," the gruff officer ordered. "Or I'll escort your visitors out of here."

"Visitors? Then I haven't been released?" Jane began to cry, no sound but with large tears coursing down her cheeks. She backed away from the bars. "Where's Hannah? How is my baby? She needs to be fed."

"She's fine. Miss Belle has her in the other room. She's demanded to see the officer in charge and is trying to insist Hannah be allowed to see you." The officer retreated a few feet, and Lily stepped as near to the bars as she could. "We fetched goat's milk from the neighbors. You should have seen the faces she made at the bottle's nipple, but she drank it. Miss Belle has taken a great interest in her and even had her own crib brought down from the attic and set up for Hannah."

Jane sniffled. "Hannah's in the big house?"

Lily nodded, forcing herself to smile. "And Miss Belle bought her some new gowns and nappies. Hannah is being very well taken care of. And luckily she's used to so many of us. She's doing fine, Jane, really. We'll get you out of here soon, but in the meantime, I wanted you to know you needn't worry about Hannah. We're all looking out for her."

Nathan tried to smile but the effort was more like a grimace. "They feeding you okay in here, Janey?"

"I—I couldn't eat. I'm sure it was fine though." She stared at her brother. "They said I murdered her, Nathan. If I wanted to kill Mrs. Karr, I would have had plenty of opportunities. Lord knows I had reason, but I wouldn't do anything like that."

"I know you wouldn't, and we'll convince the police."

"How?" Her voice was desolate. "They're convinced."

"Do you have any idea where that butterfly went?" Lily asked. "If we can just find that thing, we might be able to figure out what happened."

Jane went still, and her blue eyes widened as she thought it over, then she shook her head. "I've thought and thought about every moment. I should have thrown her out of the house the minute she showed up. Why, oh why was I so stupid?" She began to cry again.

"Stay calm, Jane. We need you to help us." The quiet strength in Nathan's voice had a calming effect in the room. "Think about everything that happened, everything she said to you. Take us through every minute of the day. Can you do that? Only you can help us, Jane."

Jane started to relax and she nodded, then exhaled. "All right, yes. I'll try."

Nathan nodded. "Good girl. Were there any other visitors before Mrs. Karr arrived? What other servants were around?"

"I started the pies around ten. I was planning on veal cutlets for dinner with herbed potatoes and vegetables. Emily helped me peel the potatoes, then she left to run some errands for Mrs. O'Reilly."

"Where was Mrs. O'Reilly, and what was she doing?"

Lily stared hard at Nathan. "We want to exonerate Jane, but I don't want to implicate Mrs. O'Reilly."

"I'm just trying to get to the bottom of what happened yesterday." Nathan looked back at Jane. "Where was Mrs. O'Reilly?"

"We were having weekend guests, so she was upstairs preparing the room for their arrival. She left me the keys so I could get into the wine cellar."

Nathan frowned and glanced at Lily. "Did any guests arrive?"

Lily shook her head. "They canceled at the last minute."

"Okay, so Mrs. O'Reilly told the truth. Then what happened?"

"I was pounding the veal to tenderize it. I heard a tap on the window of the back door, so I wiped my hands and went to answer it. I saw Mrs. Karr through the window and nearly turned back around and left her to cool her heels."

"Why didn't you?" Nathan burst out.

Jane's lip trembled. "She was smiling, so I thought maybe she had finally come to apologize for what she did to me. Not that an apology could make it right, but she should at least realize how she ruined my life."

"So you opened the door," Drew prompted.

Jane nodded. "I opened it and asked her what she wanted. She said, 'I want a favor, Jane. I want you to show me Mr. Marshall's new butterfly.' I laughed and started to close the door. She put her

249

foot in it and told me if I didn't let her in, she was going to call on Mrs. Marshall. She would tell her I'd stolen silver and that she'd been appalled to find out I'd been hired at the Butterfly Palace."

"Do you think Mr. Karr sent her?" Lily asked.

"I don't doubt it. Mr. Karr was quite fond of his butterflies."

Drew leaned forward. "So you let her in and showed her to the basement."

Lily nodded. "I didn't have any choice. I knew I'd be out on the street, and then what would happen to Hannah? She only wanted to look at it, not steal it. At least I didn't think she would take it."

"Yet you didn't go down with her. I think that's what confounds the police. If she was the evil person you claim, surely you would have gone down there with her, just to make sure."

Jane bit her lip. "I had dinner to get ready and not a moment to spare. A-And I hated being in her presence. Every minute with her made me remember what he did to me." Her voice wobbled. "I hated her. *Hated* her."

"Enough to kill her?" Drew asked quietly.

"Yes." Jane lowered her head. "I almost wish I'd done it because then being here almost might have been worth it." She burst into noisy sobs.

# THIRTY-TWO

Drew hadn't seen Vesters since Belle tossed out her bait, but that was about to end. He had been shown to the parlor and left cooling his heels while Vesters took his sweet time coming down. Drew had his story all planned out, but the question was whether or not Vesters would believe him.

When he heard heavy steps in the hall, he turned from his position by the window. "Ah, Stuart, there you are. Sorry to stop by unannounced, but I have some exciting news to share with you."

The thunderous expression on the other man's face smoothed. "Oh?"

"I know your partner didn't want me to be involved, but I've hired someone to arrange the perfect distraction while I put a bullet in Marshall's head."

The other man's jaw hardened. "You've cost me all manner of inconvenience, Hawkes. Blast you! Belle overheard you."

Drew feigned shock. "Belle heard me? I never saw her."

"She said she'd heard there was a plot to murder her uncle and asked me about it."

Drew made himself take a step back, then he spread out his hands in an appeal. "That's perfect, don't you see? No one will ever suspect you. When he's dead, Belle will tell the police what she overheard, and they'll come looking for me. I'll have a perfect alibi arranged, and we'll both escape suspicion."

"How will you explain yourself to the police?"

"I'll say I was investigating the rumor because Marshall and I were such great friends. They'll believe it."

Vesters stroked his whiskers and turned to pour a drink at the side table. "It might actually work. I'll talk to my partner about it. I like the idea." He tossed back the drink, then stared at Drew. "But I must say, it was very sloppy to allow yourself to be overheard. That concerns me, Hawkes. How do I know you won't mess up the assassination?"

"I think you've seen me enough to take my measure. This is something I have the skills for." He waited until Stuart's massive head finally nodded. "You won't be sorry."

"I hope not."

"How did you explain it to Belle?"

"I simply told her I'd look into it and that she had nothing to fear." His smile held no mirth. "And of course, I'll be there to comfort her when he's dead."

"Of course." Drew held out his hand. "So can we agree to do this together?"

After a hesitation, Vesters shook his hand. "Let's just say we'll agree to talk more about it."

Drew intended to be at the meeting on Thursday to find out more. It was clear Vesters was still being cagey.

Lily had decided to talk to Mr. Ballard at his knife factory office so there was no chance of Mrs. Ballard overhearing. The waiting room was painted a soothing green, and the furniture was new and uncomfortable. She sprang to her feet when Ballard himself appeared in the doorway looking quite agitated.

"Lily, is something wrong?"

She smiled and held out her hand. "Not at all, Mr. Ballard. I took a notion to drop by. I hope it's convenient."

His frown smoothed. "Of course, my dear, I'm always happy to meet you. I just sent a customer on his way, and I've got a few minutes before my next meeting. I'll have my secretary bring in tea." He ushered her into his office.

"No need. I don't want to be a bother in the middle of your workday." She glanced around the spacious room reeking of money with its leather furniture and masculine rug. "So this is where you make all your money."

He went around his desk to drop into the chair. "Mother hates coming down here. It's too nouveau riche for her. She forgets she'd be living on the streets if all we had was her precious Bostonian name."

Lily settled into the chair. "Something is troubling me, so the best way to deal with it is to ask outright."

"Honesty is always best, my dear."

"I have been poking into my father's death and something unexpected has come to light."

His expression grew wary. "And what is that?"

"A wallet was found in his hand. I've been told it belonged to a man named Ballard."

His expression didn't change, and he leaned back in his chair. "Do you think I had something to do with your father's death?"

"I don't know. I hope not." She held his gaze. "Did you?"

He chuckled, a laugh that sounded genuine. "Is it any wonder I'm so fond of you, Lily? You're so refreshingly honest. No beating around the bush."

She managed to smile back at him. "I could stew about it for months or just ask. So I'm asking."

"As well you should." He sat his chair back upright. "But no, I did not kill your father. My wallet was stolen two nights before. Ask the police. I reported it."

She wanted to believe him, but his story sounded entirely too well planned. Did he think she wouldn't check with the police?

"I'm glad we have that settled." He rose and came around the end of the desk.

She rose to meet him, and he embraced her. The hug felt as though it held genuine warmth. Or did she just want to believe it did?

He released her. "So you believe me?"

She nodded. "Thank you for not getting angry. I had to ask." She wanted to ask him about Norris, but it might reveal she knew too much. Still, this was her opportunity. "Does Norris know a man named Vesters?"

His brows drew together. "I would suppose so. Vesters purchases some of our products, and Norris sells for us. Why do you ask?"

"I saw them together the other day."

"Where?"

"It's not important." She moved toward the door.

"Stop by anytime, Lily. I'm always glad to see you."

He closed the door behind her, and she stood blinking in the bright sunshine. Though she'd hoped to have a clear feeling about his truthfulness, she found she was still full of questions.

Thursday came with a moonless night, clear enough that the stars sparkled in a black sky. Drew's feet ached from standing in the same position for half an hour, and he shuffled a bit from his vantage point behind a stand of live oak trees. He wasn't entirely sure this was the right spot along the river walk, but he'd spent most of the day strolling the area and figuring out where a secret meeting might best take place.

Lily had been despondent since they saw Jane, and he had vowed to do his utmost to clear her. Once he'd saved Everett, he could focus on Ballard again too. He didn't buy the man's story about losing his wallet.

He crouched down when he heard voices approaching. The shape of Stuart's head was unmistakable, bull-like with big ears. He didn't recognize the other person from this distance. There was only one way to find out.

Taking a deep breath, he slithered along the bank and came out at a curve. He brushed himself off and began to stroll as if he'd been on the path all along. When he rounded the crook, he came face-to-face with Vesters.

"Stuart, how pleasant to run into you." He thrust out his hand to shake.

Vesters hesitated, then took his hand in a firm grip. Drew got a better look at the man behind him. About fifty with a neatly trimmed beard and close-set eyes. He wore a bowler, and his suit was expensive. And Drew knew the man very well.

His boss, Ian Richardson.

He sent Ian a friendly smile. "Hello, I'm Drew Hawkes."

Ian masked his surprise well and shook his hand. "Ian Richardson. Pleased to meet you."

*I'll bet.* Drew managed to keep his simmering rage from erupting. "Beautiful night." He tipped his hat. "Good evening."

He didn't wait for a reply and strode away before he could throttle Ian. What was going on? Ian never seemed to be interested in politics, but here he was embroiled in a murder plot. No wonder he'd wanted Drew to stay out of the assassination plot and focus on the counterfeiting. He'd hoped his involvement with this wouldn't be discovered. For a moment Drew considered the possibility that Ian had other agents on this plot, but after consideration, he shook his head. There was no reason to keep it from Drew. He would have been the likely person to be involved.

Ian was a dirty agent.

Drew intended to go straight to the hotel and send a telegram to Washington. He might not be able to stop Ian, but the Secret Service could. And would. A rogue agent wasn't unheard of, but the agents worked hard to make sure a bad one didn't taint their reputation.

He heard rapid footsteps behind him and turned to see Ian practically running after him. He put his hands in his pockets and curled his fingers around his gun. Ian would likely try to persuade him of a lie and then would eliminate him if that didn't work. He stood and waited until his boss reached him.

"Drew, we need to talk."

The cold steel in his pocket was comforting. "You'll be able to explain yourself to Washington."

"It's not what it seems." Ian touched his arm. "We can't talk here. Let's go to your room. Too many people are around."

"I'm not sure it's safe to be alone with you."

Ian sighed. "How long have you known me?"

Drew looked away from the appeal in Ian's gray eyes. "Four years. Goes to show you how deluded we can be about people, doesn't it? I wouldn't have pegged you as a man who would ever sell out. How much money are you getting for this? Or is it power you're after? Maybe a cabinet position?"

"I thought you had more trust in me than that."

"Don't reverse the guilt here, Ian. I'm not the one who was playing two sides."

Ian glanced around at the couples strolling the walk lit with gaslights. "This way."

Drew followed until they were far enough away to be able to speak privately but not so far that the shadows would hide them if Ian tried to harm him. "Get it over with. I have a telegram to send."

Ian steepled his fingers. "We have an agent out there who has been living as a counterfeiter for fifteen years. He's the reason we've been able to put so many of them behind bars. His work is indispensable. You're putting his life in danger by your behavior."

"Right. You'd better come up with a better story than that, or I'm leaving."

"It's true." Ian held his gaze. "Think, Drew. I've never lied to you."

Drew struggled to hang on to his temper. "That I know of. You'd better tell me more details or that telegram is going out."

Ian stuffed his hands in his pockets. "This is a ring we've been tracking for eight years. It was too important to let slip away. There are lots of nuances to the plan to bring them in. And the plot to kill Marshall involves an attempt on an even bigger target."

"Who?"

"It depends on the results of the election. If Roosevelt wins, he may be assassinated."

"His stand on ending patronage?" Drew didn't need Ian's nod to recognize those behind it. Appointments for civil-service jobs had been based on favors and not merit. The elite hated that.

"The assassination plot is already in play."

Drew took a step back. "I don't believe you. If it was that serious, you would have brought me in on it." But the level gaze on Ian's face made his stomach clench.

"I'm telling you the truth."

"Then who is our inside man?"

"I'd rather not say."

Drew took a step toward the city lights. "Then this conversation is over."

Ian caught his arm. "Drew, it's Ballard."

Drew stared at him. "You're not saying *Ballard* is one of us?"

"That's exactly what I'm saying."

Drew shook his head, unable to take in the conviction in Ian's face. "What about the fire? You told me . . ."

"An accident. I am ashamed to admit I used it to fuel your determination to find the counterfeiters. A vendetta is a good motivator for a justice seeker."

*Wrong.* Drew had been wrong about everything. "Ballard has been trying to get to the bottom of the assassination attempt. Norris has gotten close to Vesters for that reason?"

Ian nodded. "Your meddling has nearly derailed what's really important. We don't care about the counterfeiters. We need to be able to stop any plan to kill Roosevelt. You need to back off."

"Vesters is part of that plan too?"

Ian nodded. "The plot goes deep."

Drew turned and plunged into the darkness. He'd been consumed with a blind vendetta.

# THIRTY-THREE

The noise of the cicadas rose in a raucous concert around Lily as she waited on the porch with Belle. Little Hannah slept with Emily watching over her. Drew should have been finished by now. He'd promised to stop by to report on what he'd discovered. No lights appeared in the windows of any of the houses down the street since it was after midnight.

She rose and walked along the length of the porch. "Surely he's done by now."

Belle's voice spoke out of the darkness. "Calm down. I'm sure he's fine."

"The meeting was supposed to be two hours ago." Lily stepped closer to the steps and peered down the dark street with its occasional illumination of gas streetlights.

Belle turned to face her. "Everything has changed in the last few weeks. My life is upside down. I never realized before how difficult life is for people like you and Jane. I've always had enough food, nice clothing, a beautiful home. I've taken it all for granted."

"My life hasn't been hard," Lily said. "We didn't have a lavish home, but it was nice enough. I've never gone hungry, and I'm thankful my mother taught me a skill."

Belle wore a softer expression than Lily had ever seen. "She taught you to care about other people too. It's a lovely trait, Lily. I've taken you for granted as well. These last few days have shown me how selfish my life has been up to now. All I've thought about is what I want."

Heat rushed to Lily's cheeks. "I have plenty of faults myself, Miss Belle. I'm no one to admire."

"I've been raised to believe life is all about power and money. I see now how silly that is. I've watched you pour yourself into other people ever since you've been here, both to people a bit higher up the social ladder like me and to those less advantaged like Jane. You don't seem to notice status."

Lily turned away from the admiration on Belle's face. "We are all the same inside. We have the same heartaches and joys, the same fears and ambitions. Money doesn't change who we are."

"Such a novel concept, but I suppose you're right. It's something I need to learn more about. I've watched you and Mr. Hawkes, you know. You're very fortunate. I've never been loved for myself alone. Stuart only wants me for my status and money." She sighed and turned away.

A figure approached from the street, and Lily recognized the wide shoulders. "Drew." She rushed down the steps, and everything in her sighed when his arms came around her in a solid embrace. He pressed his lips to her hair.

"Where have you been?" she whispered.

"I'll explain." There was a strange weariness in his voice.

Belle came to join them. "I want to hear everything."

Lily had her hand on his arm, and she could feel the tension in his muscles. "What's wrong?"

Drew looked weary, with drooping lids and circles under his eyes. "I've failed. I still have no idea what the plan is."

Belle put her hand to her mouth. "We have to tell Uncle Everett then. There's no choice. I have to make him stay home on Tuesday night."

"He'll pooh-pooh your concerns," Drew said. "You can try, but I don't believe there is any way of making him stay home."

Lily tightened her grip on his arm. "Then what can we do? Inform the authorities and have the police stake it out?"

Belle nodded. "Could we have the police arrest Stuart? I'm his fiancée. If I turn him in, surely the police will listen."

Drew hesitated. "There seems to be an even bigger matter at stake. A possible assassination attempt on the governor or even Roosevelt. I still don't know who all is involved. Even my boss doesn't know yet. We can't tip our hand until we know."

"So you're willing to let my uncle be killed instead?" Belle pointed her finger at Drew. "Well, I'm not. If you won't help, I'll inform the police of all I know."

"Give me a few more days," Drew pleaded. "I won't let anything happen to your uncle. I have some sources to check."

"And if you are unable to find the assassin?"

Drew held her gaze. "Then we'll go to the police together."

Belle pressed her lips together. "Very well. You have until Tuesday morning. If this plot isn't terminated, I'm telling Uncle Everett."

"Telling me what?"

Lily whirled and saw Mr. Marshall in his robe standing on the steps of the porch. Close enough to have heard everything. She glanced at Belle to see if she would be able to cover what they'd said.

Belle took a step toward her uncle. "About these two sneaking around behind my back."

Mr. Marshall came down the steps. "It hardly involves a plot. You'd better tell me all of it right now."

Lily glanced at Drew who was staring at Everett. Perhaps they'd been discovered for a reason.

Drew pocketed his hands. "I've uncovered a plan to kill you after you're elected."

Mr. Marshall frowned. "What's the reasoning?"

"The person involved plans to be appointed in your place," Belle said.

Mr. Marshall laughed. "That hardly sounds like a surefire way to get to be senator. What if the governor changes his mind? Or do you think the governor is in on it?"

"No, we don't believe the governor is involved." Drew explained what they knew so far.

"Who is this assassin?"

"I'd rather not say, Everett. Give me a chance to find out the rest of the key players before I reveal his name."

Mr. Marshall stroked his chin. "More than one conspirator, then."

Belle stepped closer to him and put her hand on his arm. "And if we can't stop them, you must stay home on Tuesday night."

"Then Drew must find them because I won't hide in my house when my supporters deserve my appearance to thank them. What kind of man would I be if I huddled behind the curtains?" He patted her hand still on his arm. "Say nothing of this to your aunt. I don't want to worry her. And put the entire problem out of your head. Drew and I will handle it."

He looked at his niece. "And I have talked to the police. They admit they have no real evidence against Jane. Their best investigator thinks Jane is too small to have delivered such a deep cut. Mrs. Karr was taller, and the angle would have been wrong. She's being released tonight."

"Uncle Everett!" Belle threw her arms around him and kissed him on each cheek. "You are wonderful."

He harrumphed. "Well, I hardly want the brat squalling in the house all the time." He shuffled back toward the door.

Lily put her hand to her throat. "Let's go get Jane!"

Mr. Marshall turned back a moment. "It's already done. Nathan is bringing her back here right now. She should be to the house in a few minutes."

Once Belle disappeared into the house behind her uncle, Lily turned to Drew and went into his arms. "I was so frightened. Was it terribly dangerous?" He smelled of soap and a manly scent that was all his own.

A lone buggy rattled by in the street, and the chorus of cicadas ebbed, then roared back.

He wrapped his arms around her in a comforting embrace. "It was a little tense for a few minutes, but it wasn't dangerous. Neither of them had a gun."

"Neither of who had a gun? Who did you see?"

He went quiet a moment. "How do you know when your trust is misplaced?"

"It was someone you knew?" She'd sensed something was troubling him. "Someone you care about?"

He nodded. "My boss, Ian Richardson. I've known him for all these years, but I'm not sure if he was telling me the truth tonight." His sigh was from his heart, heavy with disappointment. "I don't want to believe he's lied to me, but even more than that, I don't want to admit what the lie means."

"Lies about what?"

"This concerns you, Lily. Let's sit down." He led her up to the porch, past the gaslight, to the darkness at the far end of the porch. He sat on the swing, then pulled her into his lap.

She nestled in his arms and wished she never had to leave. His chest rose and fell under her cheek, and she wasn't sure she was ready to hear what he was about to tell her. Was this about their fathers' deaths? She wasn't going to start the conversation until he did. Maybe she would be better off not knowing.

His lips touched her hair, then traveled down the side of her face and across her cheek to settle gently on her lips. She offered him what comfort he could find in her kiss and wrapped her arms around his neck. The scent of his breath, the firm and confident way he held her, and the roughness of his chin anchored her in this moment. Her face and chest flamed with heat at the fire in his lips, but she didn't break the kiss until he did.

He exhaled. "You'll be the death of me, Lily."

She loved the way he came to life at her touch. She loved the way every inch of her skin seemed overly sensitive when he touched her. When she was around him, she knew nothing but the wonder of the fact he loved her.

She nestled against his heartbeat until he spoke. "I have to tell you."

"All right."

"Look at me, Lily."

She sat up and looked up into his face. "It's that bad?"

His eyes were anguished. "You were right about Ballard, if Ian is to be believed. According to Ian, Ballard's not the evil man I'd thought he was all these years."

She tried to make sense of what he was saying. Drew hated Ballard. "Does that mean he didn't kill our fathers?"

Drew nodded. "He's with the Secret Service too."

"Then who set the fire?"

He sighed and ran his hand through his hair. "It's all so murky. According to Ian, Ballard has been instrumental in bringing dozens of counterfeiters to justice over the years. His cover was nearly destroyed in Larson, which is why he had to move away so quickly."

She hoped Ballard might be a rescuer, a man of justice, like Drew. "I asked him about his wallet. He said it had been stolen several days before our fathers died. He suggested we check with the police, and we'd see he reported it."

"You went to see him again? Lily, you have to stop putting yourself in danger."

She nestled against him and ignored his exasperated tone. "But what about our fathers? Who killed them?"

Drew held her close. "No one. It was what it always appeared to be—an accident. I was so blinded by my need for revenge that I took every clue and turned it into something more than it appeared." He sighed and leaned his head back. "If I could allow my feelings to so completely blind me to the truth, what kind of agent does that make me?"

She touched his cheek. "You had just cause for your beliefs."

He shook his head. "This shakes up everything I believed about the work I was doing. How can I go on with a mission this important when I could be led by the nose by my feelings? I thought I had a good smell for the truth, but I don't."

What was he saying? "You're good at what you do, Drew. Even Ian would tell you that."

He leaned back and exhaled. "I'm going to resign, Lily. I'm a failure as an agent. I'll have to find another line of work."

Even while everything in her leaped for joy because this line of work was so dangerous, she couldn't ignore the depth of his disappointment in himself. "What will you do?"

"I don't know yet. I'll have to consider everything."

"I'll go wherever you want, Drew." She kissed him, trying to infuse him with her trust and confidence. "We'll be all right."

Lily's face hurt from smiling. She watched Jane hug Hannah to her chest. The little one reached up and patted her mama's cheek. "She missed you."

Tears shimmered in Jane's eyes. "I can't believe I'm free. Thank you all so much." She glanced at Drew and her brother, then back at Lily who sat in the other chair at the table with her.

"Cook sent over some food. Are you hungry?" Lily lifted the lid on the pot of beef stew.

"Not just yet. I want to hold Hannah." Jane brushed her lips over the baby's hair.

They talked a few more moments until Jane's head began nodding. "I'm so sorry. I haven't slept at all since I was arrested. People are screaming and shouting all night long."

"You'd better get to bed." Lily rose and opened the bedroom door for her. "Hannah is falling asleep too."

The men said good night, and Nathan left for his job while Drew lingered a moment. "I'll walk you out," Lily said.

She stepped out into the night air with him and rubbed her upper arms. An engine roared from somewhere down the street. "It's getting chilly at night now."

"Well, it *is* November."

His voice was quiet. She touched his arm. "Are you all right?"

"I just don't know, Lily. My life is turned upside down right now. I've been manipulated and lied to. The worst of it is, I realize my instincts aren't what I thought they were."

"You knew Ballard was hiding a secret. That was a good instinct."

He shook his head. "Good try, but it's little comfort."

She opened her mouth to try to reassure him, but she heard something from inside. A sliding noise, then a thump as though

266

something had fallen. "I hope Hannah didn't fall off the bed." She yanked open the screen door. "Jane?" There was no answer, but the air had a still quality. No crickets chirped. She went toward the door with Drew on her heels. "I'd better go first to make sure she's decent."

She rapped on the door. "Jane? Are you all right?"

When her friend didn't reply, she turned the doorknob. "It's locked." She pounded harder on the door. "Jane, open the door."

"Let me try." Drew moved her to one side, then yanked and twisted on the knob. When it didn't move, he took a step back. "Hang on, I'm going to bust it in." His powerful kick splintered the wood around the door frame. The second one released the lock, and he shoved open the door.

The first thing Lily noticed was the cloying coppery stench in the air. Then she saw Jane on the floor with blood pouring from her throat. As soon as she fell to her knees beside her friend and touched her arm, Lily knew she was dead.

# THIRTY-FOUR

Drew's eyes were gritty as he wrapped his hands around the hot coffee cup at the table in the dining room. The police had been here all night, but they finally left, carting poor Jane's body with them. The sweet scent of pancakes made his stomach rumble, but he didn't think he could eat. Not after seeing what that butcher had done to Jane.

Lily's eyes were red and swollen from crying. She hadn't let go of little Hannah since they'd found Jane. Luckily, the baby was fine. She'd slept through the whole attack.

"How did he get in?" Christopher asked. He was pale from lack of sleep, and his red hair stood up on top of his head.

Drew's gaze met Lily's. The bed had been moved. Could the killer have come through this house, even be a member of the household? They'd told the police all they knew, but he didn't want to worry the maids or Mrs. Marshall, who had spent all night calming her servants. They were all threatening to quit.

Christopher, Lily, and Drew were the only ones in the dining room, so he decided to speak freely. "Were you aware there is a secret passage running through the property?"

Christopher's brows rose. "You mean like in that house in Chicago, Holmes's place?"

The serial killer in Chicago had been caught ten years ago after murdering as many as two hundred people. He'd conducted his butchery via hidden passageways.

Drew shrugged. "Something like that."

Christopher poured maple syrup over his stack of pancakes. "Mother has never mentioned it. Did you tell the police?"

"I told the police. They are going to check it out."

"How interesting. Could you show me how you get in? I'd like to explore such a strange thing."

"We should probably stay out of there until the police make sure there's no killer lurking about."

Lily paced in front of the window. "Can we not talk about it right now? I can't bear it. And what about Hannah? She's motherless. Nathan can't care for her on his own."

Drew wanted to assure her they could marry and help with the baby, but if he quit his job like he was contemplating, he had no idea how he'd support her.

His future yawned as black as that secret passage.

The past few days had been a blur as Jane was buried. The papers luridly speculated about how a killer might have murdered a killer, but Drew knew the truth—the killer had come to finish the job. Jane was the only one who could identify him.

Drew and Nathan rode in Drew's automobile in the middle of the morning. "Thanks for coming with me, Mr. Hawkes. I can't stand the way everyone is talking about Jane. I want to clear her name."

"We'll find what happened to the butterfly. That will lead us to the next clue. We'll get to the bottom of what happened."

Drew followed Nathan's directions to the place of business, but the area of town was a surprise. The houses along the street were small but neat, and there was no trash along the ditches. Children played in the yards, and the few shops appeared reputable.

Drew stopped the automobile where Nathan indicated, and the two men approached the bungalow. Two small boys in knickers played hoops in the side yard, and a young woman, the hem of her skirt muddy, knelt over a tomato patch. Drew glanced at Nathan with a brow lifted, and Nathan shrugged, then rapped on the door.

"Door's open," a male voice called through the screen door.

Nathan pushed open the door, and Drew followed him into a small hall that opened into a parlor. A man about thirty years old knelt among cases of insect and flower specimens. There was a peculiar odor in the air.

When he saw them, he stood and dusted his hands on his pants, then smiled. "I'm Fred. What can I do for you?"

Drew shook his hand and introduced himself and Nathan. "We're looking for a butterfly specimen for a client."

Fred waved his hand expansively. "Butterflies are my specialty. Look around and see what you think. I have a new shipment that just came in from Africa." He grabbed a box from atop a cabinet in the corner. "Just look at these glorious creatures, especially this *Euphaedra janetta*. It's a real beauty."

For a second, Drew thought it was the one he sought, then he saw the yellow mixed in with the blue on the wings. He admired it, then turned to look at another case. "How'd you get into this business? I wouldn't think there would be all that much interest in insects. Not in Austin."

"Don't you read the papers? The craze for butterflies is everywhere. I know men who have hired African explorers to bring back specimens."

"We need a particular butterfly. A Blue Morpho."

The man's smile faded. "Why that specific one? It's very rare. Found only in South America. I'm not sure I can get you one."

"I'm willing to pay double the going rate." Drew pulled out his wallet.

One of the boys banged into the house shouting for his father. Fred went to talk quietly with him a moment, then returned with a more confident air. "I'll see what I can do. It might take a few days. I do have a lead on one."

"A lead?"

Fred nodded. "It's well known I deal in insects. A woman offered to sell me one a few days ago, but the amount of money she wanted seemed outrageous so I turned her down."

"I don't care what it costs. I want one."

"Fine. I'll get in touch with her."

*A woman.* Drew turned the knowledge over in his mind. Could it be someone who worked for Karr? He was nearly as obsessed with butterflies as Everett. "Do you have her name?"

The man laughed. "Do you take me for a fool? If I give you her name, you'll contact her yourself and cut me out."

Drew shrugged. "I was just curious. We have a deal. I wouldn't back out on it. Butterfly collectors tend to be friends, and I thought I might know her."

Fred looked cagey. "A man has to make a living, you know. Come back tomorrow, and I'll have that butterfly for you. I'll tell you her name then."

"How much money should I bring?" Drew asked. The price Fred named made him gulp, but he nodded. "We'll be here."

"Make it around three. That should give me enough time." He escorted them to the door.

When they stepped out into the yard, Drew could see Fred mentally calculating how he was going to spend the money.

Drew strode back to the automobile with Nathan. "How'd you know about this fellow?"

"Mr. Karr used him quite often. He sent me to pick up his specimens a few times. I think he's honest." Nathan climbed into the auto.

Drew started the car with the hand crank, then bounded up to the seat. "Why haven't the police been here? It was clear Fred didn't know a Blue Morpho was missing, or he might have been more suspicious."

Nathan looked grim. "Because the police think the murderer is dead. I'm sure they still think Jane is guilty, even if they did release her."

Drew stared back at the house. "A woman was selling it. That was a surprise. Fred has to go see her or meet her somewhere."

"We shouldn't leave."

Drew steered the vehicle to the side of the road. "You take the automobile on home, and I'll keep watch from across the street."

"I'll come back and spell you in a couple of hours."

"Okay." Drew climbed down and trotted back the way he'd come. Then he took up surveillance in a park area. He tugged his hat low on his head and took off his jacket to change his appearance a bit.

The sun beat hot on his hat, and beads of sweat formed on his forehead, so he moved to the shade of a live oak tree. His diligence was rewarded about an hour later when the man exited the house and went to his bicycle. Drew hadn't thought about how he was going to follow if the man left, but he got lucky because Fred came his way and rode his bicycle down another side street to a general store.

The sign on the window announced the store contained a telephone that could be rented. Drew followed from a distance until the man went inside. Through the big window out front, Drew watched him use the telephone. Fred came back out with a smile of satisfaction.

Now to watch and see who showed up with a Blue Morpho.

# THIRTY-FIVE

Election Day hadn't waited for Lily to be done grieving her friend. She pulled on her gray dress and went to the kitchen. Either they'd save Mr. Marshall, or the day would end in tragedy.

"Mr. Hawkes is in the parlor asking to speak with you," Mrs. O'Reilly said. "Be quick about it. Miss Belle will be ringing for her breakfast. Emily will care for little Hannah today."

Lily hurried to see what would have brought Drew out so early. She found him pacing by the fireplace. "What's wrong?"

He turned, and his expression cleared when he saw her. "A woman tried to sell the butterfly to the dealer Nathan took me to see. We think she'll be bringing it to him this morning. Nathan and I are taking turns staking out the house to discover her identity."

She glanced at the clock on the mantel. "We only have a few hours. You saw Mr. Marshall's reaction. He won't avoid the party tonight, so we have to catch these people."

He grasped her shoulders. "I know, honey. We'll do the best we can."

"What about Ian and his team? They have to see Mr. Marshall can't be sacrificed."

Drew shook his head. "No help there. His main goal is to protect the president. He doesn't know Everett."

She put her head on his chest, taking comfort from his warmth and strength. She listened to his heartbeat: strong and steady like the man himself. If only her mama were still alive. She had been convinced Drew would come back someday. She would have been so happy to know she was right.

The future was still murky though. Standing here in the shelter of his arms, it didn't matter. They'd figure it out.

She pulled away and stared into his face. The firm lips, the fire in his brown eyes, the Roman nose all spoke of strength.

He smiled. "What are you thinking?"

"How strong you are. How blessed I am. I know you will save Mr. Marshall."

He sobered at once. "I haven't done such a great job, Lily. Like I said the other night, my confidence is shaken. Pray harder than you've ever prayed today."

"I will. And what about this woman? Do you know anything about her?"

He shook his head. "Only that she has a Blue Morpho. They're quite rare, so we hope it's the missing one."

"Even if it is, how will that lead you to the rest of the people who want Mr. Marshall dead?"

"It has to all be connected—Mrs. Karr's death, the missing butterfly, the plot to kill Mr. Marshall."

"But what if the butterfly has nothing to do with the plot?" She didn't want to shake his confidence, but she didn't see how they fit together.

"I think the butterfly was stolen to shake up Mr. Marshall. Have you noticed how distracted he's been since it went missing?"

She nodded. "He can barely function. Last night he put salt in his coffee."

"He's obsessed with butterflies. Even more than with politics. I

275

don't understand it, but someone else knows how this would affect him. I suspect the Karrs. I found out Mr. Karr ran for senator in the primaries. He has reason to dislike Mr. Marshall."

"Do you think he wants to be appointed senator in his place? I thought Mr. Vesters believed he would be the appointee."

"We don't know if Vesters even told me the truth about why he plans to kill Everett. I caught him off guard when I found the evidence. He could have covered up the real plan with a lie."

She wasn't used to so much subterfuge and lies. "I suppose you're right." Her head hurt just thinking about it.

He hugged her again. "Have faith, Lily. And pray."

"I have been, and I will. Is there anything I can do?"

"I wish there was a way to get into the Karr house. Do you know anyone who works there?"

She shook her head. "Not a soul. I could ask Emily and Mrs. O'Reilly. They've lived here longer than I have. Maybe they've worked with someone there."

"See what you can find out."

"What should they look for if we find someone?"

"A gun, any correspondence that shows what they're up to. The butterfly."

"It just feels like the butterfly must play a bigger role than we know."

He stared at her. "Lily, you're brilliant! I bet it's a symbol for something. Can you get away this morning and go to the library? Maybe you can uncover some meaning behind it. I'm going to be watching to see who shows up with the insect this morning. Send Nathan for me if you find anything."

"Perhaps Belle would help me look. Maybe we can even ask Mr. Marshall. He might know what the butterfly symbolizes."

Drew smiled. "He probably does. He'd be better than an

encyclopedia. Start by asking him before he goes to campaign headquarters."

"Wait a minute. I've heard of a political group called Novo. It uses the butterfly for its symbol. Nathan mentioned it, remember? And Emily told me about it too. Maybe that group is part of this. Could some of his own supporters be behind this?"

"It's possible. I'll see what I can find out."

Lily's gut clenched at the thought of Everett leaving the house. "He doesn't seem to take the threat seriously."

"I'll be with him every second tonight, even if we think we've found all those involved."

Would it be enough? Lily kissed Drew good-bye and went to start Belle's breakfast. She found Mrs. O'Reilly and Emily huddled together talking at the worktable. They both wore somber expressions.

Lily frowned as she went to the stove to start Belle's eggs. "Is something wrong?"

"We saw this morning's newspaper," Mrs. O'Reilly said. "You should try to keep it from Miss Belle."

An egg still in her hand, Lily went to the table. "What is it?"

Mrs. O'Reilly held the paper out, headline up.

"Oh my word." The egg fell from Lily's hand and cracked on the floor.

There would be no hiding this from Belle.

Belle arranged her skirts around her at the round table in the breakfast room by the bay window and rang to let Lily know she was ready for her coddled eggs and toast. She felt unusually cheerful this morning, and it was probably because little Hannah chewed happily on a cloth teether on a blanket by her feet. Was this what purpose felt like?

What must it be like to have a houseful of children? With the right man, of course. Being around the baby had shown her how important the father of her children was to her future. Stuart would not have made a good father, so it was a lucky escape for her.

But still a course she had to see through to the end. When he was behind bars and her uncle was safe, she'd be able to breathe again and look for a good man.

A spotless white apron covered Lily's modest gray dress when she entered the room. She carried a silver tray of breakfast food. She placed the items on Belle's plate. When Belle picked up her fork, Lily took the newspaper from the table and started out of the room.

"I haven't read that yet, Lily. Leave it."

Lily made a slow turn. "Yes, miss." She placed it with obvious reluctance back onto the table.

"Whatever is wrong with you?" Belle reached for the newspaper and unfolded it. The headline blared out at her.

### "I WAS STUART VESTERS'S MISTRESS," SAID ACCUSED MURDERESS, NOW DEAD

This reporter has discovered a secret child stashed away in the Marshall household. Mr. Marshall is running for the senate in today's election. According to Jane White, a white woman of twenty-three years accused of murdering her former employer, Mrs. Sarah Karr, she was the mistress of businessman Stuart Vesters. The arrangement was against Miss White's wishes, and the deed was accomplished with the aid of Mrs. Karr. The accused had contemplated revenge for some time. The fact the child is being cared for by Mr. Vesters's fiancée gives credence to the accusation.

The police are still investigating the murder of Mrs. Karr. Her body was found in the basement under a display of Mr. Marshall's prized butterflies. Her throat had been slashed with a knife. Miss White pointed out the body herself, a case of the attacker returning to the scene of the crime, perhaps. The police say they released Miss White to see if she would lead them to more evidence. That hope was dashed when the monster stalking the city killed her.

If you have any evidence about this crime, contact the police.

Belle tossed the newspaper to the floor. "You would have let me go about my day without knowing such terrible things were being said? How dare they publish such rubbish. I'll be the laughingstock of the entire city." Her throat tightened and her eyes burned, but she would *not* cry. "What will my friends say? If they even speak to me at all." She covered her face with her hands. "How could Jane do this to me?"

"Jane didn't do anything," Lily protested. "Lay the guilt at Stuart's feet where it belongs. Jane was the victim here. And she's *dead*."

"But she didn't have to speak of it!"

Lily took a step closer. "What would you have her do, Miss Belle? Keep silent about what a terrible woman this Karr creature was? We must fight to clear Jane's name for Hannah's sake."

Belle dropped her hands and stared at her maid. "You knew of this. When you said you knew Stuart was an evil man, this is the incident you spoke of."

"Yes. But the story wasn't mine to tell." Her eyes were wet. "There's something else we need to talk about. I spoke with Drew this morning. He suspects the stolen butterfly symbolizes something. Could you ask your uncle if he knows any special meaning for the butterfly?"

"That seems a little preposterous, but I'll ask him."

The doorbell rang. Moments later Stuart's voice boomed out in the hall. "Where is Miss Belle? I must speak with her."

"Don't break the engagement," Lily whispered. "Smile and tell him you believe him—that you'll stand by him."

Belle nodded and pasted a compassionate expression on her face before rising to face him. A big man with a big voice and an overbearing personality, Stuart's presence always filled a room. It was something she was glad she wouldn't have to live with.

He looked at the newspaper on the table, then back to Belle. "It's all a lie."

"I'm sure it is," she said, her voice soothing.

Hannah cooed on the floor and smiled up at him. He scowled at the infant. "If you hadn't taken in that brat, I'd be in a better position to counteract this story."

"I had no idea there would be a story to counteract. We can't do anything about that now. I can hardly turn her out into the streets now that she's an orphan. That would warrant another ugly front-page article."

He winced, then crossed the room to take her hands. "You do believe me, don't you, Belle? I would never do something so evil. I don't know why the chit was trying to discredit me, but I have friends in town. I can't believe the paper printed that trash—especially now that she's dead and can't retract it."

"Of course I believe you." She forced herself to brush his whiskers with a kiss. "We'll get through this, Stuart."

"Of all things to happen on Election Day. I hope this doesn't affect your uncle's election."

She stepped away from him when he started to grab her. "Why would it? He did nothing. He's the victim here. If anything, he'll win by an even bigger landslide."

His hands dropped to his sides. "Voters can be fickle. A hint of scandal, and they're gone."

"This doesn't implicate Uncle Everett at all. Are you voting today?"

"I already did. The turnout seemed strong already."

"We'll know tonight if he's won."

He turned toward the door. "I hope you're right. I'll pick you up to attend the post-election party when we'll celebrate his win." He was looking more cheerful by the minute. "The future is looking bright for all of us. This will pass. The election will push this news to the back page."

"Of course it will." She envisioned the front-page news when Stuart's assassination plot was revealed. Then they'd have proof of the kind of man Stuart was.

# THIRTY-SIX

Belle had always found her uncle's study intimidating, even as a child. The cavernous room had a domed ceiling, and the butterflies hanging in display glass seemed to be looking at her. Once Hannah was down for her nap, she steeled herself and went to find her uncle. She inhaled and knocked on the door.

"Come in." Her uncle's voice was muffled.

He looked up over the glasses perched on his nose. His speech papers were spread out on the enormous desk. "Ah, it's you, Belle."

She tried not to see the red butterfly staring at her from the wall to her left. "You look very handsome this morning, uncle." At least the aroma of her uncle's pipe tobacco was comforting.

His intent expression cleared. "You'll do me proud today, niece. It's a big day for the Marshall household." His gaze examined her. "I assume you read this morning's paper?"

"Yes, I did. It's quite ugly."

"What will you do?"

"Nothing until the election is over and we see the extent of Stuart's involvement."

His eyes smiled with approval. "You're a good girl, Belle. Wish me luck. Even as we speak, the state is turning out to cast its vote for the next senator. I plan to be giving my acceptance speech in about twelve hours."

His good humor made her smile until she remembered how serious the day truly was. "Aren't you even a little apprehensive about tonight's possible assassination attempt?"

"Not at all. You youngsters worry too much." A frown gathered between his brows, and he glanced at the butterfly display on his desk. "I'd be more comfortable if I could find my butterfly though."

"That's what I wanted to ask you about. What's so special about this Blue Morpho butterfly? Why would anyone steal it?"

He laid down his pen. "It's rare, so it's very valuable, of course. Camille was quite upset with me when she found out how much I paid for it, but I bought her a diamond necklace to soothe her."

Her aunt was easily placated by jewelry. "Beyond the rarity and monetary value. You seem more upset about losing this specimen than I would have expected. After all, you can always buy another. We're not paupers."

He stepped to his floor-to-ceiling bookshelf and selected a book. After opening it, he flipped through the pages, then handed it to her. "It has mystical powers. It's the only known specimen with that red key shape on one wing. It's quite small. You have to look at the picture with a magnifying glass to see it. It's evident on the real specimen though. I made sure I had the real one."

"Oh, Uncle Everett, surely you don't believe in magic." She knew her levity had offended him when he started to take the book back. "No, no, let me read it. I'm sorry I mocked you. You always seem so cut and dried, rooted in the present."

"It's an article about this particular Blue Morpho. To be succinct, possession of this butterfly has put kings in power and has healed those dying. It's even been reported to have brought back a king's son from the dead." He stabbed a stubby finger at the pertinent paragraph.

She skimmed the article, and it was very convincing with names and dates detailed. "It seems to be about change. Possessing it brings about the change you wish." She took the magnifying glass he handed her and studied the watercolor drawing. "I see the red key."

"I know it's a bit silly and superstitious, but I hoped possessing it would ensure my win in the election so I could bring about the necessary change for Texas. My motives were pure. I don't seek power for myself. We have many challenges facing us. My job will be substantial, and I could use all the help I can get."

"Would someone want to steal it for its supposed power?"

"It's possible, though its magical abilities aren't well known."

She knew of one other butterfly fanatic in the city. "What about Mr. Karr? Would he know about this butterfly?"

"Oh yes, he and I spoke about it after I'd purchased it. And let me assure you, it was much more costly than the usual Blue Morpho."

"Did he know its value?"

"I didn't tell him, if that's what you're asking. Karr might be an opponent politically, but I hardly think he'd steal my butterfly."

"People do strange things for power."

Her uncle nodded. "True enough. Why are you asking so many questions about it? I thought you were most worried about tonight."

She closed the book and put it back. "I wondered if they might be connected. Someone could have stolen the butterfly for the same reasons you bought it. I'm trying to uncover what those reasons might be."

He stroked his beard. "Interesting hypothesis, Belle. You're a smart girl."

"It wasn't me. Lily thought of it." She went toward the door. "Good luck, Uncle Everett. I hope you win by a landslide."

"From your lips to God's ears."

She closed the door behind her and found Lily lurking in the hall. "Did you overhear what he said?"

"I wasn't trying to listen, but I was eager to know what he said."

"This particular butterfly is special." She told Lily what Uncle Everett had said. "So maybe Mr. Karr took it. He might have thought it would help my uncle win the election, and he sought to prevent it."

Lily shook her head. "If he took it, Mr. Karr wouldn't be willing to sell it. So maybe the woman who is coming today to sell one doesn't have the same butterfly. How will we know if it's the same?"

Belle tipped up her chin. "I'll know it. I should go with Mr. Hawkes to examine the specimen."

"He's already left. He said if we had information to send it with Nathan."

Belle turned and walked toward the door. "I'd rather deliver it myself. I will know this particular butterfly anywhere. I have to get there before anything is done."

The only distraction Drew had had was Belle's arrival. She'd wanted to watch with him, but he'd sent her away, much to her chagrin. This was something he needed to handle alone.

A buggy stopped in front of the neat little house Drew had been watching for hours. He straightened when a woman stepped down, but when he squinted, he realized it wasn't anyone he recognized. He made a quick decision to follow her into the house. Fred would be unhappy, but he'd save the fellow money if the woman didn't have the butterfly he sought.

He was on her heels when Fred opened the door. Fred's

welcoming smile vanished when he saw Drew over the woman's shoulder. "I told you I'd contact you when I had the butterfly in hand."

"I thought to save you the trouble."

The woman turned to face him. She was in her thirties with blond hair surrounding a fair complexion. Her plain clothing indicated she might be a servant. One of the Karr servants?

Her knuckles were white from her grip on the box in her hands. "What's this about?"

"This man is interested in your butterfly." Fred's voice held displeasure, but he stepped aside to allow them to enter.

Her expression still wary, she turned and stepped into the house. Drew followed before Fred could shut the door in his face. The interior of the home was cool and quiet except for the clock ticking on the mantel.

"I'd like to see the butterfly." Drew took out the magnifying glass he'd brought. "There's no need for you to spend the money on the butterfly if it's not what I want. I won't try to cut you out of the sale, Fred."

Fred's scowl eased, and he held out his hands. "May I? I want to confirm it's a Blue Morpho first."

The woman glanced from him to Drew, then handed it over. "It's genuine."

"Where did you get it?" Drew asked.

She watched Fred set the box on the table and remove the lid. "My late husband was a collector, and I'm forced to sell his specimens to support myself and my daughter. He traveled to other countries to collect the butterflies himself."

"It's exquisite," Fred said. "In perfect condition. See for yourself, Mr. Hawkes."

Drew stepped to the table and inhaled. The butterfly seemed almost iridescent. There was no damage to the wings. He focused his lens over it and studied the delicate wings. His heart sank when he realized this wasn't the specimen he sought.

He straightened. "It's quite beautiful. I'll take it." Even though the cost would deplete his savings, the desperation in the woman's demeanor tugged at his heart.

Fred beamed. "Excellent. If you'll step outside, I'll finish my negotiations with the lady."

Drew beckoned Fred to follow him into the hall. "I'll only buy it if you pay the lady the price you and I agreed on minus a hundred dollars."

Fred's grin twisted into a scowl. "That is very little profit."

"You're still making a decent profit, and you have no risk. She needs the money, Fred. That's the only way I'll buy it. And I'll ask her how much you gave her."

Fred sighed. "I'm too soft for my own good. Very well." He extended his hand. "You're a good man, Mr. Hawkes."

Drew handed over the money he'd brought. "Just doing the right thing. Thank you for doing the same."

Lily pressed the last flounce of Belle's dress, then stepped to the balcony veranda where Belle reclined on a chaise with a book in her hand. Belle had come back disgruntled after seeing Drew. She'd sulked the entire afternoon until it was time to get ready for the dinner party.

"Miss Belle, your bath is ready."

Belle put down her book. "I wish I could stay home. I can't bear to see Uncle Everett harmed, and I'm so fearful."

"I am too, but he'll be disappointed if you don't go. And Drew is there."

"Where is he? He promised to let us know what he discovered."

Lily shaded her eyes and stared at a man walking their way. "That might be him." As the figure drew closer, she recognized Drew. "It is he." She waved at him, and he increased his pace until he stood under the balcony.

Lily leaned over the railing in a most unladylike way. "What did you find out?"

He craned his neck to look up at her. "It wasn't the right one. No red marking in the shape of a key. I bought it anyway though. The lady was a widow supporting a small child."

Lily wished she could fling herself over the railing and kiss him. Only Drew would think so much of others. "Perhaps it will calm Mr. Marshall."

Belle looked as if she might cry. "No connection at all?"

Drew shook his head. "I don't think so. I'm sorry. I'll be by your uncle's side tonight though. I'll do my best to protect him." He touched his hat. "I must be off to get ready."

Lily wanted to beg him not to go. What if he threw himself in front of Mr. Marshall? "Be careful, Drew."

He smiled up at her with a trace of sadness in his eyes. "I will, love. Pray while we're gone, and try not to fret."

Lily watched him enter the house. He was walking rather oddly, as though he was in pain. She dismissed it as a trick of the angle, and the way the coming night felt full of portent. It could all go right or terribly wrong.

She turned to face her employer. "Can I come, Miss Belle?"

"What about Hannah?"

"Nathan has her tonight."

Belle stared at her, then slowly smiled. "Why not? We can dress you up, and I can introduce you as a friend. No one will ever know."

"Your aunt and uncle will, of course."

"Just avoid them. There will be tons of people there." Belle walked to the wardrobe and threw it open. "I doubt I will ever wear that green dress you repaired again anyway. We're about the same size, so I'm sure it will fit you."

Lily reached out to touch the silk, then pulled her hand back. "Are you sure, Miss Belle? I never dreamed I'd wear something so lovely."

"Of course. Take off that dress and try it on."

Keeping her eyes on the dress, Lily did as instructed. When the gown settled onto her frame, it felt just the way she'd imagined. Soft and sensuous, with a whispering sound when she moved.

She touched the skirt with tentative fingers. "It's exquisite."

"You look very different. Can you do your hair yourself?" Belle walked back to the dressing table and settled onto the stool. "After you do mine, of course."

"Oh, of course." Lily looped Belle's hair up in an intricate arrangement of loops and curls atop her head. She settled a diamond pin on the left side. "Perfect." She stepped back and redid her long hair in a fancier style more in keeping with the elegant gown.

Belle watched her with an approving smile. "Wait until Drew sees you."

Lily's pulse sped up at the thought of the expression in Drew's eyes when he caught sight of her. If he wasn't upset that she'd come. "Are you sure no one will notice?"

Belle stood and looped arms with her. "If I sponsor you, no one will dare to question your presence. It's time to go."

Lily swallowed and nodded. She prayed all the way to the carriage.

# THIRTY-SEVEN

People teemed around the lighted hall at the Driskill Hotel in an excited mass. A band played patriotic songs on the red-white-and-blue-draped stage. Lily couldn't stop gawking until Belle yanked on her arm.

"Smile and look unimpressed." Belle put on that same expression and began to introduce Lily as her "good friend" from out of town.

Lily managed to follow Belle's example, even though the sea of names and faces soon overwhelmed her. She retreated into a quiet corner to observe the festivities and watch Mr. Marshall. She caught a glimpse of Drew hovering near her employer, and she suspected his pocket contained a gun.

Mr. Vesters, drink in hand, stood about ten feet away from Mr. Marshall with several other men she didn't recognize. The telegram with the election results should arrive soon, but this crowd didn't seem to care who won or lost. Lily inhaled, then left the sanctuary of the shadows and sidled closer to listen in to what Vesters had to say.

"The woman is clearly insane." Vesters took a swig of his drink. "Anyone who knows me won't believe her story."

"Have the police questioned you?" one of the men asked.

Vesters shrugged. "Just a cursory meeting."

Sickened at his self-satisfied tone, Lily edged away. Just because Jane had been poor and alone, her story was disbelieved in favor of this evil man. The only way to clear Jane's name was to get to the bottom of the entire plot. She was sure Mrs. Karr's death was intertwined with the plot against Mr. Marshall.

She wandered to the table and took a glass of punch. Sipping it, she saw a familiar face. "Well, hello, Mrs. Adams. How good of you to come."

Dressed in sober gray silk, the preacher's wife looked much grander without her gardening attire. Molly Adams joined her at the table. "I didn't recognize you at first. Your dress is lovely."

"It's my mistress's," Lily admitted.

"Mrs. Marshall? She's not usually so generous."

"No, Miss Belle loaned it to me. You don't seem to like Mrs. Marshall."

Molly lifted a brow. "I knew her many years ago. I was Christopher's nanny. He was quite . . . a handful. I'm afraid I packed up and moved on when I caught him tormenting a rat in the barn. I'm a bit squeamish that way. When I told Mrs. Marshall, it was quite ugly. First she defended him, then she beat him herself until the blood flowed down his legs. I intervened before I left, and I thought she would strike me too. I'm quite sorry I let my bias show. And how about you, Miss Donaldson? Did they ever catch the man who attacked you?"

Lily shook her head. "I don't think the police are looking very hard." Her gaze met Drew's. His eyes widened, and he took a step toward her. She'd hoped to escape his detection for a while, but there was no help for it. "I think I've been discovered."

"Ah, your young man didn't know you were here? Go along, child. I have to find the reverend anyway. I'm glad we ran into one another."

Lily answered Drew's beckoning finger, and he took her arm. "What are you doing here?"

"I wanted to come, and Belle loaned me a dress."

A frown hovered between his brown eyes. "I'm trying to save Mr. Marshall's life, and now I'll be distracted trying to make sure you're not in harm's way. Please, please stay close to me or Belle. Don't wander off into the dark."

"I'll be fine, Drew. No one will harm me." She looked back at Mrs. Adams. "At least I found out why she seemed to dislike Mrs. Marshall. She used to work for her. It appears she didn't like Christopher's behavior with rats." She told him what Mrs. Adams said, but he didn't seem to be listening.

"You seem to forget someone attacked you, Lily, and we don't know why. I would be much happier if you went home."

She smiled up at him. "What do you think of my dress?" She refused to go home now.

His frown eased. "You're the most beautiful woman here, and if we were alone, I'd have to kiss you." He leaned closer. "In fact, maybe I'll just take a kiss anyway."

She danced away. "Not in front of everyone." But her pulse skipped at the expression on his face.

His teasing smile faded as he scanned the crowd again. "I'll be glad when this is over and we can start planning our future together."

She stepped closer again. "Have you thought any more about what you'll do, Drew?"

He took her hand. "I don't know. Get a desk job somewhere, maybe a bank. I can recognize fake money." His mouth twisted.

A rock settled in her belly. "What if the bank was robbed?"

"Lily, you worry too much. Life isn't meant to be easy. Look how boring that would be."

"Is it wrong to want a little peace?" Her eyes burned, and she blinked away the moisture. "Things have been hard for me for over four years, Drew. I want to wake up in the morning and not worry about what bad thing is going to happen today. I want to smile at you across the breakfast table and not be fearful that a bullet will find you. I'm tired of struggling. For years it's been all Mama and I could do to put food on the table."

He listened without interrupting. "But look at what the struggle has done for you. You've grown into a strong, self-assured woman. The Lily I loved before our fathers died would never have donned that beautiful dress and come to this party. She would have stayed home knitting. I don't think she would have put herself in danger for a woman like Jane either. Adversity has made that change in you."

Had she changed that much? Maybe so. Though she wouldn't say she would ever pray for adversity, she could see how God had used it in her life. "I'm weary, Drew. I've changed enough."

"That's for God to say," he said softly. "He may not want you to stay a caterpillar. I don't think you're quite out of your cocoon yet."

For a moment, she struggled to comprehend what he meant, then she remembered Mr. Marshall talking about the butterfly's struggle to escape the cocoon. She twirled a little in her dress. "I think I'm out of the cocoon."

A male voice spoke behind her. "Lily?"

She turned to see Mr. Marshall frowning at her. "Yes, sir."

"What are you doing here? And where did you get that dress?"

"Miss Belle l-loaned it to me." She clasped her hands in front of her.

His frown eased. "Well, as long as Belle is in agreement, what can I say? Though Mrs. Marshall forgot her wrap, and the breeze is a bit chilly. Would you run home and get it? I think it's in the back of her closet. You may have to dig through a few things. She wanted the brown silk one. Take my carriage."

"Of course, Mr. Marshall. I'll be back as quickly as I can." She hurried away without another word to Drew. Her future suddenly wasn't as bright as she'd hoped.

The mansion was quiet when Lily let herself in. The servants had all been given the night off, but she knew Emily had opted to stay in and would likely be in the third-floor bedroom reading by candlelight.

Lily's Cinderella night had come to a screeching halt. Even though she would go back with Mrs. Marshall's wrap, it was all ruined now that she'd been recalled to her maid duties. Enough people had been standing near Mr. Marshall to know her true status.

She dropped her bag onto the hall table. The servants usually used the back stairs, but she felt just rebellious enough to climb the front sweeping staircase. Her slippered feet made no noise on the polished oak treads. She reached the landing and glanced down the hall toward the Marshall master bedroom. Most of the servants had never been inside that room. Mrs. Marshall didn't have a personal maid, and she cleaned the room herself. She felt a maid was pretentious, though she'd seen the need for Belle to have Lily.

The room was at the far end of the hall, away from the noise of the street, and looked out on the quiet rose garden.

"Lily, what are you doing back so early?"

Lily whirled to see Emily, book in hand, at the bottom of the attic stairs. She was dressed in her nightgown, and one long light-brown braid was over her shoulder. "I came back for Mrs. Marshall's brown silk wrap. Do you know where it is?"

Emily shook her head. "They're letting you in the bedroom? You know how odd they are about that."

"Mr. Marshall sent me himself."

Emily's hazel eyes gleamed as she came closer. "Promise to tell me what you find?"

"I will." She smiled at Emily's conspiratorial wink. "Sorry if I disturbed you."

When Emily retreated back to the stairs, Lily twisted the knob and stepped into the Marshall bedroom. The scent of roses hung in the air. She turned on the gaslight and looked around. The bed was enormous and covered with a gray silk coverlet. The polished oak floorboards gleamed. Several massive dressers provided plenty of room for belongings. Another door was on the far left, and she caught a glimpse of a big claw-foot tub. It wouldn't hurt to take a peek at the big bathroom.

She stepped to the door and glanced around. The room had two gleaming porcelain sinks fitted with shiny brass faucets. It was impeccably clean. She retreated and headed for the closet at the other end of the room. When she opened it, the scent of roses grew stronger.

The beautiful clothing was a pleasure to touch, but Lily pushed the dresses to the side to allow in enough light to see. She found the wrap hanging on a hook, but when she took it down, it fell to the floor. She grabbed at it and dislodged a small flat box on one of the shelves along the back. The lid fell off, and when she knelt to retrieve the box, she caught a glimpse of blue.

She carried the box out into the light where she could see it better. The missing butterfly lay nestled in silk inside. She gasped, and her throat tightened. Mr. Marshall had had the butterfly all along, yet he'd blamed Jane for its disappearance.

She glanced around the room and realized there was another closet. After laying the box on the bed, she went to the door and opened it. It contained only men's clothing. She stared back at the butterfly. That meant *Mrs. Marshall* had taken the butterfly and hidden it from her husband. Why would she do that when he was searching for it so frantically?

She went back to the bed and picked up the butterfly in its box. What should she do about this?

If she took it and returned it to Mr. Marshall, it would be her word against Mrs. Marshall's as to where it was found. She could replace it, then send him a note telling him where it was. But would he think someone had implicated his wife on purpose?

She rubbed her head. If only Drew were here to help her figure out what to do.

The floorboards outside the door creaked, and she whirled around. "Hello?" Her voice shook, and she clutched the box in her hands. No answer. Maybe it was just the house shifting.

The clock on the bedside dinged the time. Nine thirty. Mr. Marshall would be wondering where she was. What if she hid the butterfly in her room? No one would look there, and she could tell Emily what she'd found. It would be corroboration.

Her mind made up, she opened the door. A figure loomed from the shadows, and her gaze traveled up the male suit to the man's face. "Mr. Lambreth, you frightened me. What are you doing here?"

He was smiling when his gaze traveled to the box in her hand. "I told Mother you were too smart and would be sure to find it. I love being right."

His tone was deceptively mild, and Lily relaxed until his words penetrated. "You knew Mrs. Marshall took this?"

"Actually, I took it. She just hid it."

"But why?"

"She knew it would rattle Everett, and he would be easily disposed of."

"*You* killed Mrs. Karr, not Jane."

"She caught me taking the butterfly. She wasn't my type, but I had no choice."

She backed away as he approached, then whirled and rushed back into the bedroom she'd just vacated. She tried to slam the door, but his foot came between the door and the jamb. Struggling, she tried to hold the door closed, but he was too strong for her and the door flew open. She staggered back and fell onto the floor.

He loomed over her. "I'm sorry it's come to this, Lily. I really did like you."

She edged away. "And the attack in the churchyard? Was that you? Why in a holy place?"

"I was having trouble getting to you, so it was expedient." He heaved a sigh. "I'm afraid you'll have to be disposed of. I'd hoped you'd be different. You're just like my mother, so sweet and pretty on the outside and quite wanton on the inside. I saw the way you kissed Hawkes, you know. Like you couldn't get enough of him. My mother can't get enough of men either. Come along and don't make a fuss."

She opened her mouth to scream, but he leaped forward and pressed some horrible-smelling cloth to her nose. His face wavered, then her vision went dark.

# THIRTY-EIGHT

The party tempo increased when Everett's election win was announced. Drew kept an eye out for Lily, but she still hadn't returned by ten o'clock. Something was wrong.

He wound his way through the celebrating crowd to find Belle. "Have you seen Lily?"

Belle's cheeks were pink with excitement. "I haven't seen her. Isn't it wonderful though?"

"Splendid. Where's your aunt?"

"Oh, she's around somewhere, I'm sure. Any sign of an attack on Uncle Everett?"

"It's been calm." Drew spied a familiar figure. "If you see Lily, tell her I'm looking for her." He circled around the hall to intercept Ian, who seemed to be heading for the door.

"Wait up, Ian."

Ian stopped by the punch bowl. "You seem to have everything under control here. Well done, Drew."

"What about the conspirators? Have they made a move elsewhere yet?"

Ian shook his head. "I've gotten word Vesters called it off last night. He didn't want to bring any more attention to Jane's story. He feared Marshall's death would bring more focus on the family."

"Nice of you to let me know. You've disappointed me, Ian. I respected you and looked up to you like a father."

Ian put his hand on Drew's arm. "Son, it was nothing personal. I was looking out for my country."

Drew stared at the hand on his arm until Ian removed it. "You let me believe a lie. It's shaken my confidence."

"I'm sorry for that." Ian's gaze was level. "Ballard should deliver the conspirators to us this week. He's got nearly all their names. Once we have them in custody, I hope you and I can sit down with Ballard and talk this all out. I don't want to lose you, Drew."

Drew gave a bark of laughter. "I'm hardly an asset. I've been chasing my own tail for years and didn't know it."

"You've brought a lot of men to justice, son. Don't lose sight of how valuable you are to your country. Give this some time to settle."

"Where's Ballard now?"

Ian shrugged. "I think he's probably protecting Lily. He followed her out of here."

Though he knew Ballard was one of them, Drew's gut churned. He'd been suspicious of the man for too many years, and he wasn't even too sure of Ian anymore. "I don't like it that he's gone after her. Could you go check it out?"

"I told you, Ballard is one of us. I'm sorry I caused you to distrust him all these years, but let it go." Ian turned away.

Drew wandered through the crowd trying to ignore the mounting sense of worry. Ian had full faith in Ballard, but what about those knives used to attack the women? Drew had seen them with his own eyes, and he was sure Ballard had made those weapons. What implications did that have? Was it possible Ballard had deceived Ian?

He mingled with the crowd and saw Mrs. Marshall from a distance. She didn't have her wrap on, so clearly Lily hadn't returned.

By now it was ten fifteen. The party would be winding down in another hour or so.

Mrs. Adams, her hat on and her purse in hand, paused to smile at him. "I hope I didn't upset Lily."

He'd barely listened when Lily talked about their conversation. "What do you mean?"

"That talk about Christopher torturing the rat." She shuddered delicately. "I'm surprised he didn't come to a bad end, but I spoke with him tonight, and he seems perfectly normal." She laid her gloved hand on his arm. "Anyway, tell her I'm sorry if I upset her."

He watched her join her husband and make their good-byes. Tortured a rat? He recalled a book he'd read by a German psychiatrist about killers. The book had mentioned torture of animals. Christopher was living in the house. He could have found the secret passages. Drew's unease grew. He returned to Mr. Marshall's side but found no one around who appeared suspicious. If not for his duty to protect Marshall, Drew would go in search of Lily right now.

By ten thirty every nerve was on high alert. He couldn't stand around any longer. Ian had said Marshall was in no danger tonight, but Drew feared Lily might be. He set his jaw and headed for the door, stopping only long enough to tell Ian where he was going. Marshall had come here of his own free will. Drew had to find Lily and make sure she was all right.

He took the trolley and rode to a block from the house. Five minutes later he stood in front of the Butterfly Palace. It was shrouded in darkness except for a hall light burning. Inside, he called for her. "Lily!" Her bag was on the hall table. He strode through the house searching for her and yelling out her name.

Upstairs, he hurried to the master bedroom and looked inside. The closet door still hung open, but there was no sign of Lily. A brown silk wrap lay on the floor. His unease flared to raw fear. Lily would never have left the bedroom in this state.

"Mr. Hawkes?"

He turned to see Emily in the hall. "Have you seen Lily?"

Her eyes wide, she nodded. "She was here a bit earlier to fetch a wrap for Mrs. Marshall."

He swept his arm around the room. "She left the wrap here."

Emily stared past him. "She would have closed the door and straightened the room."

"Exactly. And her bag is downstairs. Did you hear anything else? Any voices?"

"Just Mr. Lambreth. I heard his voice once, but I didn't see him."

Drew sagged against the wall. "Christopher might be the man who murdered Jane and all the other servant girls."

Lily struggled to breathe. Something pinned her arms to her sides, and she couldn't see anything in the suffocating darkness. She knew she was in the labyrinth of the house somewhere because she could smell the damp and the mouse droppings. She lay on something hard and cold, perhaps the ground, though it was too dark to see.

Mr. Lambreth. He'd put something over her face to render her unconscious. Chloroform? And what was he planning? Panic closed her throat, and she struggled but made no headway. Her arms were pinned to her sides. She flexed her wrists and encountered rough rope.

*Think, Lily!*

She calmed herself and tried to sense where she was. Could she free herself? There was a bit of give in the bonds. She flexed her arms again and felt the ropes loosen. Encouraged, she tried again and managed to free her left wrist. Her hand felt numb and tingly, but she reached over and wrenched her right wrist free, then sat up. Feeling her way in the darkness, she realized she was on a narrow cot of some kind.

She staggered to her feet, her head swimming. She was too dizzy and disoriented to know where she was going, but she managed to stumble a few feet until she ran into the cold wall. It was earthen, so it was different from other areas she'd been in. Her eyes began to adjust to the dark, and she saw a glow to her left.

Mr. Lambreth's gleeful voice came from her left. He was smiling in the light of the lantern in his hand. "I see you, Lily. You can't escape me. I've been waiting for this moment. The others were much too fast with no time to enjoy the moment. This will be different."

*He is the killer.*

Her throat closed, and she pushed deeper into the shadows.

"You can't hide from me."

His feet scuffed along the floor, and she sidled along the wall. It was too dark to see well. He must be like a cat, able to see in dim light. She kept her eye on the bobbing lantern. It quit moving, and she took a few more rapid steps away. Then a hand grabbed her by the hair. It felt like he was yanking her hair out by its roots, and a scream tore from her lungs.

"Let go of me!" She grabbed his arm and dragged it to her mouth, then bit down as hard as she could until the coppery taste of blood filled her mouth.

He swore and yanked his arm away. "You'll be very sorry you did that, Lily."

The steely intent in his voice made her quail. She didn't intend to die easily. Not before she had a chance to tell Drew she understood what he'd been trying to tell her. Not before she turned into the person she should be.

While he tended to his arm, she took off blindly running along the labyrinth floor. Christopher's footsteps pounded after her, closer and closer. With his hot breath on her neck, she stumbled over a hole in the path and went down into a pit filled with water. Pain shot up from her knee.

"Gotcha." His hands came down on her shoulders, and he dragged her to her feet. She gave a despairing scream though there was no one to hear. "Why did you kill Jane? And those other women? They did nothing to you."

A cruel smile twisted his lips. In the lamplight, his pale blue eyes were like ice chips. "While I quite enjoyed their deaths, yours will be more pleasurable since I've admired you so long." Keeping one hand on her arm, he held a knife up in the lamplight. "I had this one made just for you."

She screamed and broke free of his grip, but not for long.

Drew's gut told him Lily was in grave danger and there was no time to spare. He went to the kitchen and ran his hands over the wall where he'd seen the panel door in the pantry. It was dark in the space, so he felt around until he found the lever. When he pulled it, the panel groaned and opened much too slowly for the urgency he felt.

He grabbed the lantern on the kitchen table and stepped into the blackness. The closed air tasted stale and flat. The ceiling was relatively clean from the last time he and Lily had come through. Where would Lambreth have taken her? Instinct turned him right, toward the tunnel through the backyard. The path ran downward, and the chill in the air became more pronounced as he walked underground.

There was a T in the labyrinth. To the right would take him to the old shack where Jane had died, but something made him turn to the left. It was the only unexplored part of the tunnels. With the lantern held high, he hurried along. There were no cobwebs, so someone had been in the tunnel recently. It narrowed until his shoulders brushed both sides and he had to bend over.

As the tunnel narrowed even more, he decided to turn back. This wasn't getting him any closer to Lily. Then he heard a scream up ahead. He jerked and thumped his head against the ceiling. Gritting his teeth to keep from calling out her name, he pushed through the narrow space. Four feet later the walls were wider and the ceiling higher. A wash of air cooled his face.

He saw a pinpoint of light ahead and quickly extinguished his lantern before he could be seen. With his gun in his hand, he crept forward. Dancing shadows turned into two figures struggling in the light of a lamp sitting on a table. Christopher had his arm around Lily's neck in a choke hold from behind. She thrashed and tore at the forearm cutting off her air.

They were too close for Drew to be able to fire off a shot without the risk of hitting Lily. And he had no other weapon other than the lantern. It would have to do. Christopher's back was to him, and Drew rushed toward the struggling couple. Christopher must have sensed they weren't alone because he let go of Lily and turned. Lily fell to the ground.

It was too late to stop Drew's onward momentum. With the lantern high overhead, he brought it down on Christopher's head. The glass shattered, and the acrid odor of kerosene filled the enclosed space.

The blow only knocked Christopher backward. He growled

and leaped at Drew with bared teeth. The scent of mint washed over Drew, and he grabbed Christopher by the neck. The two toppled to the floor with Drew atop Christopher.

A red mist came down over Drew's vision. All he wanted was to choke the life out of the monster. Christopher bucked under him, then he got his knee up and shoved Drew off. In an instant he had his hands wrapped around Drew's neck. The man's strength was almost demonic, and he wore an expression of intense glee.

The insane light in Christopher's eyes faded, and he slumped off Drew. Drew looked up into Lily's face. Her eyes wide, she stared at the blood on her hands. He glanced over at Christopher and saw one of Ballard's fancy knives protruding from his back.

When Drew got to his feet, Lily rushed into his arms. He held her trembling body close. "It's okay. He can't hurt you any longer."

She shuddered and burrowed closer. "He killed Jane. And the other women."

"I know. He was a monster. I want to find out what Ballard knows about him. That's one of Ballard's special knives. He only made them for friends."

# THIRTY-NINE

The party was deadly dull now that the best people had left. Belle's face hurt from smiling and accepting congratulations on her uncle's election. Mr. Hawkes's worry about Lily had transferred to her, and she watched the clock. By eleven the party began to wind down, and she was eager to get home and see what had happened to her maid.

Only a handful of people were left as the clock neared eleven thirty. Belle walked over to the food table. She was parched, and some punch would be most welcome. The servants had begun to extinguish the gaslights, and the table was shrouded in darkness since most of the food was gone. No punch remained. She turned to survey the hall and see who was still left.

An older gentleman had hovered near her uncle's shoulder all evening, and Belle suspected he worked with Mr. Hawkes to protect her uncle. Vesters hadn't wandered far from her uncle's side, but Belle was sure he would not be courageous enough to try to kill her uncle himself. So who was left in the hall that might be dangerous?

Her gaze traveled around the room and discounted the elderly couple she'd known all her life who hovered near the door. Her aunt's best friend and her husband were no threat. She walked

306

toward the red velvet curtains that dressed up the hall. The servants did their work behind the scenes here, and it was possible a sniper lurked there. And she might be able to get a glass of punch. There were no servants behind the curtain, only her aunt.

Aunt Camille's back was to Belle, but she was turned enough to the side for Belle to see her pouring a white powder into a drink. Frowning, Belle nearly said something, but following some inner compulsion she couldn't name, she melted into the shadows.

Her aunt swirled the powder with a spoon, then threw the spoon into the trash. Odd since it was a silver spoon. The hair on the back of Belle's neck prickled when her aunt pushed through the curtains and called her uncle's name. Belle followed, still keeping to the shadows.

Aunt Camille approached Uncle Everett with a smile and held out the cup. "Here's some punch, Everett. You look parched."

He took it. "I am, Camille. Thanks for thinking of it. We'll be able to go home soon, but I need to be the last one to leave."

In slow motion, Belle watched him lift the glass toward his lips. Her love for her aunt warred with her sense of danger. What could she possibly say to interrupt him? He wouldn't believe his own wife would try to harm him, and Belle wasn't sure of it herself. What if Aunt Camille had mixed in some medicine he took all the time? But wouldn't she have told him it contained his medicine? Instead, she'd merely offered him refreshment.

Something was very wrong, and Belle couldn't let him drink that. She stepped from the shadows when the cup was only an inch from his lips. "Stop!"

Her uncle paused and lowered the drink. "Whatever is the matter, Belle?"

She rushed to his side, then turned to stare at her aunt. "Aunt Camille, what did you put in the drink?"

Her aunt blinked. "Whatever do you mean? It's merely a glass of punch." Her voice quavered a little.

"I saw you, Aunt Camille. You put a powder in the drink." Belle pointed. "Back behind the curtain."

"Are you feeling quite well, darling?" Aunt Camille started to put her hand to Belle's forehead.

Belle flinched away. Her aunt was acting very strange. "I *saw* you. With my own eyes. The powder was white. You stirred it with a spoon, then threw the spoon away. Go look, Uncle Everett. She threw away a *silver* spoon. Don't you find that odd?"

Her uncle stared at his wife. "Camille?"

His wife's face remained impassive, but a bead of perspiration popped above her upper lip, and her gaze darted away. "You would believe a lie like that of me, Everett?"

He stared from her face to Belle's, then glanced toward the curtained-off area. "Let's see, shall we? It's easy enough to get to the bottom of this misunderstanding."

When he started for the curtain, his wife whirled and ran for the door. Belle stared after her. It wasn't her place to stop her. Her aunt vanished through the front door of the hall. "I think you'd better keep that punch and have it tested, Uncle Everett."

His expression was troubled, and he strode to the curtained area. Belle went with him and showed him the trash. "There's the spoon. I stood in the shadows and watched her empty the powder into your drink."

"Why were you watching her?"

"I don't know. I was looking to see if there could be anyone left who meant you harm, and I checked behind this curtain. When I stepped back here, I saw her stirring in that powder. Though I didn't know what it was all about, I said nothing and waited to see what she intended to do with the drink. When she denied putting anything in your drink, I knew something was wrong."

His eyes showed his hurt. "I can't imagine why she would want to harm me. I give her everything she wants."

"You're very wealthy, Uncle Everett. Her last husband died under mysterious circumstances, didn't he?"

"He had a strange wasting ailment and died in Germany. It was assumed he contracted a disease there."

"What if she poisoned him? And what if she's part of the plot to kill you? She would gain your fortune, and someone else would be implicated for political reasons."

"I don't want to believe Camille would do something like this, but the evidence is irrefutable." He put his hand on Belle's shoulder. "I think you just saved my life again, niece. Thank you."

Drew emerged from Christopher's lair with Lily on his arm. His chest still heaved with the emotion of the rescue. The last door was in the carriage house, and when they stepped outside, he saw Mrs. Marshall dragging a suitcase out the back door.

She stopped and called out, "James, are you here?"

Drew stopped Lily from moving forward. "Wait," he whispered.

Ballard stepped from the shadows and hurried to take her suitcase. "What's happened? I came as soon as you called."

"Your henchman called off the shooting, so I decided to dispose of Everett myself. Belle saw me put the poison in his drink and intervened. I couldn't believe it when Everett believed her. We have to get out of here. The police will be after me any minute."

Ballard set down the case. "Do they know I'm involved?"

"Of course not. We can go to my estate in Spain."

"What about my mother? I don't want to leave her behind. And Christopher. Vesters will tell them he's his partner and complicit in this. My involvement will come out." He rubbed his head. "There are so many threads to this, Camille. I don't like surprises. We have to think this through so we're not suspects."

Mrs. Marshall stamped her foot. "There's no time! Christopher will land on his feet. We'll leave money for your mother."

"You're not much of a mother, Camille."

A siren wailed in the distance, and she grabbed his arm. "We have to go, James! They're coming."

Ballard stared down at her, then his hand went to his pocket. The moonlight gleamed on the gun he pulled out. "I haven't clawed my way up to be taken down with you, my dear."

Her mouth gaped and she took a step back. "No, James!"

The gun barked in the night, and Mrs. Marshall slumped to the ground. Ballard put the gun back in his pocket, then turned to go.

Lily put her hand over her mouth. Drew pulled his gun from his pocket and charged forward. "Stop right there, Ballard."

Ballard made a slow turn to face him. "I should have known it was you."

Drew stared at the man he'd tracked for so long. "You killed her."

He shrugged and looked down at the dead woman. "She was just a tool."

Drew's finger twitched against the trigger. "Does Ian know?"

Ballard shook his head. "I think he was beginning to suspect I'd turned, but we've been friends a long time. He wouldn't believe ill of me too quickly."

"And Vesters? The assassination plot? That was you too?"

"It was a rather brilliant idea of Camille's. Get Marshall out of the way. I marry Camille. Belle is married off to Vesters with

310

no right to Marshall's money and no longer our responsibility. Vesters gets what he wants and I get what I want. I had all the right associations to get the job done." He glanced around. "You realize Christopher is likely watching right now with a gun on your back. He's not a man to be trifled with."

"He's dead." Drew took great pleasure in the way Ballard's eyes widened. "You deliberately worked with a man butchering women. You provided him with the knives."

Ballard took a step back. "I had nothing to do with his little hobby. I didn't even know he was the killer until Camille told me a couple of weeks ago. She has gotten him out of more scrapes than this one. He first started his killing sprees back in eighty-four, but she got him out of the city. When I realized how evil he was, I began to have doubts about this little venture."

Drew grimaced. "Camille covered for him nearly twenty years?"

"He was her son. She loved him. Well, as much as she could love anyone. They had a most peculiar relationship. One minute she would strike out and hit him with anything nearby, and in the next moment she would fawn over him. It wasn't healthy." He heaved a sigh. "Now what? You should let me go, you know. My arrest will bring disgrace to the Secret Service. I think Ian would recommend you put your gun down and let me walk away."

Ian stepped from the shadows by the side of the house. "I would not recommend such a travesty of judgment." He motioned with the gun in his hand. "You're under arrest, Ballard. I'll take great pleasure in turning you in myself. We handle our own problems." He glanced at Drew. "And I owe you an apology. I let my longtime friendship with Ballard blind me to his true character. Good work."

Drew took a step toward the men. "How did you know to come here?"

Ian approached them. "I followed Mrs. Marshall, of course."

Drew struggled to understand the past four years. "I have one question. What about the fire?"

Ian glanced at Ballard. "I was never really sure about that. I didn't want to believe he was guilty, but I had a few doubts. I wanted to allow you enough rein to find out if he played any role in that. Did you start that fire, Ballard?"

The man shrugged. "I believed my cover was about to be blown. I did what had to be done."

Drew launched himself at Ballard. Squeezing the life from the man would give him the greatest pleasure.

Ian dragged Drew off him. "Let the law handle this."

Drew stared at Ballard on the ground, who seemed to have no remorse for what he'd done. Lily stepped to his side and took his hand. He curled his fingers around her comforting warmth.

Ian frowned. "I'm sorry, Drew. I was wrong about a lot of things." The siren wail grew louder, then stopped out by the front of the house. "I believe your ride is here, Ballard. Move."

Drew pulled Lily tight as the men moved toward the officers running around the side of the house. Justice wasn't as gratifying as he'd hoped.

The police had just finished putting Ballard in the back of the wagon. Lily sat on the steps to the front of the house with a wool blanket around her shoulders.

Drew approached with Officer Pickle, who seemed to be regarding her with more respect. Drew helped her to her feet, then slipped his arm around her. She relaxed against his warm strength. They'd nearly lost everything tonight. It was a miracle from God they hadn't died.

"We have everyone in custody now," Officer Pickle said.

She glanced at Pickle. "Vesters has been picked up too?"

He nodded.

It was over. She sagged against Drew. "What about Jane's reputation? Lambreth killed Mrs. Karr. He told me so. He was taking the butterfly when she came to the basement."

Pickle lifted a brow. "If you'll both give a sworn testimony, we'll issue a statement about it. I suspect we'll find the evidence in Lambreth's lair." He nodded at them. "Thanks for your help."

She burrowed against Drew as the officer went to the police wagon. "Now what happens?" she muttered against his shirt.

He pulled her away so he could look into her face. "The first thing you should do is take a bath. You have mud all over your face."

She laughed and rubbed at her cheeks. "That's the pot calling the kettle black. You should look in a mirror."

"We made it through though, Lily. I've never seen anything like the way you leaped at Lambreth with that knife. You're a strong woman."

A warm sensation lodged under her ribs. "We make a pretty good team."

"I'd like to make sure we never break up that team." He cupped her cheek in his hand and grinned. "I'm beginning to see you under that mask of dirt."

When she smiled, more mud fell off. "If you make me laugh enough, I might not need a bath."

His eyes were warm staring down into her face. "I love you, Lily Donaldson. You're the most beautiful butterfly I've ever seen, and I want you to marry me."

She smiled as his words sank in. "You think our adversity is over?" The thought of finally being able to relax was enticing.

He shook his head. "As long as we're living, we'll face adversity.

God is never finished refining us. But at least we can face what comes together. Our wings may get a little tattered, but I won't leave you if you won't leave me."

She hugged him, smelly shirt and all. "You'll find it impossible to get rid of me." She lifted her head again. "When I thought he was going to kill you, I realized I can't manage to keep you safe, Drew. It's not my job. I could have died first in that horrible place. I've been trying so hard to make sure nothing bad happens, but it's out of my hands. I don't care what you do. If law enforcement is where your heart is, I have to trust that God is going to take care of us no matter what happens."

A smile curved his lips. "I'm glad to hear it, honey. Didn't it feel good today to see justice prevail? To see the good guys win and the bad guys end up behind bars?"

She nodded. "And it's something you can be proud of, Drew. And I can be proud of you doing such a good work. I'll go wherever you want."

One corner of his mouth quirked up. "How about Africa?"

She punched him in the stomach. "Now you're making fun of me."

He hugged her, then turned her toward the automobile. Hand in hand they walked away from the place that had nearly cost them everything.

He lifted her up into the vehicle, then sprang onto the seat beside her. "Where to, future Mrs. Hawkins?"

"Wherever you decide, sir. But kiss me first. I need strength for the journey."

He let go of the steering wheel and pulled her onto his lap. "I think I need some strength too."

His lips found hers, and she sank into the promises he made her.

Life wasn't meant to be safe, but it was meant to be shared. And that was enough for her.

Dear Reader,

*Butterfly Palace* is a very special book to me. The past few years I've watched my sister-of-the-heart Diann Hunt fight ovarian cancer. In spite of the pain and struggle, Di has held on to a spirit of joy. She's worked hard to make each day count for Jesus. She's such an encourager as she has clung to God's hand while she's walked this path. Her faith is such an inspiration to me.

Struggle and pain aren't something to fear. We will all face trials while here on earth. What matters is how we're dealing with the challenges that come our way. Do we let them mold us into stronger, better people, or do we grouse and complain about our lot in life?

I hope you will take encouragement from Lily's struggle to embrace the unknown with joy. Let me know what you think! I love hearing from you.

Love,
Colleen Coble
colleen@colleencoble.com
colleencoble.com

# READING GROUP GUIDE

1. We all have trials that come our way. What struggle in your life has helped define who you are?

2. Lily and Drew were ashamed of their sexual behavior when they were engaged. How do we let shame change us for the better?

3. I'm a crusader for justice just like Drew. It's why I write romantic suspense. Is justice important to you? Why or why not?

4. Belle was used to going after what she wanted, no matter what. Have you ever been determined to have something, but you later found out God knew better?

5. Mr. Marshall was obsessed with his butterflies. What can fuel obsession, and how do we bring balance to our lives?

6. I was sad when Jane died, but I had to put it in because evil sometimes wins. The good thing is, we know justice will prevail in eternity. Has there been a time when evil won in your life and you've had to turn justice over to God?

7. The more I've lived, the more I realize many people wear a mask and it's hard to see the person inside. Is there some part of your personality you find hard to share with others? Explain.

8. Lily resolved to accept trials in the future and to try to grow through them. Are you going through a trial right now for which you need to be thankful?

# ACKNOWLEDGMENTS

I'm so blessed to be a part of the terrific Thomas Nelson dream team! I can't imagine writing without my editor, Ami McConnell. I crave her analytical eye and love her heart. Ames, you are truly like a daughter to me. Our fiction publisher, Daisy Hutton, is a gale-force wind of fresh air. Love her dearly! Marketing director Katie Bond is always willing to listen to my harebrained ideas and has been completely supportive for years. I wouldn't get far without you, friends! Fabulous cover guru Kristen Vasgaard works hard to create the perfect cover—and succeeds. You rock, Kristen! And, of course, I can't forget my other friends who are all part of my amazing fiction family: Amanda Bostic, Becky Monds, Jodi Hughes, Kerri Potts, Ruthie Dean, Heather McCulloch, and Laura Dickerson. I wish I could name all the great folks at Thomas Nelson who work on selling my books through different venues. I'm truly blessed!

Julee Schwarzburg is a dream editor to work with. She totally gets romantic suspense, and our partnership is a joy. Thanks for all your hard work to make this book so much better!

My agent, Karen Solem, has helped shape my career in many ways, and that includes kicking an idea to the curb when necessary. Thanks, Karen, you're the best!

Writing can be a lonely business, but God has blessed me with great writing friends and critique partners. Hannah Alexander (Cheryl Hodde), Kristin Billerbeck, Diann Hunt, and Denise Hunter make up the Girls Write Out squad (www.GirlsWriteOut .blogspot.com). I couldn't make it through a day without my peeps! Thanks to all of you for the work you do on my behalf and for your friendship. Thank you, friends!

I'm so grateful for my husband, Dave, who carts me around from city to city, washes towels, and chases down dinner without complaint. As I type this, he has been free of prostate cancer for two years, and we're so thankful! My kids—Dave, Kara (and now Donna and Mark)—and my grandsons, James and Jorden Packer, love and support me in every way possible. Love you guys! Donna and Dave brought me the delight of my life—our little grand-daughter, Alexa! She's talking like a grown-up now, and having her spend the night is more fun than I can tell you.

Most important, I give my thanks to God, who has opened such amazing doors for me and makes the journey a golden one.

# AN EXCERPT FROM
## *SAFE IN HIS ARMS*

The town of Larson, Texas, was busy on this warm February day. Cowboys in their dusty boots eyed the women attired in their best dresses strolling the boardwalks. Margaret O'Brien strode down the boardwalk in front of the feed store toward the mercantile. Things seemed to change daily with new stores sprouting like winter wheat. Every day more cowmen arrived in Larson, drawn by the lush grazing land and the water of the Red River.

Pa should be around here somewhere. She nodded to the ladies clustered in front of the general store, the familiar discomfort washing over her. Why couldn't she look like them? No matter how hard Margaret tried, she remained what she was: too tall and more at home with her hands gripping horse reins than a teacup. She ducked into the store and inhaled the aroma of cinnamon, bootstrap, sweat, and pickles. She busied herself with collecting material for their housekeeper, who had a bee in her bonnet about making curtains.

A cluster of women were talking in hushed whispers about the latest Zulu atrocity in Africa. These early months of 1879 had been full of bloody battles. Hearing such things always made Margaret wince, remembering her brother's death at the hands of the Sioux.

At least a national monument had been established earlier this year in memory of those who fell during the Battle of the Little Bighorn.

The women fell silent when Margaret paused. "Good morning," she said in as confident a voice as she could muster. "Anyone know what kind of material to buy for curtains? I thought this was pretty."

When she held up a lilac-flowered fabric, one of the women tittered, a tiny blonde Margaret had never seen before. Her face burned, and she put the bolt of fabric back.

"How about this one?" a woman said behind her.

Margaret's heart leaped at the sound of her friend's voice, and she whirled with a smile. "Lucy, I didn't know you were in town today. Should you be riding in a wagon in your condition?"

The blond woman laughed again at Margaret's indelicate mention of Lucy's pregnancy. Lucy linked arms with Margaret. "I feel fine. You like this pattern? I think Inez will love it."

Margaret eyed the red-and-white plaid. "It's a little . . . loud."

"Cheerful," Lucy corrected, smiling. Her head high, she led Margaret out of the group. "Silly twits. Now, don't start moaning about how they don't like you. They don't know you." Lucy shook her head. "And they won't bother to get to know you if you don't take a little more care when you come to town."

Margaret smoothed her hands on her rough skirt. They had come after cattle feed, and she had work to do in the barn when she got home, so she hadn't bothered to change. She should have put on a nicer dress. "It was too much bother since I had to help load feed."

"It's worth it, Margaret." Lucy glanced at the watch pinned to her dress. "Nate is going to be looking for me." She hugged Margaret. "I'm so glad I saw you. You're coming to the party, aren't you?"

"Sure. I'm not going to dance, but I'll come keep you company." Smiling, Margaret watched her friend waddle away. Dear Lucy. She had barreled past Margaret's prickly exterior, and they'd become fast friends. Lucy was easy to trust. She was all heart.

Margaret had her purchases put on account, then stepped out into the sunshine.

Cattlemen had driven herds of cattle through here more than an hour ago, but the dust and odor still lingered in the air. Her father motioned to her from in front of the stagecoach station. Calvin stood close behind him.

She started toward them, but the man beside her father arrested her gaze. He was tall, even taller than her father, which meant he had to be at least six foot three or four inches. She guessed he was in his early thirties. The man's Stetson was pushed back on his head, revealing shiny brown hair, and his bronzed face was chiseled with planes and angles that spoke of confidence and determination. He cast a lazy grin her way.

Immediately Margaret's hackles rose. That kind of self-assurance—arrogance, really—always reminded her of her uncle. She'd had to assert herself strenuously with him around the ranch because he thought a woman's place was in the kitchen, not in the stockyard. This man was the same type, the sort of man who would demand to be catered to and obeyed. No one who looked that strong and proud would listen to a woman.

She forced a smile. This man was probably nothing like her uncle. But her trepidation slowed her steps. Her father motioned her forward, though, and she reluctantly moved to join them.

Her father put his hand on her shoulder. "Here's my daughter, Margaret."

The man's gaze swept from the top of her head down to the dusty boots just peeking out from underneath her serviceable skirt, and Margaret's lips tightened. People in Larson were used to her attire, but this man's eyes widened. He'd probably never seen a woman dressed for ranch work. She wore a man's chambray shirt, and her red hair hung over her shoulder in a long braid. The bits of cow manure on her skirt and boots didn't add much to the general picture either. He'd really be shocked if he saw her in her britches when she was helping with the cattle.

She lifted her head and stared him down. His dark eyes betrayed none of his thoughts. She didn't think she'd ever seen eyes that shade. Like a buckeye nut, they were a rich brown color. Heavy brows accented the strong planes of his face.

Margaret thrust out her hand. "Pleased to meet you. And you are . . . ?"

He could have stared over the top of her head without taking notice of her at all. But he didn't. He gazed straight into her eyes, and her breath caught in her throat as she felt the magnetic pull of the man.

"Daniel Cutler." His handshake was firm and as self-confident as his appearance.

Margaret pulled her hand away. "You been in town long, Mr. Cutler?" He'd given his name but not his business here in Larson. Pa seemed almost proprietorial toward him, but she clamped her teeth against the questions clamoring to escape.

"He just got in today," her father put in eagerly. "He's our new foreman."

"New foreman?" Margaret's heart dipped like a bronco about to arch its back to the sky. "We don't need a new foreman, Pa. I can handle things by myself. I've spent the last ten years of my life proving it."

Their ranch hand Calvin straightened as well. "That ain't right, O'Brien. You said if I did a good job, you'd promote me. This shave-tail"—he gestured toward Cutler—"ain't what the ranch needs."

Her father glared at Calvin. "Get that feed loaded and keep

your nose out of my business." Her father skewered her with an even sterner stare. "Now, Margaret, I told you it's time you let go of some of these notions about running the ranch by yourself. I'm getting too old to be of much help, and I'd sure like for you to set your mind to finding a husband and giving me some grandchildren."

Her father's gaze traveled over Margaret's apparel and displeasure shone in his eyes. "Though what man would have you when you make no attempt to look like a woman is another concern altogether."

She had begun to find her composure, but at her father's words, blood rushed to her face. They didn't need to air their disagreements in front of this stranger. Pa had never understood how his words burned her spirit like a brand. She never let on how he hurt her, and she didn't now. She narrowed her eyes at this stranger who was set to disrupt her life.

Daniel Cutler seemed to be taking it all in with interest, and a small smile played around those firm lips of his. He probably agreed wholeheartedly with her father's assessment. Like all the rest of the men in her acquaintance, he would be looking for some dainty young thing with a simpering smile and golden curls.

She tossed her head and glared at him. His smile faltered, and she felt a stab of satisfaction. "I'm sorry you've come all this way for nothing," she told him. "But we really don't need a foreman. Not you and not Calvin."

"The thing's done," her father said. "Toss your belongings into our wagon, Daniel. We'll head back to the ranch as soon as we get this feed loaded."

She caught her breath at her father's blatant dismissal. "Pa . . ."

He held up his hand. "Enough, Margaret. Daniel is here. Zip your tongue and help get the wagon loaded."

*I will not cry.* Biting her lip, she walked to the back of the wagon.

Daniel threw his satchel into the wagon. He didn't wait to be asked but went to the pile of feed sacks and began loading them. His muscular arms handled the heavy bags with ease. For a moment Margaret stared at the muscles in his back as they rippled beneath his shirt. In spite of her dislike of the man, he was a fine specimen of masculinity. Other women strolling by paused and cast surreptitious glances his way. Glances he seemed not to notice.

She helped load the sacks, but he threw the heavy bags into the back twice as quickly, with not even a labored breath. She bristled at his strength. He was probably trying to show her up in front of her father. She'd teach him she didn't need his help—not for loading feed and not for running the ranch.

She and Daniel worked side by side for several minutes until all she could smell was burlap. Daniel tossed the last of the feed into the wagon and turned to her with a grin. "What now, Boss?"

*Boss*. The way he said the word with a hint of mockery made her grimace. Just as she opened her mouth to put him in his place, shots rang out down the street. Five men, their revolvers blasting at anything that moved, rushed out of the bank and mounted their horses. The horses came thundering toward Margaret.

"Get down!" Daniel tackled her to the dusty ground.

The breath puffed out of her as he fell on top of her. She struggled to free herself, but his strong body kept her pinned beneath him. She could smell the clean scent of soap underneath the scent of his skin. Never in her life had she felt so helpless and dependent. And protected. The word whispered through her brain with a gentle allure.

*The story continues in* Safe in His Arms *by Colleen Coble.*

Exciting tales of danger,
romance, and faith
played out under
Texas stars

UNDER TEXAS STARS

SAFE IN HIS ARMS

BEST-SELLING AUTHOR

COLLE
COB

UNDER TEXAS STARS

"Colleen Coble's books have it all—romance, wit,
suspense, action."
—Mary Connealy, best-selling author of *Doctor in Petticoats*

STARS ABOVE RANCH

BLUE MOON PROMISE

COLLEEN
COBLE

The best-selling
UNDER TEXAS STARS

series available in print and e-book

# The *USA Today* Best-Selling Hope Beach Series

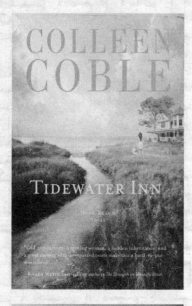

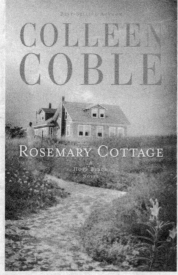

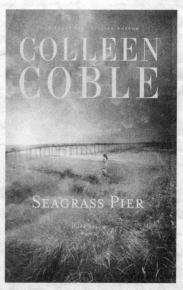

## "Atmospheric and suspenseful"
—*Library Journal*

*Available July 2014*

**Available in print and e-book**

# ABOUT THE AUTHOR

Photo by Clik Chick Photography

RITA finalist Colleen Coble is the author of several best-selling romantic suspense novels, including *Tidewater Inn* and the Mercy Falls, Lonestar, and Rock Harbor series.